A Gyrfalcon for a King

Stormclouds, Book I
Prequel novels to the **Harbingers** fantasy series

Jane M. Wiseman

Shrike Publications

Albuquerque and Minneapolis

Shrike Publications
Albuquerque, New Mexico
Minneapolis, Minnesota
www.janemwiseman.com

Publisher's Note: This is a work of fiction. Names, characters, places, and incidents are a product of the author's imagination. Locales and public names are sometimes used for atmospheric purposes. Any resemblance to actual people, living or dead, or to businesses, companies, events, institutions, or locales is completely coincidental.

Book Layout © 2017 BookDesignTemplates.com

A Gyrfalcon for a King/ Jane M. Wiseman -- 1st ed.
ISBN 978-1-7328141-9-6

For Will and Wallace

An Eagle for an Emperor. A Gerfalcon for a King. A Peregrine for a Prince. A Tiercel for an Earl. A Lanar for a Squire. A Sparhawk for a Yeoman.

Adapted from the list in **The Boke of St. Albans** *and similar medieval lists prescribing which rank of the nobility was entitled to keep which type of hawk or falcon*

Trigger warning: *This book is a work of fiction and fantasy, but it reflects some harsh realities about sexual abuse. Please take care of yourself if such references cause you distress.*

Contents

A Map of the Known World

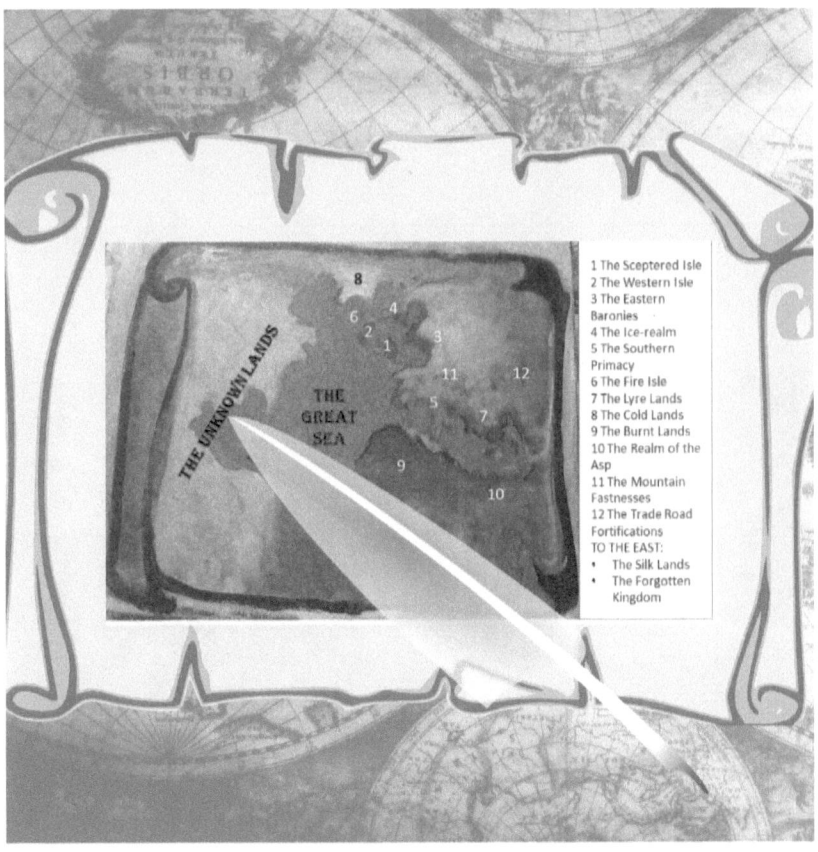

The Stormclouds/Harbingers Fantasy Novels

Stormclouds: The Prequel Series

Book I, *A Gyrfalcon for a King*
Book II, *The Call of the Shrike*
Book III, *Stormbird*

The Harbingers Series

Book I, *Blackbird Rising*
Book II, *Halcyon*
Book III, *Firebird*
Book IV, *Ghost Bird*

Betwixt & Between: The Companion Series

Book I, *The Martlet is a Wanderer*
Book II, *The Nightingale Holds Up the Sky*

Stand-alone novel set in the world of the
Stormclouds/Harbingers fantasy series:
Dark Ones Take It: being the origin story of Caedon and his brother Maeldoi

Urban fantasy novella set in the Stormclouds/Harbingers world. . .and ours!

Witchmoon (available only in e-book format)

All novels in the series available in paperback and for Kindle at <u>www.amazon.com</u>

Opening Gambit

It all started with a comet.

It started before the boy was even born, when the gods known as The Three, Trioditis, assembled the other four of them, The Children. Time out of mind, creatures on the world beneath the Spheres looked to their night sky in awe at seven fiery points of light. The Seven Sisters, they called them. The Three, and then the four Children. This one time, the time before the boy, the creatures underneath the Spheres had angered The Three beyond all measure, with their wars and their squabbling.

"The nonsense beneath the Spheres must stop," The Three told the Children. "We are tempted to wipe the whole Plane out. You'll have to start all over. Make better creatures. Build a new world."

"Let's wait and see," The Children advised. They loved the creatures—all the kinds: the ordinary folk, the mages, the witches, the gwrgi, the eala. They didn't want these poor creatures destroyed.

"We smashed them once. Smashed their whole Plane to splinters, and the creatures with it. We'll do it again," The Three warned. "The noise is giving Us a headache. But we're not tyrants. We're all about justice. We're going to send the creatures a warning. A fireball streaking across their sky."

"Let's wait and see," The Children said, wringing their hands. "Some of the mages have a plan."

"But other mages have an opposing plan," The Three snarled.

The Children shuddered. They knew what The Three meant. "One of the mages, mostly," they whispered among themselves. *Gilles*, They whispered. The mage who cared more about his own power than the creatures he was supposed to be helping. "But the boy will be born," The Children consoled Themselves. "The boy may make a difference."

The Three sent the comet anyway. When the creatures beneath the Spheres saw it, they all cringed.

"At least they've been warned," The Children told Themselves. "Especially that king. He's a problem, that one."

The Arch-mage—Myrddin, or Merlin, or Mervin—whatever you care to call him—assembled the entire Magisterial High Council, both upper and lower houses, for an emergency meeting.

He and his good friend the mage John Dee had been playing a game of chess. It was time for the meeting to begin, however, so Myrddin rose to put the board away.

"You know I had your queen in a tight spot. I was about to say garde, just as a friendly gesture," Dee groused.

Myrddin laughed. "Why, Dee, what an old-fashioned gentlemanly thing to do. You're something of a fuddy-duddy, you know that?" He settled his features into more serious lines. This meeting would not be pleasant. The comet had been spotted. It was clear to Myrddin, and ought to be clear to the rest of them—The Three were angry. With a swirl of his robes, Myrddin strode down the corridor and into the council chambers.

Behind the two of them, another mage waited out of sight in the shadows of the niche on the far side of the massive hearth where his two colleagues had been playing chess. Gilles de Rais, almost as powerful as Myrddin. As powerful as Dee. He watched the other two through narrowed eyes, as they went away. This was his chance to whisk unseen into Myrddin's private quarters.

There. The scrying stone that Myrddin always kept so very close. Myrddin had just been using it. Gilles sniffed the air. He could smell the magic emanating from it. If he moved close to the stone and peered in, perhaps the last vision Myrddin saw there might still be swirling in its depths.

Gilles sidled closer. He darted to the stone and looked. He could just make it out. A young man, barely out of boyhood. A young man with a musical instrument of some sort. He was playing and singing.

That's the boy, Gilles thought with a thrill. *That's the young mage. Myrddin and Dee are pinning their hopes on him. They think he's the one to allay the anger of The Three. The boy isn't born yet, but when he comes into the world, he'll be weak. Vulnerable. Myrddin and Dee think they will guide him. They won't. I'll make him mine.*

Gilles smiled. He glanced around, making sure he was not observed, then took a devious route to the council chamber.

The meeting of the highest of all the mages beneath the Spheres was just getting under way. At the big stone pulpit, its marble facing stained with the ages, Myrddin took a steadying breath.

"I've brought you here today because of an alarming situation, a sore on creation about to fester and rot and burst underneath the Spheres," Myrddin proclaimed to the assembled mages.

Out of the corner of his eye, Myrddin watched Gilles de Rais bustle into the meeting, interrupting everything, making his way to his accustomed seat, pretending to look apologetic and attentive. He wasn't fooling Myrddin. Myrddin saw Gilles wasn't fooling Dee, either. Myrddin could tell Gilles was aware of the apprehensive glances many of the mages cast in his direction as he brushed past them to take his seat. Myrddin could tell Gilles was enjoying the stir he made.

Myrddin made himself go on. He pretended he didn't notice Gilles's interruption. "A crack in the Spheres themselves," Myrddin boomed out, drawing everyone's attention back to himself. "A crack, I tell you. A hairline crack, to be sure. But widening. The farwyds have foreseen this dis-ease of the Spheres, and they've called on me. They speak for The Children, they are far-seers, of course, and they've given me warning. Now I'm passing their warning along to all of you. It's this: The Children are worried." Myrddin gazed out over the sea of rapt faces. "And if The Children are worried, there can be only one reason. The Three are angry."

Myrddin saw how shaken all the mages of the High Council were at his words. *Almost all*, he told himself, glancing at Gilles.

Perhaps he was about to lose this game, just as he was losing at chess only moments ago. But the stakes were so much higher than the outcome of some game. Worlds higher.

He kept going, past his fears and the unrest his words were causing. He had to.

"Comes with the job," Dee murmured at his shoulder, seeing how unsettled his friend was.

The mages grew silent. They stilled their fidgeting and listened.

"The farwyds have told me we need to get our people in line, or there will be trouble. Do I have to remind you what happened last time?" Myrddin's voice, a penetrating basso profundo, rang into the council chamber.

The assembled mages cringed and shook their heads. They had all read the books of lore recounting the horror of the times Myrddin spoke of. The Three had split the Spheres with Their wrath. All beneath the Spheres had died agonizing deaths. Every man, every woman, every child. After the Three had wiped the slate clean, they had angrily demanded that the Children (the other four of the Seven Sisters who control the

Planes) do better. The Three had made Them start all over. Make a new beginning. Fashion better creatures. Build a new world.

"Here we are," said Myrddin to his fellow mages, opening his arms wide. "We are that new world. And we mages, and our farwyds, are the creatures the Children have put in place to mediate between Themselves and their creation. We're Their safety valve. Their canaries in the mine.

"For a while, the Three were placated. Now They've become displeased. When they look down upon the Twelve Realms, and the Unknown Lands, and all the other places beneath the Spheres, they see eruptions in the Balance. They see creatures who refuse Balance, who arrogantly set out to control things themselves. And they blame us, the mages, for not keeping such an explosive situation within acceptable bounds."

"Could Their anger have something to do with the star of fire we've seen streaking through the Spheres?" cried one of the mages.

"You've seen it, then." Myrddin nodded grimly. "The comet."

"It's only a small star," said another. "It will burn itself out. Nothing to fear."

"Maybe it's a sign," said a third. "A sign of the Children's displeasure."

"The displeasure of The Three," said still another.

And another murmured, low, "Trioditis."

"Hush," another cautioned. "The likes of us do not presume to speak Their name."

Myrddin steeled himself, because Gilles de Rais was rising to interrupt. As he loved to do.

Gilles stroked his clean-shaven chin and looked around him, fixing this mage and that with his severe eye. "Why should the Children blame us? And beyond Them, the Three?" He cast a scornful eye on them all. "Trioditis. Yes, I'll name Them. I'll not cower away from Them. We mages shepherd creation as best we can. Is it our fault if some of its creatures get ideas above their station? Is it our fault if some of them want power, and seize it? That's the way of the world. Those with the power control the weak. Any of them with intelligence and will and drive? Any of them possessing those noble traits? Of course they'll try to seize control. Surely the Three must appreciate that. Must appreciate any of their creatures who have such drive. Must reward them. Such creatures are only mirroring the best qualities of their gods."

Dee started to break in, but Myrddin restrained him with a hand.

Gilles drew a breath. Myrddin saw he was about to go into full ranting mode. Gilles's voice, its harshness concealed by a charming Baronies lilt, turned insistent. "Myrddin tells us the gods are worried we are upsetting the balance of the Spheres. With all respect, Myrddin, I doubt they are." Gilles looked a challenge directly at Myrddin, who worked to achieve an impassive expression. "The Three, and The Children, too, must know that those who seize control aren't opposing balance." Gilles turned again to his fellow mages. "The powerful among us are actually the creators of balance. The powerful weigh their extraordinary, commendable strength against the general weakness and pusillanimity of all the others of creation. These strong ones deserve to rule over the weak." Gilles's voice vibrated with conviction. His teeth glinted as he smiled at his fellow mages. "As I'm sure we all agree."

Myrddin wondered if he should shut Gilles down. Before he could, Dee raised an eyebrow. "Sounds to me as if you're encouraging these creatures hungry for power, Gilles. And we've just been told not to. We've just been told it's dangerous. That this kind of creature creates imbalance, not balance."

"Mind your own business, and let me mind mine," hissed Gilles, the mask of his charm dropped.

The whole meeting began to buzz with talk.

Myrddin pounded his staff for order. "Dee is right. The Three want such creatures reined in. Let me speak frankly, Gilles. The Three have noticed a special disturbance originating on the Plane where you've been operating. One of the Planes. I know you operate on several."

"Are you accusing me, Myrddin?" said Gilles, his face darkening with anger.

"Gilles," said Myrddin. "Balance. Remember. That's the key to justice, at least the justice known underneath the Spheres."

"There's a higher justice, Myrddin," said Gilles. A number of the mages nodded and began clustering nearer him.

"There is indeed, Gilles." Myrddin strove for control. "But you know very well, and the farwyds have warned us, that The Children reserve this higher justice to Themselves. It's not for us to meddle."

"If we don't stand together, the creatures underneath the Spheres will find themselves at terrible risk," said Dr. Dee.

"So the farwyds tell us," replied Myrddin.

"Then let's stand together for might, not cowardly abasement," said Gilles. "And let me raise a concern. The farwyds say they speak for The Children. It's possible, just possible, that the farwyds want to keep their own power for themselves, and not share it with the others of creation. It's possible they're exaggerating."

Myrddin closed his eyes, trying to shut out Gilles's act of blasphemy. Gilles probably didn't believe his own words. But he must know that a certain coterie of the lesser mages would find him convincing. For some of them, even thrilling. Better to reason with Gilles. Too heavy a hand could lead Gilles into open rebellion, and then what? It would mean war.

"We have a responsibility to these creatures, especially the ordinary folk crawling helpless beneath the Spheres. We can't go running off after power, nor let the creatures do so," Dee was arguing.

"You're overruled, Gilles," said Myrddin.

Gilles subsided into his golden chair with mutterings and frowns. A few of the bolder mages of the lesser kind moved even closer to him.

"Might makes right," said one of these, looking around him for applause, seeming to think he'd invented the idea.

"Among the ordinary creatures, there are men," said another, ticking the ranks off on his fingers, "and among these men are the strongmen, the rulers. Beneath them, the followers. Next are women, mostly weak and in need of protection, ruled by emotion and irrationality. Finally, at the bottom, animals. Brutes with no understanding."

"And the other kinds of sentient creatures, all with their own ideas of hierarchy," another chimed in. "Always, the strong are on top."

Myrddin ignored them. Gilles was up to his old tricks. He sighed. He'd have to keep an eye on Gilles before his belligerent attitude got them all into worse trouble than they were in already. They'd been given their warning. The mages were charged with shepherding the other kinds. They'd already come to the attention of The Three for their lapses of attention to their duties. The Children had already given their directive to the Council, and The Children would be displeased to see their express orders flouted.

Myrddin decided not to fan the flames.

"For now," he said mildly, "let's watch and wait. We'll do nothing without consultation." He seated himself in the golden chair that was his. The council broke up into small groups, milling about the chamber to talk earnestly among themselves.

Myrddin raised his voice above the hubbub. "Which of you mages operate on the Plane where the Sceptered Isle is the strongest of the realms?"

The assembled mages looked over at him. A few of the lesser mages hesitantly raised their hands.

"Come here to me. I'm commissioning you to keep an eye on things." The others resumed their chatter. Myrddin looked over the ones clustered around him. They were a motley lot. He considered which one might be of best use. "Aderyn," he said, waving the others off.

"Yes, my lord?" She came to stand beside him. She was one of the lesser mages, but dedicated to her Plane.

"You're closest to the power struggle I fear will soon break out. Looks like the worst of it will bubble up from discontents on the Sceptered Isle."

"Yes, my lord."

"But your Child is the Child of Sea, isn't that right?"

"Yes, my lord."

"Hmm," said Myrddin. "Yet most of the Sceptered Isle is under the sway of the Child of Earth." He looked around at some of the others he'd called over, already being swallowed up by this or that group of gesticulating, arguing mages. None of them seemed particularly suitable to the work he had in mind. He turned to the one by his chair. "Well, Aderyn, Little Bird, see what you can do to contain the situation. Meanwhile, I'll look around for a mage answering to the Earth Child, someone who may be able to relieve you if things get out of hand, or if you're called. . ." he paused delicately. ". . . elsewhere," he said. Myrddin didn't mention that he had already seen this new mage in his scrying stone. A boy not yet born.

"Yes, my lord," said Aderyn.

"I'll expect regular reports from you, Aderyn, as the situation develops."

"Yes, my lord," she said. "There's another who can help?"

"A mage in the Sceptered Isle? Not at the moment. There will be. I've foreseen it. So try to hold on until he comes into the world."

"I'll do that. We have a thin line of defense, in our realm."

"Yes," said Myrddin with a sigh. "It's dangerous." Especially dangerous, he thought, when so many mages failed to live up to their potential, or died before they could. It was a terrible calling, full of hidden traps for the unwary.

A mage might not even know he bore unique abilities, and live out his life peaceably without ever wielding his powers. Myrddin counted such mages lucky. Or a mage might discover her powers but choose not to develop them. If she could stay quiescent and not attract the attention of the mighty through any noticeable burst of power, she too might live out a peaceful, natural life.

But woe to the mage who recognized himself and set out to wield and develop and refine his powers. He'd draw the attention of malign forces. Gilles, for instance. And these were only the worst. A young, inexperienced mage could easily draw unwelcome attention, too, from his own neighbors, who would see how different he was, and become suspicious. They might not have the power of a Gilles, but they could do a lot of damage to the hapless young mage in the ordinary course of ordinary village life. Stonings. Burnings at the stake. And so on.

At Myrddin's elbow, Dee looked particularly agitated.

"What is it?" Myrddin said, more sharply than he intended.

"Someone will come, you say. Someone will be born, and he will help."

"I'm sensing this, yes," said Myrddin. "I've engaged in some discreet scrying. After the meeting, I'll see if I can find out more."

"The poor fellow," said Dee. "If his neighbors among the ordinary folk discover he's a mage, those good people are likely to cry witchcraft, especially on this Plane, with all its ignorance—"

"Yes, yes." Myrddin reminded himself not to be so testy with Dee. "We know the risks, my good friend. Haven't we survived them ourselves?"

"Long ago," said Dee. He shuddered. "I remember that incident I faced, you know the one. That one time."

"Another mage on the Plane where you operated."

"He got jealous. He set traps to kill me."

"You escaped him, Dee. We've all experienced the unpleasant consequences of our powers." Myrddin had his own bad memories to get past.

Only the most advanced of mages learn to use the protections of the highest spells. Only then might they live down the generations and centuries and across the Planes. Few mages lasted long enough to do so. Few mages lasted long enough to cast their first spells. Myrddin knew that, and so did Dee. Few mages lasted long enough and became adept enough to grow near-immortal, like Dee or Gilles or Myrddin.

And here was this young mage who glimmered at the edge of Myrddin's consciousness, a boy not yet born on the Plane where they needed to act. Unless this young one were incredibly lucky, he doubtless faced a tragic fate. That's if statistics were any measure. Not even great skill could save him. Not that often. Skill was one thing. Bad luck, bad timing, determined enemies—these could easily overset such a mage in his inexperience, as he tried to make his way.

Myrddin decided to go to his scrying stone immediately after the council's meeting, to see what else he might find out about the young man.

Dee's eyes were far away. He kept on. "A jealous mage might kill this young one you envision. A rogue mage might take possession of him."

Myrddin followed Dee's gaze and saw where his friend's thoughts were leading him. A rogue mage like Gilles, one who dabbled illegally in the dark arts. One who had every reason to thwart Myrddin and Dee, and had just demonstrated it. Not for the first time.

Thank the Children for Aderyn, the caretaker Myrddin had just appointed. She was a mage of great talent, and completely dedicated. But her talents were probably limited to one time and place. Myrddin knew—and she herself knew—that she would probably live only an ordinary lifetime, subject to all of the dangers of her era. Myrddin would have to arm her as best he could. He turned back to Aderyn and placed an affectionate hand on her arm. They resumed their conversation.

Dee had stopped paying attention. He was staring with puzzled eyes over at Gilles, who was glaring back. "I don't understand Gilles," Dee murmured aside to Myrddin as Gilles looked from one of them to the other, his eyes narrowed suspiciously. "I've known you for a long time, Mervin, my friend," said Dee, "and during the course of our friendship, how many times has Gilles tried something like this? The last was the worst. Now look at him. Stirring things up again. Say he were to succeed. He'd bring the Spheres crashing down on his own head. So why?"

Forcing a smile, Myrddin dismissed Aderyn back to her family among the ordinary folk. He turned to his friend Dee. Both stood examining Gilles de Rais as he moved from group to small group of the mages who supported him. "The man's so arrogant I think he believes he'll forge a new order to replace the Spheres." Myrddin kept his voice down. That particular rumor didn't need any momentum from him, and if he took notice of it as anything more than a fool's notion, it would gain momentum.

Myrddin gazed out over the vast conclave of the Magisterial High Council. "Dismissed, all of you." His booming voice carried over the commotion the departing mages were making. "And Gilles. I'll see you in my office after the meeting."

Gilles returned a look of intense dislike.

"Unleash me, Mervin," Dee was saying at Myrddin's elbow, a familiar grim light in his eyes.

"No, good friend. I know how you feel. Not now. I need to try to reason with Gilles."

"Reason with Gilles?" Dee's voice was incredulous.

Dee was right, of course. It would be no use reasoning with the man, thought Myrddin with an inward groan. Gilles was intractable. It was as clear to Dee as it was to him. Gilles himself stood at the heart of the farwyds' warning. Gilles knew just how far to press his advantage without drawing the attention of The Three. He trod a thin line, and clearly he loved it, the danger, the rush of power he got when he manipulated himself into some advantageous position.

Myrddin pressed Dee's hand, he hoped reassuringly. He moved away to some of the others, gave an encouraging word here, a smile there.

But he never took his eyes off Gilles.

Gilles was almost as powerful in the Council as Myrddin himself. Myrddin realized he'd have to handle Gilles carefully. Diplomatically. Gilles could make trouble if he were directly confronted.

Power. Myrddin sighed.

In a way, Gilles was right. Gilles craved power, and Myrddin—with the help of the strongest of the mages, such as his friend Dee, especially Dee—needed to exercise all of his own power to keep Gilles in check.

There was a time when Gilles's power, while not overtopping his own, joined with some lesser powers to incapacitate Myrddin. That time was over, but it didn't stop Gilles from pushing. And pushing. And pushing.

As for Dee. Myrddin looked over at his fellow-mage with affection. Not as powerful as Gilles, but vastly more well-intentioned. Still, Dee was a loose cannon.

Myrddin shrugged and set that problem aside for another day. The anger of The Three was too pressing. It threatened all underneath the Spheres. He must see how best to use his own power in the service of balance.

Power itself was not the problem. It was a tool. But a tool that could too easily be misused. He must get ahead of this most recent attempt of Gilles to overtop balance. He must do it now, while it was still a gleam in Gilles's eye.

Gilles was out to destroy them all. He had the power, and he had the will to use it.

If this new mage were born into the world, into the realm of the Sceptered Isle. . .Myrddin's mind drifted back to the glimmerings of foresight promising this. . . that might give Myrddin a bit of an advantage. But for how long? There was only so much protection Myrddin was allowed to give a new mage.

As for Gilles, he observed no such ethical boundaries. He'd have no compunctions about destroying such a person. Or luring such a person into his own orbit.

Myrddin could only hope to keep the new one away from Gilles's attention. Sneak him under the radar and hope for the best.

Dee had kept hovering at Myrddin's shoulder. "We're not to interfere. I understand, Mervin. I do. But suppose we sent a messenger, with a warning?"

"The boy hasn't even been born yet," said Myrddin.

"You know," said Dee. "These things never do start with just a boy, do they? They go back, and back, and back. Suppose we send a messenger to the father of this boy?"

"What good will that do?" said Myrddin, and strode away.

Behind him, Dee called after him. "What about our chess game? I was winning, you scoundrel."

In spite of the troubling thoughts weighing heavily on him, Myrddin couldn't suppress a grin.

But then he did head for his scrying stone, and what he saw there gave such a wrench to his inwards that he nearly doubled over with the pain of it.

Myrddin slips the orb from its velvet bag and sets it up before him. It seems filled with some cloudy white substance. Myrddin begins the rite.

His murmurings wake a light deep at the heart of the orb. The light blossoms until the entire orb is throbbing with a golden radiance. Myrddin ceases. Then begins again, this time with gestures of power.

Tiny figures resolve in the heart of the glowing orb. Myrddin looks closer. He moves so close to the surface of the orb that his eye, seen from the inside, must appear to be some strange planetary body in the sky of the creatures within.

There he is again, Myrddin thinks. *There's the boy. He's playing that music of his.*

A young man pushes his way through a thick woods of oak and pine. He comes to a clearing, finds a fallen log, and slumps down on it. After a while, he unships his instrument, a beautifully carved rebec, from the embroidered bag slung over his shoulder. He fishes around for his bow. Softly he begins to bow his instrument, and after a moment, his voice rises with the notes.

She stepped away from me
as she moved through the fair,
and fondly I watched her
move here and move there,
and she went her way homeward
with one star awake
as the swans in the evening
move over the lake.

He pauses. Tries to drive the memories and longings away. Fails. Puts his instrument down.

A noise distracts him. High in the trees at the edge of the clearing, something large has settled. He peers upward. Falcon.

If I'm not mistaken, he says to himself, *a gyrfalcon.*

He holds himself still, as still as he can, so as not to frighten the bird away. It's a beautiful bird. The young man yearns to reach out for it, make a connection, one mind to another, as he has learned he can do, but he's afraid.

From the top of a tall oak, out a good way onto a bare branch, the creature turns its head from side to side, surveying its domain. The king of birds. The falcon cocks a head, seeming to peer down at the young man. The sun, slanting through the forest, glints on its beak and the sheen of its feathers.

"A gyrfalcon for a king," the young man says softly.

After a moment poised between one breath and the next, the falcon utters a harsh *kak kak kak* and leaves the tree in a flash of feathers. Something has disturbed it.

The light changes. John doesn't notice, not really, but he senses the change in some deep inner place. A hooded man steps from underneath the tree canopy. "John," says this stranger.

The young man, John, looks up, alarmed. How is it this stranger knows his name? Reaching automatically for his rebec, to make sure it's safe, he feels with his other hand for the dagger at his hip.

"No need for that, John," says the hooded stranger with a low chuckle. "I'm not a threat to you."

"Who are you, then?" John's voice is hoarse. He tries to clear it. Fear is making his throat dry. He knows he has taken a risk, leaving the safety of camp to move into enemy-held territory in the middle of a war. His troubling thoughts have driven him to find some isolated place to play his music and ponder his deep misgivings. Going into the woods, moving so far away from his friends and his companions in the army of King Ranulf, though. It's dangerous.

The enemy, it is said, employs shamans and sorcerers. There are tales about what they do to unwary stragglers from the Sceptered Isle army.

"I'm neither shaman nor sorcerer," says the hooded man. "Not the way you think of them, anyway."

John's fear deepens. This stranger can read his mind.

"Your powers—connections with your music, and with the birds—overtop any of the enemy's magic wielders by far," the hooded man says. "Problem is, you're not trained to employ your own powers. Not yet. There's your danger, John. You need someone to guide and train you."

John cringes back. He knows he is set apart. He has never liked it, the feeling he knows things others don't and can't know. The feeling that his music somehow summons up . . . something. Who knows what it summons.

All he knows is how afraid these summonings make him feel, especially since they seem connected so closely to his music. Yet all the while, he feels compelled to play his instrument, and to sing. It is his greatest comfort in trouble. His greatest joy.

Hearing this stranger reveal he too knows how John's music controls him and is controlled by him—and John's attachment somehow to birds—John shudders. He darts a glance to the man standing so close to him, too close. Had the stranger moved a bit closer than he was before? How could John not have noticed?

John sends up a wish then. *I wish I were like others.* But John thinks of a time when these deep-seated feelings of his, the uncomfortable, dangerous kind, helped someone he held very dear out of a terrible situation. When he thinks of this time, he can push himself past the fear.

But mostly he thinks that if only he could cut this hidden inborn part of himself out, he could cut out the frightening feelings at the same time, and be at peace.

He can't make himself do it. His hidden side is too much a part of him. His music is too much a part of him.

Thank the Children, or the Lady, or whoever he's supposed to be worshipping now, that the bad feelings usually stay tamped down and so far inside him that he can pretend they aren't there.

But sometimes. Sometimes they come out.

The hooded man continues talking, his voice a calm soothing thread of noise. "These people around here," he says, gesturing. "They know about bards. They know the power of music. Most of the villages here on the Western Isle actually employ a bard, if they can scrape the coin together. If you were one of these people, you'd do well for yourself, John. Do you know why?"

John looks at the stranger sidelong. He thinks about running. The man seems to have come a step or two closer. John is surprised to see how close.

"I'll tell you why." The man's hypnotic voice goes on. Almost dreamily, John notices his odd accent. *Not from here on the Western Isle. Not from across the straits to the Sceptered Isle, either. Somewhere else. The Baronies, maybe.* The man's voice is harsh, John realizes. But the harshness is overlaid with a charming Baronies lilt. A man from across the Narrow Sea to the east of John's own home.

"Bards, now." The man has continued speaking in his soft, hypnotic voice.

John realizes with terror that the man is sitting just beside him on the fallen log. He had been far across the clearing. Now he is here. In an instant, right here. He smells odd. Not bad. Not perfumed. Astringent.

"These villagers around here employ bards to help them with a very homely problem." The stranger smiles at John from under the shadow of his hood, and his smile is somehow disturbing. Something about the sharpness of the teeth. "The villagers reap the barley, they store it, then if they're not careful, rats eat all their stores, and come winter, they starve. But a good bard. Now there's a useful person to have around. A bard sings and plays those rats right out of the village."

In spite of himself, John feels himself drawn into the man's improbable tale, and now he finds himself grinning. "I sing and play, good sir, but I don't think I've ever sung and played to rats."

"You could make a fine living out here, John. Believe me, you could." The man's hand, the one nearest John, had been in his own lap. Now, as John looks down, he sees it's resting on the narrow space between them, not a handspan away from his own, as the two of them sit on the log together. "But perhaps," says the stranger, his voice dropping to a murmur, "perhaps your music does not draw rats. Perhaps your own music draws a different creature entirely. I know what you need, John. Let me train you. Place yourself in my hands, a gift freely given."

"I need to find my friends." John starts abruptly to his feet, feeling as if he is heaving off some strange weight trying to keep him rooted.

"But if you stay here with me, you'll learn about the curse."

"What curse?"

"Your father's, the one he has brought down upon you all."

"I must go." John has to force the words past his fear. "My commander will be wondering where I am."

"Off to kill more of the savage kerns?" says the man, undismayed, raising an eyebrow.

"It's wrong to kill them!" John finds himself blurting this out. "This is their land, and we're taking it from them."

"Oh, John. For shame. That's treason, you know. Those are dangerous words you're uttering."

With a cry, John sprints away from the clearing, his rebec thudding at his shoulder.

Behind him, the stranger's laughter follows him all the way to the edge of the forest.

Myrddin jerks himself away from the orb with the little scene enacted inside. He passes a hand over the orb, which returns to the milky whiteness it possessed before Myrddin set it to scrying. Myrddin bundles it back into its velvet bag. *I must keep my stone safe*, he tells himself. *No eyes must be upon it but mine.*

He thinks with a chill of what he has just seen. *These things haven't happened yet. No real danger*, he tries to tell himself. He supposes the young man is the mage yet to be born. Mere supposition. He supposes the young mage will be named John.

But he doesn't have to suppose who the other man is, and the recognition makes him tremble. The hooded man. He is Gilles de Rais.

"Maybe something can yet be done," Myrddin whispers. "The future may be averted in some cases." He has known it to be true. Rarely, though. Very, very rarely.

Myrddin rises shakily from his golden table, inlaid with mystic symbols in crushed fragments of turquoise. He comes out of his rooms, looking around for Dee.

"Check," said Dee to Myrddin. And "Mate."

Myrddin, roused from his reverie, looked over at his friend with a smile. "You got me," he said.

"You weren't even paying attention," Dee accused. "Where's the thrill of victory in that?"

"Sorry, Dee," said Myrddin. "Too preoccupied with the agony of defeat, I suppose." Struck with a thought, he hurried back to his rooms, took his scrying stone in its velvet bag from the beautiful inlaid table, and pushed it high up on a shelf, as if, by putting it away, he could put away the presentiments it had given him, and delay the consequences.

PART I: ROSE AND BRIAR

Gilles de Rais looked over at Myrddin and Dee, where they conferred together after the conference. He showed his pointed teeth in a grin. Let Myrddin summon his allies. Gilles would make his own careful inroads into all the kinds underneath the Spheres: the mages, the witches, the eala, the gwrgi. He already had his coterie among the mages, growing and getting stronger with every turning of the moon.

Someday soon, a new mage would come into the world. A mage with special powers. Myrddin had foreseen it, and now Gilles had seen it too. Already Gilles was thinking how he could make that young man his own. Sure as he knew his own name, Gilles knew Myrddin was aware of that young man's potential. Sure as he knew his own name, Gilles knew Myrddin would work hard to make the young man his own ally. Gilles would forestall Myrddin, when the time came. The young man must be his, not Myrddin's.

That was a project for later. For the future.

Here in the present, Gilles saw a handy way to make the ordinary folk his own, as well as the other kinds. Ordinary folk had no powers, and they tended to be stupid and clumsy. But there were so many of them. Individually weak, but they had strength in numbers. Gilles congratulated himself on his foresight. He'd control the ordinary folk as well as the mages and witches, the eala and gwrgi.

He knew just how to begin. A young man with outsized appetites, soon to hold sway over an entire kingdom. Not some dim figure of the future. A man already born, already a tool to hand. A young man highly placed. A prince. He was the perfect vehicle for Gilles's plans. Gilles would infect him, and if he resisted, Gilles would crush him.

RANULF

CHAPTER ONE

Schooling a Shrew in Lunds-fort

Lady knows, this big dirty city was the last place the prince wanted to be. But the king his father had given him a good talking-to. "Now that you've pledged your fealty to me, son, and have taken your rightful place as heir to the throne, I'm expecting certain duties of you. Childhood's at an end, son."

Dark Ones take it, thought Rannie. Along with the jeweled sword of office his father had used to knight him, Rannie realized he had also put on the mantle of adulthood and all its tiresome obligations.

Now one of those tiresome obligations had Rannie in its talons.

As he rode with the young men of his party through the gates of Lunds-fort, the others began making good-natured jokes at his expense. "She's sure to be ugly," said his best friend

Brenci, also an heir. Bren was heir to the earldom on the sea cliffs at the western edge of Rannie's father's realm. Rannie punched Bren in the arm and laughed along, but he didn't much feel like laughing.

Here he was, preparing to meet his bride-to-be Emilde, daughter of one of the most powerful nobles in the Eastern Baronies. But Nine Spheres, the girl was only ten years old. It would be some years before he'd wed her and escort her back across the border to his father's realm, the Sceptered Isle. Couldn't this all have waited, all the fuss and bother?

He looked over at Bren with envy. Everything came easily for Bren. He sat his horse easily; he made friends easily. He was good-looking and easy-going. And some day soon, he'd be wed to a girl he had known since childhood, Aderyn, the daughter of one of his vassals.

Bren was so rich he didn't have to worry about marrying for advantage. He'd marry for love. Not exactly love. For friendship.

"What's love, anyway?" said Bren later that day, as they settled into their quarters. "It's a momentary pang. I can satisfy that with any serving wench who happens by. Respect is more important. I've been friends with Aderyn since we were babes in arms. We'll wed, and she'll give me many sons to manage my estate and lands after I'm gone."

They paused while a bondswoman came into their rooms with fresh bedding.

Rannie eyed her. She had ample hips, and her breasts were jostling each other and pushing the front of her tunic out into enticing peaks.

As she left the room, he turned to Bren. "Speaking of momentary pangs. . ."

Bren laughed.

Rannie stepped to the door and whistled. He returned leading the woman, who stood with her head hanging. Rannie pushed her against the wall and hiked up her skirts. He pulled down the neck of her gown and buried his head between her breasts, nuzzling and biting. He thrust into her as she stood quietly, her arms loose at her sides, while he finished.

"Better," he grunted, turning to Bren. "Want a turn?"

"Nay, brother, I'm content." Bren leaned past Rannie, where he was pulling his leggings up, and handed the bondswoman a coin. She curtsied and hurried off again.

"I'll have a little more of that after we return from board," Rannie called down the corridor after her. "Make sure to attend me."

"Aren't you worried whether she's clean, brother?" said Bren.

"Nah. I'll take my chances. I've got an appetite," said Rannie. He looked over at Bren. For all Bren's talk of wenches, Bren stayed faithful to Aderyn. Rannie couldn't figure out why Bren stinted himself like that. It certainly wasn't his own way, not where women were concerned. What were women designed for, anyway, if not to tup and breed?

At board that night, he was all politeness and smiles. Their host, Baron Marifius, greeted him effusively and seated him next to Rannie's intended, the baron's young daughter Emilde. Emilde was pale and serious. Her sleek dark hair hung in curtains on either side of her thin face, as if framing an enigmatic picture. She wasn't ugly, Rannie saw with relief, but she was a skinny thing. *Still, who knows?* he said to himself. *She's only a child. What she'll look like in ten years is anyone's guess.* She could turn into a real porker with spots on her face.

He figured he had ten more years of freedom from her at the least. His father, for a man of his age, was hale and strong, not as he once was, surely, but not due to cross that river into the Land of the Dead any time soon.

The holdings of his bride-to-be Emilde's father Marifius were well into the Baronies mainland, far away across the Narrows. But the baron had agreed with Rannie's father to make this visit to his Lunds-fort kin just across the border from the Sceptered Isle, and bring his daughter along. That would put the baron's party conveniently much closer to the king's royal seat at Tambourne, conveniently close to arrange a visit between Rannie and Emilde.

"It's worth a journey. The two of them should become acquainted," Marifius had said to Ranulf the Third, the prince's imposing father, when they had met the year before and had sealed the deal to betroth their children. The children actually meeting. Ranulf huffed in a breath at the thought. Marifius was new-fangled that way, it seemed.

As Ranulf the Third had informed Rannie of these plans and had then launched into another boring harangue about marriage, the prince had tried to get his father to consider one of the court ladies of their own land, a winsome girl much closer to the prince's own age, a delicious little piece with a roving, lecherous eye and a charming gap between her two front teeth. The thought of that little gap roused the prince again, even now, as he sat at board with his intended. *Everyone says a little gap like that means a woman is a hot and frisky thing*, he thought.

Back when he had posed this delicate matter to Ranulf the Third, his father was having none of it. "Marriage is good coin that must not be spent carelessly, son. Every one of those barons over there across the Narrows is scratching and biting and clawing at the others, trying to get a better hold on Lunds-fort here on our side of the water. Every one of them sees it as a base to encroach into more of the territory that by right belongs to us. We need an alliance with one of the most powerful of their barons, to keep our borders safe."

The king had been standing by the big hearth stones of his great hall, instructing his son as the prince fidgeted to get geared up for hunting later that day. Rannie wanted to get down to the mews and choose which peregrine he would bring with him this time. He had an entire row of them, and he loved them all. At the very end of the row, his father's gyrfalcon stood solitary and neglected on its perch. The king didn't particularly care for hawking, but it was his son's passion.

As the prince's thoughts strayed to which of his birds would be most suitable for landscape and weather, his father continued to drone on. "Someday, my son, with the help of Baron Marifius, or if not him, his sons after him, you may be able to get your hands on Lunds-fort again yourself. You may be able to drive the barons across the Narrows where they belong. Then Lunds-fort will be part of our own realm once again. I doubt I'll live to see it. The Lady knows I've tried. But this last war has sorely depleted our treasury."

"Yes, Father," said the prince.

"And that's another thing. Marifius is rich. You'll get your hands on some of his gold. If you're canny, maybe a lot of it."

"Maybe one day all of it, Father," said the prince, getting interested now in spite of himself.

"Careful there, son. The young lady's brothers are stronger than you. Especially the third of the sons, Mabire. A gallant young man. They'll fight for what's theirs. The oldest is a bit long in the tooth. The second, not so bright. But that young Mabire. You watch out for that one, son." The king's tone was admiring.

The prince bowed, to show he heeded his father's warning, but he had to suppress a little twinge of resentment. The king never spoke of his own son the way he was speaking of this Mabire. The prince thought of his future father-in-law's gold with longing. If he had that, no one would be able to show the Sceptered Isle any disrespect.

No one would be able to show any disrespect to him, either.

And now here he sat, beside this skinny sullen slip of a girl, making the first move toward possessing himself of her father's riches.

He leaned over to her to make charming conversation.

"Don't bother," she said under her breath. "They'll make us wed, but that doesn't mean I have to like you."

"Rude little chit, aren't you," he murmured in her ear.

He put out a hand, under the table, and waited with well-practiced patience til she half-rose to reach for a piece of fruit in the bowl in front of her. He thrust his hand beneath her skirts and grabbed her hard by the privates under the bunched cloth. With satisfaction, he watched her stifle a gasp, squirming against his hand. "You see how it is, Mistress Sour-face."

Looking straight ahead, visibly struggling to school her expression, she hissed, "I'll tell my father it's all off."

"If he lets a child set his policy, I doubt I'd want any shrewish offspring of his to be siring my sons." In the cheerful roar of jests and conversation and toastings, no one had noticed the muted flurry of their struggle, the prince to keep his grip and the girl to get out of it. Ranulf the prince smiled pleasantly to Emilde's father and leaned over to ask him about the productivity and management of the vineyards on his lands. Under the table, though, he didn't let go. He squeezed harder.

Out of the corner of his eye, he saw tears of rage threaten to spill over down Emilde's cheeks. Rage and pain.

So the evening was not a complete loss. It had its amusements. It had its consolations for the unpleasant task the king his father had set him to perform, and it whetted his appetite for more of the pillowy charms of the little maid, afterward.

CHAPTER TWO

The Heavens Themselves Blaze Forth

B y the time the party of the prince saddled up for the ride back to Tambourne and his father's royal seat at Tam Fort there, Prince Ranulf felt unexpectedly pleased with the entire expedition. The season had passed pleasantly.

He hadn't had much to do with his intended bride. She kept out of his way, and he was glad of it. He didn't lay hands on her again. The day after their first meeting, reflecting on his actions, he decided he'd been wrong to taunt her in the way he had. He needed to take a gentler tack with her, just in case he really did have to wed her one day. He saw Bren looking him askance after that first dinner and realized he might not have been as discreet about what he'd done to Emilde as he thought.

But he'd not allow himself to marry a shrew. Not marry one and let her get away with it. When he thought of it that way, he felt justified. But also relieved that he didn't have to see her much.

During his visit, he sampled many of the city's delights, but the little bondsmaid was his favorite. After a few days of the bother of tracking her down, he had simply moved her into his bed, where he could get at her as often as he liked. As he made ready to return home, he gave her a gold piece, in case he'd left her with an unexpected burden. *I'm not some churl*, he told himself. *I take care of my obligations.*

Now, at the start of a warm harvest-tide day, the ride back looked to be shaping into a pleasant time as well.

"I've no doubt we'll enjoy some fine hunting along the way," he leaned over in the saddle to say to Bren. On the road back to Tambourne, they planned to stop for a while at his kinsman Oswine's estate, and he knew Oswine kept an excellent stable and mews.

He also thought with fondness of his cousin Aelfhild, Oswine's oldest daughter. The woman who'd taken him in hand at only fourteen (Here he laughed to himself at the joke he'd just made, and reminded himself to tell it to Bren later) and taught him everything a man needs to know about a woman.

She'd been twenty-two when she'd caught him behind the rose arbor in the garden one summer evening and had given him his first lesson. The prince felt himself stiffening at the memory.

She'd be over thirty now, and he heard she was a mother thrice over. She probably wouldn't even remember him. Besides, didn't she live far upriver, with that old husband of hers? Wouldn't she be fat and complacent by now? Or if not fat, then wrinkled and wizened? The prince tried to steel himself to disappointment of one sort or another when he saw her. If he saw her.

With amusement, he realized how unsettled he was at the idea of seeing her. Or not seeing her. He'd have to tell Bren about that, too.

When they got to Oswine's estate, and had dismounted, and had handed their horses off to the manservant, and had waited in the courtyard for their entourage and baggage train to wind into the courtyard after them, and when they had been welcomed heartily by Cousin Oswine and brought to his hearth with flagons of mead to await dinner, the prince saw with a stirring of his vitals that Aelfhild was by her father's hearth to greet them.

She was in looks, he saw. Older, but still as lush. Lusher.

"Little hawk," she whispered to the prince as she passed him to her place at board. "I remember you."

She was dressed in black. "I'm a widow now," she said demurely.

After they had supped, she murmured to him, "My room is the one farthest down the corridor."

And so their stay at his cousin's manor passed pleasantly away. The hunting was fine.

"Now for a long slog of it back home," he told Bren as they said their goodbyes and mounted up. Dawn was just turning the skies a faint gray.

"Don't forget me, little hawk," Aelfhild murmured, pressing his hand and retreating to her cousin's side.

"Don't think to have her, brother," said Bren as they rode away. The sun had risen. The day looked to be fine for traveling. "She's in the king's gift. By the next time you see her, she'll be married again to whatever lord your father chooses for her."

The prince snorted. "Why will that matter a whit?"

But then he and Bren both pulled their horses sharply up. They all did. The prince felt his mouth gaping open. Riding high above them, blindingly bright even against the brightness of the bright morning, a malign star with a flaming tail.

They all dismounted and knelt in the road.

"Child keep us," Bren whispered beside him. "What is happening to us?"

Such a star, descending from its proper place attached to its sphere, presaged a dire fate for the realm.

After the first shock, the prince got up from his knees and dusted himself off, carefully ignoring the blasphemy Bren had just uttered. It was forbidden to speak of the Children. "To horse," he shouted to his party. "We must get to Tambourne as quick as ever we may."

But as he started to spring into the saddle, he hesitated. Stumbled. Fell.

He was dimly aware Bren was by his side, shouting for help.

The sky turned black, only the bright streaking star illuminating the landscape in sharp and lurid shadows.

Something descended from the Spheres and hovered over him. It was as if a bird with a vast wingspan, blotting out the heavens, rode just overhead, boring down at him with its baleful eye.

I see you, Ranulf the prince. That's what he thought he was hearing, from some voice rebounding off the surrounding hills and valleys. *I know you for what you are.*

Who are you? he heard himself quaver. He could feel the beat of the enormous wings as they whipped the air about him into cyclonic bursts that buffeted him and left him gasping.

A mighty one who judges those abusing their power.

What do you want of me? he cried out in despair.

You are in danger, Ranulf, and it's your own doing. You must change.

Change? His mind was a blank. Change how? Had he done wrong to any? He'd schooled a silly girl. He'd taken his pleasure of a serving wench. Surely these were not wrong.

Change and wait.

Wait for what? he whispered.

You are a man judged. Now wait for your sentencing.

"Rannie," a voice was urgently calling him. "Ranulf."

The prince blinked up at the sky. There rode the star, but in everything else, the sky was the same blue it always was. He saw no hovering mighty bird. He heard no admonishing mighty voice.

Bren was helping him to his feet. His friend looked frightened.

Rannie shook his head, hard.

"What happened? Have you taken ill?" said Bren.

"I don't know," the prince said. His tongue felt thick in his mouth. He felt as though he were waking from a bad dream. "My father," he said, remembering. He stared up in fear at the star. He lunged for his horse and got himself into the saddle.

He, Bren, and some of his other courtiers rode hard for the fort, leaving the baggage train to get there as soon as it could.

Even before they reached the city gates, they heard the tolling of the bells.

The prince got down off his horse, feeling himself go white.

Bren was there beside him.

"My lord," said Bren. Then Bren knelt. "My liege."

The bells could mean only one thing. Ranulf the Third was dead. The prince would now be proclaimed king.

As soon as they got to the city gates, his father's counselors were there to meet him with sober faces. They led him immediately to his mother.

"Son," she said, putting out her hand to him.

When he rushed to her, she fended him off. She rose painfully from her chair and went down on her knees to him. "My king," she said.

"Mother, no, don't kneel," said the prince in a panic.

She looked up at him under the hooded lids of her eyes. "Ranulf," she said. "You are king. Behave like one."

"What must I do, Mother? How did this happen?"

"You must spend the morning with Wemba. He'll tell you everything you need to know." She motioned to her chief lady-in waiting, who hoisted her to her feet and led her off. She did not turn back to him when the prince cried out to her.

The old counselor Wemba was there at his elbow. "My prince," he said, bowing low. "My king. Let us retire to your father's study. I'll tell you everything. Your poor mother is overwhelmed with grief."

With relief, more like it, thought Ranulf the crown prince, looking with bitter longing after her as she disappeared down the corridor to her private apartments.

"What happened, Wemba?" said the prince as the door to his father's study closed behind them.

Wemba swept his arm wide, bowing and pointing to his father's big chair.

I must sit there, thought the prince blankly. *It's my chair now*.

"The king was out for his morning ride," said Wemba, when Rannie had seated himself. "His horse shied at something alongside the road. The king fell and struck his head against a stone. Last night, the king died."

"The star," stammered Rannie.

"Indeed. It has come to us, to signify a change. The king is dead. Long live the king."

"What must I do, Wemba?" said Rannie.

"There is a ceremonial order to follow, my liege. All the necessary events, all in their proper places. Now that you're back, we'll inter the body of your father in the High Temple of the Lady Goddess. After we have seen our good king to his crypt, we'll move in procession from the High Temple to the city gates. You'll be at the head of it, on the king's horse. When we reach the gates, the bells will cease tolling, and you will be proclaimed king."

All this while, the bells of the fort had relentlessly tolled, pounding Rannie's skull.

He put his hands to his head. "Can't we stop them, the bells?"

"No, my liege." If Wemba was dismayed by this outburst, he didn't betray it.

The bells tolled and tolled. Somehow, in their relentlessness, they reminded Rannie of the dark hovering bird, and its accusations. The bells were accusing him.

The prince pressed both hands hard against his temples. He tried and failed to speak. "And my mother?" he got out at last.

"As the queen mother and the king's widow, of course she'll know every comfort. She'll go to her own palace to live," said Wemba, placidly. If he had noticed the stark moment of panic in the new king's eye, he said nothing.

Ranulf the prince, now almost the king, cleared his throat, trying to speak and act normally. "And I'll live here in Tam Fort."

"Indeed, my liege. You and your bride, when you wed."

"But my intended is only a girl of ten." The bells tolled and tolled. *They're accusing me over her*, he thought. *But how is that possible? She's only a troublesome child. Only a girl. I gave her a lesson she sorely needed*. The bells tolled, telling him *No. No. No. No*. They tolled, saying *You. You. You.*

Wemba nattered on, oblivious. "It's customary to wed her immediately, in cases such as this. I'll prepare a scroll to send to her father, with Your Majesty's permission."

"But she's only ten years old."

"It may be—" Here Wemba made a scrupulous little pause. "It may be she will stay with her parents for a time, after the marriage, until she crosses that boundary to womanhood. Such a practice is common, in cases like this one. Shall I suggest that in my message, Your Highness?"

"Please. Yes. Please do." *Please*, he begged that dark presence. *Please*.

"But the wedding should take place at the earliest opportunity. I'll begin the planning, Your Highness, shall I?"

"Yes, please do," said Rannie automatically, but in his mind, he was saying *No. No. No.*

"Shall I have your Gentleman of the Bedchamber lead you to your room, Your Majesty? You must be fatigued after your journey, and you must be distressed by this news."

"Thank you, yes," said Rannie.

A man Rannie only dimly recognized as one of his father's courtiers steered him along, and Rannie stumbled ahead of him, numb with shock. He realized they weren't going to his own rooms in the fort. The man was showing him the way to his father's bedchamber. Rannie had been there only rarely.

"I'd like to be alone," he said to the man, who bowed and left him there.

As soon as he'd gone, Rannie wished desperately he had made the man stay. Rannie stood before the big bed as it loomed up out of the dimness.

What do I do now? He was working himself into a panic. When his mind strayed to the sullen young girl who would soon be his wife, and to the hovering of the dark, judging presence, he had to get a stern grip on himself, to keep himself from running from the room in horror.

As for the bed. Rannie eyed it. Could he ever bring himself to sleep in it? The bells over him, high in the fort, tolled and tolled and tolled. In the end, he pulled some of the furs off the big bed and rolled himself in them at the hearth. There he fell into an exhausted sleep.

In the morning, the courtiers came in to him and dressed him in the black clothing he needed to wear. They led him to his father's destrier and helped him mount. The beast laid back its ears and looked menacingly around at Rannie.

Even this horse knows I shouldn't be king. Even this horse knows I have done wrong. I am not worthy, thought Rannie.

Thank the Lady it wasn't the same horse that had killed his father. That one was his father's gentle old rouncey, his favorite for riding about. The horse, Wemba told him, had been destroyed.

The one Rannie mounted now was his father's warhorse. His father hadn't been to war in five years, and this last war he'd conducted from a litter, not from the back of this imposing black beast.

This was the horse the prince needed to ride, in the procession. Suppose this horse threw him from its back and trampled him, the malefactor.

I've done nothing wrong! he cried out inwardly.

Something told him, *No. You have.*

Prince Ranulf managed to get through it all.

He steadied himself through the lengthy ceremony of interring his father in the High Temple, in the tomb where his father's father and that man's father were buried. The tomb standing tall and imposing, surrounded by the lesser tombs of his older brother and sister, both long dead of plague, shouldering aside the small tomb of his father's first wife and the baby that killed her within a year of their marriage, decades before the prince was born.

When he bent to kiss his father's dead cheek before Ranulf the Third was shut up in the dark with his forefathers, the crown prince had to steel himself to do it, and as his mouth brushed the cheek of the dead king, he felt that dark wings were brushing just over him, waiting to descend.

Somehow, he got himself out of the tomb and back onto his horse. The procession wound from the temple end of the town of Tambourne through the town's crooked streets to the gates of Tam Fort.

But as the prince reached the gates and his counselors bowed low and his best friend and most important vassal Bren helped him dismount from his horse, the bells stopped tolling, and the prince felt a relief so strong he nearly shouted. The pressure lifted. The dark wings retreated.

Everyone but the prince fell to their knees, even Bren. Only his father's herald stayed standing. The prince stood looking out over the bent heads of the kneelers in the roadway.

The herald shouted out his proclamation. "Hear, all ye under Ranulf's protection. Ranulf the Third of the Sceptered Isle has gone to the embrace of the Lady Goddess, may Her mercy shine on us all. Men of Ranulf, fast and pray. Men of Ranulf, fast and pray. Tomorrow Ranulf, crown prince and heir in his father Ranulf's line, will become our king. The Sceptered Isle will be his. Men of Ranulf, fast and pray. Men of Ranulf, fast and pray."

That other Ranulf the herald is shouting about. I'm that Ranulf thought the prince.

In the morning, he returned in a second procession, dressed in his richest and most colorful clothing, as they all were. The green cloak of his dynasty flowed and rippled behind him as he rode the destrier again, and all the people lining the way cried out in joy.

As he rode, he squinted up into the clear blue day, and he saw the malevolent star riding the skies along with him. He wended his way once again to the Temple of the Goddess, this time to have Her high priest settle the crown upon his brow.

The prince became King. Ranulf the Fourth of the Sceptered Isle.

At that moment, he felt himself the loneliest man underneath the Nine Spheres. He felt himself judged. As the voice had promised he was, Ranulf the Fourth felt himself a man awaiting sentence.

That night, with trepidation, he allowed himself to be led once again to the bedchamber of his father. His gentleman of the bedchamber waited upon him as he climbed into the big bed. There was no escaping it: he must sleep there.

In the night, he had a dream.

He was called to account before a mighty court.

Presiding was a formidable man, and in his dream, Ranulf recognized this man as his judge.

Two men spoke of him to the court. One, a shrewd man with a pointed beard and piercing blue eyes, the accuser. The other, thin, saturnine, his eyes dark and brooding, Ranulf's defender.

"I charge this man with abuse of power," said the first man, the man with the piercing blue eyes. "In doing so, he opens himself to great evil, reaching far beyond himself to damage others."

He addressed his words to the judge, a tall, powerfully built man with gleaming dark skin, as if perhaps he came from the Burnt Lands, a man with a basso profundo voice.

"He has been given great power," said his accuser to this imposing judge. "The leadership of one of the most powerful realms underneath the Spheres," his accuser emphasized, the blue of his eyes blazing. This accuser pointed at Ranulf. "Yet he wastes his realm's resources on frivolity. He menaces the young girl intended for his bride. There is good in him, yet he squanders it. This is the way of the world. This is the reason The Three may end it. They see how futile it is for the world to go on. Why should it, if people like this are in power. The Three demand justice. This man, so young, in such a position of power, has already set his foot on the way of injustice. Let him be cursed. And not he alone. The curse of the father descends to the son."

The judge turned to the second man. "Gilles?"

This second man, the saturnine man with the brooding eyes, stepped forward. He leaned toward Ranulf and looked deep within him.

Ranulf felt seared by his gaze.

"This is one of creation's powerful," said the second man. "Young yet, but I see great promise in him. He has made the most of the gifts the world has given him, and he'll continue to do so. Why should he care about some silly girl and her over-dainty feelings? He has important tasks to perform, a realm to run. Wars to fight. This is the way of the world. Might will prevail, and he is one of the mighty of the world. Let him chart his own course. Cursed? Superstitious nonsense. Get out of his way and let him make his own justice."

The two men who had spoken looked now to the judge.

The judge pointed to the skies, where the comet pressed on, the hairy star, casting its unnatural shadow over the land.

He crooked a finger, and Ranulf knew he was to stand forth.

Hesitantly, this dream-Ranulf crept out under the wide sky. And then the hovering dark wings descended again.

A booming voice echoed in his head. *Your own blood*. The words reverberated, as if spoken into a hollow space of unimaginable proportions. *Your own blood will be charged with it. Punish. Or vindicate. Await your sentence.*

Ranulf woke up trembling.

"It's only a dream," he whispered to himself, but he quaked in fear.

After a time, he fell asleep again, and he didn't wake until morning.

CHAPTER THREE

The Bliss of Marriage

Wemba would not let Ranulf be. He was there every day with more arrangements for the wedding, and still more. Early on, Ranulf had shocked the good man to the leathern soles of his shoes.

"Lord Wemba, I must ask your advice," said Ranulf from his big chair (*his father's big chair*) in his study (*his father's study.*).

"And what is that, Your Majesty? I assure you, I'll give you the best advice I can," said the old man, bowing low.

"I know you will, my good lord," said Ranulf with a warm smile. "As you always advised Father." *How soon*, he wondered, *before I can surround myself with younger men and send this old fellow out to the countryside?* He drew a breath. "Here's my question. How can we get me out of this marriage? Give me some good suggestions how we can get that done."

Every night, as he closed his eyes in sleep, the pinched, unpleasant features of his bride-to-be rose up before him. Every night, he prayed she would not appear before the mighty dream-court to accuse him. Some nights, she did.

He distracted himself by bedding every woman in the fort who crossed his path, near about. Still the face of skinny nasty little Emilde would keep haunting him, and the thing he had done to her, and the court of the mighty ones, and the great hovering dark bird.

Am I cursed? he thought.

At last the comet disappeared. It diminished, and little by little, it faded from the skies. When it had completely gone, he felt the judgment lifting off him. The visitation of the mighty bird, some bird of prey, he told himself, was only the act of his grief-stricken imagination. Nothing more. He was not cursed. Surely he was not. Only children and fools believed such things.

But whenever he thought of Emilde, the faint beat of dark wings caused sweat to bead on his forehead, a cold trickle of sweat to gather at the back of his neck and dampen the back of his tunic.

And whenever he thought of the mysterious pronouncement: *Your own blood. Punish, or vindicate?* he felt a sort of chill settle over him.

This marriage. With, some day, its offspring. *My own blood.* It must not happen.

Well. Of course he must have offspring. The realm expected it. Needed it. Still, couldn't it be possible to have other offspring, from some other wife? Maybe that would lift the curse, if the curse was focused on Emilde. If there was a curse. Surely there was no curse.

"But brother," Bren had protested mildly, not understanding the other part of Rannie's trepidation. Rannie hadn't mentioned anything as outlandish as a curse to Bren. "It will be some years before the girl comes to live here, and anyway, plenty of men hate the women they're married to." Bren clapped Rannie on the back. "They get themselves concubines."

Ranulf reflected gloomily that his own father had had several of these convenient women stashed about the fort's grounds. His parents had clearly disliked each other. Why should his own marriage be any different?

His father's concubines had miraculously all now disappeared, their bastards with them. He wondered idly whether his mother had had them done away with. More likely those women had seen their danger, when his father lay on his deathbed, and had gathered up their offspring and gotten safely out of Tambourne.

The bastards of plenty of powerful men grew up side-by-side with their legitimate brothers, and no one thought a thing about it. The bastard brother of one of the most powerful of the barons, in fact, was that overlord's chief counselor. Ranulf had met the man.

But, he thought, *those powerful lords weren't married to my mother.*

She might have disliked his father, hated him even, but no bastard child of his nor their strumpets of mothers would be safe while she had any power to make it otherwise.

Ranulf had encountered a few of these bastard half-siblings of his, but only in passing. He'd never been allowed to be with them or make friends of them.

At least he hadn't been a completely lonely child. He'd always had Bren. Bren's father had fostered him out into the king's household when Bren was a small boy. Bren was Ranulf's brother, just about. Just as good as.

"And when I marry and have a son, and you marry and have one, they'll be brothers too," said Bren.

There it was again, thought Rannie, his mouth going dry. *My own blood.* But of course there would be children. His mind kept going in circles. There had to be children. For a king, children—sons, especially—were necessary and right. They weren't a curse. They were the Lady's blessing upon the realm.

In spite of Bren's practical and reassuring words, Ranulf's heart seized whenever he thought of marriage to such an unpleasant child as Emilde, and of the dark bird, and of the booming, judging voice.

I'm king, he said to himself. *I can just make this problem go away. Why be king at all, if I can't do this.* This thought chased away the dark fears.

He thought again of the saucy daughter of one of his courtiers, the girl with the little gap between her teeth, and he felt a surging thrill. Of course, by now he didn't need to wed the girl. He'd already enjoyed her. But someone like her.

Someone he'd want in bed with him. He'd wed someone like that.

As the moon turned, and turned about, and turned about again, as one season suceeeded to the next, the dark wings became a fading nightmare, and the nightmare didn't repeat. After a while, Ranulf hardly thought of it at all.

When he thought of Emilde in bed with him, though, he actually shuddered.

"Of course you're repelled, brother," said Bren. "She's a child. If you wanted her in that way, I'd be worried about you. Later on, things will be different. She'll move across the boundary to womanhood, and then you'll see her through different eyes."

At first, whenever he talked the matter over with Bren, two thoughts rose inside Ranulf, vying for dominance. He thought uneasily about what he'd done to Emilde, uneasily about the nightmarish wings and the nightmare of the judging voice.

But eventually, with Bren's sensible words, a more reasonable train of thought took over. Nothing had happened, had it? What had the voice threatened? Something about a sentence to be passed? Some curse. *Your own blood*. Nothing of the sort had happened or was likely to happen.

Of course, if Emilde had told any of her kin, there might be unpleasant repercussions. Surely she would have been too ashamed. But maybe she told her old nurse, or her best friend. Girls did things like that.

But some dark curse? Nonsense.

His thoughts turned more and more to the practical. The matter of actually having to wed and live with a girl like Emilde.

He knew he'd made a bitter enemy of her. He knew she wasn't likely to forget. Spending his whole life with her had seemed a remote thing only a season ago. Now it was a looming, distasteful reality. Suppose his sentence was the curse of having to spend the rest of his life with her. To look up from whatever ordinary thing he was doing, every day, and feel her judging eye on him. That would be curse enough.

"Maybe she'll die of plague," Ranulf had muttered. "Maybe I can arrange it."

Bren had just laughed at him. Ranulf glanced at him. Bren didn't really know. Bren didn't know how bad it was, what he'd done. *And*, the thought kept coming at him, *Bren didn't hear that dark voice.* He thrust such an addlepated thought determinedly away from him.

What he needed was action. After the latest discussion he'd had with Bren about the unpleasant matter of his upcoming marriage, Ranulf decided to take action that very day. He summoned Wemba to his private room, his private study, to suggest getting out of the entanglement his father had gotten him into. A murrain on his father. Ranulf felt a surge of confidence in Wemba. The man was a diplomat. He'd know what to do.

He presented a new task to Wemba: to hammer out the practical details of nullifying his betrothal.

From across his big desk strewn with parchments, Ranulf saw Wemba's eyes widen in shock.

Nothing Ranulf could say or do seemed to shock the man. Not the hordes of women Ranulf summoned to keep him company in his father's big frightening bed. None of the outlandish requests Ranulf made of him, some of them (*Ranulf knew this. He just couldn't help himself.*) deliberately designed to get the old man's dander up.

Nothing. The man's expression was just as bland when Ranulf spoke about maybe lining up all the daughters of the villagers nearby and deflowering them one by one as it was when Ranulf suggested the cook might bring him one of those jellied confits he'd so enjoyed in boyhood.

But this. To call the marriage off. Finally Ranulf got a rise out of the old man.

"Your Majesty," Wemba quavered, his eyes growing ever more alarmed. "Don't think it, I pray Your Highness. Remember, this marriage was arranged by your own father to further certain important policies of state. If you go back on your father's word, it could mean war, Your Majesty."

Ranulf sat back heavily in his chair. "I'm displeased," he said, watching with satisfaction as the counselor trembled under his gaze. "Dismissed," he said. Wemba bowed silently and backed out of the room.

There, thought Ranulf. *I like that.*

But his satisfaction was short-lived because, he realized, the marriage was still on, and drawing closer every day.

He might have intimidated the old man, but he hadn't derailed the marriage plans. Worst of all, he knew Wemba was right. He didn't derail them because, practically speaking, he couldn't derail them. Ranulf would still have to serve his sentence.

The fortnights went by. And now the marriage day was nearly upon him.

Ranulf endured being fitted for the rich bridal garments as the royal tailors fussed over him and tugged at him.

He went out to Tam Fort's paddock to examine his new horse, the one he'd ride in the bridal procession. That at least was a pleasure.

The fierce black destrier had been killed, along with his father's gyrfalcon. "It's customary," the man in charge of the royal stables had explained at Ranulf's shocked inquiry. "At a king's death, his horse, his hounds, his hawks follow him across that river into the Land of the Dead."

"In earlier times, his wife accompanied him too," Bren pointed out, later.

Bren the scholar. Bren knew his letters. Ranulf did too, a little, but he hadn't been very interested, and his father hadn't insisted on it. After all, a warrior didn't need to know his letters, and a king, of course, had to learn the arts of war above all else. His father had been a warrior. In his day, a very great warrior.

Ranulf had had to bite back a laugh, though, at Bren's interesting piece of information. He'd like to see anyone suggest to his mother that her duty lay in following her husband to the Land of the Dead. As it was, she was forced into retirement in a remote manor far from Tam Fort. He had seen her exactly twice since his father's funeral, and he doubted he'd see much of her again, not until he presented her with a grandchild.

He supposed she'd be at the wedding, though. The dowager queen.

"Yes," said Wemba. "Yes, she'll be there. Now as to the food, the head cook has provided this list. . ." and on and on the man had rambled, his age-spotted hands trembling and the white tufts of hair sprouting from his ears quivering.

Wemba's urgency dampened Ranulf's vital humors. He listened to the old counselor in a state of gloom. The bridal party was due tomorrow.

After Ranulf's earlier visit to Lunds-fort, there to meet his bride-to-be (and insult her, as it turned out), Baron Marifius and his entourage had all gotten themselves back to the Baronies mainland, to the baron's estate. Marifius hadn't heard the news of the old king's death in time to prevent the return journey. But at least that inconvenience had given Ranulf a brief reprieve, almost a full year before he'd had to make good on his father's treaty and marry Marifius's daughter.

Ranulf stirred in irritation. He had to force himself to keep his attention on Wemba. That year of grace once seemed to stretch out comfortably before him. How was it the day was upon him so soon? How could that be? Now here it was.

The bride and her family had spent the past turning of the moon in Lunds-fort, preparing. They had crossed the border just outside Lunds-fort into the Sceptered Isle, and had spent the past sen'night in a progress from manor to manor across Ranulf's territory, being handsomely entertained at each place. Including, Ranulf knew, his cousin Oswine's manor.

Some turnings of the moon back, he'd thought of Aelfhild and his most satisfying encounter with her at Oswine's manor. *How strange*, he remembered thinking. Why hadn't she been on his mind? The death of his father, and that frightening experience on the road, had driven her out of it.

He remembered what Bren had told him. As a rich and noble widow, Aelfhild was now in the king's gift. That had meant his father could bestow her hand in marriage on anyone he chose for her. Now that task was Ranulf's.

Marry her off? Why not take her for a concubine instead, he thought. *Wouldn't it be much the same*? As his marriage to Emilde loomed, he found himself casting desperately about for stratagems and evasions. He brought Aelfhild up with Wemba. Why not make some convenient arrangement with Aelfhild?

By now, Wemba had dropped any pretense that Ranulf didn't shock him deeply. "No, Your Majesty," Wemba had told him, his jowls wobbling. "A woman of the nobility, and a kinswoman. You must arrange a proper marriage for the lady."

"See to it, then, my lord." Ranulf recalled turning indifferently away. If he couldn't have her, he didn't care who did. But now, now that the marriage was upon him, he was sorry he hadn't taken a firmer stand. Or at least found someone else to install in some convenient little house in town. Some refuge.

In the morning, the bridal party would arrive in Tambourne. They'd stay at the manor of one of his most important nobles. The next day, he and Emilde would be wed.

In a daze, Ranulf went through the motions. He summoned up the energy to greet Marifius, now become his new father-in-law, and to extend him every hospitality. He met the powerful brothers at last, and through his fog he was able to register that his father was right about the youngest of Marifius's sons.

Mabire, Ranulf remembered. He was stalwart and shrewd. He looked to be a bit younger than Ranulf. Now this young man eyed his brother-in-law to-be with barely-disguised suspicion and dislike.

And Ranulf encountered his bride again. Emilde.

Just as he had remembered her, she was thin, pale, and unpleasant.

She stared up into his eyes with hatred.

He bent over her hand, his behavior toward her faultless. *See?* he found himself desperately telling that dark presence, just in case it was listening. *I am blameless.*

He cringed away from the thought the way he'd cringe away from a poisonous serpent of the Realm of the Asp. The dark presence. Thank the Lady it didn't haunt him now. Not much. Not that often.

The next morning, in a splendid ceremony in the High Temple of the Lady Goddess, he and Emilde were wed. He found himself praying a lot to the Lady these days. He never had before.

For instance, he fervently thanked the Lady he didn't have to consummate the marriage with Emilde, at least not now. *For the Lady's sweet sake, she's only eleven,* he thought, glancing over at her with dismay as they knelt for the priest's blessing.

But they did have to spend an entire uncomfortable turning of the moon together, feasting and dancing and celebrating.

The whole thing was a gorgeously presented sham.

All except one moment on the last day, before Emilde would return with her father and brothers to her home in the

Baronies, to wait until she reached womanhood before coming to Ranulf's bed.

A whole party of them went out to the mews to admire one of the rich gifts Marifius had brought to his new son-in-law.

"A gyrfalcon for a king, you know," Marifius told Ranulf. The bird sat proudly on its perch in Ranulf's mews while the members of the wedding party milled around and laughed and talked.

A peregrine for a prince or a noble, thought Ranulf. *But a gyrfalcon for a king.*

Everyone else soon crowded out of the mews into the formal gardens beyond, where they could enjoy the fine spring weather and eat and drink their fill.

Only Ranulf and Marifius remained behind.

Ranulf loved his peregrines, and he had always yearned after his father's gyrfalcon. Only a king could possess one. When Ranulf learned the bird had been killed, he felt a pang greater than the pang he'd felt when he'd learned of the death of his father. Of course he'd never admitted this to himself.

Now here was a gyrfalcon of his own, and he could see she was a noble bird.

He approached her to admire her close up. She was of the black morph, a presence so dark at the end of the mews that she seemed almost like a shadow, with a dark unsettling eye.

At his approach, she mantled and made several harsh cries. It was the usual thing, with birds of this type. She didn't know him yet.

But Ranulf jerked back in a kind of spasm. The bird that had accused him, he thought. What kind of bird was that. What kind of bird had the standing to accuse a king?

"Thanks for this rich gift, my lord," he said to Marifius, bowing low to his father-in-law, trying to hide the unaccustomed thrill of fear that pierced him through. Then he added, smoothly, "and for the richer gift by far of your beautiful daughter."

Marifius stood admiring the gyrfalcon too.

After a moment, though, he turned to Ranulf and looked him in the face. "My daughter is moody and difficult," he told Ranulf. "She's but a child, and she's in that period between child and woman where women especially are at their most melancholy. I wish you to take utmost care of her, my son. I love her dearly. I wish to see her happy."

"Of course," said Ranulf, bowing again, but he was taken aback.

"I believe the two of you dislike each other," said Marifius. "This grieves me."

"I'm sure any uneasiness between us will change as we come to know each other better," said Ranulf.

"I'd like that very much," said Marifius quietly. "You, as the elder, and her protector, will no doubt do your best to make it so." It was not a statement. It was a command.

Who is this baron, to command me, a king? thought Ranulf resentfully.

But as the thought formed, a shrill scream from the gyrfalcon brought him up short.

"Indeed I will, my lord," said Ranulf hastily. "I will cherish your daughter, and I will rejoice when she crosses into womanhood and we become one."

Marifius bowed, a stiff, curt bow, and moved out into the garden, leaving Ranulf with the gyrfalcon.

Ranulf found himself shaken by these words. By his father-in-law's frankness, his obvious love for his difficult, unsettling daughter, his obvious distrust of Ranulf.

Most of all by the bird. Her eye bored into Ranulf, seeing him.

Ranulf tried to shed himself of his dismay and found he couldn't. He stood for many minutes gazing at the gyrfalcon and getting a hold on his emotions, warding off the dark shadows that threatened to come crowding in on him.

The gyrfalcon was a noble bird. Why should he be afraid of her? He loved birds of this kind. Nothing to fear. *I'm letting my imagination run away with me*, he scolded himself. He approached closer, scrutinizing the bird.

She opened her beak once more to scream.

Your blood! You have been sentenced. That's what the magnificent dark bird appeared to be screaming at him.

He felt himself grow paler, his trembling becoming more pronounced. He stumbled out of the mews, driven by an unacccountable terror.

There were all his guests. There was Emilde. Their backs were turned to him.

Thank the Lady they haven't seen me in this shameful state, Ranulf thought.

Once out of the dimness of the mews, he steadied himself against the trunk of a tree. Its bark underneath his hand was rough and ridged. He flexed his hand, feeling the reality of it. Nothing terrible in the world, just sunlight and green and this solid tree.

But he couldn't help glancing back through the dark doorway into the mews, and shuddering.

He moved quickly to join his guests and his bride before he could fall prey to any more sick fancies. Before any of the guests noticed anything amiss.

He knew that he must stride into the garden smiling and confident. He knew that must be how he'd need to present himself to them all.

He knew, too, how far removed this outer self of him was from the inner, cringing little truth of him.

EMILDE

CHAPTER FOUR

A Consummation
Devoutly to be Wished

Emilde lay weeping in the little glade, her lady standing watch discreetly nearby.

"Please no," she begged. "Don't say I have to do this thing." She lay huddled for a moment, drawing her cloak about her. "Please," she whispered.

The wind whispered answering through her unbound hair.

She began her prayer again. "Child knows I don't desire the company of any man. Especially not that man. Yet I'm wed to him, and now, everyone tells me, I must go to him and be his.

But dear Child of mine, I'll serve you, only you, all my days, if you'll allow me to remain a virgin."

Now the wind died back. Only silence answered her.

Urgently, she began again. "I won't ask to know love. I won't ask for another, better husband. I'll stay just as I am, all my days. All my days. Please. Please."

Silence.

"If it is Your wish, I will gladly move across that river to the Land of the Dead, rather than do this thing," Emilde pled.

"My lady Emilde."

It was the quiet voice of Agace, her lady-in-waiting.

Emilde rose. She knew it was time to go. She wiped the tears from her eyes and moved toward Agace and let Agace help her mount her horse.

"It's no use," she said.

"Lady—" Agace hesitated. "Many young women have these fears, as they go to their marriage beds. Many young women have their mothers by them, to reassure them and tell them how it is, yet you have none. Shall I tell you what to expect, when you come to your husband?" Now that Emilde had become a woman, she was making ready to go across the Narrows, travel to Tambourne, and take her place as Ranulf the Fourth's wife in deed, not just in name.

"It's not that, dear Agace. It's the man himself."

"He's noble, lady. And a king."

"He's a churl," she bit out. "I hate him."

Agace was silent. She smiled a bit, but clearly she struggled not to let Emilde see.

You must think I'm stupid, Emilde thought. *That man has bedded every woman in my father's court, including you.*

"He's a proper man, your ladyship," said Agace as they rode out of the glade. "I think you'll find he treats you well."

Emilde said nothing. They all knew. Surely they had all seen how he had shamed her, when they first met. The memory of it, returning tenfold, threatened to undo her. But she forced herself to sit her horse proudly and say nothing.

"They say—" Agace began carefully. "Everyone says your father had a stern talk with him, after you were wed. Everyone says the king was properly chastened by your father's words."

Emilde stayed silent. She saw how Ranulf operated. He had sugared words for all around him. She had no doubt he'd used them on her father, to reassure him. But that's not who Ranulf was, underneath. She had seen him for who he really was.

When she thought of her father's love and care for her, and the love and care of her brothers—Mabire especially, and when she thought she must leave it all for a life of disrespect and insults, it nearly destroyed her.

I must not think about that right now, she told herself. *I must wait until I'm alone. Then I can weep.*

Her resolve was shattered as they rode into the courtyard of her father's manor. Mabire was there to help her off her horse. She fled into his arms and lay there sobbing.

"My dear, dear sister," whispered Mabire. He stroked her and led her inside and sat her by the fire. Agace brought her a hot posset, and then Mabire waved Agace away.

"Emilde," he said to her, tilting up her chin to look her in the eye. "Sister. You're about to do a hard thing. But you have courage. More courage than any of us. You're smarter than all of us. Remember who you are. Remember always. You are noble. That man cannot diminish you, though he may try."

Later Emilde allowed Agace to undress her and put her bed garment on her.

"Look at you, my lady," said Agace softly. "You're a woman indeed now. You are beautiful, my lady. Your husband will be overjoyed and astonished by you."

Emilde gave Agace a half-smile.

"But my lady. I've noticed something. I must warn you. I must. It's my duty."

Here it comes, thought Emilde. *The lecture about my duty to my husband. Whether I want it or not, whether I need it or not, Agace is determined to provide it.*

Agace surprised her. "My lady, I've heard you pray. Forgive me. It was a private matter, and I didn't mean to overhear. But I did, and now I must speak."

Emilde suppressed a small thrill of fear.

"My lady, it's forbidden to worship the Children. Yet you pray to your Child."

"I know it," Emilde whispered. "I do."

"I'd not see you put yourself in danger, when you go over there to that unfriendly land." Agace leaned over to Emilde and kissed her forehead, as she had done when Emilde was a small child.

All pretense at cheerfulness had dropped away from her lady-in-waiting. Emilde was touched by the concern she saw written on Agace's face.

"We all love you here, lady. None would betray you, here. Over there, you may find yourself surrounded by hard people. I beg you, lady. Don't let them overhear your prayers, as I have. Promise me you'll take care."

Emilde took the woman's hands in hers. "You are kind to me, Agace. I promise I'll be careful. But I won't stop praying to my Child. She didn't speak to me in the glade, but I know She hears me. You've given me good advice, though. I'll pray at the temple of the Lady Goddess and go through all the motions there. I promise I won't let anyone see my true beliefs or overhear my thoughts."

Agace kissed her again, and left her to her bed.

In a strange way, Emilde felt herself answered. Her Child had not spoken to her to tell her she didn't have to go through the ordeal ahead of her. She knew she wouldn't be able to escape it. But through her brother's love, and Agace's concern, she felt her Child was watching over her just the same. So Emilde was comforted, and at last she could sleep.

In the morning she made herself ready to go across the Narrows to be with her husband.

How very odd, Emilde was thinking as the boisterous party of Ranulf's nobles escorted her, and Ranulf with her, to their marriage bed. *These last days have been exactly like our wedding. Everything except the vows before the Lady Goddess in Her temple. We've already done that. But all the parties, all*

the feasting, all the gifts. They're much the same. One wedding. Now another. This, she realized, was the real one.

Through the first one, the actual wedding, she'd felt nothing but a numbed despair. Now she felt abject terror. Now she saw there was a difference between the earlier ceremonial wedding and this one, a big frightening difference.

You have courage, Emilde. She pulled the words of her brother around her as a protective mantle. She didn't feel very courageous.

She wondered, now that it was too late, whether she shouldn't have allowed Agace to tell her about the whole thing. What she'd have to do. What that man would do to her. But she'd been too proud.

And she did know. Of course she knew. Just not exactly how it would be, the motions and mechanics of the thing. Maybe nothing Agace could have told her would have kept this fear from her.

The smiling, shoving crowd of Ranulf's courtiers had them to the bedchamber now.

"Let's see the bride!" someone called out, and they all took up the howl.

This is just their way, Emilde had to remind herself. *Just what they do over here. They don't mean any insult.*

But she was frightened and repelled.

In all the riotous lot of them, only one face stood out, reassuring and steady. Ranulf's friend the Earl Brenci. She didn't want to look away from him.

His eyes, locked on hers, gave her back the courage she felt leaking away from her. He, among them all, seemed to understand her terror.

A lady-in-waiting drew Emilde aside. Over her arm, she had Emilde's bed gown, the richly embroidered one she'd wear to this consummation of her marriage. Shielding Emilde from the crowding courtiers, she undressed Emilde rapidly. Emilde stood stiffly still, trying not to tremble, and let her.

"No fear, my lady," whispered the waiting woman with a smile. "All will be well, and soon you'll be a woman indeed."

The courtiers jostled and pushed to get a look at her, while the lady-in-waiting playfully fended them off.

"I'll have a look," Ranulf her husband loudly proclaimed.

"Oh, no, you won't, Your Majesty," exclaimed the waiting woman. "Not before your time."

His friend the Earl Brenci made as if to pull Ranulf away, and Ranulf made as if to burst from his restraining arms.

Emilde felt her resolve fading from her. She knew she was shaking.

"There now, my lady. All done," whispered the waiting woman. The bed gown was over her head and clothing her modestly, and the waiting woman was leading her to the big bed and helping her up into it, and pulling the rich coverlet up to her chin.

And now Ranulf was beside her.

"Take the bride! Take the bride!" the courtiers chanted.

Half of them, Emilde could see, were drunk. The other half, blind drunk. Falling down drunk. Throwing up in the corner drunk.

Emilde looked sidelong over at Ranulf.

He was staring at her. "You are beautiful," he whispered to her.

He sat up and shouted at the others, "Clear out of here, you lot, while I claim what's mine."

"Take the bride! Take the bride!" they chanted, crowding in around the bed to see.

Abruptly Ranulf rolled over on top of her. Emilde shrank back.

Ranulf reached down under the covers and yanked up her bed gown.

He raised up on one elbow to leer at the guests, and they all burst out into guffaws and cheers.

Emilde felt how hard he was against her. She squeezed her eyes tight shut and steeled herself.

"Don't fear, my lady," Ranulf whispered at her ear. "We'll give them a little show, shall we?"

He made vigorous thrusting motions under the covers, while the guests roared and capered around the bed.

"Let out a little cry," Ranulf whispered in her ear.

She did.

More cheers erupted.

Ranulf sagged down on top of her. Then he sat up. Through her slitted eyes, she saw him beaming. He shoved the covers aside and all the guests moved in to look. But his body covered hers.

They did see the blood, though, staining the white of the sheets. Emilde looked over at it, too, dumbfounded.

Her lady-in-waiting reached for her, and Ranulf eased off her so she could be led away to be cleaned up. Looking over her shoulder, she saw her husband leap out of bed, shielding his nakedness with the coverlet. He motioned to Bren, who seized up the bloody sheets and tossed them at the crowd.

The courtiers grabbed them and capered off with them, waving them bawdily above their heads, to hang them off the balcony of the king's quarters in the fort for all to see.

The marriage had been consummated.

All was right and good, and the realm was safe.

CHAPTER FIVE

A Tricky Matter

Emilde's lady-in-waiting, the woman named Silfleda, was combing out her hair and exclaiming over how silky and thick it was.

Emilde was in the little rose arbor off her bed chamber, with a hot posset to fend off the morning's chill, and a bowl of berries too.

After Silfleda had finished with her, Emilde sat silent, absently toying with the quill from her writing box. She wanted to write to her brother, to tell him all was well, but she didn't know how to put her strange feelings into words.

Silfleda moved in and out of the arbor, directing a servant girl carrying piles of newly laundered clothing. "And you know your letters, lady," she marveled, looking over Emilde's shoulder to admire what she was doing. "No woman in this realm knows her letters."

"It's common, in mine," said Emilde.

"Now this is your realm, lady," said Silfleda.

"Maybe I'll start a new custom, here," said Emilde.

Silfleda gave her a guarded smile.

Emilde saw Silfleda knew a lot. She knew the ruse Ranulf had perpetrated on his court. She knew Emilde was still a virgin. And now she saw Emilde had odd foreign notions about some important matters.

But Emilde also sensed Silfleda had been chosen to attend her because of her discretion. Silfleda had comforted her during the raucous practice of bringing the king's wife to bed. Silfleda wouldn't tell.

Silfleda looked up suddenly and stepped aside. She swept down into a low curtsey. "Your Majesty," she said.

Emilde started to her feet.

Ranulf was standing in the door to her pretty garden. He quickly went to Emilde, half-risen from her bench, and gave her a little push, to let her know to stay seated. He sat down at her side.

"Leave us," he said to Silfleda, and she silently backed out of the arbor.

Ranulf sat looking at Emilde. Emilde tried to keep herself quiet. She looked down at her hands. Ranulf was big and blond and sitting far too close to her. She could smell his maleness. He was strange to her. She wanted to inch away from him, but she knew she must not.

"So we are wed in reality now," he said to her at last.

"Not exactly," she said.

He laughed. "No," he said.

"Why didn't you—"

"Why? Lady, I saw you were terrified."

"But the blood," she began.

"Oh, that." He smiled. "That's an old trick. One a woman uses on a man, to make him think she's an intact pure virgin when in fact she has known many men. A small pig's bladder filled with blood, and a pin."

"But you used it on me."

"Clever, no?"

She felt an unwilling smile stealing over her.

"See? I knew you could smile," he said. His tone was gentle.

"Why not just take me, Your Majesty?" she said to him, her voice gone sharp. "You own me, after all."

"I don't own you, Emilde."

"But you do," she said.

His expression was sober. "Let's take it slow, you and I, shall we?" Then he said, "I was remiss, when we met." He hesitated, and an unsettled expression swept over his features. She couldn't read it. What could he be feeling? she wondered. It couldn't be fear. That wouldn't be possible, would it? "I beg you to forgive me, lady, for—for that thing I did."

"You have many sugared words, when you choose to use them."

He let out a rueful little laugh. Finally he said, "I see I'll have to earn your trust."

"People don't change, you know." She turned stiffly away from him. "Not that easily. Not that quickly."

"Well," he said, picking up one of her hands in his. She forced herself not to snatch it away. "Eventually you must bring yourself to let me do what husbands and wives do," he told her. "We must produce a child, you and I. The realm expects it."

That strange fear seemed to have settled over him again.

"Yes," she said, breaking into the thick dread pressing down on them both. "I know it, lord."

As they sat quietly, the dark mood left them. After a moment, Emilde looked over at this stranger who had become her husband. She found she was curious. "So. What did prompt this seeming change, my lord? Why protect me from your rowdy courtiers the way you did? Why protect me from yourself?"

He sat beside her shaking his head and looking down at his shoes. He had let go her hand. "I don't know, lady. I just—it just happened that way."

"But you were prepared. With the pig's bladder and the pin. It didn't just happen. You prepared for it." She had a sudden insight. He was as reluctant to bed her as she was to be bedded.

He nodded. "Yes."

"Perhaps I'm not pleasing to you. That would be convenient, would it not? We've hated each other from the first, and we know it, both of us. But here we find ourselves trapped together. Both of us. We will do what we must, and then, when we produce a child, we won't need to have anything to do with each other in that way. We can declare a truce."

"Truce," he said, his eyes brightening. He reached out his hand again to her, and this time she took it and pressed it.

She was able to smile at him now, a real smile.

"Yes, when we produce a child, then we can. . ." The fear had come back into his eyes, and she wondered at it. He must find her quite unattractive. She was glad.

But as he stood, he said a bewildering thing to her. "Truce. But that's not the reason. That you are unpleasing to me, Emilde. No. You are very pleasing to me. So that's not why." Then he went away.

For a while after that, life got better. Emilde began to enjoy learning about the new land where she lived now, and its people and customs. Not all of them were as barbarous as the custom of bedding the bride.

Silfleda was a quiet comfort to her. Many times, she found herself silently thanking Ranulf for her, if Ranulf were the one who had made such an arrangement.

But maybe he hadn't. *What do men know of ladies' maids,* she thought to herself. Even maids who are high-born ladies-in-waiting. Maybe Silfleda was a happy accident, or maybe someone else in the king's household had her best interests at heart.

A little of both, she discovered. Ranulf had indeed chosen Silfleda for her. But he had had help.

One of the unexpected delights of her new life was making a friend. She had never really had one of those. Her brothers were her friends, especially Mabire, and her lady-in-waiting Agace had served her as a friend.

But she'd never made a friend of another girl, in her childhood. She didn't know what that was like.

Now she did.

Her new friend was the wife of the Earl Brenci, the best friend of Ranulf.

Bren and Ranulf had grown up together, as close as brothers, she'd discovered. Shortly after her own marriage to Ranulf, but several years before she'd come across the Narrows to be his wife in fact, Bren had married his childhood sweetheart Aderyn. His father had died, he'd inherited the earldom, and he and Aderyn had wed. Unlike herself and Ranulf, the two of them were of an age, more or less. Bren was maybe a year or two older than his wife.

And now Aderyn had come to Tam Fort to live with Bren there.

Aderyn was diminutive, suiting her name, which meant, Emilde discovered, "little bird." She had long curling light-brown hair. Her bright, inquisitive eyes were gray. "I'm the Sea Child's," she told Emilde matter-of-factly.

"And my Child is the Earth," said Emilde. "But Aderyn. Surely we may not speak openly of the Children."

"Nay, it's not allowed," said Aderyn placidly.

"I shouldn't have mentioned my Child at all," Emilde whispered. She'd forgotten her promise to Agace.

"You may speak of Her to me, though," said Aderyn. "But your woman back there in the Baronies was right to warn you. Don't speak of Her to anyone but me."

"How is it you took the risk of talking to me about this?" Emilde demanded.

"Hush," said Aderyn, looking over her shoulder where Silfleda was making the servant re-fold the bedding, because the girl had done it wrong. "Not that I don't trust Silfleda. I picked her out for you myself. "

"I knew it!" Emilde exclaimed.

Aderyn smiled. "I took the risk of speaking to you about the Children because my Child told me it would be fine."

"She told you?" said Emilde. She was staring at Aderyn. "She speaks to you?"

"Yes, She does."

"I wish my Child would speak to me," Emilde whispered.

"Maybe She speaks to you too. Maybe you need to listen more closely to Her."

Then they both looked up.

"I need my wife," a voice outside Emilde's rooms was saying.

"Bren!" Aderyn called out. "Here we are, in Emilde's arbor."

The young earl came striding into the sunlight, smiling at them both. He bowed to Emilde. "How are you this fine morn, my lady queen," he said to her.

Emilde laughed. "So formal!"

He straightened up and took his wife's hand. "I need Aderyn about a matter," he began.

"Husband," said Aderyn. "Explain about the Children to our friend."

Bren looked hard at his wife, then at Emilde. His smile had disappeared. "We don't speak of Them at all. Not to anyone."

"Not even to Ranulf, your best friend?" said Emilde.

"Especially not to Ranulf." Bren looked around. By then Silfleda was elsewhere. He turned back to Emilde. "Ranulf knows my beliefs. Of course he does. We're as close as brothers. But long ago we agreed never to speak of it. He's king and must uphold the law. The law says everyone must worship the Lady Goddess. So we of the Children stay silent, if we value our freedom. And our heads."

"You worship the Children too."

"The Earth Child is mine, my queen," said Bren, "as I see She must be yours. My wife's Child is the Child of Sea, as anyone can look at her and tell." He glanced over fondly at his wife.

Emilde knew he meant Aderyn's gray eyes. All those of the Sea Child had them.

"So now, my wife, if I can have a word with you—" and both of them bowed to Emilde and left her in the arbor.

She could see what a tricky matter this was, the matter of belief. Agace had been right, and Bren and Aderyn were right. She'd speak of her Child to no one, certainly never to Ranulf. But she could talk about it with Bren and Aderyn, if she were careful. Especially to Aderyn. Aderyn knew things. Things others didn't and couldn't imagine. She thought then, *I can talk to Aderyn about anything, when I need to*. And that, she found, was the greatest comfort yet in this perplexing new realm.

CHAPTER SIX

Close Your Eyes and Think of. . .

The dreaded night finally arrived. Aderyn helped Emilde prepare herself. Bren had known about his friend Ranulf's ruse all along, and anything Bren knew, Aderyn knew.

"Ranulf was kind to me," Emilde whispered to her friend as Aderyn helped her into her bed gown. Aderyn had sent Silfleda away and was serving as ladies' maid on her own. Now Aderyn helped Emilde climb into the high unaccustomed bed in the royal bedchamber. Emilde remembered that bed.

She shivered. "An uncomfortable room." She couldn't stop shivering, even though Aderyn had seen to it that the fires burned briskly.

"Even Ranulf doesn't sleep here," said Aderyn. "Now then. Are you easy, my friend."

"No," said Emilde. "But I have to go through with it sometime, so it may as well be tonight."

"My poor friend. It's not so bad. It can be a bit difficult, at first, especially if you don't love the man, or if the man is clumsy."

"You weren't there, that night. The night we were supposed to consummate our marriage."

"No. I don't hold with such displays. I wouldn't go. But I sent Bren to comfort you."

"He did. And so did Ranulf. He was kind to me," said Emilde again. "But Aderyn, you must see it. I don't love Ranulf."

"It's not necessary. Bren and I don't love each other, not in the way people suppose. We just have a high regard for each other."

"I had a low regard for Ranulf," said Emilde. "Until that night. When he showed he could be kind."

"I know what he did to you, when you and he first met," said Aderyn, her mouth settling into a grim line. "But he received his punishment for it. Partly, anyhow. I think he's sorry the two of you started off on the wrong foot. He's a peculiar one, Ranulf," she said after a moment. "He's Bren's best friend, his brother, more or less. But I can't make him out. Something has wounded him, I think."

"Wounded him?" Emilde looked over at Aderyn blankly. Aderyn was lighting rushes and placing them in brackets around the room. And then she thought of another thing Aderyn had said. "He was punished?"

"His punishment is dark and will taint all that come after him." Aderyn's voice deepened. It seemed to come out of some other place, not from her.

Emilde felt a prickle of fear as she stared at Aderyn. For a moment, she didn't know her friend. But then Aderyn smiled at Emilde, and the moment passed. "I don't know how to describe Ranulf," she said. "A part of him is loving and generous, but inside him there's another part that is not, and these two parts are constantly at war. As for punishment." She finished lighting the last of the tapers. "The Children see to punishment. Sometimes you may not see that They do, but They always do. Anyhow," she said, and her voice turned playful. "You may not love Ranulf, and he may not love you, but no one can call the man clumsy. He is accomplished with women. He has bedded just about every woman you've met here so far, with these exceptions: the extremely old, the extremely young, and the diseased and disordered and ugly." Aderyn came to the bedside and smiled down at Emilde. "And me," she said.

"How did you avoid him?" In spite of herself, Emilde was amused.

"He does have a sense of honor, you know. He wouldn't bed the wife of his friend and brother. Unless she were willing, of course. And I want only Bren."

"But everyone else?"

"Everyone."

Emilde stared up at Aderyn and shook her head. "How will I get through this?"

"You will. You'll surprise yourself. Just close your eyes and think of. . .well. . . think yourself elsewhere, if you find yourself hating it."

There was a knock at the door.

Emilde felt herself tense.

"I must go, my dear friend. If you need to talk about anything afterward, you have only to send for me. Silfleda will attend you, after. But don't feel you have to tell me anything. I don't need to know anything. Anything at all." Aderyn kissed Emilde on the forehead and slipped away.

And there in her place stood Ranulf.

He bent down and kissed away her tears, which had leaked from her eyes in spite of her best intentions.

"Have you never seen a man naked before, Emilde, my wife?" he whispered.

She shook her head no.

"Then we'll save that for another time." He turned his back to her, pulled his tunic over his head and stripped off his leggings. He slipped into bed beside her. "Do you know what happens, at least? Shall I explain?"

"I think I do know," she said. "I have seen the dogs in the streets and the beasts in the fields."

"It's like that, but then again, it's nothing like that." He pressed his body against hers, and she felt the thing that had alarmed her most during the mock-occasion of their consummation night. He stiffened against her. "So, my wife, first let me help you settle," he told her. "You are like a cat backed up in a corner by some vicious dog. I'm not a vicious dog. I promise I'm not." He began to kiss her and to fondle her, and gently, gradually, he brought her to it and past that barrier, and it was over.

She lay blinking up at the ceiling.

His arm was about her, and he drew her to him.

"That was fine," he said to her.

"I think there's some bleeding," she said.

"Yes, probably. Usually. Don't worry about it. We won't have to show the bedding to the whole fort this time. Silfleda will take care of it for you. And how are you feeling now?"

"Relieved," she said.

"You see how I felt about it."

"Yes." She looked over at him, puzzled, and frowned. "For you, it seemed. . ." She paused. "Most intense."

He laughed. "Indeed," he said. "But not for you."

"No."

"If you wanted me to, I'd teach you how to feel great pleasure in the act."

"That's not necessary."

"As you wish. And you're right. To sire a son, it's not necessary for you to feel pleasure. But it's necessary for us to do this act if we are to get a son."

"To sire a son, it seems, or the attempt, anyhow, gives you great pleasure, Your Majesty."

"I don't have to work at it. I just do. And you don't have to call me Your Majesty. Not in bed."

"How often do we have to do this?"

"Often, until I've gotten you with child."

"It wasn't so bad," she admitted.

"I'll take that as a compliment, Emilde." He turned to her and ran a finger down her cheek. "You're so young. I'm twice your age. Yet I've known women as young as you who are as pleasure-minded as I myself."

"Perhaps I'm not made for pleasure," she said.

He stared seriously into her eyes. "Perhaps not. But I doubt that. I do. I know a lot, Emilde. You feel things intensely. If the right man were to rouse what's inside you to answer him with equal intensity, I wager you'd feel as strongly as I do." He sighed and looked away from her. "I tell you truly, Emilde. I wish I were that man. And it's my own fault that I'm not."

So it began between them. In several seasons, she was with child, and he stopped coming to her.

Nine turnings of the moon later, their son was born in a day-long session of pain that astonished Emilde with its savagery.

"Here now, here's your son," said Aderyn, handing the babe to her and helping her suckle him.

Emilde looked up at her with gratitude. "What would I have done without you here, my dear friend?"

"Tush," said Aderyn with a smile. "I wasn't that much help. I've had no babes of my own, have I?" She and Bren had tried. Aderyn lost every baby she tried to bear, either early on or in one case, shortly after the poor little mite was born. "I might not be built to be a mother. You are, my girl," she said to Emilde, all smiles. But as she turned to go, Emilde heard her murmur to Silfleda, "Emilde is too young to be a mother. I fear for her, what this will do to her body."

Emilde was not afraid. She had her son.

Ranulf had been out hunting. When he heard the news, he came joyfully to her rooms and gazed down on the tiny lad. "We'll call him Artur," he decreed.

"Artur, after the hero in the story?" said Emilde. She'd expected the infant crown prince to be proclaimed yet another Ranulf.

"Artur, yes, the very man," said Ranulf. "My son will be a mighty king, so let's name him after one."

Emilde locked eyes with the father of her child, and felt an unexpected rush of emotion. Ranulf loved this baby of theirs. Ranulf didn't seem to consider himself a mighty king. He didn't seem to consider himself the proper model for their son. He was a mystery to her. A contradiction.

"Perhaps this marks a new day for us, my wife," Ranulf leaned over to whisper in her ear.

"Perhaps it does," she whispered back.

But Aderyn was right. It took Emilde's body a long time to heal and for her to return to full health. In the meantime, the gossip of three or four more conquests her husband had made in the act of love came filtering back to her through the wagging tongues of the court. So that tender moment between them passed.

RANULF

CHAPTER SEVEN

Forsaking All Others

Sometimes Ranulf found himself thinking wistfully of Emilde. Now that they had their son, Emilde resisted his overtures, and Ranulf was often too preoccupied to insist on his rights as king and husband. There was a new gyrfalcon to train in, or a new mistress, or there was a war to fight.

Always, Emilde was completely circumspect. She gave Ranulf no occasion at all for uneasiness. She did not have a wandering eye. Ranulf knew all the signs. He knew them well. He himself was a living, walking example of them. If she were playing him for a cuckold, he'd have known it. But she never did.

Perhaps she's right, he told himself sometimes. *Perhaps she really isn't made for pleasure. Some people lack that capacity.*

The Lady knew he had too much of it, had it in abundance. Not that it bothered him much, especially since it never seemed to bother Emilde. And by now, the strange forebodings of long ago had dwindled away into a bad memory. Even less than that.

The most troubling of all these fears was his worry that he would hate the child they bore together. Sometimes he recalled the words of the dark presence. *Your blood!* What did that mean, really? That someone born of his blood would enact some terrible curse against him? The first glimpse he'd had of his infant son had dispelled all fears of that sort. He needed an heir, no matter how he felt about it. And now that he had one, he found he loved the little boy beyond anything else in the world.

But Ranulf worried about other matters. He remembered too well the plague year that took his older brother. His brother had been the son destined to become king, not Ranulf. But his brother, and his older sister, too, lay long dead. Ranulf was older now than all the combined years his brother and sister had lived on this earth.

If he let it, fear would place its icy fingers on his heart when he looked at his son. Artur was a delicate boy, dark like his mother, and finely made like her. What if something happened to Artur? He and Emilde needed to have another child. Maybe several more.

Thinking about that, he was more assertive with Emilde, insisting they engage more often in the act of love. But she didn't have another baby. She miscarried once, a daughter. The years went by, and nothing.

Strangely, as she grew older, she grew more beautiful. Some women blossomed early. He knew to rush to pluck that blossom as soon as he spotted it, because the next year, or the year after, the petals would be blown and blowsy. That was not the case with Emilde.

She didn't possess the kind of beauty that attracted him most, golden and lush. Hers was a dark, delicate loveliness that stopped the heart.

She was like the picture of a queen, not a real woman. She didn't appear to have a real woman's emotions.

Perhaps, he thought, her strangeness came from the strange way she had been brought up. She'd been given the training of a scholar. She was always writing. Letters to her father, to her brothers. Especially to Mabire, her favorite brother. Letters to other writers she admired, writers whose books she had read. Baronies writers. Writers in the Southern Primacy. She knew the language of the Old Ones. It was unnatural, especially in a woman. Yet Ranulf couldn't help admiring her for it. He knew Bren admired her skills as well. But then, Bren himself was something of a scholar.

By now, Emilde was beginning to teach what she knew to their boy.

Ranulf loved his son dearly. When he was home from his campaigns, he had Artur by him always. He especially loved to take the little boy down to the mews to see the hawks and falcons.

"There," he'd say to the child. "See there? That big one? That's a gyrfalcon. Only a king is allowed to have a gyrfalcon.

Someday you'll be king, my boy. Then you'll have a gyrfalcon of your own."

He knew that other men of the court, his vassals and courtiers, looked at him askance. Of course now that Artur was old enough to wield a small practice sword, he was out in the courtyard with the royal arms master for a short while every day. But even at such a young age, as it was fairly clear to all who saw him, he didn't have the makings of a warrior, as his father did.

The person this bothered the most was Ranulf's mother, the queen dowager. "You're spoiling that boy!" she'd exclaim to Ranulf during her rare visits to the court. "You're turning him into a dainty little thing with no backbone."

Her words, he knew, only echoed the unspoken thoughts of many others about the court. But Ranulf found this did not worry him, or not much. He doted on the boy utterly.

Everyone whispered that he was mishandling his son. Everyone but Bren. Poor Bren had no children of his own. Aderyn hadn't given him any, although the Lady knew they tried. But Bren loved Artur too. Even better, Bren appreciated Artur for who he was and didn't look sidelong at him, wondering why he wasn't the boy he couldn't be, the rough and tumble kind of boy, or wondering why Ranulf didn't insist he be the boy everyone thought he should be.

Ranulf loved Bren for that.

And Ranulf also saw that while Emilde might never love him, not in the way he sometimes wished she did, she had put aside her distrust and dislike. First, because of how gently he had handled her, when they were finally wed. And now because of their son. She saw how much he loved Artur. How much he loved Artur for Artur's own sake.

I may not be a good man, thought Ranulf, sometimes. *But it was a good thing I did, when I married Emilde. I made amends. And I love our son.* He sent these thoughts of his into the sky. *I have made amends!* he told the dark judging presence, wherever it had gone. Maybe it had left him. Maybe it was satisfied.

No one knew he felt these things about his son and wife. No one but Bren, and Bren, of course, didn't know about the visitation of the terrible bird of prey. To everyone else, Ranulf showed no doubts, no vulnerabilities. He was a demanding and intimidating monarch, and he wanted it that way.

He was perpetually at war. He went on campaign to the north, to secure the realm's borders there and then to extend their reach. Now he had encroached on the large savage isle to the west of the realm. He wasn't making much headway, but he thought someday he would. He was a large, physically powerful man, his bright head and the golden flow of his beard kingly. He was always at the front of the battle line. Always, he'd been athletic and bold. Now he had become an accomplished strategist and leader of men. His men respected and feared him. The enemy feared him.

Always, he watched and waited for his advantage in Lunds-fort and the surrounding area belonging to the Baronies. *Really, it's ours*, he said to himself. *It's on our side of the Narrows, and in my grandfather's day, we owned it. Someday I'll get it back.*

Right now, though, a rare interlude, he was home. He looked at his young son and realized how much time had gone by since the boy's birth. Six years. High time the lad had a brother. It was dangerous to the realm, otherwise.

He went to Emilde, to let her know.

"We must try harder than we have, my wife. We must try every night I'm home. We must have another son."

Emilde bowed her head in obedience.

"Am I so repellant to you, Emilde?" he said, turning to her in the firelight.

He had come to her after the board had been put aside. He had dismissed her lady-in-waiting, Silfleda, and had come to her to let her know his inmost thoughts.

"Of course not, Your Majesty," said Emilde. "You're not repellant to me, not at all. You're the father of my dear son."

Yet, as he put his hand out to caress her cheek, he saw how she almost imperceptibly flinched away from him. He set himself to change that.

By the time the winter season was over and he was getting ready to go on campaign again, he felt he had made some progress toward that goal. He'd put all other women aside, in his pursuit of Emilde's affection.

Lying in bed together on their last morning before his departure, he turned to her to caress her, the small high breasts, the narrow hips, the silky smoothness of her hair and skin. "How beautiful you are, Emilde," he whispered. "I think you may love me, at least a little."

She smiled at him. "Ranulf, you have filled me with pleasure, these last turnings of the moon. You are right about the pleasures of the body. You've taught me that at last. If only these pleasures would go on forever. But they won't. You'll leave, and soon things between us will be back the way they always are."

"Do you think so, my darling wife?"

"I know so. I know you well by now, Ranulf. Some beautiful girl will catch your eye, and then—"

"But they mean nothing to me, those girls. None of them."

"Then why pursue them?"

He shrugged.

"Maybe you can't help it. Maybe it's the way you are made," she told him, but she looked skeptical.

"When I return, we'll try again for a son," he said.

"That's it, isn't it. We're trying for a son. It has nothing to do with me, not really."

"That's not true, Emilde. Look at how beautiful you are. Surely you know this about yourself."

"When I get old, I won't be. Any beauty I may have will fade."

"Let's not think of that. Let's think of how we feel right here, right now," he said, and turned to caress her again, to bring her to the height of pleasure and then to take his own.

Later, he thought maybe that last time they spent in each other's arms was the moment they made their second son.

When the news reached him in his camp far to the north, it filled him with joy.

"Be happy for me, brother," he told Bren. "Emilde is with child."

And of course Bren was happy. But Ranulf also saw the shadow of sadness that came over him. Bren had no son. No child at all. Ranulf prayed to the Lady to grant him one.

CHAPTER EIGHT

Fostered Out

When Ranulf flung himself off his horse and through the big gates into the keep of Tam Fort, he became even more alarmed than he already was. His mother stood there to greet him.

"Mother. How is Emilde? How is the child?"

"You have a son, Ranulf," said his mother.

"Thank the Lady," Ranulf exclaimed.

"I'm thinking you should name him Audemar, after my brother," she told him.

"But Emilde?"

"He's a fine strapping boy. What do you think of Audemar as a name?"

"Fine," said Ranulf. "A fine name for him. What about Emilde?"

Aderyn was there at the gate now too. She pushed past the queen dowager, who looked over at her with irritation and dislike. "Emilde is not well, Your Majesty. You should get to her side as soon as you may."

"She's in danger?" Ranulf felt his heart nearly stop.

Aderyn nodded gravely.

"Take me to her at once," he said.

At her bedside he knelt and brought her limp hand into his and kissed it. "Emilde," he whispered, feeling his heart break seeing her lying there so pale and still.

She stirred and her big dark eyes opened. "Ranulf," she said. Her voice was so weak. He saw how she could barely push the words past her parched lips. "We have a son," she said.

"Yes, my darling," he said, and felt the hot tears start into his eyes. He vowed to himself, and to the Lady, that if Emilde lived, he'd devote himself to her, to her only.

"Come away, Your Majesty," Aderyn murmured at his ear. "You must let her rest. She's exhausted."

He stumbled out into the corridor and covered his face with his hands. He prayed to the Lady for her.

Bren was there by his side, then, steadying his elbow. "Come to the hall for something hot to eat and drink, Ranulf. You'll need your strength in the next days."

He was right. Aderyn busied herself seeking out a wet-nurse for the babe. Emilde was too weak to nurse him. She'd insisted on suckling Artur far longer than was seemly, but she wasn't in health to suckle the little Audemar at all.

For once, Ranulf's mother was a strong support to them all. She was the one who eventually found the wet-nurse, a woman in her own entourage.

For at least a fortnight, Ranulf daily expected to be called to Emilde's bedside for a last goodbye. She lingered on, just barely.

In the second turning of the moon after the baby's birth, Ranulf's mother began making preparations to go back to her own estate.

"Son," she said, as they gathered in the hall while the board was removed from its trestles after the evening meal, two nights before her departure. "I'm minded to take the baby back with me. He has formed a strong bond with his nurse, my own woman. I'll bring him back with me to foster him until our poor Emilde gets her strength."

Ranulf looked over at his mother with gratitude. Had she ever been this loving? Now she was. The crisis, he thought, was bringing out her finest qualities.

Aderyn stepped to them then. "How generous and fine, Your Ladyship," she said to the dowager queen. "But Bren and I stand ready to foster the child, and then he'll be right here in Tam Fort where his mother can see him and hold him."

"Nonsense," said Ranulf's mother. "That will disrupt his feeding. And it will put our poor Emilde under too hard a strain. She must have complete rest. There's already one child in the household to tax her. I'll take the babe."

In the end, Ranulf bowed to his mother's experience and grandmotherly love. The tiny Audemar was packed off with her to her estates a day's travel away. As it turned out, he wasn't returned to the arms of his mother for three years, not until the dowager queen dropped dead of an apoplexy one evening after too heavy a meal of herrings and cream.

But at least Emilde lived to see her son again. At least there was that.

CHAPTER NINE

A Rose

I can deny you nothing, my wife," Ranulf had whispered to Emilde, when she'd proposed it.

"Now that Audemar is back with us, do you think we can journey with him, and with Artur, to see my family? Life is chancy, Ranulf. My father is as old as your mother, near about. He too could die soon. He's never seen the boys." That's what she had said to him.

Any of us could die at any time. That's the way of the world underneath the Nine Spheres, Ranulf had thought with a pang, when she said this. *And you. You especially.* Ranulf felt his heart wrench. "You're not strong, Emilde," Ranulf had told her, holding her hand. She had never recovered from Audemar's birth. In all that time, he'd never made love to her.

But now Marifius was traveling to Lunds-fort to meet with other barons over the management of the city, and his son Mabire with him.

So now Emilde had brought it up again.

"I'd do anything to please you and make you smile," he told her.

She had smiled back at him, but her smile was skeptical.

"I would," he assured her.

"I know," she said to him. "Anything in your power."

The unspoken thought stretched between them. *So much of what you do is out of your power, or so it seems.* That's what Ranulf knew Emilde was thinking. And she was right. Why couldn't he be like Bren, in perfect, easy control of his own impulses? He intended to be. He meant to be. And then.

Instead of pursuing these thoughts to their gloomy conclusion, he said, "We'll go to Lunds-fort. That's not as long a journey as the trip across the Narrows to your father's lands. We'll go to Lunds-fort, and your family will see our sons. We'll bring Bren and Aderyn with us, and Aderyn can help you with the children."

He was rewarded with Emilde's joyful smile and a rare kiss.

Of course there were plenty of waiting-women to help her with the children, Ranulf thought, but Aderyn would be there to guard Emilde and protect her from over-doing.

The visit was just as he thought it might be. Taxing. Taxing on the children, and on Emilde's strength, and on his patience. Emilde's father and brother had never warmed to him, so he had to be on his guard during the entire turning of the moon to say nothing improper, do nothing improper, even though his own wife had banished him from her bed and the city was teeming with flirtatious beauties.

Artur, a boy of eleven, was quiet, withdrawn, and disappointing to his relations, as anyone could see. He was nearing manhood with no hint that he'd turn into the kind of stalwart warrior king the realm seemed to need.

And Audemar was a whirlwind of bad behavior, whining, throwing tantrums when he didn't get his way, sticking his finger in the confits while the cook's back was turned, pulling the cat's tail and blaming it on his brother.

Only Emilde was happy. Her wan cheeks bloomed. She flourished under the fond attentions of her father and brother, and she was oblivious to the bad impression her sons made on all.

"Just let her be happy," Aderyn murmured to Ranulf as the visit drew on. He nodded. She was right.

He found himself walking the city restlessly, as often as he could get away without offering any offense. Emilde certainly didn't notice. She was completely occupied.

One day, he got on his horse and rode out into the countryside. His heart lifted. It was a mild springtide day, fresh and green.

He trotted his courser Volatîn down the lane, wishing he could hunt. He and Bren had talked about trying to organize a hunt, but it was just too complicated, so they left the idea alone.

On impulse, he headed into a field and took Volatîn to a canter. Volatîn was a three-year-old, and fairly inexperienced, but he was a spirited animal that made Ranulf's heart glad. He knew he probably shouldn't be riding Volatîn over broken ground neither horse nor rider knew. His father's fate briefly passed through Ranulf's mind, but passed right out again. The wind blew by him and he rode the courser hard, whooping like a lad in his exhilaration.

Time to ease back, he thought with regret, and so he did. He leaned over to pat Volatîn on the withers. "That was fine, boy, was it not?" he said to his horse.

He took Volatîn back to a trot, riding him in a winding path back to the road, encouraging him to stretch out long. Then he brought him to a walk on a long rein. After the courser had settled down, Ranulf swung out of the saddle and leaned against him, breathing with him and counting his breaths. Ranulf was a large man, and Volatîn was young. He didn't want to damage the horse, but just in the past year, Volatîn had grown tall and solid. Volatîn felt good against him. *I must do this more often*, Ranulf thought, and he could tell the horse felt the same. "You and I do well together, do we not?" he whispered to Volatîn. He loosened Volatîn's girth a bit and walked him down the road.

Then he stopped. Was that a cry? Probably not. He resumed. But then he brought Volatîn to a stand and listened again. Surely that was a cry of distress. A woman's cry.

They had come to a crossroads. He took Volatîn to the boundary post and tied him there. Then he ventured into the fields in the direction the cry had come.

He heard nothing beyond the whispering of the trees and an occasional sleepy mid-day bird call.

There, he thought. There it came again.

He rushed in the direction of the cry.

Three men had cornered a young woman against the stones of a wall. One of them had her by the long golden fall of her hair, and another was at her clothing.

With a roar, Ranulf sprang to the men, drawing his sword.

They looked over their shoulders, startled. Then all three of them were away, leaping over the wall and disappearing into the forest beyond.

The young woman crumpled down weeping.

Ranulf helped her up. "There, my girl. You're safe now," he said to her, soothing her with his hands.

He saw it. She was only a girl, perhaps fifteen. She'd moved beyond the barrier into womanhood, he speculated, but only just.

She was crying hysterically.

Holding her hand, he sat her down against the stones of the fence and leaned her head over onto his chest.

As she calmed, he found himself planting little kisses on her upturned, tear-stained face.

And then, without really meaning to, he found he'd possessed her himself.

He'd run those men off. *Villains*, he had thought. Now he himself was the villain.

He cradled her against his chest as they lay in the meadow grass at the foot of the wall.

With dismay, he brought his hand blood-stained and sticky away from where he was stroking her thighs and flanks.

"It's your first time," he said to her quietly.

She nodded, burying her head into the crook of his arm.

"I'm sorry," he whispered. "I didn't mean to do that. You are just so beautiful that—"

"My father will kill me now," she said dully.

With alarm, he sat up and scrutinized her.

She was no village maid, no peasant there for the taking. Now he could see it. She was gently born.

Lady keep me, he thought. *I am a terrible man.*

"You were overwrought. I took advantage of you. I am to blame," he said. "I'll go to your father and explain."

"No!" she exclaimed.

"No," he agreed. "Maybe not. What shall we do, lady?"

He was miserable. Why was he asking her this, a man who had just deflowered a young girl. How would she know what to do about her predicament? He berated himself for an addlepated scoundrel.

"I must pretend it never happened," she whispered.

"Who were those fellows?"

"One hoped to marry me, but I rejected him. I hate him, and I persuaded my father not to give me to him. So he and his brothers lay in wait for me. They said if Cob couldn't have me, they'd ruin me so no one could."

And now I've ruined her, thought Ranulf, hating himself more.

"I was thinking to rescue you from them, the villains, and now I find I've taken you for myself." He reached into his belt pouch and produced a gold piece. "Here," he said, offering it to her. "In case there's—"

The intensity of her stare silenced him. She stared and stared at the piece of money. Then she raised her eyes to his. They were heartbreakingly blue. "You think I'm a strumpet. You think you can pay me and walk away."

"No! No, I don't think that, I just—"

"You must marry me. You must make it right," she said firmly.

"But lady." His voice sank to a whisper. "I am already married."

"Then I am lost," she said, getting to her feet and brushing off her skirts, settling her clothing back around herself. "I must get home and think what to do."

In a confused flash much like a thunderclap sounding about his ears, Ranulf realized something truly strange. He realized he loved this girl.

Oh, tush, he told himself. *That's impossible. What a fopdoodle you are, to think such a thought. You don't even know this girl. You've done wrong to her, but you can't possibly be in love with her.*

Another part of himself insisted otherwise. Another part of him felt certain he was right.

"My lady," he said, kneeling to her. "My name is Ranulf. I think I'm in love with you."

Her incredulous laugh made the forest around them ring out.

"Leave me be," she told him. "I must get home. I must think what to do."

"Tell me your name," he cried after her desperately.

She whirled to face him. "Cicely," she said. Then she was running. Then she was gone.

He sank back into the grass. *What have I done?* he thought. *What have I done?*

As he stared blankly around himself, he spied a flash of white underneath a thorny patch by the wall.

It was an apron.

Cicely's apron.

He put it to his face to see if there might be a trace of her fragrance, the headiness of her that he had inhaled as he had taken her in the grass.

"Ow," he said, putting the apron down. He spread it open. She had filled it with pink dog roses, and their thorns along with them. She must have been gathering the flowers up when those three churls had attacked her.

He, the fourth churl, sucked at his thumb, where one of the thorns had pricked him hard.

He sat against the stone wall, thinking of the music of her voice. She spoke in that charming hybrid language so many of the country people used in these parts. Not quite his own language. Not quite the language of the Baronies. Some pretty mixture of the two.

After a while, he sighed. He knew he'd better get back to the city.

Absently, he tucked a rose from her apron into his belt pouch.

He wandered back to Volatîn, untied him from the boundary marker, and swung back into the saddle.

Before he turned Volatîn's head toward the city, he stared down at the boundary marker. *Ecga Green*, it read.

He wasn't sure how long it took him to get back to the city, and back into the comfortable big house belonging to Emilde's kin where they all had rooms.

It was near time to sup. No one had seemed to miss him. He went wearily to their own room to change out of his muddy, grass-stained clothing.

Emilde came in to ask him something, and she saw his belt pouch thrown aside in the corner.

Before he could think how to stop her, she had darted to it and was taking the faded dog rose out of it.

"These wild roses! I remember these," she exclaimed. "When I was a girl, I used to go out into the fields and meadows to collect them. I'd put heaps of them into my apron."

"Mind the thorns," he said hastily.

She wasn't listening. She was deep into her memory. "But," she said, her voice turning sad. "They always faded by the time I got them home."

PART II: HARVEST OF THORNS

"It hurts me when they suffer," cried Dee to Myrddin. They both watched while one of the ordinary folk, supposedly powerful, a king, endured the same kinds of trials endured by all those who crawl beneath the Spheres.

"He might be a king, and that woman might be a queen, and that one—that other woman, the young one, not powerful at all, not by their lights, not by anyone's lights, might cry her eyes out every night in her father's house. But they all share the struggles of their kind. And even though we may think we know better, and see farther, still we may not interfere," Myrddin told his friend and best colleague among the mages. He sighed. "We give them what comfort we can, Dee, and it's little enough. This is the hard part of our role underneath the Spheres, we mages. The Three have placed us betwixt and between. It's never easy."

Behind them, Gilles de Rais didn't bother to stifle his laugh. "That man down there? That king? He's the perfect example of what I mean by power. Let him suffer if he can't hold onto it. My curse on him if he can't."

Myrddin turned to him with a frown.

Gilles smirked and moved away from the others. He stood twirling the tassels of his robe. "I stood for him in Myrddin's silly tribunal," he whispered to himself. "But he's a paltry little king for sure. Power? I'll shape him into my own instrument, for my own   power."

BREN

CHAPTER TEN

The Loving Man and the Wise

To see how Emilde glowed in the affectionate arms of her father and brother made Bren so happy he thought he might burst. Of course they were all glad to see it. Poor Ranulf. He was as glad as any.

She showed off her children, not realizing how her kin stared at the two boys with dismay. Artur because, they could all see, he'd never grow into a strong king.

And Audemar. Was it possible to see evil in a person at so young an age? wondered Bren. When he looked at Audemar, that's what he saw. A sly, malicious child. Maybe the others just found him overly-boisterous and annoying. Maybe that was all. Maybe Bren was wrong, and crazy, to think this of a small boy who had just reached his fourth year.

In spite of himself, he still found himself thinking it. Was the child born that way, or did that vicious woman, his grandmother, make him that way, he wondered. If only he and Aderyn had insisted harder that they be the ones to keep the boy. But they were all too worried about Emilde and whether she was dying to pay enough heed to Audemar and what was happening to him. And they would have had to convince Ranulf.

Bren knew this about Ranulf. All his life he had tried and failed to please that old woman, his mother. Bren wondered if, over the years, the queen had enjoyed watching her son's futile struggles. Bren wondered if her cruelty to their son might not have been part of the malice the queen wielded as a weapon against her husband, Ranulf's father.

Bren had seen a lot of things during his boyhood at Ranulf's side.

Fatherhood. Bren sighed. What did he know of it? He decided he was probably wrong about little Audemar. Ranulf took pride in the boy. Bren wondered if Ranulf saw himself in Audemar. The serious older boy destined to be king—that was Ranulf's older brother, the one groomed to be king. The Children decreed otherwise, and that noble boy died at fourteen. The ignored rowdy little brother—that was Ranulf himself, not supposed to be king, the despair of his father. And here he sat on the throne.

Perhaps Audemar was much the same kind of boy.

But no. The Lady knew, Ranulf had his faults. In many ways, though, Ranulf had a generous heart. Bren thought about that uneasily. Thought about all the contradictions in his friend. He was capable of spite. Bren thought of their first visit to Lundsfort, the time Ranulf had treated Emilde so shamefully. But then he thought of how gentle Ranulf had been with her when, a frightened thirteen-year-old, she'd first come to his bed.

When Bren looked at little Audemar, he saw no generous spirit at all. He saw nothing but spite. He saw glee at causing others pain. He could be very wrong about the boy. *What do I know of fatherhood, after all?* he thought again, sadly.

Aderyn kept trying to bear a child. Son. Daughter. Nothing. Everyone blamed her. *A barren woman*, they whispered.

It may be they should blame me instead, if they want to blame someone, thought Bren.

Aderyn was fine and honorable. A good person. Beyond good. She had some qualities he didn't quite know how to describe to himself. As if she knew things others didn't know. He didn't love her and never had. She didn't love him. Not in the swooning way of the stories. But they held each other in the highest regard. They'd never play each other false.

That's another reason why Bren was so dissatisfied with himself. Was he himself honorable, the way Aderyn was? Maybe he wasn't.

He had never acted on the dishonorable impulse that lay hidden in his heart. At one time, he had thought if he kept quietly denying it, it would stop gnawing at him with its sharp teeth and leave him in peace.

It never had.

The source of his gnawing pain was Emilde. Bren was in love with his best friend's wife, and had known it from the time he first saw her, a courageous little girl of ten beset by the problems of her elders, problems she didn't and couldn't possibly understand. At first he loved her for her gallantry and thought nothing wrong in it. When she came to womanhood and arrived to be Ranulf's bride, though. Shortly afterward, he really began to know what he was up against. He didn't just love and admire her. He desired her in the way a man desires a woman, and the longer he was around her, the more his desire grew.

He had never breathed a word of it to her. It would be wrong and cruel, and in so many ways. When she first came to the Sceptered Isle, she had been friendless and frightened. If not for him, and for Aderyn, she might have remained so, and her first seasons and years there would have been a torment. To reveal, even after so long, that his friendship was a sort of sham. No. He couldn't do it. He wouldn't. And of course there were all the other reasons. His brother Ranulf. Aderyn, his faithful wife.

Aderyn saw so much. He wondered if she saw the struggle he waged with himself. She'd never spoken of it. Never even hinted.

He shoved these painful thoughts aside. It was time to go to board. He was making himself ready, and he saw that Aderyn was nearly ready, too.

"I'm stepping out for a breath of air, my wife," he told Aderyn.

She was pulling her kirtle over her head. She never liked having a maid fussing around her. She nodded and waved a hand at him. "I'll see you below, Bren," she said.

He went down to the street and looked about him at the bustling, noisy city. *What a stench*, he thought, almost sorry he had come. But the streets were so fascinating. He could watch all day.

The door opened and someone stumbled out against him.

"Mind your footing," he said, steadying the person. Right away he saw it was Ranulf. Ranulf looked miserable.

"Brother," said Bren.

"Bren, I have done wrong."

"Again?" said Bren, trying to make his tone light.

"No, you don' t understand. I've hurt someone I love."

"You've hurt Emilde?"

Ranulf stood gazing at Bren, his expression unreadable. Bren stirred uneasily. He could almost always tell what Ranulf was thinking.

"Her too."

Oh, he thought. *This is about yet another of Ranulf's women.* "It will soon pass, Rannie," he said.

"This time it won't."

That, thought Bren. *That sounds unusual. And dangerous.*

Before they could talk of it further, they were summoned to board, and then their wives had summoned them to bed.

"What's the matter?" said Aderyn, as they prepared for sleep.

He turned to her in the dark and caressed her. She always knew.

"It's Rannie only."

"Some new woman."

"I suppose so."

She made an exasperated noise. "You'd think he'd grow out of it, after so many years. A father, too."

"You'd think." Then he despised himself for his own hypocrisy.

"Well," she said. "As we both know, there's nothing to be done about Ranulf and his appetites. Emilde just deserves better, that's all. He seems to love her. I really think he does. But then I think a loving man wouldn't behave so to her. Surely a loving man would not. Nor would a wise man."

She turned over with an irritated little shrug, and soon he could hear her gently snoring at his side.

But Bren lay a long time awake in the dark. Was he a loving man himself? A wise man? He was loving, but maybe in the wrong way. Wise? Surely not. Not wise at all.

CHAPTER ELEVEN

Hard-Fought Battle

You should see her now, my lord," the midwife whispered. "While there's time."

With dread, Bren stepped into the darkened room.

"Don't be afraid, dear Bren. Come here to me," said Aderyn.

Bren knelt at her bedside. They had both been so happy, when they realized that after all this time, Aderyn was with child. But her body was too old to bear a child safely. Now it was clear to all. Aderyn was dying. Bren leaned over to kiss Aderyn.

"We have a boy," she said. She sounded sleepy, as if she were trying and failing to rouse herself from sleep.

"Yes, a fine boy," he whispered.

"At last we have made a child. After all this time, when we'd given up. The Children are gracious to us. Always gracious. Afterward, praise Them and give Them thanks."

"I will," whispered Bren.

"Will you name our son for my father?"

"Drustan," said Bren. "I will. I promise it."

"Thank you, my husband." She lay quiet. He could see how she struggled to breathe. "And he's strong? He's well?" Bren thought she sounded a little panicked.

He gripped her hand. "A marvel of a baby. Strong and well," he assured her.

"That's good, then," she said after a while. Her breathing was coming harder. Then her eyes opened wide. "Tell Myrddin," she gasped out. "Tell him I tried to last a bit longer, until the other one came. Tell him. Promise me." She clutched at Bren's arm.

"Don't try to talk, Aderyn. You need rest." Bren didn't know anyone named Myrddin. Someone from her childhood, perhaps.

"No time to rest," she choked out. "You'll be a good father to our boy," she said after a while, her voice dreamy.

Thank the Children she wasn't talking out of her wits any longer, thought Bren, filled with sudden hope. But then his hope died.

"You'll be a good father. I know this. You are a fine man. Always kept faith. . ." She rallied, but he saw the effort it cost her. "Always, you did. Even when it was hard. So hard. You fought. I know it. I saw it. The many reasons you fought—"

"Aderyn," he cried.

"Shh. Comfort her. Promise me."

"I promise," he said, the tears streaming down his cheeks.

"She needs it."

"Many of the reasons will still be there, why I shouldn't."

"Yes," she said. "They will. Give her what comfort you can."

"I will."

"I've seen something in her, Bren."

"Don't leave me, Aderyn," he begged.

"She's fought as hard as you. You didn't know that, I think. She doesn't know I know that."

Bren could see it now. Aderyn was failing. She struggled to get each word past her lips. He took her hand, and it was cold.

The midwife was gently tugging at him. "Her ladyship must rest, lord," the woman was whispering. So Bren let himself be led away, and when he saw his wife next, she lay in her shroud.

"My thanks for coming," Bren said to Emilde. "I didn't have anyone else I could ask." After Aderyn's death, he had felt broken with grief. But the baby needed all of his attention. Of course, as a wealthy noble, he had had plenty of help. It probably seemed strange to all the others, he thought, that he spent every moment he could spare just holding the little child and gazing into his eyes. Unmanly, maybe. Bren didn't care.

"Of course I've come, Bren." Emilde put her hand on his arm. "Hand over that baby."

Bren passed his son Drustan to Emilde. "We didn't think we could have children. It never happened. And now, when it seemed like Aderyn was beyond her child-bearing years. . . ." He trailed off. "It was too much for her." It seemed a bitter thing to him. Some malign fate had decreed this for Aderyn. She didn't deserve it. *But then*, he thought, *can any of us say we deserve our fates?* The purposes of the Children were mysterious to all underneath the Nine Spheres.

He and Emilde walked together down the winding path to the secluded place in the forest where the priestess of the Child of Earth had her bower.

The priestess stepped out quietly to greet them. "My son. My daughter," she said.

"We've come to you on behalf of my wife Aderyn and my infant son Drustan," said Bren.

"Tell me how I may help," said the priestess.

"We are both of the Child of Earth, the infant and I," said Bren.

"And I, too," Emilde said quietly.

The priestess directed a sharp look from one of them to the other.

She recognizes both of us, surely, thought Bren. *The queen. And one of the highest nobles of the land, the king's best friend. How shocking that must be to learn. Worshipping the Children is treason. But our secret is safe with her.*

He shied away from the other secret he was harboring, about Emilde, hoping that the priestess's insight did not reach so far. He blushed. *And suppose Emilde sees it? How shameful. How I will drop in her regard, if she sees.*

He steadied himself. "My wife was of the Child of Sea. She died giving birth to our son. We had to bury my wife in a tomb at the High Temple of the Lady Goddess."

"I understand," said the priestess, her expression carefully neutral.

They were all engaged in an act of treason here. Bren hoped that's all the woman understood, but treason was enough. He and Emilde were putting the priestess in danger, coming to her. And she, if she chose to betray her calling and her vows, could become a rich woman by betraying the two of them.

"I have this armlet that belonged to my wife," Bren told the priestess. "Since we couldn't bury her in the way appropriate to her Child, we were hoping you would bless it." He handed it to the priestess. "I'll take it to the sea cliffs where she was born, and I'll place it in her family's barrow."

"I can surely do that," said the priestess.

The three of them bowed their heads while she intoned some quiet words. She stayed quiet for a bit longer. Bren worried little Drustan would fuss, but he didn't. The priestess got a faraway look in her eyes and cocked her head, as if listening to something the other two couldn't hear.

She raised her eyes to Bren's at last. "I have commended your wife to my Child, begging Her to intercede on your wife's behalf with Her sister the Child of Sea. She assures me She has done this. Don't fear, good man. The Child of Sea has taken Her daughter your wife across the river to the Land of the Dead. She sends you assurances that your wife watches over you and the infant from those shores. She sends you assurances that your wife is valued highly among the Children, always has been, always will be."

"Thank you," whispered Bren.

"I want you to know something," she said insistently to Bren. "Mine are not just words of comfort. Your wife is one of the most precious to her Child. One of her Child's true servants, one of Her little birds. Now her tasks here among us will pass to others. But she'll always watch over you and your child."

Bren bowed his head in assent.

What the priestess said just confirmed for him what he realized he'd always known about Aderyn. His wife had wielded some special power bestowed by the Children. She was like no other he'd ever known beneath the Spheres. Always, in life, she had watched over him. He knew in his bones she'd keep on doing it from those far shores.

"You've brought the infant to me for blessing?" The priestess broke into his thoughts.

"Yes," said Bren.

Emilde transferred the little child to his father.

"I believe him to be of the Earth, as I am, and not of the Sea, as his mother was," said Bren, handing him to the priestess.

She cradled him gently and looked into his eyes. "I believe you are right, my son." She blessed the baby and handed him back. "And you, my daughter?" she asked Emilde.

"I'm just here as witness, but if the Child of Earth could bless me in the difficult undertakings we all face beneath the Spheres, I would be grateful."

"Of course," said the priestess. She placed her hand on Emilde's forehead and said some quiet words. She did the same for Bren.

They knelt and kissed her hands.

As they rose, Bren caught a glimpse of the look she directed at them both, deeply compassionate, as if she saw the connection between them.

That's just the guilt talking, he thought. *And Emilde can't possibly know what I feel for her.*

They went back the way they had come, neither of them saying much, neither wanting to break the sacred quiet of the blessing and the glade.

As they parted, Bren hesitated. He wanted to speak to Emilde of his deep emotions, and of what Aderyn had revealed to him on her deathbed.

But he couldn't. As he had told Aderyn, there were too many other reasons to keep silence. Ranulf was his brother. That was the biggest of them.

Emilde leaned over and kissed him on the cheek. "Thank you for everything the two of you have meant to me," she whispered. "Without you and Aderyn, I don't know what I would have done, when they brought me here as a frightened girl. And now here is Aderyn's legacy. It's a hard thing, what happened to her. But look at this beautiful baby."

They both gazed down at the infant where he kicked and squirmed in his father's arms.

Emilde thinks of me as a valued friend, and I won't break her trust, thought Bren. *I won't break my trust with my brother.*

Aderyn's dying words to him echoed inside him, that maybe Emilde felt the same and had waged her own inner battle.

But he shook his head as Emilde looked up at him, puzzled. *I have to keep fighting,* he told himself. *I must.*

CHAPTER TWELVE

Impossible Mission

But Rannie. Remember what you said to me when you first met this girl? That you must keep your love for her hidden because it would break Emilde's heart to know of it?" Bren sighed inwardly. Rannie and his women. But this woman seemed to be different. A woman named Cicely, someone he had met during that trip they had all made to Lunds-fort.

"I know, brother, and you're right, I don't want to hurt Emilde," said Ranulf. "But now things have changed. Cicely is with child. My child, Bren."

"How can you be so sure?" Bren argued.

"I'm sure. I've had her carefully kept. She's with her family near Lunds-fort, and they watch her for me."

"Then why not keep her there, where her family can look after her."

"I love her. I want her here with me. Other men have their concubines and bastards. Even my father. But I don't want my bastard in the shadows, the way my father's were. I want to raise him with his brothers."

"Or her," Bren reminded.

Ranulf's stubborn look just deepened. "It doesn't matter. Son or daughter either one. Cicely must come here to be with me."

"Under Emilde's nose, where she can hurt and shame Emilde every day."

"I seem to remember you telling me, long ago, that men didn't need to love their wives. That if they didn't, those men could take concubines."

"Foolish to say such a thing," Bren muttered.

"I know that you, Aderyn, and Emilde were all fast friends, Bren," said Ranulf. "But Nine Spheres, man. Emilde and I haven't had anything to do with each other in—you know, in that way—since little Audie nearly killed her. Hardly anything."

"I see that you're determined to do this thing," said Bren. "But I'm begging this as a favor. Go ahead and do it, brother. I see you're determined. Bring her here. Just don't ask me to help with it." He turned away, his guilt gnawing at him. What was his own inner wish, but just this one? To be with the woman he loved, in spite of the consequences. Bitter irony that the woman was Rannie's wife. And his own dead wife's best friend.

"I'm asking you," said Ranulf firmly.

Ordering me, though Bren bleakly.

"I have to go on campaign," said Ranulf. "You know I do. And I don't trust anyone else to bring Cicely here. You're the only one I trust. I need her settled here long before the event, so no jostling or troublesome commotion during Cicely's travels over rough roads will harm my child. I don't want Cicely worried or stared at or bothered. You're the man I trust to see to it."

In the end, Bren had to agree to go to Lunds-fort and take Cicely from her father's hands and bring her back to Tambourne. To set her up in a little house close by Tam Forest. To get word to Ranulf later on, when the bastard child was born.

I won't have to do this thing for a full season, he thought desperately. *Maybe I can talk Ranulf out of it*. But he couldn't. Ranulf just dug in his heels.

The time drew near. Ranulf made his plans to leave on campaign to the Western Isle. With great fanfare and pageantry, everyone came down to the river to see the ships off. From there, Ranulf's proud fleet of cogs, flags fluttering, would proceed down river, out to sea, around the southwestern nose of the Sceptered Isle where it poked itself into the Narrows, and head across the Western Straits.

They all stood on the banks of the river and waved. Bren. Emilde. Artur and Audemar and their minders. All the courtiers.

"Go with your minders, children," Emilde said to her boys, hugging them, as the last of the fleet rounded the bend in the river and was lost to sight. Artur gave her a hug in return and turned to follow his tutor. He had a book under his arm. Audemar broke away from Emilde at a run, leaving his flustered minder to hustle after him.

Bren waited while Emilde thanked the courtiers for coming and gave them all little gifts in honor of the occasion. They stood in a line, doffing their caps to her and bowing, and she smiled at each and presented the gifts prettily to each one. It took a long time, and Bren waited patiently by her side. The nearness of her unsettled him. He tried to make his mind a blank. He'd doggedly kept away from her presence this past season. Now his resolve needed stiffening.

As soon as this ceremonial duty was finished, he was to walk Emilde back to the fort. The very next day, he'd have to set off on his own journey, the journey to get Cicely, and he was beginning to brood about it again after a period where he'd felt resigned to it.

He offered his arm to Emilde, but his mind was elsewhere.

"So, is it true, what I hear?" said Emilde, smiling at him and putting her hand on his proffered arm.

He glanced over at her and stopped, dumbstruck. He'd never seen her look so beautiful. She was radiant. She actually radiated some inner light, shining from her eyes, shining like a halo around her glossy hair, her pale cheek. "What's that, Your Highness," he got out at last.

"Hush with that, Bren. No formalities. No one's near to hear us. They've all gone off to the banquet. I suppose I should be there to preside at board, but I'm too tired. I'll leave that to Ranulf's chancellor. As for the news I've heard, I mean, of course, the journey Ranulf has asked you to undertake. The journey to bring that concubine of his back to Tambourne."

Bren stopped short in the path, his head down, a deep flush rising to his cheeks.

"You thought I wouldn't know?"

"My lady, forgive me. Forgive the part I play," he said miserably. "It's not my choice."

"Is it true, that she's with child." Emilde had stopped, too. She turned her face away. He could hear the effort she was making, to keep her voice even.

"So His Majesty tells me," said Bren. "Emilde," he burst out. "Believe me. I tried talking him out of this."

"Keeping her here. Keeping her in Lunds-fort. Tush, what's the difference? It's much the same, wherever the woman lives. Everyone knows Ranulf has this concubine. Everyone knows she's carrying this bastard of his. Don't treat me like a child, Bren. We've been friends too long."

"Friends," he said bitterly. "What I'm about to do tomorrow, do you think of it as a friendly act? Besides," he said, his voice dropping low. "I don't think of you as a friend." The words whispered out of him before he could stop himself.

He heard her draw in her breath. He lifted his gaze to hers.

What possessed him to keep going, he was never sure, later. The velvet darkness of her eyes, maybe. Her nearness. The ineffable fragrance that always seemed to surround her. "Emilde. I'm in love with you. I've loved you from the moment I first saw you at board in Lunds-fort, trying to free yourself from my brother, who was acting a villain's part with you. And then, when you came to his bed that night, the night of our little sham, our performance, I fell in love with you the way man and woman do. I fell in love with you for your courage and your honor."

He stopped. He had said the unsayable. The unthinkable.

"I fell in love with you because of your beauty, and the bell-like quality of your voice, and the delicate scent of you when I'm near you. I fell in love with you for the fineness of your mind, the depths of your emotion. I've struggled for years not to feel these things, but I do. There," he gasped out in a kind of desperation. "I've told it all. Now you have good reason to banish me from your sight forever. You won't have to think about it and wonder whether it's the right thing to do, when I'm the one who commits this betrayal, bringing that woman here. For perfectly sound other reasons, it will be right and good to banish me."

He looked down again, waiting for his sentence of exile as the condemned wait for the axe.

Instead, he felt her hands warm in his, then her arms about his neck.

"They'll see," he said, looking around in a panic for the others who had come from the fort to cheer Ranulf and his departing troops.

"Then let's step under the trees," she murmured.

They were in each other's arms, kissing, pilgrims in the desert yearning for water.

He stepped away from her. She was looking at him, incredulous, and he knew the same expression must be on his own face.

"What are we doing?" she whispered.

"Meet me back there," he said hoarsely, jerking his head in the direction of the fort.

They walked quickly away from each other, but within a bare candle-measure, they were in his bed, her legs twined about him, he drinking her in as deeply as the deepest spring. They stayed together all night, never stirring from each other's arms except when he stepped to the door and barred it, late, as the moon went down.

In the morning, they woke together and exclaimed in wonder. "I thought it was a dream," he told her.

She nodded, smiling. "As did I."

"We're doing wrong," he said, after a while.

"Are we?" she said.

"Aderyn told me before she died—"

"Ha. She told me too."

"But there's Ranulf. What about Ranulf?"

"What about him?" she said.

"He's my brother," said Bren uneasily.

"He's a man with this new woman he has as good as married, and you're about to bring her here to supplant me."

"But he isn't going to marry her. He's married to you."

They moved apart, troubled.

So in the morning all their bright love was undone and dimmed.

She slipped back to her own wing of the fort, and Bren stayed brooding in his.

Brooding until a pounding came at the door. "My lord? The horses are ready."

Child keep me, Bren thought, a thudding in his head. The journey. He'd forgotten having to head out today to Lunds-fort.

"I lay abed too late, man," he called out, trying to sound jocular. "Get the men something to eat, and some ale. I'll be there as soon as I've dressed."

His spirits dragging, he left his rooms and made his way down to the stables in the outer bailey of the fort. His heart was a jumble of jagged warring shards that cut and bit and damaged him beyond bearing.

But he had this impossible task to do, so he did it.

EMILDE

CHAPTER THIRTEEN

Sneaking Around

S iflede, I need to know something," said Emilde. *If Aderyn were here, I could ask her*, she thought. *But Aderyn is not here.*

Then she thought about Aderyn in the Land of the Dead, and whether from that shore she watched over the ones she loved. Bren. The infant Drustan. And if she were watching, whether she had seen the lovemaking between her best friend Emilde and her beloved husband Bren.

When she thought about that, her face burned with shame. But Aderyn had told her. Had told them both. Aderyn knew and had always known how she and Bren felt about each other. Somehow, it didn't lessen the deep shame she felt now.

"What is it, my lady? My lady, are you ill? Your face is so flushed."

"No, a momentary thing. I believe my stomach is a bit unsettled, that's all," said Emilde. Her courage failed her just as she had screwed it up to ask Silfleda her question.

She went to her bed, got in, and drew the coverlet up to her chin. Silfleda, who had risen from her seat at the window, where she was doing some embroidery, sank back down and plied her needle again, but she kept looking over at Emilde with concern.

She could ask Silfleda her question, and Silfleda would tell her, and advise her, and help her, and she'd never tell anyone else. Emilde knew this. But she was too ashamed.

Instead, Emilde set her own mind to her problem. It was this. How to get out of her rooms in the fort, walk down the lane that ran along the forest, and spy on the little house where Bren was bringing Ranulf's concubine.

In spite of all her fine words to Bren about how the woman didn't matter, how her presence in Tambourne didn't matter, Emilde found it did. She found she had a deep-seated compulsion to see the woman, but she didn't want the woman seeing her looking. She was too proud to let the woman see. And now she was too ashamed of herself and her sneaking ways to ask for Silfleda's help.

Why should I care what this woman of Ranulf's is like? What she does? Emilde asked herself. *I told Bren I didn't. Why is it that I actually do?* Ranulf treated her with all respect. Except for that early terrible incident, he always had. But he didn't treat her as a wife, and no wonder. She didn't allow him in her bed. She hadn't for years.

Except that one time, she reminded herself. Then she pushed the thought away, returning to her shame.

Why shouldn't he have a concubine? Other men had them. She wondered if her father had had a concubine. If he had, she'd never known about it. Her mother had been dead for so long. She died when Emilde was a small child. Emilde didn't remember her. She wondered now why her father never remarried. Now that she knew more about men, she thought he must have sought comfort among women at least sometime during all those lonely years.

Maybe with bondservants. That would have been more discreet.

Ranulf, she knew, had gotten every likely-looking bondswoman about the fort into his bed at one time or another, and that never bothered her.

Why should a concubine be so different?

She knew why. It was the public shaming.

Everyone would see this woman. Everyone would know who she was. Everyone would compare her youth and beauty to Emilde's fading looks. And they'd all talk about it.

Somehow, Emilde thought, if she could only see the woman with her own eyes, deliberately, not in some chance embarrassing encounter, she'd learn something.

She wasn't even sure what she'd learn.

The truth, maybe, and under circumstances where she could think about it and confront it honestly without others scrutinizing her while she did it, to see how she managed it. Maybe that.

Here's this beautiful young girl. And here am I, getting old and looking like it. Here's this girl my husband desires. And here am I, the woman he does not desire and never has.

The night she had spent with Bren just sharpened the contrast and threw it into relief. *Here's the man who does desire me, the man I desire, and we were never allowed to speak it or act on it until it was too late to do anything about it.*

Now that they had done something about it, she somehow felt worse. A fine thing between them, spoiled and ruined by long years of holding themselves back. A single night together could not undo the damage of that. It just made her feel more keenly what she had missed.

Emilde wanted to toss on her bed and groan in anguish, but she knew if she did, Silfleda would get worried, maybe call a healer.

She had had a scheme. She'd veil herself, and Silfleda would arrange for her to be driven in a closed cart to the woman's house. When the woman came there—*no*, thought Emilde, forcing herself to say it, at least in her mind—*when Bren brought her there*, Emilde would watch her from behind the hanging tapestries of the cart.

Just once, she thought. *Just that once. Just so I can see, and be private while I see.*

She couldn't bring herself to ask.

This very afternoon, Bren would escort the girl to the little house beside the forest, on the other side of the fort. Emilde would miss her chance.

If she saw, right now, before anyone started speculating about it, she could arm herself. Later on, everyone would be watching her to catch her least reaction.

Everyone would be watching the chance encounter that was sure to come, and everyone would judge her, and compare her to this girl, and gossip about it all.

In a sudden burst of imagination, Emilde understood how she might manage to achieve her wish.

"Lady Silfleda," she said.

"Yes, Your Highness?"

"I'm uneasy. I've had bad dreams."

"Oh, my lady, how can I help? Would Your Highness like me to brew you a hot posset?"

"It's more serious than that, Silfleda. Shall I tell you? Maybe you can advise me."

"Of course, my lady."

"It's my husband the king. When he's off on campaign like this, I can usually keep my fears away. Not this time. I keep dreaming that he is injured. Dying, even. The dreams are haunting me, Silfleda."

"Oh, my lady!"

"You know," she began carefully, "You must have seen that I'm not a very devout person. I go to the temple of the Lady Goddess on important occasions, but I'm not good like you, Silfleda. I don't go every Lady Day."

"The Lady keep you, Your Highness. I'm sure She loves you dearly. She wouldn't hurt the king over a thing like that."

"Surely not," said Emilde hastily. "That wasn't my thought. But I'm wondering. Maybe I'd like to go to the temple to pray, even though it's not my usual practice."

"That's a fine idea, Your Highness," said Silfleda.

"I just don't want to exhibit my fears before the whole fort."

"We could drape you with veils, Your Highness."

"Yes," said Emilde, as if such a thought had never occurred to her. "That might be the perfect thing. Could you find me some, dear Silfleda?"

"I will, my lady," said her lady-in-waiting, and bustled from the room.

And then, thought Emilde, *veiled like that, I can go to the temple. I'll have to walk right past that little house on the way. If Bren and the woman aren't there yet, I can wait praying in the temple until they are. Then I can walk back past. And I can see. And no one will see me.*

It seemed like a good ruse until she actually did it.

Rejecting Silfleda's offer to accompany her, she set off heavily veiled for the temple. She moved past the little house, which stood empty.

She presented herself to the priest of the Lady, who kindly showed her to a place where she could kneel and pray. She made sure to position herself so she could see the road.

When the harness of the horses jingled outside, and when she looked out and saw Bren getting down off his horse and handing a slight figure off another, she finished her praying, got to her feet, and instead of breaking into a run, made herself go slowly out of the temple. She headed down the lane on the other side of the lane from the little house.

Through her veils, she watched.

The girl was young and beautiful. She somehow glittered, as if her skin, her hair, everything about her were golden.

Is she pregnant? Were the tale-tellers right? wondered Emilde. It was hard to be sure. If this young woman were indeed pregnant, it was early days.

Before she could be observed lingering there, Emilde walked on. When she got back to her rooms in the fort, she told Silfleda she needed to be alone and sent her away.

Silfleda looked at her with sympathetic eyes and pressed her hand. *She knows*, Emilde realized with a fresh pang. It would surely have been more honest to tell Silfleda her wish, as she had first planned.

Now she felt more shamed than ever, caught behaving in such a childish way. She spent a miserable day and night closed up in her rooms, huddling in her bed, berating herself for a sneak and a coward.

I have to come out of these rooms sometime, she told herself.

She called Silfleda to her and let her lady-in-waiting comb her hair and help her put on rich clothing. Each of them pretended she didn't know what the other was thinking.

Then, holding her head high, Emilde went to the great hall to preside at board as always.

But she had the unsettled feeling that everyone in the fort had known she'd gone out disguised to look at Ranulf's concubine. They all no doubt pitied her, and maybe scorned her for her weakness, too.

Bren was not there. That made things easier. How could she face him after that night they'd spent together, she wondered.

We've done wrong, he'd said.

Surely he must blame her. She had violated her husband's trust, and through her, he had violated his brother's.

Then he had brought that woman to the fort.

At least now she knew. In the end, though, her spying didn't give her the relief she'd hoped from it.

The reverse, in fact. She felt uneasy and ashamed. Uneasy in spirit. Uneasy in body, too.

Bren was right. She'd done wrong. And in ways he didn't even suspect.

CHAPTER FOURTEEN

Uneasy

A bare turning of the moon later, Emilde was sitting in her arbor with her writing box when Silfleda came to her to tell her the Lord Brenci was there to speak to her.

"Please show his lordship to the arbor. Then leave us, please, Silfleda. I believe he has come on a confidential matter," she told the lady-in-waiting, but her heart pounded.

She hadn't seen him since their night together, except of course for the brief glimpse of him she'd had as he had escorted Ranulf's concubine into her new home.

A moment later, Bren was bowing before her.

"Please sit and tell me your news, your lordship," she said, as Silfleda backed out of the arbor and into the rooms, and then closed the door behind her.

Bren sat down heavily on the bench across from her. He was looking tired.

"I've been away," he said.

"I've noticed."

"After I—" He stopped and drew a deep breath. "After I performed that errand of Ranulf's, I left again right away. I had to go to my estates, to arrange for little Drustan to be fostered with a new wet-nurse there. The milk of the first one dried up."

"I hope all is well with him. I hope you are well," she said. Then she disgraced herself by bursting into tears.

He was beside her in an instant. "Dear Emilde," he said, stroking her hand, her hair.

She got a good grip on herself and pushed him away. "No," she said. "We must not start touching each other, Bren. You know what it will lead to. And then how we'll feel. It's too painful."

"What I said, about how we were doing wrong—" he began.

"You were right to say it."

"Aderyn understood, Emilde."

"I know she did."

"It's Ranulf. That's the part I can't stand—"

"Hush," she said, and tried to smile. "I should have told you something. I was remiss."

"What is it?" He gave her a look of dread.

"I'm with child."

"Emilde! Emilde, I—"

"It's not our child, Bren. At least I don't think it is."

"Ranulf's."

"Yes, I believe so. I believe I was with child when we—"

They sat in silence.

"Please let me explain. It's hard to explain. Let me try."

"But Emilde—"

"Let me try," she repeated.

He sat still, looking at her.

Does he hate me now? she wondered.

"When Aderyn died, I was so distraught. I was beside myself. And Ranulf saw, and he—"

"I understand," said Bren.

"But I should have said something," said Emilde.

"My darling Emilde. The night we spent together came upon us so fast, we didn't have time to think about anything. We were swept away. And then."

"And then the night was over, and we thought about it."

"Yes," he said.

"And anyway, I never dreamed that one night with Ranulf, after all those nights alone in my bed, would produce this. Seasons. Years alone. I didn't plan for it to happen. I didn't want it to happen. It just did." She looked up at him. "But you came to see me about something, Bren. You came to tell me something, and instead, I've told you this. What have you come to tell me?"

"I came to tell you that in spite of the difficulties, I meant what I said about loving you."

"Now this. The gods are unkind. Now surely you think otherwise."

He shook his head. "No," he whispered. "No, I feel the same. But now, Emilde. Now I'm frightened. You shouldn't be having a child."

"I'm having one." She tried to smile. "Nothing bad will happen to me, Bren. You're just thinking of what happened to Aderyn. But that won't happen to me. Aderyn was past child-bearing, but then it seems she wasn't. I'm still in my child-bearing years. It will be fine."

She could see it in his face. *Our child killed Aderyn. Audemar nearly killed you.*

"I'm much stronger now. The bad time I had with Audemar won't happen again." They sat in silence, both of them knowing no one could say such a thing. No one could predict what the fates had in store for a woman when she birthed a child. "Meanwhile," Emilde said, breaking the silence, "not far from this place, down the road in that little house by the forest, another of Ranulf's children is coming into the world."

He nodded. He wouldn't look at her.

"We women, you know. This is what we do. You men go to war. It's dangerous, but you do it. What we women do is dangerous, too. But we do it."

"I should be at Ranulf's side, over there in that savage land," he said. "I should be with him and the army."

"Instead, he left you here, to take care of all this messy business with his woman."

"And now it's done. And I won't have anything more to do with it."

"I hear she is a beautiful and pleasant lady."

"If she is, I wouldn't know," he said. "I suppose she is. I suppose people will say she is. I tried to look at her and speak to her as little as possible. I couldn't. Poor lady, she's all alone." He sat staring at his shoes. Then he looked up into her eyes. "When will your baby be born?"

"In six or seven turnings of the moon, I believe," she said.

"And so will hers."

"That's a strange thing," she said. "But how convenient for Ranulf. He'll come back for the birth and he'll get two for one, like a thrifty merchant."

"It seems he will," said Bren.

And so their uneasy conversation trailed off, and he left the arbor. She saw him around the fort from time to time, but they had no more private conferences about babies, about love, or about any other matter, interesting, difficult, or mundane.

A Garden Path

Emilde lay still, letting the midwife examine her, and letting Silfleda fuss over her.

"How are the pains now, Your Majesty?"

Emilde braced herself for another one. "They're starting to get bad."

"Everything is looking fine, Your Majesty," said the midwife, a knowledgeable woman named Cwenegund. "The baby's lie is good. It won't be like the last one. Put your mind at ease."

Thank the Children, thought Emilde, but what she said was, "Thanks to the Lady." She trusted Cwenegund, and was reassured.

Silfleda leaned over her. "Your Highness, Artur is most distressed. He remembers, the poor lad. Remembers about his brother, and the bad time you had then. Shall I send him a word of comfort from you?"

"Bring him here to me," she said.

Silfleda and the midwife exchanged a look of dismay.

"It isn't done," Emilde heard the midwife mutter.

"Bring Artur to me," she said, her voice firm.

In moments he was kneeling at her bedside.

"Artur. Dear boy." She stopped for a moment, to collect herself, as another wave of pain took her. She looked over at him with affection. He was sixteen, really no longer a boy. "Everything is fine with me. I'm well. Soon you'll have a new brother or sister." She reached out and smoothed his dark hair from his high white forehead. "Don't fear, my son."

"Yes, Mother," said Artur.

"Are you deep in your studies?"

"Yes, Mother."

"You must tell me all about them tomorrow. All about the fascinating things you've learnt."

"I will, Mother." But now Silfleda was tugging at him and hustling him from the room.

It was dawn before Emilde's third son came into the world. Cwenegund put the child in her arms, and Silfleda rushed to tell the king.

Emilde looked into the child's eyes and loved him. Any doubts about who had fathered him faded immediately. If any boy were Ranulf's, it was this boy.

Ranulf shouldered into the room and came to Emilde's bed.

She pulled the cover aside so he could see his son.

"A fine boy," Ranulf breathed. "A fine son." He bent to kiss Emilde's forehead.

She felt drowsy. She gave him a smile. "I hear you have yet another newborn son, my husband."

Ranulf's smile faded. "Yes," he said curtly.

"You must be a happy man," she said.

"Yes. Indeed," he said. "Lady be thanked."

"Sire, you must let your wife rest," she heard Cwenegund saying to the king, and he silently withdrew.

"You must rest, my lady," Cwenegund bent over her to whisper.

"How can I rest? How can I know a moment of peace? But I have this fine boy, so all is well."

Silfleda and Cwenegund drew the hangings at the windows close together so the sun wouldn't disturb her, and after she had nursed the child, they bore him away.

Then she did try to sleep. She thought she wouldn't be able to, her thoughts were so disturbing to her. That other woman. That other son.

But she fell almost immediately into a deep sleep.

At first her dreams were dark, restless visitations. Then it seemed to her she saw a misty light blooming ahead of her in the distance, as she moved through the dark space of the dream.

And now, as the light strengthened, she saw she walked in a beautiful garden, green and golden.

In the midst of the dreamscape garden, Emilde turned a corner, and there, coming toward her, was Aderyn. Aderyn threw her arms wide in welcome.

"Aderyn," whispered Emilde.

She thought to herself, *How odd to see Aderyn here.*

She thought to herself, *This can't be. Aderyn is dead.*

Then she thought to herself, *I'm dreaming.*

"My dearest friend. I'm here to comfort you. You must not grieve."

Emilde looked at her friend, suddenly stricken. "Aderyn, have I done wrong by you?"

"Nay, Emilde. You have loved truly and honorably."

Emilde felt tears prick her eyelids. "I'm so unhappy. Bren is unhappy."

"Bren's unhappiness will go on for a while, and we won't be able to help him with it, you and I. But your unhappiness will come to an end this very night," said Aderyn. "Your Child promises you this. And now prepare yourself, because you have a road ahead of you. Your Child has sent me to give you companionship along the way."

"My Child is good to me," said Emilde, falling into step with Aderyn along the garden path. "But Aderyn. I don't want to leave my sons."

She and Aderyn had moved out of the garden now, and were going deeper and deeper into a forest.

"It's a sad thing, yet you must." Aderyn's voice echoed among the trees. "You'll watch over them from that far shore. That will be your comfort."

"If only I could see Bren before I leave."

"You and I will watch over him, too."

"And poor Ranulf. What will he do? How can he go on living like this?"

In her mind, she drifted to that moment long ago when she had seen the faded rose in Ranulf's belt pouch. She remembered her delight, the memories of girlhood it had evoked. But then, later on, as she had thought about why it was there, she had realized what it meant.

"Ranulf must go on, and he will." Now it seemed to Emilde that Aderyn whispered into her ear. "You've given him what help you could. Now he'll have to muddle through by himself. A darkness hovers around him. But his Child will reach out to him."

"His Child? He worships the Lady."

"His Child will make Herself known to him." Aderyn's words were like the whisper of the breeze nosing against the hangings at the window of Emilde's bedchamber. "His Child will come to Ranulf at last," Aderyn whispered.

"And that will give him comfort?"

Aderyn's voice was sad. "Nothing will give him comfort, or not for a long time."

"His sons will comfort him."

Aderyn's words rang out now, like the ringing of a gong. Her words echoed through the forest, causing every flower and every leaf to vibrate with the force of them. "One son will damage him deeply. One son will wish him well but not be able to help. One son will help him and comfort him through the power of the Children. One son will justify him. One will be cut off before he truly lives. One will carry on after him, until, by the Children's decree, his task is done."

"Well, then," said Emilde, recognizing Aderyn for who she really was. She knelt to Aderyn, not sure what the deep bronze ringing words meant.

But inside Emilde, it was as if a book had closed. "I'm ready to go on our journey." She was in the dream garden. She was in the forest. She was in her bed at Tam Fort.

Aderyn moved to her and took her arm. She guided her from the bed and led her gently from the room. The journey was not very long, and with Aderyn there to help her, it was not even very hard.

As they approached the banks of that river, drifts of mist began to waft between her and Aderyn. Aderyn looked back at her with an encouraging smile.

"Come on! It's not far," she said to Emilde, beckoning.

Emilde had a hard time seeing Aderyn now. Rosettes of mist bloomed up ahead of her, expanded, merged into each other.

Roses bloomed all around her as she lay in her bed, as the part of her left behind lay there. These roses bloomed deeply crimson and spread, and merged into each other in dark, overlapping patterns like petals, and the thorns of these roses hurt her. Emilde felt a moment of panic.

Aderyn's voice echoed from the mist, so then she felt a burst of courage. She knew which direction to go. She too stepped into the mist, which swirled about her, cool and refreshing.

She moved further in, and the further in she moved, the more she couldn't tell where she herself ended and the mist began.

But that was all right. These pale roses had no thorns. She had gotten so tired. Now as she reached the other shore, she knew peace, and could rest.

BREN

CHAPTER SIXTEEN

To the Sea

Bren thought he must be dreaming. Aderyn was there beside the bed, reaching out a loving hand to him.

"My wife," he whispered.

"Dear Bren. You must be strong for our son."

"I will," he promised. "And if that means that Emilde and I must not—"

She leaned over to stop his mouth with a kiss. Her lips were cold.

"That's not what it means. The Children smile on you both, but your paths take different turnings. You must be strong and bear it."

He woke groggy and late, shaking the shreds of dream away from him. He sat up in alarm. By now, Emilde must be delivered of her child. He'd meant to keep watch, if only in his own mind, all night with her. But he had fallen asleep instead.

He threw on his clothes and rushed from his rooms at the fort.

Everyone stood about wreathed in smiles. Down the corridor came Ranulf. He moved to Bren and embraced him. "I have a son!"

"How is Emilde?"

"She's well, brother, Lady be thanked."

"And have you named the child?"

"It's Avery. After my uncle."

"A fine name," Bren was saying, but as he started to ask another question, a cry echoed down the corridor.

He stopped. Ranulf stopped. Everyone, standing around and buzzing with the news of the birth, fell silent.

Again. A cry.

The smile on Ranulf's face faded. Pure panic, that was what Bren read in his face.

Bren tried to speak, but his lips were numb.

Suddenly the dream from the night before came crowding into his mind. The visit from Aderyn. Her message that his life and Emilde's would take a different turning. This cry. It was about Emilde. Something had happened to her.

As he was thinking this, the Lady Silfleda, Emilde's lady-in-waiting, burst down the corridor and threw herself at the king's feet.

"The queen is dead," she got out.

What happened after that was a blur to Bren. He couldn't speak or think, just sag against the stones of the corridor's wall. *No*, he kept thinking, when he finally could think. *No*.

He stood back as her lady-in-waiting and some of the courtiers carried Emilde's slight body past him to the courtyard, to make it ready for entombment.

He caught only a glimpse of her, the sheen of her dark hair, the paleness of her face.

Then bondswomen hustled past carrying armloads of bedding stained a deep crimson.

He couldn't move. Everyone was shoving out into the inner bailey of the fort, headed to the great hall, Ranulf in their midst, leaving Bren alone in the corridor.

After a while, the midwife crept down the corridor. He remembered her, from Aderyn's lying-in. He put a hand out, stopping her.

"Mistress Cwenegund," he made himself say. "I heard the birth went well. But now."

"Your lordship," said Cwenegund, bobbing a curtsey. "It were not like your wife. The birth were not hard, and the child is well. We left the poor queen sleeping, and when we went back to check on Her Majesty—" The woman lost her composure and began to weep.

"Steady, mistress. The Children have plans for our lives, and we don't know what they are."

She looked up at him, startled.

He realized he had mentioned the Children. A forbidden thing. *Well, then*, he thought. *Let Ranulf punish me for it.*

"Your lordship, you have the right of it," said the midwife, wiping her eyes with a corner of her apron and ignoring his dangerous words. "I've seen this before. The mother seems well, but then the strings of her life are cut, and her life's blood flows out of her. None can do aught, if that happens."

"Poor lady," Bren whispered. "Child keep her."

Staring back frightened over her shoulder at him, the midwife hurried away.

After that, Bren moved through his life in a daze. He tried to give Ranulf what comfort he could. Ranulf's own distress kept him from seeing how shattered Bren himself was, and that, Bren thought, was the Children's own mercy.

A fortnight or more later, Bren was toiling up the steep path from the coast to his ancestral manor on the sea cliffs at the western edge of the Sceptered Isle. His men lugged his gear behind him.

His chief servant, Mistress Guenbrith, was there to meet him, the infant Drustan in her arms.

"You got my message, I see."

"Aye, your lordship. And here's your lordship's lusty boy. See how hale he is."

Bren looked down into the eyes of his son as he lay in Mistress Guenbrith's arms. The little child stared back. Then he began to root and grizzle.

"He's hungry, lord. I'll take him to his nurse, shall I?"

"Yes, please, and send one of the bondswomen to me with ale, if you would be so kind."

He sank to the stones of his hearth fire in relief. How good it was to be home.

"You'll be back soon?" Ranulf had said to him, as he'd prepared to leave. They'd all gone through the painful time of interring Emilde in the big tomb in the High Temple to the Lady Goddess (*where she should not be*, Bren thought desperately) and the painful early days of mourning.

"Aye, I'll return soon," Bren had told Ranulf, and at the time he had believed the words he'd said. Now he recognized them for a lie. If it were in his power, he'd never go back to Tambourne and Tam Fort.

Ranulf had been grief-stricken at Emilde's death. But Bren saw he also made use of a ready source of comfort, Mistress Cicely, his young concubine.

Bren tried not to think badly of Ranulf. He had two baby sons to provide for, and the two older boys. But of course he had plenty of help doing so. *That's a cynical thought*, said Bren to himself, thinking of his own grief and the means he had to buy the help of servants and nurses. And Bren saw Ranulf did care. He even put aside his plans for a new campaign of war so he could see to his sons' comfort. Had he ever done such a thing before?

He loves his sons, Bren thought. *He'll make sure to be around, at least for a while, until they all get past the worst of their grief.*

Emilde's infant, Avery, of course had no inkling of his motherless state. As far as Bren could see, the child was thriving.

Audemar. Who knew what that boy thought? He seemed the same as ever.

But sixteen-year-old Artur was devastated. Bren sat looking down at his hands, thinking of the day Ranulf took the lad to meet Cicely and her child. Bren was dubious about it all, Artur so grief-stricken, his mother's death so recent. But then, of course, Ranulf hadn't consulted Bren. Bren did go along, though. Ranulf asked him to do it, and he forced himself to say, as graciously as he could muster, that he would. He loved Artur, and he worried about how the lad would take this meeting. *I owe it to Emilde to be there*, he thought.

"I want you to meet your brother," Ranulf explained to Artur, as he walked his oldest son to the small house where Cicely lived. "Someday this boy will be your vassal and under your protection. You should meet him right away. He should grow up knowing his obligations to you, my son."

"Yes, Father," Artur had said.

Behind the entire party, Avery's wet-nurse bore him along too. Audemar, Bren saw with relief, was not part of their group.

"Audemar won't need to have much to do with his half-brother, as a vassal. That will be Artur's task. I'll leave him with his minder," Ranulf had said privately to Bren before they'd set out.

As for the infant Avery, Bren wasn't sure what that was all about. Why bring an infant along to this meeting, he wondered. But Ranulf had looked over his shoulder at the wet-nurse carrying Avery. "For this youngest child of mine, knowing his brother will be a far different knowing than Artur's," Ranulf told Bren, hanging back to walk beside Bren. "This young one will grow up with his bastard half-brother. They're of an age, and will become friends. I've known of many men whose most faithful retainers have been bastard-born brothers of theirs. Perhaps this boy will be Avery's squire, when he heads out to war, who knows?"

Bren had just nodded.

His opinion actually wasn't wanted or needed. Let Ranulf do as he pleased. He'd do that anyhow, no matter what Bren thought about it.

The whole party of them crowded into Cicely's tiny house.

The meeting between Artur and Cicely had left Bren cringing with embarrassment.

Ranulf didn't seem to notice.

Artur looked into the cradle at the young woman's infant, then quickly away.

Was that a look of hatred, Bren wondered.

Later, when they all got back to the castle, Bren noticed him with the same hostile look on his face as he gazed at Avery.

So it's not about bastardy at all, Bren thought. *This boy hates anything that damaged his mother—the boy who killed Emilde, the child of the woman who supplanted her.*

The visit to Cicely might have been ill-advised for Artur, Bren didn't know.

But he did know that for himself, it was too much. That visit decided Bren. His grief was too raw, and it had no safe outlet.

He'd make some excuse about needing to see to his own son, and then he'd leave Ranulf's court.

Seeing Artur's struggle almost undid his resolve.

Shouldn't he be here to watch over Artur?

No, he told himself. Others might have their doubts about Artur and treat him dismissively, but Ranulf never had. He was a father who loved his son. Bren saw that Ranulf would give Artur the love and protection he needed.

But I. I need to get away from this, he thought.

And now here he was.

Bren needed to see to his son. And he needed to see to himself. His grief cut into his heart. There was no way he could properly show it, not in Ranulf's court.

He needed to get away so he could attend to it.

The dream of Aderyn came back to him. *You must be strong for our son*, she'd said.

Now he saw what she meant. First, of course, to be the strong and loving father little Dru needed and deserved. That first. Of course that.

But the other thing was this. If Bren's grief over Emilde went untended, he wouldn't be able to fulfill his first obligation. He'd be a shattered thing with no will of its own.

He had loved Emilde so long, and with nothing to nurture or acknowledge it. Then they had had that one night in each other's arms. One. Now she was gone.

Bren had always been able to rely on his Child, knowing She was kind, knowing Her love would see him through life's terrors and disappointments.

But now he was shaken. Were They indeed kind, the Children? Perhaps the concerns of petty human beings were so insignificant to Them that They didn't see or care.

Aderyn's visit in his dream told him he needed to heal. Aderyn knew the best place to heal was the sea.

Child of the Sea-Child, of course she knew that.

Bren stepped to the door again and breathed in the sea air. The waves crashed in a muted roar underneath the cliff on which his house was built.

I'm here, he thought. *If I heal at all, here's the place I will do it.*

CHAPTER SEVENTEEN

Summons

The message Bren dreaded was finally here. *It had to come sometime*, he thought, a thudding in the pit of his stomach. He handed the messenger a coin and unrolled the parchment. He knew what the message probably said. It was probably his summons from Ranulf to bring his son to court. Bren took the parchment to the pleached garden on the protected side of the manor to read.

It was good to sit there in the sun. His hopes here at his house on the cliffs above the sea had been realized. As the years unfolded, as he watched his little son grow and flourish, he knew peace.

But I'm feeling my age, he told himself. He settled himself on the little bench there and raised his face to the sunshine, trying to put aside the unsettled feelings Ranulf's message roused in him. Besides, here he could watch little Dru at play, and that was his greatest delight.

The message wasn't exactly what he thought it would be.

Ranulf had penned it himself, which touched Bren greatly. Ranulf was awkward with his letters.

Brother. Dear friend I hope you come to me, it read. *Artur marries next turning of the mon bring Dustan for fostered with my boys.*

Bren and Ranulf had always talked of it. How, when they had sons, the boys would be fostered together. Now here it was. A request, but really, a command.

In the past few years, things had changed for Bren. He still thought of Ranulf as his brother, but he didn't want to part with Drustan, and he didn't want to go back to court.

He had had no falling out with Ranulf. He'd just left, and Ranulf hadn't summoned him. Bren wondered what that meant. Bren had returned to his cliffs and his lands when his son reached his first year. Now the child was six. Five years. The first few years, Ranulf hadn't gone to war, but he had last year, and he hadn't insisted Bren join him on campaign.

Bren sighed. Here was the summons to go back at last, and it was for Artur's marriage. Bren had always loved Artur. Of course he'd return for Artur's marriage, and when he did, of course he'd bring his son. Once he and his son were back within Ranulf's reach, it would be difficult to leave. Bren knew it. Ranulf knew it. Ranulf knew Bren knew it.

Yet deep inside, Bren understood a return to court would be—well, the death of him, that might be too dramatic. But it would hurt him deeply.

Everywhere I look, I'll see Emilde, he told himself. *Every time I look at Ranulf, I'll think of his concubine. Every time I see that boy, her son, I'll think how much his birth hurt Emilde.*

Why doesn't the hurt ever lessen? He cried this out to Aderyn. She was the only one who understood. And that, he had to acknowledge, was most unusual, since she was dead. She visited him often, though, in his dreams.

How could he judge Ranulf, when he himself loved Ranulf's wife? But then again, Ranulf's wife was dead, too. Five years dead.

It was too big a muddle. Bren found it easier to stay away.

I'll think of a reason not to go, he told himself.

He looked hard at the little piece of parchment. Something else was written there, written on the back. Bren flipped it over. He sucked in his breath.

Brother you will find this strange. My Child has found me. I pray to Her now.

Bren stood and called out. The little boy, Drustan, turned and waved. He left his minder and came running across the garden to his father.

I have my hurts and my fears, Bren thought. *The Children have other ideas. So now I must answer when They call.*

"My son," he said. "You and I will go on a journey together. Will you like that?"

The boy's eyes shone. "Yes, Father," he said.

"You and I will go to court. You'll meet some friends there."

This place is beautiful, he thought, *but lonely. My boy doesn't have other boys to play with here, and he'll never have brothers or sisters, because I'll never marry again. I'll take Drustan to Ranulf. He'll have a good life there.*

He knew he'd return to his cliffs. He knew Ranulf's summons was really a command, and he knew he had no choice but to obey it. He knew he'd know even greater hurt, without his son nearby. But he saw now. It had to be.

CHAPTER EIGHTEEN

An Eagle for an Emperor

B ren and Ranulf were off hunting together. The beaters had flushed some fine game for them, and the courtiers accompanying them were having a good day, Bren saw. Ranulf lifted his glove with his bird and stood with his head thrown back, ecstatic, watching his gyrfalcon take to the sky.

This kind of hunting was Ranulf's delight and always had been. Bren smiled at the easy familiarity of the scene, at how easily he'd resumed his place at Ranulf's side. His own borrowed tiercel from Ranulf's mews stirred restlessly, and Bren released him too.

Bren had been dreading his return to the court. Yet he was surprised at how good he was feeling, now that he was back.

Right away, Drustan had taken to the two little boys, Ranulf's youngest sons, and they to him. He was off playing with them now.

And Bren had been surprised at the uprush of emotion he felt when he saw his brother, his dear friend, after so long. He fell upon Ranulf's neck, thanking his Child for the good feelings.

"It has been too long, brother," said Ranulf.

Hunting wasn't very important to Bren, but he knew how much it meant to Ranulf. When Ranulf suggested they go out hunting, he'd readily agreed.

"Pick out one of the peregrines," the king urged Bren, as they looked over the birds in the mews.

Bren grinned at Ranulf. "But," he teased, "I'm no prince."

"If you want to stand on ceremony, brother, take one of the tiercels, then. Tiercels for earls."

The whole matter reminded Bren of their boyhood, where they were continually pretending to out-do each other—Ranulf to pull rank and Bren to pretend undermining him.

Now here they were, in fine country on a fine day. They had nearly come to the limits of their hunting, and then they'd head back toward Tam Fort before dark took them. Ranulf spoke quietly to the courtiers, who reined their horses in, and then he and Bren turned their horses into a secluded glade. On Ranulf's arm was his favorite gyrfalcon, a great white bird named Goda.

"Good hunting here?" Bren called ahead to the king.

Ranulf didn't answer. After they'd moved in a little further, Ranulf wheeled his courser around. Volatîn. That was the courser's name. Bren remembered now. He remembered how much Ranulf loved that horse. Volatîn was old now.

I'm old, Bren thought.

Ranulf waited for Bren to catch up with him.

They sat their horses in the glade, their breathing and their horses' breathing becoming slow and peaceful in the green surroundings.

"A beautiful place, is it not, brother?" said Ranulf.

"Indeed. Very peaceful."

"I brought you here to show you something."

Bren looked around him, confused.

"To show you the place. This is where it happened. The farwyd of the Child of Earth came to me here."

"You've mentioned this in passing, brother. I am amazed. And I am very glad for you, too. To know the Children and Their love. That's a fine thing."

"You may have seen. I haven't torn down the High Temple of the Lady Goddess. Anyone may go there to worship."

"I did see that, brother."

"I talked to the farwyd about that. I told her she had convinced me, but I couldn't accept hurting anyone who wasn't convinced. The priests of the Lady Goddess used to urge me to hunt down the Children's believers, find their bowers, tear them down. Execute their followers. I refused to do it. You may not know that. And now I told the farwyd I couldn't do the same to the followers of the Lady."

"What did the farwyd tell you?" said Bren.

"She told me I was right."

"The Children are merciful."

"You know that, brother. You've always known it. And Aderyn."

"Yes."

"You never spoke of it with me."

"Remember? I did once."

"Then we agreed you never would again."

"For my own safety, Rannie," said Bren, putting a hand on the king's arm. "That's what you told me. You said to me, *Don't put me in that cruel position, brother*. So I never have."

"But now I see."

"Did you know Emilde worshipped the Children too?"

Ranulf looked startled. Then he looked down. Bren saw he was having trouble composing himself. "Another way I failed her." He looked up now. "Now I see why she was such fast friends with you and Aderyn. Well, of course she would be. But now I see a deeper reason."

Bren nodded, his heart full.

"I had thought—" Ranulf hesitated. "For a while I had thought—"

Bren swallowed hard. But the moment passed, and Ranulf didn't say it. Bren felt grateful and cowardly at the same time.

"You know, after the farwyd's visit, I decided I should take poor Emilde's remains to the Child of Earth's barrow. But then I thought, no, she worshipped the Lady."

Bren laughed a little.

"I'll do it, Bren!"

It touched Bren to see such a look of happiness flash across Ranulf's face.

But then he said, "Cicely worships the Lady."

"Oh," said Bren. *Now I see it,* he thought. *He won't persecute those who love the Lady because he doesn't want to hurt his precious Cicely.* Then Bren felt ashamed of himself. Ranulf's impulse was good and noble. If Cicely played a role in that, she deserved praise.

"But anyway, I wanted you to see, Bren. This is where it happened."

"I don't understand that, Rannie. Help me to understand. As I've always thought it, the farwyd never leaves her cave on the promontory far to the east. How is it she came here? It's such a long journey, and she is very old."

"Were you a bit skeptical, once you'd heard my courtiers talk about it behind my back? They're a bit skeptical too." Ranulf laughed.

"The Children are mighty. I know that, brother. But explain to me. If it's allowed."

"I was out hawking," said the king. By then, Goda had returned to his arm with her catch, and Ranulf stopped to stuff the animal into the game bag at his saddle. The borrowed tiercel had returned to Bren without anything to show for his effort, but he sat preening himself and looking around with his fierce eye as if he weren't disappointed or jealous at all.

"This is how it happened," Ranulf resumed. "Goda, here, had brought down her prey. We all saw the stoop. If you want to know the definition of mighty, that's it. Goda, as she screams down on her prey." Ranulf looked over at his bird proudly.

"But then she disappeared into some brush, and she didn't reappear. That gave my heart a wrench, you can believe it did," he went on. "I went into the thicket after you, didn't I, girl?"

Goda sat placidly on the king's arm and didn't reply.

"I came into this glade. Where we are right this moment."
Ranulf stopped, clearly moved. "Around me, I heard a kind of
thrumming in the air. Then a mighty pounding of wings."

"Goda?" asked Bren.

"No. It was an eagle. An eagle for an emperor, Bren. But I tell
you, it was the largest eagle I've ever seen."

Bren thought to himself that he'd never seen an eagle up
close. Just the sea eagles as they swerved and rocked on the
wind over the cliffs.

"This eagle came into the glade, and as it descended, I was
terrified." Ranulf stopped for a moment, and a strange look
came across his face. "Do you remember the comet, when my
father died?"

"Of course," said Bren.

"Do you remember that when we looked up and saw it,
something frightening happened to me?"

"Yes. I do remember that. I remember the panic I felt,
thinking you'd become ill, fearing the comet was about that."

"I've never spoken of it. A mighty bird came to me. It came
to judge me for my wickedness. I was so full of dread I couldn't
speak or move. So when this happened, the great eagle
appearing again, here in this very glade, I knew a terrible fear. I
knew I hadn't sufficiently changed my wickedness. I'd changed
some things, but in other ways I was the same as always. Out of
the mercy of my Child, she came to me."

"Who?"

"The farwyd, man. She was the eagle."

"I see," said Bren.

"The farwyd. She's a kind of emperor, you know. The empress of a vast domain, the lands where the Child of Earth's star fell. The bird was massive. Then it dwindled away. And there she was. She was tiny, shriveled. I had to bend down to get a look at her. I got off my horse, and I bent down to see her, see what she might be. I was so startled."

Bren looked at Ranulf. Maybe he had fallen and had hit his head. Maybe he'd fallen asleep in the glade and had had a dream.

Ranulf laughed at him. "You're a follower of the Children, Bren, and you don't believe my story either." He sat his horse and smiled at Bren. "Look, man. Suppose it were a dream," he said, just as if he'd read Bren's mind. "If it happened to be a dream, it told me just as true as if the farwyd really did appear to me in the form of a bird. So I'm easy."

Bren thought of all the comfort that dreams had brought him lately. He thought of Aderyn, traveling from the Land of the Dead to speak words of comfort. "In whatever form you saw her, you saw her, brother. I believe you."

"And then she told me about my Child, and how my Child loved me in spite of myself. For the first time since Emilde's death, I felt peace. I told her I knew myself too well. I told her I was sorry about Emilde, but I knew I'd go back to my old ways."

"What did she say to that."

"She said my Child understood this. She said my Child would keep helping me fight. She told me people were suffering, and my Child wanted me to help them, and that these matters were much more important than my own puny failings. So that's what I'm doing, brother. I'm taking food to the hungry. Sending out healers to the sick."

"That's admirable, Rannie."

"That's not enough. I'm powerful. I can do these things. But people need to be able to do them for themselves. So I'm thinking about how to help them do it. And Bren—"

Bren marveled at the resolve he saw in Ranulf.

"Bren, here's the best part. I've enlisted Artur to help me. The farwyd told me I was right to trust Artur and his path. But then she said—"

Now Bren felt a pang of concern.

"My sons. Bad things may happen to them. May happen because of them. She told me a thing about John that frightened me, Bren."

John, Bren thought blankly. Then, *Oh, John.* The little bastard. Cicely's boy.

"If you pray, your Child will help you through it, brother," he said to Ranulf.

"That is my hope, Bren." He heaved a sigh. "Because whenever I look at him, that little boy, I feel the fear all over again. He's just a little boy. But she told me a thing about him that—" Ranulf took a breath. "Then I stay away. I stay away from Cicely because of it. In many ways, I'm the same weak man I always was."

The two of them sat their horses, letting the green quiet of the glade descend on them with its mercy.

"So," said Ranulf at last. "I wanted to tell you. You are the person who means most to me in this world, aside from my sons. Whatever other failings I have, at least I am bringing up my sons to honor the Children."

As they rode back to the hunting party, Ranulf continued telling Bren about his plans for his sons, and all about them. How Artur had already made his profession of fealty to his father. "But not in the High Temple, as in ages past. Artur went up to the mountains of his Child for his vigil. It was a beautiful thing, Bren. And now," he said, looking over at Bren, beaming. "Artur will wed and give me grandsons, and your son and my two little ones will become the best of friends, as you and I are."

"Rannie," said Bren uneasily. "This is hard to explain. After the wedding I must return to my cliffs."

"You are happy there," said Ranulf. "After the hard things you've been through."

"Yes," said Bren, wondering again how much Ranulf suspected about his feelings for Emilde. Ranulf was maybe hinting at such a thought, but after a moment Bren saw he wasn't pursuing it. Bren wouldn't, either.

No point in bringing it up. Let the dead rest under the thorns and briars of their graves. His friendship with Ranulf was long-standing and solid. Their sons would probably be friends for life, too. They knew the mercies of their Child. That was enough. The two of them left it at that.

PART III: BEAUTIFUL BOYS

"And how is the young one, Aderyn?" asked Myrddin. "He doesn't know himself yet, what he is. Watch over him, Aderyn, Little Bird. He is the hope now. See that the birds befriend him."

Aderyn nodded her assent.

"This may be unfair to you, Aderyn. You've worked hard underneath the Spheres. One of the best and most faithful of the mages. Now you've moved to a place of rest. Yet I'm asking a difficult task of you." Myrddin watched her uneasily.

"I am happy to undertake this task, Lord Myrddin," said Aderyn. "When I look at this young boy, I see my own, and I feel sorrow that I'm not beside him to help him. And besides," she added. "Do I see in this young one a special ability?"

Myrddin smiled. "Indeed you do. An ability very like your own. And another ability not so like yours, but very valuable to the art."

"An accomplished mage with many facets. A rarity," she breathed. "I'll help him any way I can."

"Thank you, Aderyn, Little Bird." Myrddin bowed to the bird-mage with deep respect. She might not be as powerful as himself and Dee, restricted—as they never had been—to only one of the Planes. But she was beloved of The Three for the depths of her compassion.

Standing in the shadows, Gilles overheard. His lips drew back from his teeth in a snarl.

This boy. He stared down through the layers of crystal to the land beneath, where new life had come into the world. This boy was the threat, then. What foolish King Ranulf had started with his heedlessness and lust, Gilles swore to himself he'd finish.

Ha, Gilles thought after a moment. The king has other sons. I'll go after them too.

All unwitting, Ranulf will become my instrument. I'll make Ranulf my own, and Ranulf will never realize. Anything of Ranulf—his boys, his very kingdom—and especially that one boy—will belong to me.

And then.

Then, Gilles swore, he'd turn it to his use.

CICELY

John

Whon John was born and opened his big blue eyes onto the world and looked into hers, Cicely thought her heart would burst.

She expected Ranulf would come by to see. She didn't expect Ranulf would be waiting impatiently outside her little house to be let into the room by the midwife, and to throw himself on Cicely in love and relief, and to marvel alongside her at every marvelous feature of their marvelous son.

She fell in love with John the moment he was born. And then, to her amazement, she fell in love with Ranulf only a few moments later.

After he left in order to give her some rest, and she had John in the crook of her arm and was nursing him, her mind began to wander back to the other day she had thought she was in love with Ranulf.

The day she thought he was rescuing her from attack. She was dazzled by him. Blond, virile, older, strong. Like one of the heroes in the stories, there to right the wrong about to be done to her, and then to declare his undying love for her and sweep her away to riches and comfort.

But then almost immediately she saw what he really was. A predator chasing away the other predators so he could take her instead.

Even then, stupid girl that she was, it took her a while to understand. What he was doing seemed, in the moment, so overwhelming, so exciting, that she fell right into his hands.

She remembered the bitter taste of the aftermath, lying in the grass realizing what had happened to her. She blamed herself savagely.

When she got herself home, somehow she'd explained to her mother's satisfaction that she had fallen while trying to climb over a wall. That's why her clothes were all disarranged. That's why she'd lost her apron. That's why her hands and knees were scraped and scratched.

So her mother hadn't gone to her father, Lady be praised.

Cicely was already in her father's bad graces.

He'd begun calling her Mistress Prideful.

Cicely knew her father had come upon hard times.

He could no longer go to the wars or serve his overlord, because he had injured his leg too badly one day when he was out hunting. Besides, that baron he served was across the Narrows somewhere on the mainland and almost never came over to the Lunds-fort side to see about his vassals. He didn't even know her father.

Her father got a pittance of a pension from the man, barely enough to feed them. He hadn't been injured in his overlord's wars, just on his own look-out, and too bad for him. Three daughters, no sons, no money for a dowry.

Certainly her mother couldn't be expected to help. She could hardly head out to find work as a servant. If she did, the disgrace would destroy them. They were gentles. In name, anyhow.

Her father wouldn't allow it.

So when Cob of the neighboring farm started paying Cicely court, and when Cob indicated he'd not expect a dowry, or not much of one, and when her father saw a way to get his oldest daughter off his hands and out of his household, just one more mouth to feed, he was overjoyed.

Cicely wasn't.

Cob was an ill-smelling, dirty, drunken man with two brothers just as dirty, all living together in a dilapidated manor house, passing themselves off as gentles. Everyone knew they weren't, not really. Cicely despised Cob, and she didn't like the way the brothers eyed her, as if they were calculating when they could get their hands on her too.

She begged her father not to make her wed Cob. He refused to budge. She begged her mother to intervene. Her mother refused to take Cicely's part.

Finally, in a panic, she rushed to the Ecga Green village temple of the Lady to pray. There she encountered the raw young priest assigned to give them all spiritual comfort. He was only a year or so older than she.

"You are distressed, my daughter," he had said to her. She remembered the day and the look in his eyes.

"Oh, Priest Archard!" she had exclaimed. "Lady help me! My father is trying to force me to marry Cob."

"That's very wrong, my daughter," he had said. "Cob is a dirty thing. He doesn't deserve to have such as fair a flower as you in his bed."

Cicely remembered looking up from her prayers at him, startled. Priests weren't supposed to notice the appearance of the worshippers they counseled, and they weren't supposed to use terms of endearment such as "fair flower" to or of the young women who prayed at the temple, nor to think at all of matters of the bed. But if Priest Archard would help her avoid a horrifying fate, she didn't care.

"Please, Priest Archard. Please talk to my father."

And so the silly man did. Silly because he refused to grant the Lady's blessing to Cicely's marriage against her will, and then, for his misplaced scruples, the very next season, was removed from the temple at Ecga Green to be placed somewhere else. Cicely knew her father complained to the young man's superior about Priest Archard sticking his nose where it didn't belong.

Cicely was glad for Priest Archard's want of sense. At least she had avoided her fate. But then, that day in the woods, it looked like Cob and his brothers had devised a worse one for her.

She remembered how she fled, stumbling and looking back over her shoulder at her evil pursuers. She remembered her kerchief flying off, and her hair streaming unbound behind her. She remembered how they cornered her against the wall. "Share and share alike, brothers," one of them had said. Which one, she could never remember. In her panic, they were just a collection of sets of eyes and hands and red slavering mouths.

And then, or so it seemed to her, she reeled from a bad fate to a worse to a worse. The man she looked to for protection turned out to be no protection at all. Even more terrible, afterward, he offered her money, as if she were a peasant girl he could just take along the roadside if he pleased.

But so handsome, a little voice niggled at her. *He has disgraced and ruined you*, another voice raged.

Then, strangest of all, the odd thing this man had said to her. *I think I'm in love with you.*

Was the man daft? Surely he was.

The next turning of the moon had settled her mind a bit. Her parents hadn't found out she was disgraced and ruined. She wasn't with child.

But life kept on in its miserable creeping course. Her father's recriminations. The panic in her mother's eyes as they fell further and further into poverty. The meagerness of the broth in her mother's kettle. No meat. A few old, limp vegetables floating around in it, with their spotted, ragged leaves. Her sisters' faces getting thinner and thinner. And it was all her fault.

Their much more prosperous relations in Lunds-fort wouldn't help. They enjoyed casting a disapproving eye. Her father had had fallings-out with all of them. Now, they seemed to suggest with their disdainful glances, he and his family were only getting what they richly deserved, and they should shut their complaining mouths.

Then, one day, when Cicely came in from one of her surreptitious expeditions into the woods to seek out edible plants to supplement their diet, careful not to let the neighbors see the straits and stratagems they'd been reduced to, she found her mother and father sitting at their ease around the hearth fire, waiting for her.

"Daughter," said her father. "You can at last redeem yourself in my eyes."

"Yes, daughter," her mother put in. "No more disobedience."

"If the thought is distasteful to you, well, that's something you'll have to bear," said her father. "And this time, my girl, disobedience will get you a taste of this." He looked down at a thick stick he had beside him.

Cicely began to tremble. What were they going to make her do now?

"It's not what we'd wish for you, Lady knows," said her mother. "But it's something. And we'll keep body and soul together. And your sisters may have a chance at marriage."

"Silence, woman. Cicely doesn't need to know our reasons. Cicely needs to obey."

Cicely clasped her hands together and looked down at her shoes.

"Make ready, Daughter. You're going away."

"Where, Father," she whispered.

"Going away to be a rich man's concubine. He's bought and paid for you, my girl. You have to do it. I've signed the parchment. He'll be coming to take you before sundown."

Cicely had thrown herself into her mother's arms, sobbing.

Her father had brandished his stick.

She had gotten together her few belongings.

As sundown approached, the three of them sat rigid at the hearth fire.

Then the knock at the door.

Her father opened it.

Cicely's mouth gaped open.

"Cicely," said Ranulf, her attacker. "Has your father told you?"

She nodded dumbly.

This rich man, this Ranulf, had turned to her father then. "There's a change of plans, my good man."

She saw her father bristle at being addressed in this manner, as if he were some fellow, and she saw her mother's eyes widen with fear.

Maybe he won't be taking me after all, Cicely thought, a little hope blooming in her.

Before her father could do what he always did, antagonize and bluster, a man stepped into their small house and addressed Ranulf.

"Sire," he said, bowing low. "Shall I see the horses stabled?"

"Nay, my thanks. I won't be long."

"Very good, Your Majesty," said the man, and disappeared again.

Cicely looked dumbfounded from one side to the other, where her parents had hastily thrown themselves onto their knees.

"Please," said Ranulf, "Please rise. I'm not your monarch. I'm the king of the Sceptered Isle, and I'm only a visitor in your realm."

Her parents stayed kneeling.

"Cicely," said Ranulf, looking straight at her. "I hoped to bring you back with me. I return to my own realm in the morning. But a slight problem has presented itself, and I see I can't bring you with me, not yet." He felt behind him, pushed the door of the house open, leaned out of it, and motioned to someone. Then he stepped aside.

Two men came in with a heavy chest.

Ranulf nodded, and they set it down, and then they retreated.

"My good man, I'll have to beg your indulgence. I'll have to beg you to keep your daughter safe for me until I can make better arrangements. I'll visit her whenever I can, if you will humor me. Meanwhile, here is the price we agreed on."

Cicely's father sprang to his feet. He rushed to the chest and opened it and looked in. He looked back at Ranulf. "Yes, I agree," he said.

"Good. Is there a place your daughter and I may be alone for a while?"

Now Cicely's mother got to her feet too. "Please, my lord, follow me."

She led Ranulf to the door of the bedchamber where she and Cicely's father slept, and opened it for him. She stood aside and looked over to Cicely. "Daughter," she said. "You're to go in too."

"Beauty's as valuable as good coin," Cicely heard her father murmur to her mother.

So then Cicely belonged to the king.

But love? No. She was deeply ashamed.

Ranulf was as good as his word. He sent chests of goods. He sent gold. He sent rich clothing for the family to wear.

And every few turnings of the moon, he arrived to spend a few days with his concubine Cicely.

The family grew so prosperous that they moved to a bigger house. Their hopes for their other two daughters came to nothing, though. No family of gentle birth wanted their son to have anything to do with the family of a concubine. It was disgraceful.

Cicely's mother cried, and her sisters pouted and threw hateful looks in Cicely's direction.

But Cicely's father was cheerful. "Someday they'll come around. You'll see," he told Cicely and her mother. "Money drives the world. Meanwhile, we are living well. Very well indeed. I'm thinking of getting a horse."

They'd had to sell the last one several years ago so they could eat.

From time to time, Cicely didn't see Ranulf for a full season or more, because he was off at the wars.

Early on, she conceived a child. A bare few turnings of the moon later, she lost it.

She was glad.

And then, last year, she had conceived again.

"I'll be off to the Western Isle to do a bit of knocking about of heads," Ranulf told her when she let him know. "But I'll send my best friend and most trusted confidant, the Lord Brenci, Earl of the High Sea Cliffs, to bring you to Tam Fort while I'm gone. I don't want my child born in some other realm. He must be born in my realm."

But he'll never be king after you, thought Cicely, *because he'll only be your bastard.* Then she thought, *Suppose this child is a daughter.* What would Ranulf do then? He appeared to want sons. That was strange to her. She knew he had sons already, legitimate sons.

She realized she knew little of Ranulf's life in that other realm. She knew he had a wife, who would certainly be displeased to know Cicely was being moved to her own city. She knew this wife had borne Ranulf two sons. This wife would certainly be dismayed to know Cicely was bearing the king's child.

"Suppose I lose this child, the way I lost the last one?" she said to Ranulf.

"I want you with me, Cicely, no matter what. I've been remiss. You must come to be with me, whether my wife likes it or not."

So that's it, thought Cicely. Just as she'd thought. The problem and impediment to her moving out of her parents' house had been this wife of Ranulf's all along.

A fortnight later, the earl, a man as handsome in his darker, slighter way as Ranulf was in his big blond strapping way, arrived to take her with him across the border to the Sceptered Isle. Her parents were almost as overawed by Earl Brenci as they were by King Ranulf.

The earl handed her up onto a horse he'd brought for her, and they rode off. He was perfectly polite to her, but stiff and remote.

He disapproves of me, thought Cicely.

He installed her just the same in a comfortable little house that she explored with delight. A house of her own! And seven or so turnings of the moon later, she was giving birth in that house, and Ranulf was rushing to take her into his arms, and to gaze with eyes of love on their beautiful boy.

Cicely thought of her grandfather, the only man in her life who had loved her for her self alone, and not her yellow hair. "I want to name him John, for my grandfather," she told Ranulf.

"John. A fine name. A name from your side of the isle," he said. He put out his big hand, and laid it on John's little head. "Do you know," he whispered to Cicely. "This is the happiest day of my life."

And then at last she gave in and loved Ranulf back.

CHAPTER TWENTY

Avery

Cicely wasn't the young prince's minder, but she might as well have been. Young Prince Avery, the legitimate brother, and John, the bastard brother, spent all of their waking time together, just about, and mostly at her house. The two children were not just brothers. They were fast friends. And now here was the earl's boy, too. Drustan.

The three of them, little savages, roamed the forest beyond her house at the edge of Tam Fort, fishing, playing at war, whooping, chasing each other.

As she watched them and tended to them, she sometimes felt a pang of envy. If only her own childhood had been this free. This joyous. But then she had to remind herself that if she'd grown up a king's daughter, or even a king's bastard, she would probably have had to sit quietly and mind her manners. That was the burden girls had to bear.

The boys had their spats. Avery could be high-handed. *After all*, she sighed to herself. *He is born to it. His father is Ranulf.* How could he help it?

But John's father is Ranulf, too, she reminded herself, *and John is nothing like Avery*. It's not that John was diffident or meek. Far from it. But while Avery was loud and boisterous, John was quiet and determined.

Then there was Dru. Cicely wanted to gather all three of them to her and hug them tight, as she had when they were younger. She thought with fondness of the soft little cheeks, the downy hair, the little boy sweet smell of them. Now, as the three boys crowded to her hearth, poking into the kettle, looking for something to eat, they were much too big for that. She ladled out bowls of stew for them, and they crouched together at the hearth stones, slurping it down.

"You boys are growing faster than the bondswoman can keep you in leggings," she told them, laughing.

Dru looked up at her, nodding thoughtfully. "Yes, Mistress Cicely. She tells me that, too," he said in his clear piping voice.

Dru was just as sturdy, just as dauntless as the other two. But Dru was a careful lad. He considered everything he did. He was like a little man. Meanwhile Avery threw himself at life. And John stood a bit aside, always his own self. He'd been that way from birth. Sometimes, looking into her son's eyes, Cicely wondered what she saw there. It made her shiver, sometimes.

Avery shouted and hallooed and laughed. Dru carefully talked things over. Talked and talked and talked. As for John. John sang.

Where did that come from? Cicely wondered. No one in her family was musical. And she didn't know of any musical people in Ranulf's. The Lady's own gift, she thought fondly, listening to her son's silvery voice as he ran singing about the place.

His singing made Ranulf uneasy, though. She wasn't sure why.

One day, as she sat sewing in the door to catch the spring sun, she heard upraised voices.

"I'll be king. You have to bow down to me," Avery was screaming at the other two.

John stood with his fists balled up. "I won't," he said.

Dru just leaned against the side of the house, looking. "That's not true, Avery," Dru said. "You won't be king."

"My father is the king. I'll be king after him. Bow, varlets." Avery had made himself a little wand out of a willow stick. Now he waved it around. Then he lunged at John with it, as if it were a sword.

John laughed scornfully and pushed it aside.

"You must obey me, Johnny," said Avery, coming at him again with the stick. "You're only a bastard. You have to do it."

"I don't," said John. "I won't."

"I'll make you."

"Just try it," said John.

"You're only the third son," said Dru. "You'll not be king, Aves. Artur will be king, and if something happens to Artur, Audie will."

Cicely had half-risen from her joint stool. Her heart broke for John. Here it was, the first time in his life anyone had thrown it in his face. *Just a bastard.* And it had to come from his brother, his best friend. Cicely wanted to cry.

She made herself sit back down. These boys would have to sort it out themselves, she decided. They were only six years old, but they had to learn these things for themselves, where they stood with each other. Where they stood in the world. John had to learn it too.

If she started interfering every time John had to face what he was, he'd have a hard row to hoe.

She looked over at Avery with dislike. What a handsome boy, she thought. And how ugly his features were right now, distorted and sneering.

Well, she thought. *He's Ranulf's look-out, not mine.*

She thought of Audemar and what a little beast he was turning out to be. Not so little any longer. Fourteen, entering manhood, about to make his vigil and swear fealty to his father as second-in-line for the throne.

As for Avery. Cicely realized she actually cared for poor motherless small Avery. She wouldn't want him to go the way of his older brother.

Avery rushed to John and pushed him hard. He drew back his stick and slashed it across John's face.

John stood still and looked down at himself, surprised. Avery hadn't budged him, though. He reached out, snatched Avery's stick out of his hand, broke it in two, and threw it at Avery's feet. Then he stalked away.

"I'm going back to the fort, Aves," said Dru, after a shocked moment. He turned on his heel and left too.

Avery stood quiet, his head drooping.

He looked over at Cicely. Suddenly he was pounding over to her and casting himself sobbing into her arms.

"There, Avery. There, lad."

"I'm sorry!" he got out. "I hurt John."

"I doubt that stick could hurt him much."

"No," he sobbed. "I hurt him, Mistress Cicely. I hurt my brother."

Then Cicely understood. She realized the little boy wasn't talking about hitting and shoving. He was talking about something else.

"Why, Avery," she said, making her voice gentle. "Look what a fine man you'll make. You understand what you just did. I am proud of you."

"I love John. Now he'll never love me back."

"Of course he will, Avery. You and John are each other's best friends. You're brothers."

"And Dru," said Avery.

Cicely wiped his tears away with her apron.

"Yes, and Dru. There now."

"But I might be king some day," said the little boy with a stubborn set to his chin. "I'm third, you know, Mistress Cicely."

"Well, if that ever comes to pass, Avery, you must begin to think right now about what a king needs to do. How a king needs to reign with justice and honor."

Avery burst into tears again. "What must I do, Mistress Cicely," he said.

"I think you know, Avery."

"I must go find John and say sorry."

"Yes, that sounds like a good idea."

"Is my mother watching me from the banks of the river where the dead people go? Nurse says she is, when I do wrong," Avery whispered, stealing his hand into Cicely's.

"Does that scare you, Avery?"

"Sometimes," he said softly. He wouldn't meet her eye.

"Your mother loves you, I'm sure," said Cicely, pressing his hand. "I'm sure if she's watching, she's as proud of you right now as I am."

"I'll go to say sorry," said Avery. He squared his thin little shoulders and marched after John.

Wonder what his mother does think, watching from that place over there where the Children's dead wander. Watching me help her son when she can't, thought Cicely, miserable. *Watching me take her place in Ranulf's heart.* She wondered how much the dead queen, dead Emilde, must hate her.

But later she looked out into the dooryard, and there were the three friends again, playing as happily together as if the incident had never happened.

CHAPTER TWENTY-ONE

Drustan

M y lord!" Cicely said with a gasp. She stood up from her joint stool, her workbox falling from her lap.

"Here, let me get that," said the Earl Brenci, bending over and retrieving it and handing it to her. "I didn't mean to startle you."

"I heard you had come to court. Your son told me. But I didn't look for you here."

Bren gazed across the dooryard to Dru, where he played with the other two boys in the dirt at the edge of the garden. They were constructing some sort of fort over there with sticks and mud.

Dru spied his father and came pelting over to him. "Father! Father!"

Bren caught Dru into his arms, then held him out. "How big you've grown, son," he said.

"I'm seven," said Dru.

"Near a man," said his father. "The age of reason."

"Father, we're building a fort. Come and see." He grabbed Bren by the hand and pulled him to the place where the other two boys knelt in the dirt.

Cicely watched while Bren squatted down, talking to the three boys and looking at everything they pointed out to him and commenting on them. She saw that throughout, he kept a hand on his son.

He misses Dru, thought Cicely. As uncomfortable as she always felt around the earl, she admired him, too. He loved his son.

After a while, Bren stood and wandered back to Cicely. "It's just as we hoped, Ranulf and I. The boys have become fast friends."

"Yes, indeed they have, your lordship."

"I'm here at court for the blessing of Artur's and Gelvira's daughter," he told her.

The prince had married last year, and now he and his bride had a child, a girl named Diera. Tomorrow she'd be dedicated to the Children.

"I hear the birth went well," said Cicely. "Mistress Cwenegund is a skilled midwife."

"Yes," said Bren. He looked sad.

Cicely was appalled at herself. Of course. Cwenegund had been the midwife who had presided at Dru's birth. But she couldn't save Aderyn, his mother.

"She tried her best," said Bren, almost to himself. "But the Children willed otherwise."

Cicely realized how much the death of his wife must have hurt Bren. Everyone said so. He'd become almost a hermit, out there on those sea cliffs of his.

"Cwenegund and the lady-in-waiting left with Avery, so she could get some rest, and when they returned, she was already dead."

Good sweet Lady, thought Cicely. *He's not speaking of his wife. He's speaking of Emilde.* She looked at him sidelong.

Suddenly she realized. He was in love with Emilde. *And he's heartbroken still. No wonder he keeps away from court.*

"A terrible thing," Cicely murmured. *How the gods torment us all*, she thought.

"But then, Ranulf has his fine son to comfort him." Bren looked over at Avery. "Three fine sons. Now a granddaughter."

"People say he is very pleased," said Cicely, overlooking the omission Bren had made. *Four fine sons.* At Bren's quick look, she said with a smile, "I don't see His Highness much these days."

The gods really do torment us, she thought, remembering the tender feelings she'd had toward Ranulf after John's birth, and how he'd seemed to return them. But now. Now things were different.

Cwenegund had come to her, when she was going through some dark days. "Mistress Cicely. It may be you'd want to avoid having a child just now. Save your strength for little John. I know some things, lady. If you wish it, I'll brew you a potion."

Cicely thought of Cwenegund with gratitude. The king still did come to her from time to time, but most of his attention was fastened on the exotic new bondservant he'd acquired from the Lyre Lands. Under the circumstances, Cicely didn't want to carry the king's child. She wouldn't be able to stand it, if the king turned indifferently away from the child. Already, she knew deep hurt because the king, who had doted on John, now seemed to avoid him.

Over the last few years, Cwenegund's little potion had kept her safe twice over.

Cicely realized she hadn't said anything for many long moments. She realized Bren was watching her with a concerned look in his eye.

"I'm fine, your lordship. John and I are fine."

"He's providing for you? For John? Ranulf's not stinting?"

"No, by no means, your lordship. You're kind to ask."

Bren's mouth had settled into a grim little line. "Dark Ones take him. It's that woman, the one from—"

"Your lordship, please don't worry on my behalf. Did you know that poor woman died?"

"No, I didn't know that," said Bren.

"She gave birth to a daughter. The birth did not go well. She's dead now."

"And the child?"

"I believe the child is well. I'm not sure. I don't hear much court gossip. My life is quiet here, Lady be thanked."

Cicely realized Bren was regarding her with different eyes. Somehow, she thought she had won his respect. She wasn't sure how.

"Your son is a fine boy," she said now, breaking into the moment.

"I miss him sorely. But Ranulf is right. It's better for him here. I came for the dedication of Artur's daughter, as I said, Mistress Cicely, but I came for another reason, too. I wanted to sound you out about it before I approached Ranulf with my idea."

Cicely was astounded. "You do me honor, lord," she murmured.

"It's this. Dru is seven. He has reached the age gently-born sons begin training with the sword. I'm sure Ranulf knows this. He may have already made provisions. But I want to talk to the king, to urge him to allow Dru to go to the arms master. The royal arms master is a very skilled man, although getting a bit old. But now, I believe, he has his young son to assist him in practical matters. It would be a fine thing for Dru if this young man trained him. I've heard impressive things about this lad's skills in the arts of war. Young as he is, he went with Ranulf on his last campaign and acquitted himself well. Now he helps his father with the training."

"I see that training with this young man would be a good thing for Dru. I do indeed," said Cicely, wondering how this could possibly concern her.

"The other two boys are only six. Some might think them too young. But Mistress, splitting them up, forcing the other two to wait, may do more harm to the three of them than good. I'm thinking of urging Ranulf to let Avery and John begin training too. What do you think about that?"

When Cicely didn't reply right away, he smiled. "As you see, I've come around to Ranulf's way of thinking. These three boys will be friends and allies their entire lives. I want to preserve and encourage their bond. I think Dru is ready, though. I'd hate to hold him back just to wait for the other two, and I'd hate for the other two to stand idle while Dru's skills advance ahead of theirs."

After a moment, more hesitantly, he spoke again. "Mistress, you must think this a bad idea. You must be thinking how you can safely disagree with me. Please don't think I'm making a demand. I do want to know your thoughts. I'll abide by them, mistress. When I look at these boys, playing, I see men who will be each other's best support, later in their lives, and through difficult times. I see how carefully you've tended them, not just your own son. All three. I value your judgment, mistress. And I tell you truly, sometimes I distrust Ranulf's."

Now Cicely had to laugh. "I think your idea is a fine one, Earl Brenci. I'm just astounded that you would ask me, a woman you've always distrusted and despised."

"Never think it, mistress! I did you wrong, if I ever gave you cause to think so. Let me be honest, since the matter is out in the open. I thought Ranulf was wrong to make you his concubine, and very wrong to bring you here. It was a torment to his wife, whom I regarded very highly. But none of this is your fault. I know my friend and brother. I know him well. And perhaps you and he—" Bren hesitated.

"Love each other? At one time, I thought so. I'm not so sure, now," said Cicely. *And that wife of Ranulf's, whom you regarded so highly? I don't think that's the right way to put it. I think you loved her desperately. I think you were trying to protect her.*

"I've known Ranulf my entire life. He tries to overcome himself, mistress."

"He fails." *Lady help me*, thought Cicely. *I've committed treason, saying so.*

Bren just heaved a sigh. "What complicated lives we lead, mistress." Almost to himself, he said, "We all fail." After a moment he looked up. "But my plan for the boys? What do you think?"

"I think you have the right of it," she said. "I think you see exactly how it is with these three." She looked over at them with affection. "They're fine boys, all three of them, and I will do everything I can to make sure their friendship continues. You can count on my support, Your Lordship."

But now, like any proud and fond father, Bren rushed to question her closely about Dru. What was he like? What had she seen in him? Was he as wonderful a lad as his father thought him?

Yes, yes, yes, she said to him in her mind, as well as out loud. *Dru is a wonderful boy. You are right to be proud of him. My son John loves him dearly, and he loves John back. Both of them love Avery dearly, and he loves them back.*

As he stood to leave, she assured him again of her support. "Training them together will be a fine thing."

"And there's another matter, mistress. Training for war is important for a gently-born boy. But these boys should know their letters. What do you think of that?"

Know their letters? Cicely thought doubtfully. But if the earl thought it important, she was sure it was.

"Yes. They should all know their letters," she told him.

He beamed at her. "I'm glad we are agreed."

He called Dru to him and embraced him again. Then he left Cicely's garden.

"I miss Father," said Dru to Cicely, looking after him. "Sometimes I wish I could go back to the sea cliffs with him and live with him there. But then I wouldn't have my friends by me."

"Your friends would miss you, too, Dru," she told him, pressing a sweetmeat into his hand, and one for Avery, and one for John.

BREN

CHAPTER TWENTY-TWO

Daughters

The ceremony to bless Ranulf's new grandchild was arduous. First, the entire royal party traveled to a cleared place in the forest to sleep in sumptuous tents set up by bondservants the day before. After a banquet laid out on boards spread in the king's own tent, everyone bedded down.

Bren suppressed a groan as he lowered himself into his makeshift bed. His bones were getting too old for this.

Ranulf, out on campaign half the year, was troubled not a whit. Some bondsmaiden was with him in his bed to entertain him. Bren looked over at the woman—really just a girl—but Ranulf didn't appear to be paying much attention to her, beyond the usual perfunctory smilings and hand-kissings and the girl's cow eyes back.

So, thought Bren, no important rival for poor Cicely. He had changed his mind about Ranulf's concubine. He reminded himself to tell Aderyn that, when she next visited him in his dreams. He thought Aderyn would be pleased by his new feelings. She saw so much deeper than the rest of them, and always had. She'd always regarded Cicely kindly, and Bren had always found that odd, seeing as Aderyn was Emilde's best friend.

It was not until Aderyn died that Bren fully realized about her. He couldn't call her a witch, because witches were evil. He didn't know what to call her. But he knew she had certain powers granted by her Child. The priestess's words later had confirmed it.

Maybe Aderyn didn't fully belong to this time and place, he thought. Maybe she could move around between the Planes. In his reading, he'd come across descriptions of such beings.

He had to laugh at himself then. If he didn't fully believe Ranulf's account of being visited by his farwyd in the form of an eagle, why would he allow himself to think these thoughts about Aderyn and not call himself a credulous fool?

Alongside these doubts was a certainty that set the doubts aside. He knew he was right about Aderyn. Maybe not right about her exact nature, but right that she was something at least a little bit outside of nature. When he tried to have conversations with her about it, in his dreams, she just laughed at him and turned his questions to other matters.

He hoped the night in the glade would produce one of these dreams, a visitation from Aderyn, but it didn't.

The morning dawned chill and brilliant.

Now a procession formed. At the front of the procession was Artur, the crown prince. Beside him was his bride Gelvira, a girl of around fifteen. She'd been brought from the southwesterly parts of the Southern Primacy, the country of the Old Ones, to be wed to Artur.

Poor girl, thought Bren. She'd been brought to Artur only a little older than the age Emilde was when she was taken to Ranulf to consummate their marriage. He wondered if this girl, too, had been terrified to be hauled off to an unfamiliar realm, an unfamiliar court, and Artur's bed. If she had been, she didn't seem to be now, a year or so later. She was all smiles, a dark-haired beauty. She and Artur made a striking pair. Maybe, with her by his side, Artur would make a powerful king after all, thought Bren.

In her royal mother's arms, the infant screamed as if she were being murdered.

Just behind man, wife, and baby walked Ranulf, the proud grandfather.

The rest of them wound in after, and they all moved silently through the trees. Even the little granddaughter was quiet now. The walking must be jiggling her into calm, thought Bren.

When they reached the bower of the Child of Earth's priestess, Bren remembered it well. He remembered bringing Drustan here to be blessed, and Aderyn's armlet. He remembered Emilde accompanying him. He still fancied he could feel her light touch on his arm, and his eyes filled with tears. He blinked them away.

The priestess came out to bless the little girl-child, Diera, and to pray for her. The priestess prayed for them all.

Then they all processed quietly back.

Ranulf caught up with Bren on the way back. "A peaceful place," he said.

Bren nodded.

"This is where I mean to bring Emilde's bones. This is where she should rest."

"I think she'd like that," said Bren, when he could trust himself to speak.

"Do you think she watches over us, beyond that river?" said Ranulf.

"I know Aderyn watches over me," said Bren.

"That must give you great comfort, brother."

"It does," said Bren. He wanted to ask Ranulf a question, but he didn't want to disrupt the sacredness of the place to do it. He'd wait.

As they all got caught up in the hustle and bustle of dismantling the tents and packing up to ride back to the fort, Bren saw his moment.

"Rannie. I hear you're to be congratulated on the birth of another child as well."

Ranulf looked over from adjusting his horse's saddle with a bark of surprise. "It's a gossipy court," he grumbled. Then he nodded curtly. "Yes," he said.

"Pardon me, brother, if I overstep."

"No. No," he said, putting a hand on Bren's arm. "I'm just distressed. The mother died. It was a girl-child, and she killed her mother."

"I'm sorry to hear it, brother."

"She was a fine vigorous young woman. Not frail, like Emilde."

Or too old to be having a child, like Aderyn, thought Bren.

"It came at me a bolt fired straight from the blue. Everything was fine. The child was fine. The mother was fine. Then, a sen'night later, a fever set in. A day later, she was gone."

"That's what happened to Aderyn. A fever."

"It's a wonder the land is peopled," said Ranulf. "So many of the mothers die."

"And the babes die. But I am glad to hear the child is fine. And Artur's child is fine."

"Yes, this child of my bondswoman did live, in spite of the fate of her mother. That is the glad side of my sad tidings. The child is fine. A girl-child only."

"What did you name her?"

"Her mother named her, before she left me to cross over that river. One of the last things she said to me, before she died. Told me to name the child Eris."

"Eris," said Bren blankly. "That's an ominous name, brother."

"Oh, aye?" said Ranulf, looking amused.

"Yes, for if you read the texts of the Old Ones—"

Ranulf began to laugh. "Bren, I love you, brother. This woman was completely unlettered. No scholar like you. None of us are your equals, in that endeavour. Well—" he paused.

"Artur is. But anyway, this woman wouldn't have known about anything ominous."

I wonder, thought Bren. In that part of the world, even the unlettered knew all their old gods and all the stories about them. Could this woman have borne Ranulf some great resentment? Great enough to name their child after her goddess of strife, of death and destruction? The child was like a living curse she inflicted on him. Bren shuddered.

Ranulf was smiling a little, looking off into the trees. He didn't see Bren's expression. Bren schooled himself to look completely neutral. "What a woman her mother was," Ranulf said. "Fiery. Making love to her was like going to war. She was a war captive, you know. When I brought her to my bed, though, I wooed her in a different key."

If Bren were a worshipper of the Lady, he knew he'd be making that warding motion against the Dark Ones they all use in situations like this one.

But he said only, "Will you raise her with John and Avery and my son?"

"What?" Ranulf looked startled. "No. No, certainly not. The mother was a bondsmaiden only. And the child is a girl."

"I see," said Bren. Then he said, "What about little Diera?"

"You have some strange notions, Bren. You must come back to court. Out on your windy sea cliffs, you're becoming something of a hermit. No, Diera will be brought up a proper princess, no truck with unruly little boys for her. Very soon I'll start looking out for a proper marriage for her. When the time comes, she'll be ready to carry out her role in the world."

"Just as your father betrothed you to Emilde."

"Yes," said Ranulf. "Indeed. The Baronies might be a good place to start my search. One of the most powerful of the barons, Gilles de Rais. . . ."

He paused. "But no, he's too old. Someone. Some young princeling over there."

Bren didn't pursue his questions any further. He saw the irony was totally lost on Ranulf.

He had intended to go back to his manor as soon as little Diera had been blessed. But Ranulf persuaded him to stay a fortnight longer.

"You can see more of your son, and you'll be here when Audemar makes his vigil," said Ranulf.

Inwardly Bren sighed. As ever with Rannie, what he said was not a request. It was a command. But the joy of it was, Bren would have more time with Dru. So he made no objection, and settled his mind to staying.

CHAPTER TWENTY-THREE

Sons

"Artur, my boy, how happy I am for you!" Bren exclaimed, folding the young man into his arms. "How proud your mother would have been this day."

They had all come back to the fort and were milling about the great hall, warming themselves at the hearth stones. In spite of the mild weather, the cold inside the gloomy stones of the fort was penetrating.

"I'm glad you're here, Uncle Bren," said Artur. "Come to the fire and take a look at my daughter."

He and Bren stepped to his wife Gelvira, where she was holding the tiny girl.

"How perfect she is. She reminds me so much of your mother," said Bren. Then he looked up at Gelvira and smiled. "Although it's hard to tell, with babies. Maybe she looks most like you, my lady."

Gelvira nodded to him, acknowledging him. She looked over at her husband. Artur spoke rapidly to her in her own language. Bren could tell it was much like the language of the Baronies. And the Old Ones, too, he thought. All those tongues were close. Their own tongue was nothing like it, and on the sea cliffs, the people who had lived there time out of mind, Aderyn's ancestors, spoke a language completely incomprehensible to all but a few.

Gelvira looked back at Bren and smiled at him now in return. She bowed her head to him.

"They say, when the world was new, we all spoke the same language," Bren said to Artur. "But we angered the gods with our pride, and they struck us down. As we shattered into many peoples, so did the language we spoke. And now it is many languages, not one."

"A pretty story," said Artur. "I'll look into my books and see if I can find it."

"When you do, let me know," said Bren. "I am so isolated on my cliffs that I have only a few books, my own, and no library to consult, as you have." Then he realized Artur could act as his ally in an important matter. "Artur, I may need your help with your father."

"How's that?" said Artur.

"The little boys are nearly ready to begin their arms training."

"They've grown up fast," said Artur, marveling.

"Indeed. But Artur. Do you believe arms training is the only kind of training they need? I do not, and John's mother agrees with me." *Better make it look like my own idea*, he decided hastily. *I don't want to get Cecily into trouble or have the idea brushed aside.*

Artur saw immediately what he meant. Bren's comment about Cicely passed right by him. "They must know their letters," he said.

Bren beamed at him. "Exactly."

"I believe I can convince Father. Besides, as soon as this little daughter of mine is old enough, she'll learn her letters, too." At Bren's look of surprise, he added, "as Mother did."

"You are exactly right," Bren exclaimed. "Your mother was a fine scholar. In the Baronies, it's a common practice, I believe."

"Something we should emulate," said Artur. "Well," he said after a moment's reflection. "Gelvira will have to give me a son. No matter how well educated Diera becomes, she can't inherit the throne, being a woman."

"You'll have plenty of chances to have sons," said Bren with a conviction he didn't feel. *After all*, he thought, *look at my own history. But then at last I did have a boy, and he'll be earl after me.*

A commotion interrupted his thoughts. Into the hall burst Ranulf's second son, Audemar, surrounded by cronies of his. They were loudly laughing at some joke the prince seemed to have made. He stopped still in the middle of the assembled guests, leered in their faces, farted loudly, and capered off, followed by his bellowing, guffawing friends.

"And that's my brother," said Artur with a shrug. His wife was crimson with embarrassment.

"Well, my boy, he has always been like that. No changing him now."

"I'm glad to hear you're staying for his vigil, Uncle Bren," said Artur.

"Yes," said Bren. "And I hope he takes it seriously. It's a serious matter."

But of course Audemar didn't. At least, Child be thanked, he did manage to uphold minimal appearances, thought Bren, after it was all over. In spite of the stories filtering down the mountain about his rowdy, blasphemous behavior during the vigil itself, Audemar came sedately enough off the mountain at the appointed time, leading his horse, and he knelt without incident before his father, swearing fealty to him, and then to his older brother.

Bren, standing close by, watched Ranulf with concern. Audemar was a dismaying boy. But Bren couldn't tell how dismayed Ranulf might be by his discourteous second son. *It used to be,* Bren thought sadly, *that I always knew what Rannie was thinking. No longer.*

The little boys behaved well, considering. Avery made a breach of court etiquette, and Bren's own son Dru helped him do it, but in the overall scheme of things, it didn't matter. Everyone was watching Audemar too closely to notice what Avery was doing.

Avery stood quietly and respectfully enough with Gelvira and some of the others of the royal party at the head of the procession, although at one point Bren turned to find him smirking over some solemn out-of-character words Audemar was repeating during the rite. Mostly, though, especially for a six-year-old boy, he behaved well.

But then at one point Bren noticed he had disappeared. *Oh, no*, he thought. *Not you, too, Avery. Your father has enough work for nine fathers just keeping Audemar in line.*

But a moment later he saw where Avery had gone. He'd backed out of his designated spot close to the royal party, edged down behind the line of spectators, and had moved in again to stand right next to Bren. Bren put out a hand and tousled his hair. The boy grinned up at him. Now the lad had inched over beside his friend Dru, whispering something to him. *That's what he wanted*, thought Bren. *Just to stand with his friend.*

But then. Then both boys disappeared from Bren's side. The ceremony was nearly over. Bren tried not to let his annoyance get the better of him. He'd have words with both boys later, about how inappropriate and disrespectful it was to sneak off to play before the ceremony had drawn to a close.

As the ceremony ended, he saw that wasn't the way of it. Not at all. The boys had simply moved down the line of spectators. Far down. Almost to the very end of the line. And there they stood beside John, all three of them arm in arm.

I should scold them all, thought Bren, smiling at them and marveling. *But I won't.*

CHAPTER TWENTY-FOUR

Friends

Bren's visit, which he'd planned to last barely a sen'night, had now stretched into a full turning of the moon. Every time he made to leave, Ranulf had a new excuse why he shouldn't. By now, he saw through Ranulf's ruse. If Ranulf had his way, Bren would settle back in at court and never leave.

It was a tempting thought. He'd be near his son. One impediment to life at court, his fear that Cicely would be a constant reminder to him of matters that disturbed and enraged him, had turned out to be baseless. *Like many fears*, Bren thought. It was the fear, not the feared thing itself, that created the problem.

But in the end, the reminders of Emilde all around him were too much for him. *Why can't I get past this?* he berated himself. Others grieved, and then as time went by, they managed to deal with their grief. Why couldn't he? He decided he must have some character flaw that prevented him.

Those people, those other grievers, might have a lifetime together to look back on, he realized. As he had his satisfying life with Aderyn. As Ranulf had his life with Emilde, even though it was less than satisfying.

But Bren had nothing. Not with Emilde. Only a day together. Not even a day. It was worse, he decided, than having had nothing at all.

As soon as he'd think that, though, he'd scream at himself, *No! I had that, at least. And I had her friendship for many years.*

When he looked at Ranulf, he had to tamp down a smoldering fury. *You had her, but you didn't appreciate what you had. Or if you did, you couldn't, wouldn't, didn't act on it, just selfishly kept it close.* Of course he knew that was unfair. Ranulf hadn't chosen Emilde. She'd been forced on him, and he on her. Ranulf had no idea he was standing in his brother's way, and if he had known it, what could he have done about it? He was king. Emilde was his queen, the mother of his heirs. The king can't step aside and let some fellow take his wife, no matter what he might privately think about it.

So Bren was riven.

And he was old.

He had lost his chance at happiness. Worst of all, he'd seen it just outside his grasp.

He needed to get back to his cliffs, where he could know quiet.

Meanwhile, his boy was flourishing here.

"Come down to the little courtyard by the mews and stables, brother," Ranulf said one morning shortly before Bren's departure. They were breaking their fast together at the hearth stones in the great hall. "The boys are having their first lesson with the Royal Arms master, Master Derian. You remember him, don't you?"

"Of course I do. He gave us our lessons. He must be very old by now."

"He's not so very old. He seemed so much older than we were, back then. But he was only a bit older than Audemar is now, I'm thinking. Still, I can tell by watching him. He's slowing down. His son helps him now."

"Derian wasn't the head arms master, back then. The man your father had training his vassals and most valued warriors was that old fellow—" Bren scratched his head. "I don't remember the man's name now."

Ranulf laughed and nudged Bren. "I don't either. You and I must be the ones getting old."

"But Derian trained us lads. That I remember well. Every bruise. Every fall. Every word of praise. Every triumph."

As they talked over old times, the two of them were heading to the little courtyard.

They came to the arch and looked in. Derian was drilling a line of warriors.

Huddled in one corner were the three boys, gaping with awe at Ranulf's battle-scarred troops.

Avery saw his father the king and Bren first. He came running over. "Father! Uncle Bren!"

"We're here to see you have your very first lesson," said Ranulf.

Avery beamed with pride.

Now Dru and John had jumped down off the bench where they were sitting and had come to join them. All three boys hopped up and down with excitement.

A compact, wiry, hard-muscled lad of maybe fifteen or sixteen noticed them and came over to them. He knelt to the king.

"And who's this?" said Ranulf. "Young Conal, is it?"

"Yes, sire. I'm helping my father with the young ones."

"Earl Brenci and I were just reminiscing about your father. He was around your age when he started helping us learn the sword," said Ranulf, extending a gracious hand. "You seem cut from the same cloth as your worthy father. I believe you were part of the company that made the assault on the port city of Waes Inlet, in my recent war."

Conal kissed Ranulf's hand. "I was proud to fight under your banner, Your Majesty."

Ranulf motioned him to his feet.

"I hear you led a party of the street fighters who secured that city in my name," said Ranulf. "Brave doings, young master."

"Bloody doings," murmured Conal.

"Here are your charges," Ranulf said to him. "Boys, introduce yourself to your arms master, Master Conal."

"I am Avery," said the little prince.

"Bow to your arms master, lad," prompted Ranulf. Avery made a pretty bow.

"I am Drustan," said Bren's son. He made his bow.

"That's my boy," Bren told young Master Conal. He turned to John and urged him forward. "You, too, John," he whispered to the boy.

"I am John," said the boy, bowing.

Conal looked at him quizzically.

Avery shoved over to John's side. "John's my brother, Master Conal."

Bren saw realization dawn in Conal's eyes. *Poor John*, thought Bren. *This will be the way of it his whole life. Who's that? people will ask themselves. Then they'll think, Oh. The bastard.*

But none of that seemed to bother John. He and Avery looked at each other and grinned and punched each other in the arm.

"Likely lads, all three of you," said Conal. "Follow me, and I'll find practice swords for you lot."

And so their first lesson began, and they were all in it together.

Bren walked away from the courtyard, satisfied that his son would have a good start in life.

"Thanks for taking my boy in hand, brother. It's just as we hoped, back when we ourselves were boys. These three will be friends their whole lives."

Ranulf nodded. "A good start," he said, echoing Bren's thought.

"And now, brother, much as I hate to leave you, and to leave my boy, I have to make my way back to my cliffs."

"I suppose I knew this day was coming," said Ranulf. "I hate to see you go, though."

"But brother. Did I see warriors drilling in there? I'm thinking you're about to go on campaign."

Ranulf laughed. "You're right, I am. Back to the Western Isle, and those stubborn kerns." After a moment, he said, "I'd like very much to have you by my side, Bren."

"My days as a warrior are done," said Bren with a sigh. "Of course, I'm your vassal. You can order me to do it."

Then Ranulf was punching Bren in the arm, very like the small boys they'd just been watching.

"Nah," said Ranulf. "Just send me all your men. And all your gold."

"That, brother, I can promise you I'll do," said Bren.

CICELY

CHAPTER TWENTY-FIVE

Wickedness

What a relief to have John out of the house so often, thought Cicely, with a guilty twinge. Right now, she needed help. With the boys over so often, she didn't feel right leaving them to themselves, especially not that mischievous little Avery.

These days, the three of them had their morning lesson with Master Conal, and then, after they had eaten a midday meal of bread and cheese, they'd head off to the priest at the High Temple of the Lady Goddess to learn their letters. Not the main priest. He was far too busy. One of the young ones.

With the example of the royal family before them, many in Tambourne had forsaken the Lady to worship the Children, the gods of their ancestors. Cicely was glad to see Ranulf understood how much better it would be to send the boys to school at the temple than to some impoverished tutor, even though the worship of the Lady was in decline. The priests all knew their letters. Everyone knew that.

Ranulf, she thought quietly. More like, Artur had arranged it all. He was the one who really knew. He worshipped the Children, as they all did, but he spent a lot of his time in the library of the High Temple. It was said he was gradually amassing his own library.

Cicely didn't pretend to understand why Ranulf not only tolerated but encouraged this eccentric behavior in his son and heir. It had something to do with Ranulf's experience in the forest. Something about some farwyd. A farwyd, she knew, was some sort of high priestess connected with the Children.

Ranulf had tried to explain it to her once. She had nodded along, but she hadn't understood a word of it. Something about some eagle coming to him with a message.

Crazy stuff, Cicely thought privately.

She told Ranulf she wouldn't change her god. When she told him that, she wondered if she were putting herself in danger. Apparently not. Ranulf had just nodded. "As is your right, my dear girl," he told her.

That was when he was feeling very loving toward her. Now, he hardly bothered with her at all. But every fortnight or so, he showed up at her gate and spent the night in her bed.

That's why she needed quiet to think things through. She needed Cwenegund's help. She was with child.

Especially now, she didn't want to make herself vulnerable by having a child of Ranulf's.

He was occupied with other children. Other women.

If she only got a sliver of his attention now, she wanted it focused on John, not divided between John and another babe of hers.

Although that worried her, too. True, the king hadn't withdrawn his support from John. John trained with the others. He went to the Lady's school with the others. Avery and Dru were his best friends, and no one, least of all Ranulf, was intruding on that. But Ranulf's love for John seemed to have dwindled away. It hurt Cicely, because she saw that it hurt John. John wasn't even old enough to understand it, but he felt it.

He'd felt it especially strongly, she could tell, when Earl Brenci was here. Earl Brenci was so kind to him. Kinder than Ranulf. Ranulf was busy and preoccupied, with little time for Avery, so John didn't have to compare himself there. But he could see how much Bren loved Dru. And he could see he didn't have that kind of father-love for himself.

In a way, then, she was glad Bren was gone. But in another way, a selfish way, she wished he were still here. *How strange,* she thought. *We were enemies. Now we're allies. We distrusted each other. Now we place great trust in each other.*

How strange that she'd become a kind of surrogate mother to Bren's son Dru.

Now I have two women across the River of the Dead to be angry with me, she thought with dismay. Dru's mother, and of course Avery's mother, who had other reasons to hate her, too.

How many ghosts of the dead hating you does it take before you are cursed? she wondered.

She didn't want to be pregnant and cursed. The curse might hurt the baby. She needed to go to Cwenegund.

So that very day, she walked into the town of Tambourne and found Cwenegund's small house.

A stranger came to the door in answer to Cicely's knock.

"She doesn't live here any more," said the woman.

"Where is she?" said Cicely, feeling a little spurt of panic.

The stranger shrugged.

Asking around Tam Fort, Cicely discovered a new midwife was helping the women of the fort and the town.

She went to the house of this new midwife. She was a tall, severe woman with gray hair pulled back in a knot at the nape of her neck.

"Mistress, I came to ask your advice," Cicely began.

"What about?" said the midwife.

"I think maybe—"

"Hmm," said the woman. She reached out and touched Cicely's cheek, feeling it, and bending over to look into Cicely's eye. "With child," she said.

Cicely nodded. "But mistress, having this child right now will be distressing to me. In the past, Mistress Cwenegund was able to give me a potion—"

"Wickedness!" the woman burst out. "Dark Ones at work there, mistress. It is evil to wish the death of your child. It is evil to help another realize that wish. This mistress Cwenegund has done evil, if she's done what I think you are telling me. She did wrong. You too, mistress. You've done wrong."

Cicely stood up in alarm. "It's just a health drink she gave me," Cicely lied. "I'll not bother you further, mistress." She started backing out of this frightening woman's house.

"You," said the woman, ignoring Cicely's excuse-making. "Aren't you the king's concubine? It's wickedness to rid yourself of a babe. But the king's babe? That's dangerous, mistress. That's treason. If I were you, and I were minded to do anything like that, I'd keep a wickedness like that to myself, I would."

"No," said Cicely feebly. "No, I wouldn't do such a wickedness."

"I hope to the Lady not, mistress," said the woman.

Cicely found herself making the warding sign against evil.

She nearly ran back to her own house. She got into bed and pulled the covers over her head. John was alarmed when he found her there. Then she got up and fixed him something to eat, and tried to act cheerful so he wouldn't be afraid.

But she was afraid. She was most afraid.

I'll have to have this babe after all, she thought dully to herself.

Several turnings of the moon later, she finally discovered where Cwenegund had gone.

Cicely was at the High Temple to get John after his lesson from the priest. When his lesson ended, he usually came down the little corridor that led from the temple's library into its main hall, and he'd find her there.

Two other women of the town were in the back of the hall, waiting, too. They were waiting their turn to prostrate themselves at the feet of the statue of the Lady, to beg Her for some boon.

There was a long line that day.

Maybe I should be in that line too, begging the Lady to take my baby away. Kill it. Rid me of it, she thought. But after the frightening words of the new midwife, she saw how wicked she must be in the eyes of the Lady. She could hardly pray to the Lady to grant a wish as wicked as that.

The other two women were talking about Cwenegund. One of them was pregnant, just as she was, but this woman was already carrying a big belly around. Cicely knew her own belly would be showing soon.

"Nine Spheres, how I wish Mistress Cwenegund were still in the town," said the big-bellied woman. "I don't trust this new one."

"But did you hear what happened? Mistress Cwenegund has given up the business of midwifery."

"No, that's terrible. She was the best. Everyone said so."

"She let the queen die."

"No, she didn't. That she died was only the will of the Lady. The queen's cord of life was ready to be snipped. No one can stop that."

The two of them argued about Queen Emilde's fate for awhile.

The line inched forward. John still hadn't come out.

The women's chatter had circled around to Cwenegund's whereabouts again. "She's gone for a lady's maid to Lord Piers. She's living in that little village just outside his manor," said the woman who wasn't pregnant.

"But why?" said the woman who was.

"This is the sad part. She was helping deliver her own daughter's baby, and the daughter died. Right there under her own mother's hand. They say Cwenegund can't get past it. They say she swore she'd never go as a midwife to anyone again."

Just then John did burst down the corridor with other noisy boys, to a great deal of shushing from the priests.

John ran up to Cicely and put his arms around her neck and kissed her.

She knew she'd miss it when he suddenly realized no other boy his age was doing such a thing, and that he was now too old to be kissing his mother. So far, that hadn't happened.

"You're getting so tall, Johnny," she said, ruffling his hair.

"I'm bigger than Avery now," crowed John. "Bigger than Dru, and he's older, Mother!"

You're going to be a tall man, like your father, Cicely thought wistfully.

Artur was slight and fairly small, for a man. He took after his mother. Audemar was big and robust, like Ranulf. If she had to guess, Avery would be tall, too. Tall and blond, like his father. Just maybe not as tall as John. As for Dru, Bren wasn't very tall. Dru probably wouldn't be as tall as his two friends. It was hard to tell about the little boys, though. In a few years, it would be easier to figure out what their adult selves would look like.

Cicely smoothed the hair off John's forehead. One stubborn fair lock of it fell straight forward into his face. They walked home together. *I need to keep you safe*, she thought, glancing aside at John. *I need to keep any remaining attentions of the king focused on you.*

In the morning, when he was off to the practice court, she set out to walk down the road to Lord Piers's estate. It was not very far. She'd look for Cwenegund. Maybe it wouldn't be too late to do something about her looming problem.

Lord Piers was one of Ranulf's most important vassals. Cicely had never liked him. Most of the few times she'd encountered him, he looked straight through her, as if she were a piece of trash. But one time, he'd looked straight at her, and that was even more disturbing. He'd examined her, looked her all over, and he hadn't hidden that he was doing so.

He had leaned over to her and whispered in her ear, "Girl, when Ranulf gets tired of you, come to me."

She had walked as quickly away from him as she could without actually breaking into a run.

Lord Piers had a bored and elegant wife who looked down her nose at Cicely. He had three daughters, one maybe a year or two younger than John, one just a toddler, one a babe in arms. The little girls were always richly dressed. They wouldn't be allowed to associate with any dirty boys, certainly not a boy as lowly as John. They amused Cicely. One day they'd all change their tune, the silly things. But then, she realized, their father would make them marry someone awful.

Cicely shivered. If she had this baby, she hoped it wouldn't be a girl. She found herself feeling actually sorry for Lord Piers's daughters.

Cicely paused outside the estate of Lord Piers. The little village where many of his servants and retainers lived was just beyond. But it was the middle of the morning. No point in looking for Cwenegund there. She would be at the estate, working, not in the village. That meant Cicely would have to go into the big kitchen house to ask after her there. The thought of setting foot on Lord Piers's estate frightened Cicely a little. Lord Piers and his haughty wife were sure to be elsewhere, though, so she felt a bit calmer.

When she asked in the kitchen house, one of the bondswomen rushed out right away to bring Cwenegund to her.

"Mistress Cicely!" exclaimed Cwenegund. She embraced Cicely. "As you see, I've changed my employment," she said. She drew Cicely out to a bench in the sunshine.

Cicely didn't know how to begin. She thought of what she had overheard.

"Mistress Cicely. I can tell. Ye're with child."

"Is it already that obvious?"

Cwenegund nodded. "To me, it is. But I know you well, mistress. Maybe not as easy for others to see, I'm thinking."

"I need to rid myself of it."

Cwenegund was shaking her head sadly. "I don't do such things any longer, mistress. Maybe you've heard. First the queen. Then my own daughter." She began to cry quietly. "Maybe the Lady is displeased with me, mistress."

Cicely reached over and stroked her hand.

Cwenegund got possession of herself again. "And anyway, mistress. Seeing how far along you are, you couldn't take my potion. Not and do it safely. I'll not be responsible for any more deaths, mistress."

"I understand. It will probably be fine. It's only that—well, you know what we discussed. Ranulf doesn't love me any more."

"He may, and just be distracted, mistress."

She laughed at that. She knew she must sound bitter. "Well. I'm glad to see you anyway. I hope your life goes well, Cwenegund."

"Thank you, mistress. And if I may say so. You look in health. I'm thinking the babe will be healthy and strong. I'm thinking the birth will go well."

"I hope you're right, Cwenegund. I'm more worried about after."

So Cicely went back home, and six turnings of the moon later, her second son Walter came into the world. As Cwenegund had predicted, it was an easy birth.

The severe midwife who had called Cicely wicked was the one who attended her. Cicely cringed away from her, worrying the woman would somehow put a curse on her and her child with her ill-will.

But all was well.

"You have a baby brother, John," Cicely whispered when he was allowed to tiptoe into her room to have a peek.

John's face lit up. "What is his name, Mother."

"Walter, after my uncle. We'll call him Wat."

"Wat. That's a brave name, Mother."

Ranulf was back from the wars by then, but he didn't come to see his new son for three turnings of the moon. By then, enough time had gone by that he could come to Cicely's bed.

After all, she thought. *That's the main thing he wants. This new son doesn't interest him at all.*

He did take a look at little Wat, kicking in his basket.

"I've named him Walter," said Cicely.

Ranulf grunted. He put a finger out and touched Wat's tiny nose.

Then he turned to the more pressing business he had with Cicely, in bed.

But Cicely loved her little baby, and she was glad she hadn't taken Cwenegund's potion to rid herself of him.

CHAPTER TWENTY-SIX

The Tax-man

With a baby to nurse and keep clean and keep track of, as he crawled around getting into everything and trying to pull himself to his feet, and a boy shooting up as rapidly as John was, Cicely had more than enough to keep herself occupied. Today, as John came leaping into the house after his training, famished for something to eat, she had to shake her head.

Hadn't she just made him a new pair of leggings? But look at him. He had grown out of them already.

She sat him down at the hearth stones with something hot.

He pushed the empty wooden bowl aside with a clatter.

"Aves and Dru and I are meeting behind the tavern," he told her, running out of the house.

Behind the tavern? She thought blankly. What about his studies at the temple?

She stepped to the door and called after him.

He stopped mid-stride and turned around. "Mother. I'm late."

"What about your schooling?"

"Called off today. Some Lady thing. Some festival," he shouted over his shoulder, bounding down the road that wound between the forest and the fort.

She hauled Wat up to her shoulder and smiled after John, shaking her head. His religious training left much to be desired. She should be teaching him about the Lady. But then Wat began clamoring and drumming his little heels against her, so she set him carefully down in the dooryard.

She stood there thinking about John and his future. How hard it was to know what to do. Perhaps John should worship the Children, as his father and brothers did. She wasn't at all sure of the right course to take.

Before she could think it through, her attention was distracted to Wat.

"What do you have in your mouth? Holy Lady," she said, extracting it.

So the day passed pleasantly, and she didn't even notice that John was late for dinner. It was growing on toward midsummer, and the evenings were still light.

But at last she did start to worry.

She hadn't worried long when there was a flurry at the door.

She opened it to a tangle of boys who burst into the house, heaving and panting.

"You lot. You look like the Dark Ones are after you."

The three of them stared up at her, their mouths gaping open. They were all trying to speak, but none of them could.

From outside, there came a sound of male shouting and tramping.

Cicely felt her eyes narrow. "What have you boys been up to?"

"Nothing, Mother," John got out.

"Nothing, Mistress Cicely," stammered Dru and Avery.

They were looking everywhere but into her eyes.

"You're up to something. Are you in trouble?"

A chorus of noes answered her, but to her mind, they were faint and hesitant noes.

The noises outside grew louder. Then they began to fade.

The boys looked around at each other, and Cicely could see they were all shaking with relief.

"Sit down here at the hearth stones. I'll bring bowls of stew for all of you lads. Then," and she looked at each one of them firmly. "Then you will tell me about it."

They hung their heads. But they were a bit more cheerful after they'd filled their bellies.

"Now, then. Tell me."

They all stared around at each other.

"We found a way into some tunnels, mistress. Old tunnels under the fort," said Avery. "Secret tunnels," he said with relish.

The other two were nodding vigorously.

"Let me guess. You weren't supposed to be in them."

Heads, two bright, fair ones and one dark one, shaking no.

"And someone found you there," she prompted.

Heads nodding yes.

"And then we ran here, and they were chasing us, and it was exciting, Mistress Cicely," Avery burst out.

"Boys," she said. "It seems you did wrong. What would have happened if they'd caught you?"

They all mumbled.

"Speak up, lads. I didn't hear that."

More mumbling. Avery's voice, more distinct. "Told my father."

"And then?"

"Whipped for sure, Mistress Cicely," said Dru, looking up at her through scared eyes.

"I know it's a pleasing thing, to explore, but—"

"You don't understand. We had to find a treasure," said Dru.

His sober little face almost made her laugh. She turned to Wat, who was starting to fuss, and gathered him into her lap and dandled him until she could compose herself. "A treasure?" she said, finally.

"Yes, for John."

"John?" She looked hard at her son.

He hung his head. Now she saw he had an embroidered bag in his hands.

"Is that the treasure?"

He nodded.

"You boys stole something?" She was astonished. They weren't bad boys. They could be over-exuberant. They'd been known to break things. Very occasionally, they fought with each other and came to her with tears and bloody noses. But stealing? No.

"It's just trash," Avery said. "Nobody cares about it but us. Well, John, really, but we all sneaked in and got it."

"If it's just trash, why were those men chasing you."

The three of them looked at each other sidelong.

"Not supposed to be in there," Dru said finally.

"John, you haven't said a word. I'd like to hear from you what happened.

John looked up at her. "We were just exploring, and those guards told us we couldn't go in there—"

"The tunnel," Avery put in.

"—so we waited until they thought we'd gone away, and then Dru—"

"I created a distraction," Dru said proudly.

The other two looked over at him and grinned. Avery punched him in the arm.

"—and then we sneaked in," said John.

"Yes, and then we were treasure hunters, mistress," said Avery, his words tumbling end over end in his excitement.

"I see," said Cicely.

"So then," said Dru. "If we were treasure hunters, we needed to find a treasure, see? So we found this."

"But when we were sneaking back out, they spotted us," Avery finished.

"But you say it's John's treasure. Why is it yours, John?"

John shrugged and gave her a sheepish sidelong glance.

"Let's see it." *If it really is something valuable, maybe the boys can take it back with an apology. They'll have to take their punishment. But that won't be a bad thing. A good lesson*, she thought.

John undid the drawstrings of the bag and drew out an object.

"What is that?" she said, puzzled.

"It plays music," he said. He showed her, plucking on the strings of it. It made a discordant twanging, and she could see one of the strings had come loose from its peg and was hanging useless.

"Give it to me, son," she said.

She held it. It had once been a fine thing made of wood, a musical instrument such as she had heard the court musicians play. The wood was ornately carved, and it looked like it had been highly polished, once. Now it was water-stained and cracked.

"So, boys. Why take this?"

"John needs it, for his music," Dru explained.

"John, you don't know how to play one of these, do you?"

John shook his head no.

"But he'll learn how, and then he'll play our battle chant, when we ride to the wars. Show Mistress Cicely, John," said Avery.

John looked around at his friends. Then he stood up and opened his mouth. Out of it came an astounding thing, a song to stir the blood. *Of course*, she told herself, *he's only a boy, but his singing. Holy Lady. It's fine.*

King Avery upon his steed
Rode all his men before!
His armor glittered gold as gleed,
Bolder man was never bore.

Tell me whose these men ye are
Or whose men that ye be,
Who gave you leave to ride in my glade
In the spite of mine and me?

It is I, the mighty Earl Drustan,
I'm earl in my country fair,
Let all our men on one side stand
And all your men over there.

Avery's men had their bows bent,
Their hearts were brave and sound.
The first of the arrows they shot off,
The earl's men all went down.

The earl he set upon the king
And struck a blow full sore.
With spear made of a mighty tree,
He—

John stopped, drew a ragged breath, and looked at his toes.

"There's a lot more, Mistress Cicely," Avery said.

"Where did you hear this song?" she asked her son.

"The court musicians practice near the courtyard where we train. When Conal tells us our training for the day is over and we have his leave to go, we sneak over there and listen, mistress," said Dru.

"Then we write our own words. Dru knows his letters best, so he writes them down. And then we have wars, Mistress Cicely!" Avery's eyes were shining.

"Well, then," said Cicely, trying not to laugh. "That's very fine. But tomorrow, John, you and I will go to the king's musicians with this instrument and give it back."

"Aww, it's all broken, Mistress Cicely," said Avery.

"Nevertheless, that's what we'll do," she said, looking John in the eye.

The next day, Cicely didn't allow John to go to his training with the others. She marched him in front of her to the great hall of the fort.

Halfway there, she heard a scuffling. She whirled around. She saw two boy-forms, all knees and elbows, ducking behind some barrels. "Come out, you two. Why are you not with Master Conal?"

Avery stepped out from behind the barrels, and Dru crept out too. "We're coming with John."

"We're a fighting force," Dru explained to Cicely. "We leave none of our men behind when the enemy has captured them."

Cicely felt her lips begin to twitch. "Come on, then," she said.

At the fort, she spotted the musicians gathered before the hearth stones. Probably getting ready to practice, she thought.

She took John by the hand and went up to the master of them, the head musician. She curtsied.

He turned around, surprised. "Mistress Cicely, is it?"

"Yes, Master Electus."

"How may I help you, mistress."

Cicely pushed John forward. "Bow," she hissed at him.

He made a little awkward bow to the man.

"This is my son John," she told Master Electus. "He has something to say to you. Go on, John."

"Master Electus, I am sorry for what I did. Here it is." John held out the embroidered bag.

Master Electus eyed it, perplexed. After a moment, he took it and looked inside. "Oh," he said. He looked up at Cicely. "It's one of our old instruments, discarded in the midden. As you can see," and here he drew the instrument out, "this rebec is cracked. We can't use it any longer."

"I thought that might be the case, good sir," said Cicely, "Yet still I can't allow my son to take what's not his own."

Master Electus looked down at John now. "Ah," he said. "Your mother is right to teach you this lesson, young Master John. But tell me." He bent over to John so they were at eye level, but he only had to bend a little. John was growing so tall. "Why did you take it?"

"I wanted to play it," John said.

"And as you see, it would be very hard to play this instrument, damaged as it is."

John nodded.

"Do you like music, lad?"

John nodded again.

"Do you play any other instrument?"

John shook his head no.

"What about singing? Do you sing?"

John nodded.

"Sing me something."

"Sing our battle song," Cicely heard a voice behind her whisper, a very loud whisper that caused Master Electus, she could see, to try hard to control his expression.

John opened his mouth. "Tell me whose these men ye are, or whose men that ye be," he sang.

Master Electus held up his hand. John stopped. "What if I set someone to teach you how to play an undamaged rebec. Would you like that?" the master asked. "And give you singing lessons."

"Oh, yes!" said John.

"May he learn, mistress?" said the man to Cicely.

"Yes, he seems to love music, Master Electus. I thank you for this offer. I'll ask the king for coin to pay your man for his time."

"That's a bargain, then," said Master Electus with a smile. He looked back down at John. "Come to us tomorrow afternoon." He paused for a moment. "In fact, John, come to me," he said quietly.

"May I, Mother?" John looked to Cicely.

Cicely thought about it. These music lessons would cut into John's time at the school. But she thought too of John's voice, and what she had heard in it. The music master seemed to have heard something too. "Yes, you may," she said.

With a whoop, the two boys hovering behind her jumped on John and began to pound him.

Master Electus looked at Cicely, nonplussed.

"These boys were all in it, I believe," she said. "But John was the possessor of the—" she paused with a little smile "—the stolen goods, so he's the one I brought to you."

As the boys skipped and jumped out of the hall, Cicely rushed to catch up with them.

"You lot. Head straight to Master Conal now," she scolded.

They hung their heads.

"He'll whip us sure," said Dru to her.

"Then you'll have to take your medicine, won't you?"

With dragging feet, they went away from her.

But that afternoon, when John came home, he told her, "Master Conal didn't whip us for being late, Mother."

"No?"

"No, Avery explained how, in battle, we never leave one of our own behind, and Master Conal told us that was a valuable lesson to learn."

"Getting off scot-free," Cicely muttered. "I don't know as I think that's a good lesson to learn. You need to pay your scot to the tax-man, John, if you owe him one."

But she had to smile, because John was so excited. His music lessons would begin the next day.

CHAPTER TWENTY-SEVEN

Another One

When the joyous bells of the fort rang out, Cicely stopped plying her distaff for a moment to send up a prayer of thanks to the Lady.

As merely a concubine, she hadn't had much to do with the true members of Ranulf's family—Avery excepted, of course. But she'd always thought fondly of Gelvira, the crown prince Artur's wife. Like herself, Gelvira had been brought a stranger to Ranulf's court. Like herself, Gelvira was an outsider.

There the resemblance stopped. Gelvira was the highest-ranking lady in the land. One day she'd be queen. She barely knew who Cicely was, and if she ever encountered her, she averted her eyes.

Cicely was kind of a scandal to them all. *And I'm a scandal at home, too*, she thought. Once, she'd persuaded Ranulf to let her travel back across the border into Baronies territory, to Ecga Green, to visit her parents and sisters. She quickly saw no one wanted her there. Her parents had clawed their way back to respectability, with the help of a lot of Ranulf's gold. They'd gotten one of her sisters married off, and married pretty well.

During Cicely's visit, her mother and father talked of negotiations for the second sister's hand, but they looked at her uneasily as they spoke, and her second sister frowned and wouldn't talk to her at all, beyond the barest niceties. Cicely's reappearance threatened to undo all that her family had achieved. When she left a few days later, she saw looks of relief on all their faces.

Ranulf's gold. She wondered if he were sorry he had agreed to send it, now that he had tired of her. But as far as she knew, his payments to her father were regular and generous.

Sometimes she felt bitter about her life. During those times, she accused Ranulf, in her mind, of many wrongs. Meanness and stinginess, though. No one could accuse him of that.

But poor Gelvira. All the years Cicely was trying hard not to get another child, Gelvira was trying hard to have one. She needed to have more. Her little Diera was a healthy child, but she was a girl. Gelvira needed to bear sons. Every child, son or daughter or who-could-tell-which that planted itself inside her womb, always died, sooner or later, before she could birth it.

Cicely hoped Artur was kind to his wife. He looked like he might love her, the few times she'd been in a position to see how he treated her. If Gelvira had even met Artur before their marriage, Cicely would have been surprised to hear it.

Now, listening to the bells, she was glad for Gelvira. All those bells. They surely meant a son. Rejoicing over another girl-child would have been a far more subdued affair.

Crowding right behind Cicely's joy came worry. The bells told her the child was fine. What about the mother? So many mothers died.

Why should you care at all? she scolded herself. She tucked her distaff more securely under her arm and resumed pulling out the long fibers of flax onto her spindle. *These people don't care about you*, she told herself. *Why should you care about them?*

Then she looked up with a smile as John came shouldering through the door, his rebec slung over his shoulder. The king had allowed him the coin for one of his own.

She set her distaff aside and moved to the hearth to find something for her two boys to eat.

She wondered, now, as she sometimes did, about the look she had seen in Ranulf's eye, when she had brought up this matter of John's music and the need for the instrument. A fearful look had crossed Ranulf's features. Cicely was almost sure that's what it had been, but how could it? What was so frightening about music, she wondered. What was so frightening about John making music. It was a puzzle, so she thrust the thoughts away. *I must remember to thank him for the coin*, thought Cicely. *It means so much to John.*

Especially now that his voice was cracking. It amused her and endeared him to her. He was becoming a man.

But John had been alarmed.

"Of course I'm glad I'm becoming a man, Mother. But what about singing?"

"You have your instrument, son."

"Yes, at least I have that. I want both!"

"Master Electus told me you are not to worry. Even if you're embarrassed about your singing, you need to continue going to him and keep up with your lessons."

"He told me the same. But last time I sounded so bad."

Cicely thought what they did to boys with beautiful voices in the Southern Primacy. Even in parts of the Baronies. She shivered. Luckily, if someone were to suggest it, Ranulf would never allow it to be done to John, bastard or no bastard.

"Master Electus tells me that once you grow into your voice, and learn how to manage it, you'll be pleased with it again, son."

"I suppose." But John looked downhearted.

His gloomy mood changed in an instant. Wat, coming down from the loft, spotted his brother and launched himself at John like the arrow from the bow.

John pretended to be bowled over by him, and the brothers lay in a heap, John tickling Wat and Wat giggling and thrashing.

"No, Johnny! Don't treat me like a baby!" he protested.

"But you are. A little tiny baby," said John, holding him down and continuing to tickle him.

"I'm not." Wat's small face had grown red.

John let him up and hugged him. "I'm sorry, Wat. You're right. I'm a mean big brother. I must be more respectful. Look at you. You're a growing boy, and you'll overtop me soon. Then

I'll have to come crawling to you for protection from my enemies."

"I will, Johnny. I'll protect you," said Wat, mollified.

John grinned over his head at Cicely and touseled Wat's hair. "I'm counting on it," he told his brother. "Promise," he said.

"I promise," said Wat. But then, as if it were written there, Cicely saw a disturbing thought dawn on Wat. "When you were my age, you started training with Master Conal," he said, settling down comfortably against his brother and reaching for the rebec.

John unslung it from his shoulder and let Wat pluck at it. Wat soon tired of that.

"You were just exactly my age, when Master Conal started training you," Wat said.

"I know. I'm going to talk to him about you. But Wat, Master Conal's father just died, and now the king has appointed him Royal Arms Master in his father's place."

"So young to take on that responsibility," Cicely marveled, moving around to bring bowls and cups down from her high shelf across from the hearth.

"Master Conal is good. He's the best." Now John turned back to Wat. "Our father the king is keeping Master Conal so busy he might not be able to take on any other pupils. Not just at the moment."

"Please ask him, Johnny. Please please please," cried Wat.

"I will," said John. "In the meantime, you and I can practice in our dooryard."

The younger boy's face lit up then.

"Did you know a prince has been born to my brother Artur?" said John, looking up at Cicely.

"I heard the bells and knew that must be what they were telling out. But John, what about your brother's poor wife? How is it with her, have you heard?"

John shrugged. "No one was talking of that."

"She's probably fine, then," said Cicely. But with a chill she thought of all the women she'd known who were fine, too, after. Then, a day or maybe even a sen'night later, the fever took them. Or poor Queen Emilde, who died in a sudden gush of blood when everyone thought she had come well through Avery's birth.

Cicely began getting out bread and cheese for a light supper.

Without being told, Wat stepped outside and came back with an armload of fresh turves so she'd be ready on the morrow to get the midday meal going.

They're good boys, thought Cicely. *Praise the Lady they're healthy and strong.* They'd never taken sick, not even when plague swept through a year or so ago.

"You've heard all the news around the castle, I see," said Cicely to John.

"Yes, and Mother, I heard a funny thing about Audie."

"What's that, son?"

"You know how nobody likes him—"

"John. You must not say such things about your brother."

"But it's true. Nobody does. He's a pig. Anyway, the king sent over to the Baronies, to a powerful man he knows over there, to bring a boy across the Narrows to be Audie's companion."

"That's nice for the lad." *Lad*, she thought. Audemar was twenty. Yet he still behaved like a spoiled boy. She stayed out of his way, and tried to keep her sons out of his way, too. He was malicious and spiteful. "Your father looks out for all his children," she said instead.

"He's still a pig. I wouldn't like to be in that huscarl's shoes, the one who's to be his companion."

"John." She made him look at her. "Don't go around saying such things about Audemar. He'll be a powerful man some day. You can't afford to make an enemy of him."

John rolled his eyes.

"Hear me, John. You're nigh a man. You need to understand some things about your position here. It's dangerous not to."

John looked at her silently. "Mother, I do know that. Aves and Dru and I have been talking about it."

"You shouldn't be speaking of such things with them."

"I can speak of anything with them."

"You may think so, but—"

"Anything."

She nodded. *I hope to the Lady you're right, son*, she said to herself. But then she allowed herself to relax her worries away from her.

The friendships among those three were as strong as anything she had ever seen. Other powerful people might threaten John, if he were seen to overstep his place.

Those two, never.

It was the dedication day of the little prince. Domgall, they'd named him.

Everyone had just come back from the glade of the Earth Child, and now they were gathered in the great hall of the fort, waiting for the summons to the feast of celebration.

Cicely caught the eye of the Earl Brenci on the other side of the hearth and smiled.

He stood with his hand on his son's shoulder and smiled back.

He's so glad to be with Dru. And look at Dru. John is nigh a man, but Dru looks to have already gotten there, she thought.

Dru, like his father, would never be a tall man. But like his father, he looked like he'd someday be the most handsome man in the room.

Not in the showy big blond way of Ranulf and his sons—except Artur, of course—but in his own way, Bren was the most handsome.

Cicely saw many women in the hall cutting their eyes at Bren. Pretty soon, they'd be cutting them at Dru.

Bren was looking older, though.

I probably am too, she thought. *No wonder the king has abandoned me. There are plenty of lovely young girls vying for his attention.*

Cicely stood with her sons close by her. They were all hanging back in a corner where they wouldn't be very conspicuous. They could see but not so easily be seen.

Cicely craned her neck to catch a glimpse of the baby in Gelvira's arm. A tiny red-faced mite who in aftertime would be their king.

Artur stood beside Gelvira, his hand on her arm. And on the other side of her stood Ranulf, proud and solemn. His legacy, and his dynasty, were assured with the birth of this child.

A little further off stood Audemar and Avery.

Avery has been displaced now to fourth in line for the throne, and Audemar to third, thought Cicely. Audemar looked sullen. *I'll wager he's not happy about it,* thought Cicely suddenly.

Avery, though. He looked to be the carefree boy he'd always been. *He's getting tall, too,* thought Cicely.

"Look, Mother," John whispered beside her. "There's that lad."

"What lad?" Cicely looked over at him, confused.

"The lad brought over from the Baronies to be huscarl to Audie," John whispered back.

Cicely moved a bit so she could see this poor fellow. She agreed with her son. What a miserable way to spend your youth. But she didn't dare say it, and once again she wished John would be more discreet about it.

Cicely looked this stranger up and down. He was slender, of middle height, dark-haired, pale-complected.

She'd heard about him from the gossip about the fort. His name was Caedon, and he was the ward of Gilles de Rais, the most powerful noble in the Baronies. This Caedon was a young man who looked to be more or less of an age with Audemar.

As Cicely stared, he turned his head. He looked straight into her eyes and smiled.

Hastily she turned away. *What unusual eyes he has*, she thought. They were a kind of amber color. She'd never seen anyone with eyes that strange. They were like a cat's. A wolf's, maybe, she thought with a shiver.

As she dropped her own eyes, she noticed a boy close beside this unsettling Master Caedon. A young boy.

And that's the other one, she said to herself. According to the court gossip, another one had come with Caedon, a young boy whose task it would be to fetch and carry for Caedon.

I don't envy him, either, she thought.

PART IV: AUGURIES

"Tell me, Aderyn. Tell me, Little Bird. What sort of mage will our lad turn out to be? I know already he's a bard, with a bard's magic."

"He's a natural-born ornithomancer, my lord," Aderyn replied to Myrddin. "He speaks to the birds."

"As you do," said Myrddin. "The birds, the ones in creation who navigate between the land and the Spheres. The Children's harbingers. A powerful type of mage indeed, although as yet this young one doesn't know his own powers."

From the shadows, Gilles de Rais narrowed his eyes, listening. "This new mage they speak of is only a boy," he whispered to himself. "He will not be able to derail my plans. I have Caedon placed at court, to make sure of it."

The young mage, John, was fast friends with Ranulf's third son Avery.

Gilles's thoughts settled on his minion, Caedon. So useful to me, he told himself. Such a perceptive lad. And I was the one who saw it in him. I was the one who trained him.

Caedon, recognizing immediately what the youngest prince was made of, had already set his trap of destruction for Avery. As for the second son Audemar, the lout of a prince who would serve as Gilles's entry-point into the court of Ranulf, Caedon had matters well in hand there, too. Gilles was very pleased with Caedon.

And the crown prince. . . Gilles's very red lips drew back from his teeth in a smile. The most important of Ranulf's three legitimate sons, at least for now. Caedon had assured Gilles that soon, very soon, he'd be in a position to help Gilles with Crown Prince Artur as well.

Gilles, though, saw further and deeper than his minion Caedon. Gilles saw how easy it would be to underestimate the third of the sons, Avery—how dangerous Avery could be to him, and to his plans. And John the bastard son as well, loyal to his half-brother Avery. If I can destroy the prince and contain the bastard while they are still young, Gilles told himself, I'll put myself in a fine position to uproot that silly king's whole dynasty and install my own.

Not that Gilles cared a whit about the dynasties of the ordinary folk. But to carry out his larger plan, he needed control of all the kinds. The mages. The witches. The eala. The gwrgi. And the least and weakest of all the kinds, the ordinary folk with their small minds, their small imaginations. He needed even these.

The young mage John. Gilles pondered. He wanted John, not to crush like the others, but to possess. Gilles thought how to go about it. If he could accomplish such a thing, then the troublesome third son, Avery, would be rendered helpless, his destruction more certain. With the young mage John at his side, and his gwrgi minion Caedon, Gilles could take Avery out of the action.

Besides, Gilles wanted John for another reason. To all those around him, even his own family, John seemed like one of the ordinary folk. But Gilles had known for a long time what John really was. One of his own kind, a mage. Gilles didn't have one of those. Not a powerful specimen.

He thought about what he did have. Witches, yes. Gwrgi, yes— and especially Caedon. The eala, yes.

Gilles's eyes softened. And one of the ordinary folk, too. Reluctant, maybe, but close bound to him with no hope of release. It flew in the face of good sense, how much Gilles valued the boy. Ah, could he not have a little sentimentality in his life? Gilles shook his head at his own folly. The boy kept trying to pull away, but Gilles and Caedon between them would control him.

Yet of all his own kind, the mages who followed his lead, Gilles knew none with the potential to become a powerful tool and companion.

Most of the powerful mages were his opponents. Myrddin. Gilles's lips drew back in a snarl. He'd nearly had Myrddin if not obliterated, then rendered helpless, and with the aid of a witch. Myrddin escaped Gilles's trap only because he had Dee, his strong ally.

"I need a strong ally," Gilles muttered to himself. "Not an equal, of course. I need one I can train and shape and possess."

Now, as the mage Aderyn, the one called Little Bird, flew from Myrddin's side, Gilles followed her with his eyes. He gave a satisfied grunt. Aderyn could do much to thwart Gilles, but not as much as she once might. Not now she had gone across the river to the Land of the Dead. At Myrddin's behest, she could leave the shores of that river for brief periods. Not for long.

On the whole, Gilles felt a deep satisfaction. Caedon was becoming an ever-more useful tool in his hand. Soon, if he played his cards right, he'd have another tool as useful. More useful. He'd have John. Then he'd use those tools of his. And, in the service of the world he would build, he'd send them out to destroy, destroy, destroy.

JOHN

CHAPTER TWENTY-EIGHT

A Lanar for a Squire

John was in high spirits. Conal had promised they could all go out hawking when their training was over that day. Avery and Dru had already learned how to hunt using hawks and falcons, and they each had birds of their own in the mews. John had none.

"You can use one of mine," said Avery. "I have six, I think."

"There are plenty of extra birds in the mews. The king needs them when he entertains visitors from afar and takes them out hawking," Dru said. Actually, as they were both quick to point out to John, their birds were the noble falcons, the long-wingers, not the ignoble short-wingers, the hawks.

John didn't care. Falcons, hawks. He loved them all.

Later on, the entire group of lads would be heading to the mews, choosing their birds, and riding into the forest to a clearing where they could fly their birds. Of course John knew how to ride. All of them had been in the saddle from babyhood, or so it seemed. As soon as they were in Conal's hands, they became expert.

"A warrior needs to know how to sit a horse," Conal had said to them at the beginning of their combat training, "and to fight from horseback, too." At least once a sen'night, the whole group of his young pupils trekked out to the field beyond the practice courtyard to drill with sword and shield from horseback, ride at the quintain, and work on quick mounts and dismounts while wearing the padded gambeson to approximate the weight of armor.

But John had never hunted. Not with a hawk or falcon. Not with a hound. Never. Hunting was for the gentles, and he wasn't a gentle.

Avery and Dru were knights. When Dru had turned fourteen, his father the Earl Brenci had come from the cliffs for his accolade. The year after, it was Avery's turn for the accolade. These were purely ceremonial events all boys of their class underwent. It didn't mean they fought in Ranulf's wars. Not yet. Next year, John knew, Avery would sit his vigil and pledge fealty to his father and brothers the way Artur and Audemar had before him. That event was not purely ceremonial. It was deadly serious.

Sometimes, to tease and bother the two of them, John addressed them mockingly as Sir Avery and Sir Drustan and made elaborate bows to them. But once, when he had done this, and they had laughed good-naturedly if a bit uneasily, he detected an undercurrent of resentment inside himself. Then, ashamed at harboring sour feelings toward his brothers, he stopped his teasing. When he thought about these incidents, he blushed.

As young knights in the king's retinue, Avery and Dru did enjoy certain privileges. They went out with Ranulf's hunting parties from time to time. Since Ranulf loved hawking above all other kinds of hunting, they'd acquired their birds, and they had become proficient.

The nearest John had come was gazing at the birds with an intense longing he couldn't quite explain. Sometimes he even sneaked into the mews, which were close by their practice courtyard, to stare at the hawks and falcons hooded on their perches. They were so mysterious. He felt a strange connection with them.

He didn't let Nyles, the grouchy old falconer, catch him. He avoided the cadgers, too. They would have reported his intrusion to Nyles.

Now that Conal had decided the teamwork and strategizing of falconry would be good practice for his charges, John realized with rising excitement that he was about to get his wish: to join up with a bird in a profound act of partnership.

And today was the day! When he got to the courtyard, though, he saw something else unusual was going on. Avery and Dru, and some of the other boys, were standing in a little knot with Conal. And a strange new boy was there beside him.

Conal looked up and saw John. "Over here, Johnny," he called.

John walked slowly over to the group of them. Now he realized with shock who the new boy was. It was that lad sent over with Master Caedon to be companion to Audemar.

They'd all seen the lad running here and there on errands for Master Caedon during the last year or so. But none of them had ever talked to him.

I don't even know his name, John realized. But instinctively he recoiled from the boy. Anything to do with Audemar was nothing to do with him. Whenever he thought of Audemar's cruel slits of eyes in his fleshy face, the derisive laugh he visited upon his inferiors, the mean tricks he was known to play on anyone weaker than himself, John hoped to keep it that way.

"John," said Conal, as John drew reluctantly near. "This is Rafe. He is Master Caedon's assistant, and now he'll train with us."

Rafe looked a bit younger than he himself was, but surely too old to begin training, especially with the older boys. If he was just beginning his training, John thought with resentment, he should be made to go over with the little boys.

John's brother Wat had been much on his mind lately. Wat would soon be far too old for a beginner, yet he hadn't been given leave to learn from Master Conal. Once he was, and found himself grouped with the small boys, he'd know the humiliation John wished on this new boy.

John didn't understand why Wat was being treated so churlishly. "Why would our father the king give me leave to train, but not Wat?" he had demanded of his mother. "We're both his sons."

His mother had only shaken her head, looking downhearted.

John wondered. Was it because when he was born, his mother was the king's beloved, but now she wasn't? Had he been allowed to train because he was fast friends with Avery and Dru, and the king couldn't exclude him from the group, not now, because the king knew what a fuss those two would kick up if he hadn't let John train with them? Maybe the Earl Brenci, Dru's father, had made the king feel guilty, and that's why he'd allowed John to be included. John knew the earl felt deep respect for his mother and gratitude for her care of Dru.

As he was thinking these dark thoughts, the new boy came over to him and looked him in the eye. "Hello, John, I have seen you about the fort," said this boy, Rafe. His voice had a pleasing Baronies lilt. He pronounced John like "Yann."

"And I have seen you, too," said John, carefully schooling his tone so it wouldn't sound as unfriendly as he felt. "Rafe, is it?"

"Raoul, actually, but the prince can't pronounce it. So Rafe will do," said the new boy.

The prince, thought John. *He means Audemar.* He tried out the unfamiliar syllables in his mind. *Raoul.* For once, he was in agreement with Audie about something. *Rafe* was much easier.

"John, please pair up with Rafe during the opening exercises," said Conal.

"Yes, Master Conal," said John, but to himself he said, bitterly, *Why me? Why do I have to stop to teach this new boy everything the rest of us already know?* Because he was sure that would be the way of it.

He and Rafe faced each other. They drew their practice swords, not the lightweight wooden ones of John's childhood and the little boys' training, but heavy blunted things, their sharp edges bated. Bated or not, a blow from one of them could do a lot of damage. John had the bruises to prove it.

He and Rafe stood on their guard. During the group's warm-up exercises, they went through the fluid motions together of all the standard offensive and defensive positions as Master Conal called them out.

As he watched Rafe carefully, John was surprised. If Rafe was just copying what he saw John doing, he was catching on fast. But no, it looked like Rafe actually knew these positions.

Then the sparring began. John was hard pressed to keep Rafe from getting under his guard. He found himself sweating and breathing fast.

He was determined not to let this newcomer best him. But gradually, as they continued fighting, he found the newcomer, smaller, younger, lighter, was doing exactly that.

When Conal called time, John stood gasping for breath and staring.

"Where did you learn to do that," he got out. "You're good, Rafe."

Rafe smiled. "My guardian provides us with the best masters. I have practiced since I was six."

Us, thought John. That must mean Rafe and Caedon. But he said only, "You are so quick." *I must be generous*, he thought. *I must acknowledge when I'm wrong. Otherwise, I will show discourtesy. A knight is always courteous.* He carefully kept himself from the next inevitable thought: *I am no knight and never will be.* "I could hardly keep up with you," he told this new boy, Rafe. Then, more unwillingly, "Have you met the others?"

"Only just, and then you came, and then we began," said Rafe.

"Come over here with me and meet them, then," said John. *I must show courtesy*, he told himself firmly.

"I know about you," said Rafe as they walked across the courtyard. "You're the king's bastard."

John made a noncommittal noise.

He was surprised to find he, Avery, Dru, and this new boy were soon talking easily, animatedly in the friends' favorite corner of the courtyard.

But John put aside his complicated stew of feelings about the new boy when their combat session ended and he crowded into the nearby mews with the other boys, marveling at the rows of majestic hooded birds on their perches as the cadgers busied themselves among them. Now that he was allowed in the place, he roamed around taking it all in. Rafe was the last thing on his mind now.

The boys of the upper nobility who owned their own birds went over to Master Nyles, the falconer, to get them.

Avery stood looking over his six birds, trying to decide which one to take out. John laughed to himself. Avery's favorite was a large peregrine falcon named Lady Gray, and he knew Avery would choose her. He was right. Avery did.

Dru owned two birds, two tiercels, and he adored them both. He stood jittering from one to the other, trying to make up his mind.

Other boys claimed their birds. Those who had none waited patiently for Master Nyles to get around to them. They would each get the loan of one of the extra birds the mews kept.

By now, though, John had moved into a reverie. He felt so strongly about the birds that his surroundings faded away. In almost a trance, he went from bird to bird, just gazing at them.

So then he suddenly saw he'd be at the end of the line, the last to choose. He hustled into line. He didn't mind. Being last gave him even more time to watch the birds and to see what they did as the boys claimed them and started working with them.

He turned to Conal, who had come up behind him. "Master Conal, how will I know what to do once I get a bird?"

"That's one of the reasons for our exercise. To teach you."

"But it's not like our training with the horses. We don't need to know falconry to go to war."

"True. But working with the birds, and with each other, will teach you a lot about—" Conal didn't finish his thought. John had finally reached the head of the line.

Master Nyles stared at him for a moment. "Who's this?" He spoke past John to Conal.

"Another one of my pupils. John, this is Master Nyles."

John bobbed a quick little bow. He wondered which bird Master Nyles would match him with.

"Master Nyles, this is—"

Master Nyles was shaking his head firmly. "I know who he is. It's not allowed, Master Conal, as you know very well." He turned his back on John and began directing one of the cadgers to sort out a pile of jesses.

John looked over his shoulder in confusion at Conal. He saw that Conal's mouth had become a tight little line. His eyes were hard. "Come with me, Johnny." He put a hand on John's shoulder and walked him outside. "Sit there for a moment, will you, lad?" He indicated a bench against the wall of the mews.

John sat on the bench, lifting his face to the sun. After the winter, it felt good. He was trying not to think about what had just happened to him, but of course it was dawning on him what had. Master Nyles wasn't going to give him a bird, because John was not a gentle. John was in fact a bastard. The noble sport of falconry was closed to such ignoble folk as he.

Conal put out a hand to John that meant, "Wait right there." He strode over to the group of boys and began laying down the ground rules of the hunt. Experienced boys to go with Avery, who had progressed the furthest in his skills. Inexperienced boys to go with him, and not to make one move without his instruction.

Dru came over to John, his bird on his arm. "Where's your bird, Johnny?"

"Don't have one."

"Why not?" Dru took a step back to peer into the mews. "Plenty left," he said.

John squinted up at Dru against the sun. "Master Nyles says I'm not to have one."

Dru's mouth gaped open. Then he too realized the reason. His face darkened with anger.

Avery was beside him now. "What's wrong? Come on, you lot. We're about to get started. Where's your bird, Johnny?"

Dru was still staring at John. Without shifting his gaze, Dru said, his voice quiet, but a rage underneath, "Master Nyles isn't letting him have one."

Avery saw instantly. His cheeks flushed a dull red. "In that case," he said tightly, "I'm putting Lady Gray back on her perch."

John opened his mouth to protest, but Dru had his hand on John's arm. "Putting mine back too."

Conal moved up to them. "What's this, then."

Avery turned to him, defiant. "Johnny doesn't go, we don't." Then he added, "Whip us if you like."

Conal put a hand on Avery's shoulder. He looked long into Avery's eyes. "You think I'd do that, Avery? Whip you? Ever?" he said softly. Something changed then. John felt it. He didn't know how to name it.

Conal turned back to John and Dru, and the moment passed. Conal's voice was hard, matter-of-fact. "Master Nyles says Johnny is not to have a bird. John and I are thinking about that. So the three of you see the problem we face, lads. What do we do about it? You lot have come up with one solution. Refuse to have any part of it. Might be a good solution. Can you think of any others?"

The problem we face, thought John. *We*, he thought. Conal included himself in that *we*. He loved Conal then, and he saw the other two did, too.

"I've been knighted," said Avery. "So has Dru. Suppose we tell that prickass that John's our squire?"

"Might work," said Conal.

"No." Somehow, that seemed worse, to John, than having his lack of gentility rubbed in his face.

"No?" said Conal.

"No."

"Back goes her ladyship, then," said Avery, turning to the door to the mews. He didn't say it with annoyance. He said it as if of course that would be the way of it. Dru stepped up beside Avery to follow him into the mews and do the same.

"No, I don't want that," John burst out.

"What do you want?" said Dru, looking back at him, perplexed and miserable.

"Johnny. All in this together. Remember?" said Avery, coming to John.

John looked down at his shoes.

"Lads," said Conal to John's friends. "Take your birds over there." He nodded to the group of other boys. "John and I need to talk."

The two hesitated. Then they quietly did as they were told.

Conal sat down beside John on the bench and stretched out his legs "Nice here," he said.

"All of you should get started," John said. "I'm holding everything up."

"John. Listen to me. This isn't about you."

"What's it about, then?" John worked to keep the bitterness from his voice. He knew he wasn't succeeding.

Conal didn't answer right away. Then he said, "Explaining that. It's complicated, Johnny." He paused again. "Partly," he said after a moment, "It's about me."

John looked at him sidelong.

"I'm not a gentle, either, you know," he said.

"But you're the king's arms master." John glanced over at Conal. Conal wore his hair cropped short, like a yeoman. In fact, that's what he was. John's own hair, the despair of his mother, since it was forever falling down into his face, was long and fair and straight, held back with a thong, like his friends'. Like a boy of the nobility. John wondered whether someone would come up to him and demand he cut his hair off.

"Yes, I serve the king," Conal was saying, "which gives me some privileges I might not otherwise have. But then other matters interfere with these privileges. Matters that have nothing to do with the rule about only nobles being allowed to hunt, a rule honored more in the breach than in the observance, as the bards might put it."

"What matters?"

"The matter of Master Nyles never liking my father, and thwarting him any way he could. The matter of Master Nyles not liking me."

"Because you're your father's son?"

"That," said Conal. "That, and another thing he doesn't like about me." He looked away, his expression unreadable. "But to take that out on a boy who has nothing to do with it, and set out to try to shame him—" Conal's voice turned suddenly savage. He drew a ragged breath. "Listen, John. The world is full of boundaries and rules. Some of them make sense, and some of them don't. Some people follow them, even when the rules don't make sense, even when the rules might be hurtful. Evil, even. Because some people are rules-followers, no matter what. Other people consider the rules carefully and follow the ones that make sense and give the others short shrift. And some people use the rules as if they are weapons in a war they are always fighting." He stared down at his hands. Powerful hands. John could see he was clenching and unclenching them, getting a grip on himself.

"I just made a lot of rules for our hunt very clear to those boys over there," Conal went on, indicating his other pupils with a tilt of his head, "and I expect them to follow my rules, because it will keep them and their birds safe. So I believe." He was silent for a moment. "Rules can be most important, most useful. But some rules are not. Sometimes it's hard to tell the difference between useful rules and the other kind. Sometimes it's hard to know what to do about it when the rules are—" Conal paused. "—when the rules are the harmful kind," he concluded quietly.

"What about you, Master Conal? What do you do about the rules?"

"I respect the rules, Johnny. I follow them when I can, because life is easier that way, and the rules are usually there to protect realms and the people who live in them. But some of us find we've been thrust outside the rules. The rules don't protect us. They hurt us."

John looked at Conal, puzzled. How could Conal consider himself outside the protective fence of the rules? Conal was the king's arms master. He possessed skills so valuable that the king had given him great responsibility at a very young age. He remembered when the three of them had first met Conal, and how the king had praised Conal for his bravery in battle. John thought about how old Conal must be. Not as old as Artur. Around Audemar's age, he guessed. Not all that much older than his pupils.

Conal smiled at John. "So, Johnny. Here you sit, outside the comfortable fence of the rules. Falconry, the rules say, is a sport for gentles. That's a little game the gentles play, to keep the rest of us in our places. There are many games of that sort that certain people play, many fences put up not to protect but to exclude, and you're going to find yourself running up against them all of your life. You're not gently born. Nine Spheres, lad, you're a bastard." Here Conal gave John an unexpected grin. "Better start thinking right now what you're going to do about it."

John cracked a reluctant smile.

"But think of it. You're here being trained with your friends because, at the early age when you fell in with those two rascals of lads, your mother was the king's favorite. Now here comes your younger brother, and your mother's not the favorite any longer, and your brother is not allowed the training you're getting. Where's the protection of rules and rules-following in that? Or take young Master Rafe over there," Conal said, pointing him out.

Rafe looked over at them in confusion. He started to walk in their direction, but Conal waved him off.

"Nice lad. I like him very much," said Conal. "I'm glad he has joined us. Is he a gentle? If he is, just barely. But because his guardian is one of the most powerful men in the Baronies, and because this powerful baron has requested that Rafe be trained with you lot, and because our king, at least right at this moment, wants a good relationship with the baron, Rafe's accepted as a gentle and given his bird. What do we conclude from that, John? Sometimes the rules are sound and wise, sometimes they're foolish or even harmful, and sometimes, whether they're wise or foolish, they're inconsistently applied."

Conal stopped and looked at John intently. "So how does anyone know what to do? What do you do, now that someone has thrown up that fence of rules between you and what you need to do, and for no good reason? What do we do, you and I, when we come up to that fence? What do your friends do when they see they're on the other side of it from you, and feel the hurt of it almost as much as you do? They're taking this hard, John. What do you think you need to do about that? Anything? Nothing?"

"Pretend to be Aves's squire and beat Master Nyles at his own game," John whispered, reluctantly.

"That's what I think too, Johnny. That's what I'd do. But I'll not force you to it, just because I find such tactics work for me, when sensible means have failed."

"I'll do it, Master Conal."

By this time, Avery and Dru were hovering around just out of earshot.

Conal summoned them over. "What do you think, Avery the prince. Can you get on your high horse and charge in there and demand your squire be given a bird?"

Avery and Dru were jumping on John then, and pounding him on the back, and, giggling, dragging him to the door of the mews.

Avery stepped aside from them. He forced a frown on his face, and he drew himself up impressively. Avery had already grown tall. Just not as tall as John.

"Nine Spheres," John heard Conal muttering behind them. "And they're still growing."

"Master Nyles," Avery called into the dim interior of the mews.

The man emerged. "How may I help Your Highness."

"I must inform you of something, my good man," said Avery in supercilious tones. "As you know, my father the king knighted me this year. . ."

Around the corner, outside the man's line of sight, Dru was making grotesque faces at John. John was doubling over with suppressed laughter.

Conal, on his way past them to the rest of their group, gave them an unexpectedly stern warning frown.

So then John settled down, and so did Dru.

But afterward, the three of them couldn't stop sniggering over Master Nyles's disgruntled expression when he realized he'd have to cater to the whim of his young whippersnapper of a prince.

The man nearly had it his own way, though. "A lanar for a squire," he'd said with a sour expression, looking over his collection of birds. Then he had turned in triumph to the three boys. "But we have no lanar at the moment." They didn't realize Conal had come back into the mews with them until

Conal stepped past them to the man, his voice dangerous. "What other bird can you give the boy?"

Master Nyles had silently reached for one of the least impressive birds, a small hawk, and handed it over to John. Not the noble falcon, but the ignoble hawk.

John didn't care. He accepted the fierce little bird with joy. He was learning an astonishing new thing, how to hunt in companionship with a noble creature. Noble by nature, not by the rules of kings and realms. As John came eye to eye with his bird, he saw she had an inner nobility no one could take away from her.

Even better, he was with his friends, and they loved him, and he loved them.

There was another thing he found out. All three of them did. Conal was their well-respected teacher. But somehow, for them, he had revealed himself to be something more.

CHAPTER TWENTY-NINE

Yeomen, Sparhawks, and Outcasts

John had done what he had been told not to do. John had gotten himself somehow separated from the others in the hunt. He was violating the most important rule Conal laid out for them all. Stay together.

Now John felt frightened. He wasn't afraid because he didn't know where he was. He wasn't afraid Conal would whip him. He was afraid because he was letting Conal down. When Conal set out a rule for them to follow, it was a sound rule. They might not even like it, but they knew he had good reasons for issuing it—almost always because it would keep them safe.

"And you may think, pfft, I'm not in any danger. You may even be right, the time you think it. But if you follow this rule until it's deep a part of you, one day in the midst of battle you'll find it has saved your life," he had told them, insisting on a rule most of them found a bit silly. John couldn't even remember what it was, probably because, just as Conal had suggested, it was so much a part of him now that he didn't have to think about it any longer.

So as he realized he'd violated this rule of Conal's—stay together—and especially just after Conal had had a serious talk with him about rules, a talk you'd have with a fellow adult, not talking down to a child—John's mouth went dry and he bitterly regretted his lapse of attention. Conal had trusted him. He was violating Conal's trust.

The thing was, he and his little bird, a sparhawk, had formed themselves into a lethal hunting team almost immediately. As the others struggled with their birds, his was harrying prey across the field and bringing her catch straight back to John. Maybe she was a particularly well-trained, cooperative bird, thought John.

Conal, watching him, had shaken his head. "Doesn't work like that. Your bird has to get to know you. So I don't know, Johnny. You're doing something I've never seen before, and I have no idea what it is." Conal had shrugged. "I do know this. Whatever you're doing, it's working."

Then he'd taken John away from the team of boys new to falconry and had sent him over to Avery's team with the experienced boys. Avery, Dru, Rafe, one other. And now John.

For most of the afternoon, Avery's team hunted their birds together. But John's hawk used a different method than the others' peregrine falcons, whether tiercel or Avery's big female. Their birds gyred up high and came down on their prey in a screaming stoop. His own little bird stayed low, on the lookout. Then she tail-chased a shivering, ambushed flock of pipets or some other small fowl making melody at the edge of the forest, cut out one poor misfortunate from its fellows, came down on it, and dispatched it with her sharp curved cruel beak. Then the triumphant return to John's gauntlet with a pathetic bundle of feathers, the little hawk's jesses trailing.

A few of the others looked askance at John as their bigger birds soared majestically high to terrorize and bring down hares and even a badger.

Conal came by to look at some of John's kills. "You and that little bird are doing well," he said, and then moved on to an inexperienced boy whose bird seemed to regard him with utter disdain.

Shortly after that, John rushed away from his group into the forest. His hawk was in distress. He found her in some heavy underbrush, trapped by her jesses.

"There, my girl," he said, untangling her. She came to his gauntlet with her kill, and he let her eat this one, a mouse.

It was then he realized. He and his bird were lost.

He sat down with his back to a tree, to think what to do and to listen for sounds of the others.

That's when he realized something else. His bird was speaking to him.

In some deep place in him, she was communicating with him. Earlier, she had heard his uncertainties and had reassured him. Then she had heard his growing excitement and joy, and had shared her own with him. Now that he was in distress, she comforted him.

I should be frightened by this, he thought. But he wasn't. He realized now why he had had such an easy time with his bird while others hadn't, and the reason for Conal's amazement.

He knew he couldn't try to explain it to Conal. It's not that he distrusted Conal. The reverse, in fact. And now, of course, he trusted Conal even more. It's that he couldn't put into words what happened between him and this bird. The thoughts they shared didn't take the form of words, but he didn't know how to explain the form they did take.

He wouldn't be able to explain to Dru and Avery, either.

Now he sat still, trying to listen. Trying not to panic.

His bird cocked her head at him. It was as if she said, *Your ears are too dull, boy-person, friend of birds. But I hear those others you seek. Let me fly, and I'll lead you to them.*

That's what he did. She flew in short bursts, stopping to let him catch up to her, and after a while, he too heard the commotion of voices that meant he had found his friends.

He arrived at the clearing where they'd begun their training just as Avery's group reached it to settle their birds back into the mews. He fell in behind them.

Avery looked around. "Oh, there you are, brother."

John heaved a sigh of relief. No one had missed him. Conal wouldn't know he'd disobeyed. No one would.

John saw he was wrong about that. Rafe had seen.

"Where did you go?" he said.

"Got lost," John said, keeping his voice down.

"Good thing you found us when you did. Master Conal would have whipped you sure."

"Good thing I did," said John.

Rafe gave John a mischievous grin. "But he really wouldn't have, would he? Whipped you?"

John smiled back. "No," he said.

"That's not his way. I can tell already."

The other group had come back to the clearing now too, and the boys were all milling around. But Rafe stuck to John's side.

"Some masters beat you, when you do wrong. Or—" Rafe hesitated. "Or other things. But some masters make you want to do the right thing, and then you feel bad, when you don't, and then that bad feeling is what turns out to be your punishment."

"Yes," said John.

"Master Conal's that kind. I can see that."

John nodded. Then he blurted out, "I'll wager Audie is the other kind."

"Yes," said Rafe, with a scornful little laugh. "But I'm beholden to Master Caedon, not to the prince, so that's all right."

John looked over at Rafe in astonishment.

"Master Caedon, but really, to my guardian, the Baron Gilles. And he's far away from here." Again the grin.

"Brave little sod, aren't you?"

Rafe stopped smiling. "Not really," he said. He fingered a little amulet dangling from a thong about his neck.

What is that? John wondered. A sea bird, maybe. Rafe's gray eyes told John that Rafe must be a child of the Child of Sea.

John shivered. He wasn't sure why. Something in Rafe's expression. Something in the way he was touching the little amulet at his neck.

But now they were approaching the mews, and Conal was lining them up to turn in their birds.

When it was his turn to take his hawk to her perch, Conal was there to show him how to hood her the proper way. Before the hood shut her into her own privacy, she spoke to John again.

You're sad, she told John. *You think we won't meet again. We will. We'll hunt together, and I'll tell you many things*, she said.

What is your name, noble lady? John said to her.

My name is Striker, said the hawk.

I am honored to know it, John replied.

Conal took John aside. "You have a gift, with the birds."

"It will be hard to convince Master Nyles to let me hunt again," said John, gloomily. In spite of his hawk's reassurances, he'd seen the black look Master Nyles had given him as he brought Striker back to the mews.

"Oh, as for that," said Conal with a smile. "Avery and I have already cobbled together a plan to fix that little problem. I'm sending you here every afternoon, after your schooling and the music lessons are over. Now that I see the talent you have with the birds, I'd be a fool of a teacher if I didn't have you cultivate it. This plan of mine should work well until the Spheres revolve into the dark part of the year. Then we'll think of another way."

John felt a burst of joy. "I hope I may take the same bird out."

"She's the only hawk in the mews. A lanar for a squire, remember? But there's no lanar, so you have to settle for a yeoman's bird." He nudged John and began to laugh. "I learned on that kind of bird, a little sparhawk, myself."

Conal leaned over, as John turned away to join his friends. "And sometime, John, I'll want you to tell me what you and that little bird did together, when you two got into the woods away from your group, and how she got you back to us."

John looked over his shoulder at Conal, startled. Conal wasn't smiling. He wasn't frowning. If he had to name the look Conal gave him, John decided he'd call it concerned. Worried, even.

Then Dru and Avery grabbed him, and they ran and leaped all the way to John's house. But as they left the mews in a noisy tangle, John caught Rafe looking after them wistfully.

He and Striker and Rafe. They were all outcasts, in a way, thought John. Somehow, deep inside, John knew something about Rafe, and didn't know how he knew it.

But one thing he was sure about. He knew it, just as he had known what Striker was trying to tell him. He would become fast friends with that boy. They all would.

CHAPTER THIRTY

A Bad Thing, a Good Thing, and an Odd Thing

By the time the Spheres had wheeled around to autumn, John had learned a lot. He was learning his letters, and while he knew he'd never learn them as well as Dru nor be as interested, he was learning. Of course, under Conal's expert tutelage, he was learning the arts of war. They all were, and it thrilled them all, because they were leaving boyhood behind and soon would find themselves fighting in Ranulf's wars.

John was learning other important things. He was learning music, his instrument the rebec as well as the instrument of his voice. As his voice changed and deepened, he began to understand how to manage this new instrument of his, and Master Electus was helping him see the right way to do it without damaging his voice.

He and Striker were learning the hunt. Even more thrilling to him was that other skill he was learning from Striker, the skill he could never talk about. He was learning the language of the birds, and Striker was teaching him.

One more thing he was learning. The delight of making a new friend. The three of them had all become fast friends with Rafe, just as John had foreseen. They had been three. Now they were four.

John had gotten into the habit of singing and playing as he walked the lanes around Tambourne. Today he was doing that on the way to meet his friends. They planned to go off to the fort's stables together to look over Dru's new horse.

Dru was waiting for them in the fort's outer bailey. John slung his rebec back onto his shoulder and ambled up to Dru. They exchanged a few words about the latest lesson Conal had given them in the use of the short sword and when, in the midst of battle, to switch to the sword from the spear.

Then Rafe joined them from Audemar's wing of the fort. "Where's Aves?"

"Late," said Dru.

They waited for a while. Avery didn't come.

"Maybe he thought we were all to meet at the stables," said Dru. They walked over to the stables and admired the horse, but Avery was not there.

"This isn't like Aves," said Dru.

"Dru always worries," John told Rafe. "Dru, stop," he said. "Some princely duty probably arose to detain Aves. He probably had to entertain some countess or polish the silver or something."

"Probably," Dru agreed, and tried to laugh, but he still looked worried.

"Nine Spheres, Dru," said John, amused. "What's the worst that could have happened to him? Fell in the moat and drowned?"

Dru didn't reply to that. He said only, "See you lot tomorrow," and walked away.

So they parted. John headed down the path that wound along between the fort and the forest toward his mother's small house. It got dark early these days. He hadn't been able to take Striker out lately, and he missed her sorely.

About halfway home, he stopped short. There was a black fluttering shape in the path in front of him.

He peered at it through the gloom, trying to make it out. It was a bird. A fairly large bird. It stalked straight at him. A largish bird. *A blackbird*, thought John blankly.

The bird was making a low croaking noise. John took a step backward, but it came on. As it neared, he saw it looked ill or maybe injured. One eye was a milky white.

John felt a shiver of fear.

It began to speak to him in the way he could never describe. The way birds spoke. Not in words. Some other way.

A denizen of the mews, a lady by the name of Striker, asked me to get a message to you, said the blackbird. *Something has happened. The Little Bird has told Striker where to look. She has flown high, this one. She has seen a bad thing.*

John stood frozen. Who was this Little Bird, he wondered.

Your brother the boy-person is in trouble. You must go to him.

Where? John cried out, though no word passed his lips.

The river, where it rushes under the bridge. Go quickly.

The blackbird surged up out of the roadway and flapped off into the forest.

John felt a raw panic. The boy-person of the message was Avery. He knew it. His silly words of earlier came back to him with a chill. *What's the worst that could happen? Drowned in the moat?* But he somehow knew the danger Avery faced wasn't from drowning. He didn't know how he knew it, but he did. He stopped himself from bolting into the forest toward the river. Instead, he pelted back the way he had come, his rebec banging against his shoulder. He swerved aside into the little practice courtyard. At one end was a narrow door. The door to Conal's rooms. He pounded on it.

Conal opened it after a moment or two and looked out, startled when he saw John there.

"Master Conal," he panted, doubling over and taking in huge gasps of air.

"What's happened, Johnny?" Conal looked alarmed.

"It's Aves. He's in trouble."

"Where?"

"The river. The bridge," John got out.

"He's in the water?" Conal exclaimed. All of them, children of the Child of Earth, were uneasy around water. If any of them could swim, they swam badly.

"No," said John, although a part of himself stood amazed he was so certain of it.

Conal stepped back into his rooms, emerging an instant later buckling his sword belt around him and slamming the door to behind him.

He and John set off at a run, taking the narrow path that led to the river through the forest. As they neared the bridge, they heard shouting and scuffling.

"Get help, John," said Conal, fixing him with a hard stare. "Get the Watch. Now."

John didn't want to leave. Avery was in trouble. But he'd never disobey Conal. He turned and ran.

Soon he was dashing back down the path, two men of the Watch close behind him. The watchmen had lit rush lights against the dark and were holding them high. The lights cast fantastic jagged shadows ahead of them down the path.

As the three of them reached the bridge, they came upon a strange tense tableau. Conal was holding two men at sword point, one of them obviously wounded and moaning, the other man looking wildly about. In the crook of his left arm Conal sheltered a bent-over huddled figure wrapped in his cloak.

"Avery!" screamed John, and ran to his brother. Avery's face was white. He looked stunned. When he saw John, he turned away and buried his head against Conal.

"Arrest these men," Conal called to the Watch. "They were trying to harm the prince."

The two men of the Watch shoved past John, while he stood aside by Conal and Avery. They began binding the attackers.

"John," said Conal. "Avery is fine. He'll be fine. He's had a bad shock. John. Are you listening to me?"

"Yes," said John through numb lips.

"Go home. Go straight home. As soon as I get Avery back to the fort, I promise to come to your house and let you know how he does. Do you understand? John?"

"Yes," said John. He made himself walk back up the path and down the road to his house. All the way, his mind was in turmoil. What could the men have been doing to Avery. Had they hurt him. Conal said he was fine, but he didn't look fine. Around and around whirled John's thoughts.

When he reached his house and went in, ducking his head under the lintel and blinking in the smoky light from the hearth, his mother saw how distressed he was. She was alarmed.

"I'm fine, Mother. But something bad happened to Avery."

"Lady help us, what?"

"I don't know. I think he's all right. Master Conal is coming over in a while to tell me."

His mother made Wat go protesting to bed, and she got something hot for John to drink.

"You're shaking as if the Dark Ones are after you, son," she said.

He sat down by the hearth, and his mother brought a blanket from the chest and tucked it around him. But he couldn't stop shivering.

After several candle measures, a knock came at the door.

It was Conal. "Mistress Cicely, I hate to disturb you so late, but I must talk to John."

"Come in, Master Conal. John told me Avery met with an accident."

"He's well, Mistress." He looked past her to John. "Don't fear, John. He's fine." He looked up to the loft, where Wat was peering down. "Don't worry, lad," he called up to Wat.

"Wat," said their mother. "Go to sleep."

After refusing her offer of refreshment, Conal sat at the hearth fire with John. His mother silently withdrew.

"John, I mean it," said Conal, keeping his voice low. "Avery will be fine."

"But he's not fine right now, is he? Not really," John whispered.

Conal sat silently, dropping his head to study his hands, which he had clasped in his lap. Then he looked up at John, his expression unreadable. "John," he said at last. "Tell me how you knew to get me."

"I just knew."

"You weren't there when those men attacked Avery?"

"No."

"I didn't think so," he said. After a while, he spoke again. "I think you know you can trust me, John. Tell me how you knew."

"Sometimes I just know things. Something speaks to me."

"And this something spoke to you tonight."

"Yes," said John.

"What is this something."

John felt somehow horribly ashamed. "Birds speak to me," he whispered.

"Ah," said Conal. "That makes sense," he said, seemingly to himself.

"It makes no sense," said John bitterly.

"John," said Conal. His voice was gentle. "Thank the Children they speak to you. Otherwise Avery would be—"

"Dead? They were trying to kill him?" cried John, horrified.

"Damaged," said Conal firmly.

John looked at him in confusion.

"Did the birds tell you to come to me?" asked Conal.

"No, I just knew that was the best thing to do," said John, "when the birds told me Aves was in trouble."

"Thank you, John. You're right. That was the best thing you could have done. You have good instincts, wherever they come from."

"But is Aves really—"

"Yes. It's a bad situation, and there may be bad consequences, but your brother will be fine."

"Will be," said John.

"He will. Trust that. You and I and his other friends will make sure of that. The way you can help him most is by not asking him a lot of questions or talking with others about what happened."

"But I'll have to tell Dru and Rafe. They're already worried. When Avery didn't meet us this afternoon, as he planned, we started worrying. And you know how Dru is."

A shadow of a smile crossed Conal's face. "Yes, I do," he said. "My advice? Let Avery tell those two. And whatever Avery chooses to tell them, or not to tell them, you back him up."

"I'll do it, Master Conal."

"You're a good brother, John. The brother Avery deserves."

"I love Avery," said John.

"So do I."

John looked over at him in wonder.

"All of us do. Everyone who really knows Avery can't help loving him, isn't that so?"

"Audemar doesn't love him." John thought a second after he'd said it that he probably shouldn't have.

But Conal's expression turned so vicious, so full of fury, that John stopped talking in amazement.

"No. He doesn't," Conal bit out. He visibly got a grip on himself. "Listen, John. This is going to be all over the fort. Keep what you know to yourself. It's important. What happened to Avery was bad enough. But then—"

John saw with alarm that Conal was struggling to go on. "You must have seen. I wounded one of the villains."

John nodded.

"I would have liked to kill them both, down there by the river," he said savagely. He looked at John. "Why do you think I didn't."

"They must be taken to the king and put to the question, to find out why they did it and who put them up to it."

"Yes," said Conal, "but instead, Prince Audemar was there when we got his brother to the fort. He told the Watch to bring the two men to him, the malefactors. When they came before him, he made as if to question them. Then, as if in a rage, he lunged at them with his sword and killed both of them on the spot."

"He killed them? But why—" John began.

"Why, indeed, John. Why indeed," murmured Conal. Then he got to his feet. "This is too big a burden for you to bear, John. I'm telling you because tomorrow you'll hear it, all of it, and all the gossip and twisted crazy stories along with it. So I wanted you to know from me first. Try your best not to speak of it to anyone."

"I'll have to speak of it to Dru and Rafe," said John again.

"All in this together. That's the way of it."

"Yes."

"Well, John." Conal rose to go, clapping John on the shoulder. "As I said. Try to follow Avery's lead on what to tell, and how much. Will you tell anyone else about the birds?"

John colored up. "I don't think so," he mumbled. "They wouldn't understand."

"Few do," said Conal.

"But you do."

"Not too well. I knew a man once. . ." He trailed off. "Better if you don't speak of it to anyone. Some might call it—"

"Witchcraft," whispered John.

"Yes, some ignorant fools might. So promise me, John."

"I promise," said John.

"Thank the Child for you, John." Then Conal was out the door.

Bad enough being a bastard, thought John. *But a witch too?* He poked furiously at the turves of the fire. Then, more carefully, he banked them for the night. He thought, *Witchcraft or not, it saved my brother. So I don't care what it is.*

It was a bad winter, long, snowy, and cold. John and the others worried about Avery. He was so silent and withdrawn. Out in the woods during their falconry sessions, he'd sit alone on a log, pulling his cloak about him. If John saw first, he'd come over to the log and sit down close beside him, not saying anything. Just being with him. Then Dru might see, and after a little while he'd be close on Avery's other side. Pretty soon Rafe would wander over and be there too. And always, somewhere nearby, stood Conal.

As the Spheres made their turn into spring, a change came over Avery. From withdrawn, he became vigorously active.

He'd never be the almost-scholar Dru was, but he threw himself into his studies. John was amazed by them both. John himself did his duty by his studies. Sometimes the things they all were asked to read actually spoke to him. Sometimes deeply. But not the way they spoke to his two friends. Rafe was more of his own mind, but then, Rafe—though a bit younger— was far ahead of all of them in his skills. Reading, even the language of the Old Ones. Writing easily and clearly with his quill. Figuring.

"My guardian has Master Caedon teach me, and he taught Master Caedon himself," said Rafe. "If I neglect my studies, Master Caedon punishes me." He was matter-of-fact about it.

"Punishes you how?" demanded Dru.

"Whips me. Usually, anyway. Sometimes other things." Rafe shrugged. "But now I get to study with you lot because Master Caedon is too busy to bother with me."

"I don't like that man," muttered John, later, to Dru. John recalled with a shudder Caedon's strange penetrating yellow gaze.

"Me neither," said Dru.

Like Dru, Avery was dedicated to the skill of the book. But he threw himself fanatically into the combat skills Conal showed them. In a matter of a fortnight or so, he turned himself from one of the best of Conal's group of young warriors to easily the best. To far and away the best.

John wondered whether Avery's new dedication had anything to do with his vigil. In the spring, the friends all knew, Avery would go to the mountain to sit his vigil and come down the mountain again to swear fealty to his father and brothers.

"You're Ranulf's vassal too, Dru. Why don't you have to go through some big fealty-swearing ceremony?" John asked him.

"Oh, I do. I did. It's part of the ceremony of accolade. The duty of a knight. It's just not such an important sacred thing as Aves's vigil."

John thought back to the ceremony of accolade where six or seven young boys of the nobility, boys turning into men, knelt before the king and were knighted. Not John, of course. He watched from the sidelines. He hadn't paid much attention to the words they were all saying, just drank in the pageantry.

As they talked about it together in the practice courtyard, Conal strode through the group, forming them up for the morning's exercises. "Take these exercises seriously, all you varlets," Conal called out. "Soon the king will go out on campaign, and then you won't be my pupils any longer. We'll all be soldiers together, lads."

"All in it together," Avery whispered to the friends. "All of us. Conal too." John was glad. Avery was back to his old self. Whatever bad thing had happened to him that night at the bridge, he'd moved past it.

It was strange, how Avery put it. Including Conal in *us*. Conal was their teacher. Set apart. Then John reflected on the bad time Avery had experienced. All of them were there to help him through it. But, he thought, Conal too. Conal most of all. He could see Avery had formed a bond with Conal over it. *And I formed a bond with Conal, also,* John thought. *Not just in that matter, either. About the falcon. About other things. Conal helps me whenever he sees I might need it.*

John worked hard on his skills with Conal as his guide. He was by no means Conal's best student. Not as good as Avery or Dru. Maybe on a par with Rafe, but he guessed that as Rafe gained height and muscle mass, he'd easily surpass John.

"Don't worry about it, Johnny," Conal told him after one especially difficult session when he saw how frustrated John was. "You can hold your own. And you have other skills."

"You mean that witchy thing I did?" said John with a shudder.

Conal gave him an affectionate cuff. "I mean you're smart, Johnny, and you have a good heart. When we go to the wars together, and I'm no longer your teacher but your companion in arms, I'll be glad I have you at my back."

Conal had a kind of genius, John thought. He knew just what type of encouragement brought out the best in each one of his students. He used that encouragement as skillfully as he wielded his sword, and at just the right time.

John saw Conal drove Avery unstintingly. Mercilessly. He gave him no quarter when they sparred. Fought him as viciously as he'd fight the most vicious enemy.

At first John worried about that. Dru saw he did. During a break in a particularly hard-fought practice fight between Avery and Conal, Dru pulled him aside. "Look at Aves, Johnny. He needs this."

John looked over at his brother, breathing hard, leaning over to catch his breath after the severe drubbing Conal had just given him. He looked enraged. But then John saw something else. Underneath the rage, an exhilaration.

"Come on, princeling," Conal taunted him. "Give as good as you got."

In a fury, Avery was on him, dealing flurries of blows, blindingly fast. He was pressing Conal back to the corner of the courtyard. With a swift backhanded sweep of his broadsword, he caught Conal off-guard, a rare moment, and Conal went down.

Conal threw his sword aside and held up his hands. He grinned up at Avery. "I yield, Aves, you madman."

Avery put out a hand and pulled Conal to his feet and embraced him.

"Good fight, Aves," said Conal. He drew the others around them and began analyzing the fight, blow by blow. "And then," he said, "Notice how Avery worked around to my blind spot and took perfect advantage of my lapse of attention. If his sword had been unbated, not blunted, lads, I'd be a dead man. As it is, I'm going to be carrying around some painful bruises for a while. All of you," he said, looking around at the circle of them pressing around him. "Think about what Avery just did to me, and avoid getting yourself into a fix like that, in a fight man to man, or especially a battle, where a lot is going on and your attention can easily get distracted."

In the silence that followed, one boy muttered, a bit too loud, "He's the prince. Probably let him win."

For an instant, John thought Conal would pretend he hadn't heard.

Instead, he turned slowly around and fixed that boy with his eye. The boy blushed and dropped his own eyes to his shoes.

Conal said, in a mild voice, "No. You may be sure I did not." He stared intently at them all. "This may be practice, lads, but it's not a game. I'm preparing you for war, and I'm preparing myself. Every moment. Think about what just happened to me, lads. I'm skilled. But I'm a person, not one of the gods or a hero of old. I have attention lapses. We all do. That can get us killed." He looked meaningly around the circle, at each one of them. "That can get you killed," he repeated. "And your own lapse can get the man beside you killed. We need to think about that, all of us. All the time. Take a break, you lot." He walked away and disappeared into his rooms at the end of the courtyard. Nobody said anything. Nobody looked at the boy who had spoken when he should better have stayed silent.

Dru and John moved to Avery to congratulate him.

"Pay no attention to that little prat," said Dru to him.

The little prat sidled up to Avery. "Sorry, Aves," he said, shamefaced.

"Better apologize to Master Conal, not to me," said Avery.

"I'm going to," the boy said, looking miserable.

John and his friends saw how miserable, so they all pounded him on the back and threatened him with a dire outcome the next time they were matched up, and the boy made inventive, anatomically unlikely threats back, so in the end, they were all laughing, and it was fine. Later on, John looked over to see Conal giving the boy some special pointers about his grip and clapping him on the shoulder when he did well.

But John also saw Avery needed no reassurances about the outcome of his fight with Conal. He'd won through strength, skill, and cunning, and John saw he knew it.

Other things the friends learned that winter weren't as straightforward as swordplay. Girls, for example. *Still*, thought John, *like combat skill or learning our letters, some of us catch on sooner and easier than others.*

Some, like Avery, not at all. "Girls," he said, looking around vaguely. They were huddled about the big hearth in the main hall of the fort, trying to stay warm. A snowstorm had blown up out of nowhere, and there was nothing the friends could do except maybe study their letters. Even Dru was sick of it and itching to get outside.

Across the hearth from them sat a group of girls around their own age, giggling and entertaining each other with cat in the cradle, comparing the embroidery on the edges of their cloaks, playing with each others' hair, and similar boring girl pastimes.

"Yes, girls. You know, Aves," said Dru. "The curvy people, the kind that smell good and feel good and—"

"Stop," said Rafe. "Nine Spheres, Dru. Are you trying to drive me mad?"

He might be a bit younger than the rest of us, thought John, looking over at Rafe, *but in some ways, he's older.*

"Oh," said Avery He shrugged dismissively. "My father will arrange for me to marry one of them. Someday. I suppose." He went back to running the polishing stones over the blade of his short sword laid across his lap.

"My father too," said Dru. "I wonder which one."

"Maybe no one at court," said John, looking up with a grin from tuning his rebec. "Maybe a lass from your own part of the realm. Big hips. A heifer of a woman."

Dru kicked him.

"Ow," said John.

"Don't insult the women of my lands, varlet. I like a big woman."

Dru resumed gazing at the girls across the hearth. "Look at that one. Lord Piers's oldest daughter. She's a bit too tall for my tastes. Almost as tall as I am. Taller, maybe. Big—that's fine. Taller than I am? Not sure about that. And as for that one." He looked at the girl to the left of the first. "Isn't she a bit drab?"

"Why should that matter a whit?" said Rafe. "I can love both fair and brown," he said.

"Then that little blonde one. The giggly one. Lord Piers's tall daughter looks pretty serious. Looks like she keeps to herself. But that one—" Dru was continuing to look yearningly across the hearth.

"Pfft," said Rafe. "I can love girls who love loneness best, and a girl like that one," he said, indicating the giggly one, "a girl who masks and plays." He looked at the whole row of them, his eyes bright and hungry.

"Stop it, Rafe. They know you're talking about them," murmured John.

"They're all looking back at you, man," said Dru, a little smile playing about his lips.

Rafe kept looking. "I can love her. And her," he said, indicating them with his eyes. "And you," he whispered, moving his gaze to another one. "And you."

John hid a grin.

"I can love any," Rafe told them, fingering the little amulet he always wore on a thong about his neck, "so she be not true."

"You crazy lad," said Dru. "You want them unfaithful?"

Rafe shrugged. "Oh," he said with a laugh. "We men are not faithful. Why should they be?"

Dru laughed. John tried to laugh too, but then he thought of the life his mother led, and he couldn't laugh.

Instead, he started picking out a tune on his rebec, and then he took up his bow, and then he was softly singing. *She moved through the fair*, he sang.

And fondly I watched her
move here and move there.
And then she turned homeward
with one star awake
as the swans in the evening
move over the lake.

"Dark Ones take you, Johnny. Now you're the one they're all looking at," said Rafe.

"Musicians. Like setting out a dish of honey and watching the flies buzz over to it," said Dru with such a look of gloom John had to laugh, although he had blushed red.

Those girls, he thought. *I'll never be allowed to have anything to do with those girls, daughters of nobles.*

"Maybe I'll learn to play and sing. Turn myself into a dish of honey too," said Rafe, a speculative look descending on him.

"You don't need that, Rafe. You're your own walking talking honey-trap." Dru sounded even more gloomy.

"Tush, man. I like women, and they know I like them. That's all."

Dru said, "No. That's not all."

They were all laughing at Dru now, even Avery.

"You don't believe me. I shall demonstrate in the manner of the Old Ones examining some interesting natural effect. Rafe," Dru said. "Walk from here to the door out into the bailey."

Rafe looked at him in confusion.

"Do it, Rafe. Don't look at them, don't look back at us, just walk over there."

"Do it, Rafe," Avery urged. "I want to see this interesting natural effect too."

"Do it," said John, amused now.

Rafe rolled his eyes. "Very well." He got to his feet.

"Remember," said Dru. "No looking at them. No looking at us, just walk. Now."

Rafe brushed himself off and headed to the big doors.

"Now watch those girls," murmured Dru to John and Avery.

They watched.

As if their eyes were on strings somehow tied to Rafe, the girls swiveled their gaze away from the three at the hearth to track Rafe all the way to the doors.

Every step.

Dru summoned Rafe back. He returned to the snickers of his friends.

"QED," said Dru, spreading his arms wide.

John wasn't quite sure what that meant. Some expression of the Old Ones he was probably supposed to have learned during their studies.

But he caught the gist.

"That's amazing," said Avery to Rafe, looking at him with fascination. "You really do draw them like flies to honey."

Rafe shrugged and grinned.

John bent uncomfortably over his rebec again. *Yes,* he thought, *it's true. That's what you do, Rafe.* Each of the six or seven girls across the hearth had followed Rafe to the door with her eyes.

Except one.

Lord Piers's oldest daughter. The tall girl.

Her gaze was elsewhere.

It had been fixed in fascination upon John, and it hadn't wavered.

ODELYN

CHAPTER THIRTY-ONE

Girl Talk

Odelyn and her friend Ailys told the other girls goodbye and headed out into the cold.

Lyn put her hood up. They walked crunching through the snow from the inner to the outer bailey of the castle and through the fort's big gates. They hadn't ridden over to meet their friends. They'd walked to the fort rather than go to all the bother of getting the horses out. Now they headed back to Lyn's father's manor.

The air was crisp, almost crackling. Silver filigree outlined the branches of the trees, and where the sun shone on them, they sparkled as if in fairyland.

The day before, Ailys had ridden behind her father from their home upriver as he brought a piece of business needing Lord Piers's attention over to the manor. Some boring political thing, the girls told each other.

Ailys's father had braved the weather to go back home afterward, while Ailys stayed overnight to spend time with her best friend, Lord Piers's daughter Odelyn. The snow had stranded her there. But today it was nice enough to walk from the manor over to the fort.

"That was a pleasure, sitting around the fire back at the fort," said Ailys. "I haven't seen several of those girls for an age. Marguerite gave me a pattern for the embroidered band at the neck of her kirtle. She saw how much I admired it. I believe I'll try it."

"I'm hopeless at needlework. Cwen tries to teach me, but I always snarl the thread or somehow get it all in a muddle," said Lyn, trying and failing to remember, even after so short a time, what this embroidered band of Marguerite's looked like. She wasn't very interested in such matters.

"Did you see those lads, how they stared at us?" said Ailys as they picked their way around the icy patches of the lane.

"Yes," said Lyn shortly. "Cheeky lot, weren't they."

"One of them was the prince."

"The prince?" said Lyn blankly.

"Yes, the youngest one."

"But he's just a baby."

"Not him, silly. Not the heir. I mean the king's youngest son, Avery."

"Oh," said Lyn. "Which one was he?" She reached out to steady Ailys as her friend slipped on an icy rut made by a wagon wheel in the mud of the lane and nearly went down.

"Oof." Ailys brushed herself off. "The tawny-haired one on the end. Tall. The one just sitting there honing his sword, not paying us any mind."

"Oh, him," said Lyn.

"Honing his sword," said Ailys, bursting into a peal of bawdy laughter and nudging Lyn in the ribs.

Lyn looked over at her, a bit scandalized. "Should you be talking of him so disrespectfully? He's the prince."

"Silly Lyn," said Ailys. "He's a man like any other, isn't he?"

Lyn said nothing. She was thinking of the one with the beautiful voice, the one singing and playing his instrument. She didn't want Ailys to see how interested she was in this one. Ailys would tease her about him. "Who were the others? Do you know them?" she asked cautiously.

"Not exactly know them. Know who they are," said Ailys. "Surely you do, too."

"No," said Lyn.

"You should pay more attention," said Ailys. "We're not little girls any longer. My father is already looking out for a man for me to marry. Isn't yours?"

"I suppose he must be," said Lyn.

"After all, we are women now."

"Yes," said Lyn.

The whole matter unsettled her. She didn't want to be given as bride to some man she didn't know. She wanted to keep on with her studies. She knew very well no husband would let her continue them.

But maybe I can still find books to read, she thought, *even if I have to smuggle them into the house.*

She and Ailys had been friends since early childhood, but she felt a separation between them, now that they had entered womanhood. Ailys was all too eager to whet the skills of gossiper and intermeddler and power-wielder that she'd learned in girlhood. Lyn saw her friend would use such skills to succeed in the more complicated background roles that women played at court. Their mothers both excelled at these skills.

Lyn hadn't enjoyed such games—power plays, really—when she was a girl playing girl games with other girls, and she hated the idea of continuing such games forever into womanhood.

But she and Ailys did have something important in common, even now. Especially now that they had crossed the boundary into womanhood. Neither had brothers, Lyn because her mother hadn't given her father any sons, and Ailys because the plague had taken her two brothers a few years earlier.

So the whole of their fathers' hopes lay in arranging important marriages for their daughters.

With a sinking heart, Lyn realized that meant an older, established, wealthy husband.

Not one of the laughing beautiful lads they'd seen at the fort that afternoon. As long as she married well, her two younger sisters might be able to wed lads like those, she said to herself with a shade of resentment.

She thought of the four young men uneasily. The shy one with the dreamy expression and the beautiful voice. And the other two, who were extremely good-looking and self-assured.

Then the fourth one, Avery the prince.

He was different.

Handsome, too, but different in a way she couldn't describe. Would she or Ailys have a chance with someone like that? If either of them wanted to angle for his attention, maybe eventually his hand, it was better that he wasn't further up the royal hierarchy, closer to the throne.

The heir, Crown Prince Artur, was already married to his foreign bride, cementing some alliance important to the king. The other two sons of King Ranulf—Audemar the second son, and Avery, the youngest, least important of Ranulf's three sons, the one that afternoon at the fort—might get to wed someone of lesser importance, like Ailys. Or herself.

Especially now that the Crown Prince had a son of his own. When the king died, Crown Prince Artur would sit the throne. If something happened to him—plague, death in war, or any of the other misfortunes befalling the hapless creatures underneath the Spheres—the baby princeling would be named king.

The king's second son, Audemar, and this third son Avery would never be king. So maybe Prince Avery was available as a husband to one of the young women sitting around the fire at the fort. Why not herself? Why not Ailys?

Ailys snorted in derision when Lyn broached this thought. "We'd have not the ghost of a chance," she said. "Even though Prince Avery is the third son, and only fourth in the succession, you may be sure the king is looking to the alliances he might be able to strengthen through Avery's marriage. But he's a luscious lad for sure. Still," she said, considering. She shook her head. "He's too much like an overgrown boy for my taste."

"You'd prefer Audemar," said Lyn slyly.

"Ugh," they both said in unison.

"That pig. No," said Ailys. "Never."

"Not even if your father made you?"

"I suppose I'd have to, in that case, but it's so unlikely. You needn't worry about me on that score. I don't lie awake at night fearing it."

"Some unlucky princess will get him for a husband," said Lyn, giggling.

"The poor thing." Ailys giggled too.

"I suppose he's a stalwart proper man, though. Every time I get a glimpse of him, he's riding through the fort's gate with some poor dead animal strapped to his saddle."

"Ha," said Ailys. "It's all for show."

"What do you mean?"

"He just likes the boasting and the feasting. He can't hunt."

"What about all those dead stags and whatnot?" said Lyn.

"The way I heard it—" Ailys dropped her voice. "Bowmen hide in the woods. When the prince chases an animal into a thicket, they shoot it. Then, when Audemar's squires go into the underbrush after it, they know to pluck the arrows from the carcass and give it a couple of slashes with their swords before dragging it back out so the prince can gloat over his kill."

"Nine Spheres," Lyn breathed. "Do you think the stories are true? Do you think he really believes he kills those animals?"

"I doubt it," scoffed Ailys. "He likes the show."

"Do you think he thinks all those cronies of his believe it?"

"He doesn't care. That's my guess. As long as they don't dare act as if the reality is otherwise. Men like Audemar enjoy the show, and they enjoy watching while others force themselves to pretend to believe it."

"It's treason we're speaking," said Lyn with a shiver.

Ailys laughed at her.

Lyn had a sudden thought. "Poor Master Electus," she said.

"What? Oh, him," said Ailys. "Yes. The poor man. He's a true musician, but he's made to write and sing all those songs in Audemar's praise. The king, the crown prince, no doubt he enjoys making music for them. But to have to sing for Audemar, that pig, no. I wouldn't like to have the music master's job."

By now they were heading through the gates into the manor, and Cwenegund, Lyn's lady's maid, was anxiously waiting for them at the door.

As they entered, she fussed around them and made them come to the hearth in Lyn's rooms and change their shoes. She took their cloaks and shook the snow off them. She disappeared and then reappeared with hot possets for them to drink.

They settled down together at the hearth. Over their possets, Ailys dropped her voice confidentially. "They say Prince Avery is nothing like Audemar. Everyone says he is a matchless warrior. Lyn. Pay attention. You know which one I mean," she prompted. "The lad we saw, the one with the sword."

"He's been to war?" said Lyn doubtfully. He hardly looked old enough.

"No, but that's what they say, those who've seen him fight in the practice court. And next year, they'll all go over to the Western Isle on the king's latest campaign."

"He's probably one of those men who loves his sword, his horse, and his hound, in that order," said Lyn.

"Don't forget his hawk. His wife will come in a distant fifth," Ailys agreed, and the two of them went off into fresh gales of giggles.

Anyway, thought Lyn, *handsome or not, I don't want him.*

Cwenegund, coming in to collect their cups, shook her head at them. "Very unseemly behavior, your ladyships," she said, her lips pursed. "Unseemly to speak of our prince in that fashion."

Lyn grinned at her. "You know we're right, Cwen," she said.

Cwenegund suppressed a smile and went back to her task of supervising the cook.

"So," said Lyn, as Cwenegund left. She turned back to Ailys and tried to sound off-hand. "Who were those others. Those lads," she prompted. "Since you know so much about it."

"Oh, you want to know that, do you?" teased Ailys.

"Don't tease. Tell me," said Lyn.

"Hmm, let me see. Who were they?" Ailys pretended to think.

Lyn swatted at her with a cushion.

Ailys laughed. "Very well. The one beside Avery? Dark? Good-looking and not as tall?"

Lyn nodded.

"That one. That's the young Sir Drustan. He'll inherit an earldom, and he's filthy rich. That one's a catch. But everyone in his line marries a neighbor from the desolate coast of his ancestral lands. His father will see to that. The rest of us have no chance at him, more's the pity."

"What about the other two?" said Lyn.

"Nobodies. The young prince's hangers-on. The really handsome one, shorter but Nine Spheres, girl." Ailys pretended to swoon. "His name is Rafe. Actually, he's not Avery's courtier. He's Audemar's."

Lyn made a face.

"Right," said Ailys with a sigh. "It's too bad."

Their thoughts turned once more to Ranulf's second-born. "What an ill fate, having to marry that one," said Ailys, again. "He's closer in the succession than Avery, though," she elaborated. "Close enough that I doubt the two of us will have to steel ourselves to such a fate. But Rafe, his little minion. What a tasty morsel for some lucky girl!"

"Ailys!" laughed Lyn. "How you do talk."

"They say he's gently born, but who knows. He was brought over from the Baronies to serve Audemar, along with that other one. Caedon."

"Master Caedon. I do know who he is. He's kind of frightening, don't you think? The way he stares."

"As if he's a butcher sizing up a haunch of meat. No," said Ailys after a moment. "That's not it either. Not sizing you up as if you are a sugared almond he'd like to pop into his mouth. Sizing you up like—" She stopped, at a rare loss for words. "Like a miser counting up his horde. But kind of intriguing too, wouldn't you say?"

Lyn shuddered. "No," she said. "His eyes," she said.

Ailys nodded. "Like a wolf's."

"What about the other one," Lyn added after a moment.

"What other one? There are just the two, Caedon and Rafe."

"The tallest one. The one who was singing."

"I see. We're back to the lads at the hearth, are we?" Ailys thought about it for a moment. "Oh," she said. "That was John, the king's bastard. The prince's half-brother."

"I think I've heard of him," said Lyn, trying to sound offhand. She felt a pang. She told herself how silly she was.

"A likely-looking lad for sure," said Ailys. "No one anyone would ever marry. Some nobody. Worse than nobody, because he has the royal connections without any of the royal privileges. But if I got him alone in the hayloft. . ." She winked at Lyn.

Lyn pretended to be scandalized. She pretended to giggle.

But actually.

Actually she didn't know how to name the feeling that swept through her.

CHAPTER THIRTY-TWO

Bride Talk

Not long after Lyn's conversation with Ailys about the four young men they'd seen at the fort's big hearth, she was winding down the spiral stone staircase in her own house, yawning and rubbing the sleep from her eyes, heading to break her fast in the manor's hall, when voices filtering up to her made her stop and crouch down on the step to listen.

It was her favorite spot for finding things out, especially things her parents would never talk about while she was in the room. She waited just out of the line of sight of the people talking. Her mother and father. Talking about her.

Her next-oldest sister Merewina, coming just behind, nearly tripped over her.

"What are you doing, Lyn? Almost broke my neck," Winnie fumed.

Lyn held up a warning hand. She peered around the curve of the stairs and down into the hall. Her parents hadn't heard. They didn't look up. The clatter of the servants bringing mugs of ale and platters of bread had masked her sister's exclamation.

"Shh," said Lyn. "They're talking about me."

Winnie crouched beside Lyn to listen, too.

"Hmm. If I had to name someone, there's Sir Rowson," their mother was saying.

"I don't like that man much." The rumble of Lord Piers's voice came filtering up to the girls where they crouched.

"Everyone says he's an up and coming man," said their mother. "Very connected to Audemar, they say. And he's pretty young."

"Audemar," said Lord Piers, his voice filled with contempt.

"What about Earl Brenci?"

"A widower," said Lord Piers, considering. "And rich. Influential. His Majesty's best friend. But no." The two listening girls heard regret in his voice. "Everyone knows. After his wife's death, he took himself to that remote estate of his and he just sits up there brooding. I doubt we'd have much success, with that one. Besides, he's out of touch with court matters. No. I'm more partial to Beorhtric. Not as wealthy, but fertile bottomlands downriver. And connected to all the doings at court. That's the kind of man we need to think about, wife."

"He's so much older than Odelyn," said their mother, sighing.

"That doesn't matter. I'll tell you what, wife. The person I like best of all for Lyn is even older than that. His interests and mine are close and growing closer."

"Earl Ricbert," their mother breathed.

"Exactly."

"Very much older than Lyn," she said. But then she said, breathlessly, "An earl."

"I'm quite a bit older than you, my wife. Did that stop our fathers from joining in a bargain that has benefitted us both?"

"You're right, husband," said their mother.

Lyn and her sister looked at each other, horrified.

"He's really old, Lyn," Winnie whispered.

Lyn nodded, feeling a bit sick.

The old earl had outlived two wives, and his only son was much older than Lyn. The sisters hushed and strained to hear more.

"You know he has those lands he inherited on his mother's side. I can get him to see the advantage of settling those on Lyn and her issue. The son won't lose by it, not much. He'll gain allies, and the earl is so rich the son will still have plenty of land of his own," said Lord Piers.

"Meanwhile, we join our interests with his against those who would influence Ranulf to. . ."

Here their voices dwindled away. They had moved from their places at board over to the hearth ring.

Lyn leaned back against the stones of the staircase, disconsolate.

Winnie took her hand and held it and stroked it.

"They'll marry me off to this old man," Lyn whispered to her sister, "and then you and Aisly can marry whomever you like."

The sisters knew that wasn't exactly true. Close enough, though.

Lyn's eyes filled with tears. She stood and made her way back up the stairs the way she had come. She didn't think she could face her parents right then. If they talked to her about this plan of theirs, their words would make it too real for her, and if they didn't—they probably wouldn't, because they still needed to arrange the whole thing—she'd have to sit there directing hateful thoughts at them but need to hold it all inside.

"What's wrong, my lady?" exclaimed Cwenegund as Lyn rushed into her room and threw herself across the bed.

"My parents are going to make me marry some awful old man," she said, muffled, into the furs.

"Well, now," said Cwenegund, sitting down on the bed herself and patting Lyn. "Ye be a woman grown, my lady, and ye knew this day would come."

"But why such an old man?"

"I don't know which ye mean, Lady Lyn. Maybe not so old. At your age, all proper men might seem old to you."

"No," Lyn insisted. "Old. Very, very old. Some ancient old earl."

"An earl. My, my. Your father has your best interests at heart, I'm sure of it, lady," said Cwenegund.

Lyn sat up slowly and wiped her eyes with her sleeve. "He has his own best interests at heart, you mean."

"Now, then, my lady. We must all trust our elders and betters."

"What if I went to the Temple and pledged myself to the Lady Goddess? Then they couldn't make me marry anyone," said Lyn. But Lyn saw Cwenegund recognized her words as cheap bravado. Lyn knew full well the priests of the Temple would turn her away, and Cwenegund knew it, too. The Temple's priests would never risk the anger of such an important man as her father.

"Think, my lady. Think of having little babies of your own. Think of a son, how wonderful that would be," said Cwenegund.

"Instead of boring daughters I'd someday have to find some horrid old codger for them to marry."

A gloom descended on Lyn then. She could hardly eat. She felt sick and weepy every day.

Night was different. Almost worse. At night, Lyn couldn't help it. Her mind strayed to those lads she and Ailys had seen. Especially to that one lad. John. John the Bastard. And then.

Then an unseemly thing happened to her. She couldn't help it. She started touching herself, underneath the furs. *This is wrong,* she told herself. *Surely this must be wrong. The Lady must be watching what I'm doing. She sees everything. She must be displeased.* The thought of John filled her with such a strange, intense longing that she couldn't keep herself from doing it, in spite of her troubled conscience. In the mornings, she woke up achy and disoriented.

Whenever her mother called her to her rooms, Lyn felt sure sentence was about to be pronounced on her. Whenever her father summoned her after board, she felt sure this was the moment she'd learn her fate.

As the fortnight dragged on into a turning of the moon, and then another, and the dire pronouncement wasn't made, and as the year turned into spring underneath the Spheres, Lyn began to feel more cheerful. If she thought about it hard, though, she'd have to admit to herself that she was experiencing a postponement only, not an actual reprieve. So she didn't think about it. As if that would make the whole thing go away.

"Silly Lyn," she told herself, when the day actually came.

She had a dread feeling in the pit of her stomach when Cwenegund bustled in to tell her that her parents wanted her to come to them down by the hearth stones.

It was mid-day. Her father was usually out visiting his vassals or present at court. Her mother was almost always at court, that time of day.

How could she have missed the unusual circumstance of both of them at once, in the middle of the day, in the house, their heads together, talking something over.

Now she had a terrible suspicion what that something was.

Her parents turned almost in unison at her approach.

"Here, daughter," said her mother, patting one of the big stones beside her. "Sit here with us."

Lyn sat down beside her mother, her hands in her lap. She was gripping them to stop their trembling.

"Daughter," said Lord Piers. "You're a woman now, so I have thought much, of late, on your marriage prospects."

Lyn nodded miserably.

"Speak up, girl."

"Yes, Father," she almost whispered.

"I have chosen a worthy man for you. Most worthy. Tonight at board you will meet him."

"Who is this worthy man, Father?" asked Lyn.

Her parents exchanged glances.

"It's the Earl Ricbert," said Lord Piers. "His lands are vast. He'll take proper care of you, my daughter."

Before she could stop herself, Lyn burst out, "But he's so old!"

"Tush, child," said her mother. "That matters not a whit. For women, yes. Not for men. He'll get strong sons upon you, daughter."

Lord Piers had stood up. He towered over the two women. "None of that," he said to Lyn. "I'll not have my judgment questioned. Marriage is a serious matter that your elders and betters will decide for you. It's no matter for a child. I'll not hear another word."

"Father, please don't—"

"Silence, Odelyn. I've made myself clear. Your mother will help you get ready for tonight. In a fortnight, you'll be betrothed, and wed within this turning of the moon."

"So soon! But Father—"

An angry red crept up Lord Piers's pale cheeks.

Lyn's mother put out a warning hand to her. "It's settled, daughter," she said. "Go to Cwen. I'll be with you both shortly, and we'll decide what you're to wear to meet your husband."

Lyn ran weeping to the stairs and pelted up them.

But at the turning, she got a forcible grip on herself. She crouched down at her listening spot, to hear what they would say. Maybe there was a chance to change her father's mind. She was his favorite child, she knew.

"This is what comes, husband, of allowing that girl to learn her letters," her mother was saying waspishly. "Now you see."

"Silence, woman," Lord Piers roared out.

Even from the safety of her listening spot hidden from his view, Lyn cringed back.

"I'll have no more women questioning me this day on matters that don't concern them."

"It's true, though," her mother persisted. "You are in the wrong, Piers. You should never have allowed it."

"You forget, wife, that you yourself told me women learning their letters was all the rage, at court."

"Yes, and then once our queen died, it faded out of fashion. I told you then—"

"Silence!"

Lyn heard the distinct sound of a slap, and then a gasp. Then her mother's quick feet, coming for the staircase. Lyn fled up them to her room.

"What now?" said Cwenegund, rolling her eyes, when Lyn came sobbing in and threw herself on the bed.

But she said nothing more, because Lyn's mother was in the room right behind her daughter.

"Compose yourself, daughter," said her mother, her voice tight and furious.

Lyn hoisted herself from the furs. "Mother!" she pled, holding out her arms.

"Enough nonsense, Odelyn. You're a woman grown. Act like one." She turned from her daughter to Cwenegund. "Make sure my daughter is bathed and her hair brushed. Make sure my daughter's best kirtle is presentable. Use those brooches with the gems in the spiral pattern, the ones brought from the Great City, and—let me see. The golden armlets. We're expecting important guests at board in only a few candle measures' time."

"Yes, my lady," said Cwenegund, bobbing a curtsey.

To Lyn, her mother said, "I forbid you to cry. It will spoil your complexion and make your eyes red. Stop this instant."

"Yes, Mother," said Lyn dully.

"Lyn. You must comport yourself the way your father and I expect. The well-being of the family rests on the issue you will produce. Your sisters' well-being rides on this."

"Yes, Mother."

The woman swept out of the room then. Lyn and Cwenegund carefully did not remark on the distinct red hand print Lyn's mother bore across her left cheek.

She stuck her head back into the room before they could say anything. "Cwen."

"Yes, your ladyship?"

"You're a healer. I'll need a poultice when you're finished with my daughter, something to draw the redness out." She pointed to her face.

"Yes, your ladyship," said Cwenegund.

In spite of Cwenegund's protests and urgings, Lyn delayed and lagged as the time for supper approached.

"Lady Lyn, the guests are all down there at board. It looks right discourteous, you lurking up here and not going down to greet them. Your sisters are at board already."

"Suppose I refuse to go down," whispered Lyn. "Then that old man will see what a disobedient wife I'll make, and he'll call the whole thing off."

Cwenegund looked genuinely frightened.

Lyn sighed. She knew she had to go down there. *Lady knows what my father will do to me if I don't. If I shame him in front of this man*, thought Lyn in desperation.

"There now," said Cwenegund, relieved, fussing over Lyn's kirtle and the brooches one last time. "You look beautiful, my lady."

"What does it matter how I look," Lyn muttered savagely and pushed Cwenegund's hands away. She strode to the door, took a ragged breath, and went down the staircase.

"Here's my daughter now, Your Lordship," said her father.

Lyn came down to a sea of faces looking up at her. Her parents. Her sisters. A retinue of strangers her husband-to-be must have brought along with him.

And the man himself.

As Lyn drew level with him, she dropped him a deep curtsey. This man, the Earl Ricbert, guided her to her feet, mumbling pleasantries. She towered over him.

He was shorter than she was, but probably not by that much, she realized. Age had bent him almost in two. He only seemed markedly shorter.

He tilted his head up to her father. "Tall," he croaked.

Her father smiled a bland, faultless smile and led the way to board.

The man was richly dressed. Lyn was seated beside him, and he took her hand up in his claw-like hand and held it through the entire meal, unless he had to drop it to spoon meat into his dribbling mouth. One of his retinue stood just behind and beside him, cutting the meat into small bits for his master.

Lyn said little. She wasn't expected to say much, if anything, thank the Lady.

The earl and her father engaged in a running conversation about the state of the realm.

At least he's not senile, she thought to herself. He seemed to have a good grasp of matters at court. At least there was that.

Among the other guests were the earl's son, considerably older than she was, and the son's wife. The son addressed her politely, although he stared at her in a way that made her a little uneasy. The wife sent covertly hostile glances Lyn's way throughout the entire meal. The woman confused Lyn. Was she angry that any child of Lyn's might cut into her own children's inheritance? Angry about how her husband was looking at Lyn? Lyn didn't know.

She stared down at her trencher, trying not to catch anyone's eye.

Her mother was silent, too. Lyn noticed how artfully Cwenegund and her mother's lady's maid, between them, had arranged her mother's veil and hair to conceal the darkening bruise across her cheekbone.

Lyn saw it, though. She wondered if the others did, too.

Her sisters Winnie and Aisly were silent as well, watching everything with huge eyes. They both must have heard a lot of the shouting and weeping, earlier.

At last the meal, which had seemed endless, was over. Everyone stood around the hearth talking while the servants cleared the board away.

"My lady Odelyn," said her husband-to-be. "I yearn for the day when the two of us will be wed."

Lyn murmured something politely back. She thought with horror of the night-time feelings that visited her. She thought with horror about belonging to this old man, all those feelings she had locked inside her belonging to him.

"What say you, my lord Ricbert? The betrothal a fortnight from now?" said Lord Piers.

"Fine," he croaked. "Fine."

"And then I hope you and your family will stay here with us," Lord Piers continued.

Earl Ricbert and his family planned to ride on to court that night and stay there as guests of the king before returning to the earl's estate to the northeast.

The earl presented Lyn with a fine bolt of silk and some gems, and then he and his retinue left with many protestations of friendship. Lord Piers and his family stood at the doors to the manor to wave farewell.

The earl's son and his wife mounted horses whose bloodlines were as noble as theirs. Nobler, maybe. Servants helped the earl himself hobble out to a closed cart and several of them heaved him inside.

As soon as she could, Lyn slipped away to her bed. She lay staring into the dark all night, tears behind her now. She thought about John. *What a child I am*, she scolded herself. *What an addlepate. He doesn't even know I'm alive. And if he did? And if he yearned for me as much as I yearn for him? There's nothing the two of us could do about it.*

She had a fantasy of slipping from her bed and running off to find him. She had a fantasy of confessing all her pent-up feelings, and then a fantasy that he had the same feelings for her.

What a fopdoodle, she thought of herself.

I belong instead to some old man, she thought.

A fortnight, she thought.

CHAPTER THIRTY-THREE

Grave Talk

By that time, whenever Lyn descended the stairs from her bedroom to the great hall of the manor and heard the murmurs of her parents, she knew to halt halfway down and listen.

But also, she grew accustomed to a painful twisting in her stomach whenever she did.

The conversations were all about the betrothal ceremony in the Lady's High Temple, the new clothes that would be needed, the gifts, the dowry, the influence, the lands. The many factions at court, and which nobles were allied with which factions. Above all else, how, through this marriage, Lord Piers would now have an easy entrée into one of the most powerful of these factions.

But on a morning only three days before the betrothal ceremony, as Lyn crouched to listen, she heard something that startled her so utterly that for a moment she didn't know how to feel.

Then she did. A hint, just a hint, of hope.

"I'm sure it's nothing, wife, but a man his age can't be too careful," her father was saying.

Then her mother. "Really. Postpone the betrothal over such a trivial matter? A running nose, a slight cough? Suppose the man has had second thoughts. Suppose—"

"Nay, wife. Nothing of the kind. The man is just indisposed. We'll have to wait a sen'night, that's all. I'll talk to the priests of the Temple today."

A postponement, thought Lyn. And then, *Suppose Mother is right? Suppose that old earl is having second thoughts.*

Hope and joy fought inside her for dominance. Joy, because she didn't have to face the dreaded moment, not yet, anyhow. And hope that maybe she wouldn't have to at all.

She didn't have to wait long to tell which it would be.

The next morning, as she crouched in her listening spot, she heard her mother lamenting and berating.

"—and now look," she was saying. "The man is dead. That's what comes of picking some doddering old codger instead of a hale man like Sir Rowson."

Then her father's inarticulate roar of rage.

Lyn didn't wait to hear the details. She skipped back to her bedroom with a look so glad that Cwenegund stopped her endless folding of laundry to stare.

"He's dead! The earl is dead!" Lyn exclaimed, twirling about the room. Unbidden, the thought came into her mind, *John*. She made herself stop. What did her feelings for John have to do with anything? They weren't even real feelings. Just some girlish foolish fantasy. Still, she couldn't stop smiling.

"For shame, Lady Lyn. Rejoicing in another's misfortune like that."

"I know, Cwen, but his misfortune is my fortunate escape," said Lyn, sitting cross-legged in her furs and grinning at Cwenegund. "You think so, too, Cwen. Admit it."

She laughed as a grudging smile spread across Cwenegund's face.

"Ye have the right of it, my lady. The man was far too old for you to wed. But my lady—"

She stopped, because Lyn's mother was staring crossly into the room.

"Daughter. I see you've heard. Your husband-to-be is dead. They say it was the sweat. Merry at breakfast, dead by supper. That's what they all say, about the sweat. Thank the Lady he didn't bring it here."

"Yes, Mother," said Lyn, trying to look demure. Try as she might, she could not make herself look sad.

"I suppose you think you have your way now, Mistress Willful," said Lyn's mother.

"Mother, I—"

"Don't lie to me, girl," her mother snapped. "No false tears, if you please. Just think of this. If he'd only lasted one more turning of the moon, your fortune would be made, my girl. We'd have had to give up the dowry, but in return, we'd have some of his lands, at least some of them." She paused, spots of red angry color coming into her cheeks. "And if the old man had managed to last another year or so, you'd likely have a babe and inherit a lot."

"Not if that first son of the earl's had anything to say about it, Mother," said Lyn reasonably. "And his wife. She hated me. Anyone could see that. They would have robbed me and the babe."

"Your father would have appealed to the king," her mother grated. "I don't want to hear another word from you. We must all begin again. And this time, your father had best listen to me." She flounced out of the room.

After a moment, Lyn said to Cwenegund, "I suppose they'll find another old codger for me to wed now. But at least I won't have to wed this one."

By then, she'd gotten herself into a more realistic frame of mind.

The fantasy-John would have to remain her own secret. It had nothing to do with her actual life.

But I can enjoy my fantasy, she told herself. *Who's to know about it? It will be my own private refuge. I can visit it whenever I like, with no one the wiser. I can pretend it's the real John, with no one to laugh at me.*

The thought of the Lady's disapproving eye, that thought she resolutely thrust away from herself. She did the same with the other equally unwelcome thought. That she didn't even know the real John, and might not like him if she did.

I would like him, though, she told herself stubbornly. *I can tell. I would.*

Meanwhile, actual life carried on. As an almost-widow, Lyn had to walk in the earl's funeral procession several days after his death, as it wound through Tambourne and into the High Temple of the Lady Goddess.

At least I'm no real widow, she thought with relief. *Then I would have had to be at the front of the procession, and I would have had to pretend to cry.*

From the back of the crowd, she watched as the desiccated old earl was popped into the tomb of his forefathers. She waited with her parents to speak words of sympathy to the earl's son and daughter-in-law.

When it came her turn, she pressed the son's hand warmly, and then turned to the man's wife.

"I'm so sorry," Lyn said.

The woman sneered. "I'll wager you are sorry, you doxy," she hissed in Lyn's ear. "I'll just wager you are."

Lyn drew back in amazement as the woman smiled in triumph.

Lyn had to bite back an answering smile. She wanted to murmur, "No, I'm glad the old mumblecrust is food for worms." Instead, she just curtseyed and moved on.

As she did, though, she intercepted a stare of such naked lust from the son that she nearly yelped.

Turning hastily away, she heard his wife mutter, "Careful, mannikin, else I snip you shorter than you already are."

Then she did have to hustle out of the Temple to stifle her whoops of laughter.

Her mother rounded the corner and glared at her. "Have a care, Mistress Merriment, that your father doesn't hear."

That sobered Lyn up. "Yes, Mother," she said meekly.

She caught her friend Ailys gazing at her in wonder. "Hello, Ailys," she said with a smile. Ailys had been in the crowd of spectators.

"Don't tell me you're happy about this," said Ailys, catching up to her and murmuring in her ear. "Your fortunes were made, with that one. Chances are, he'd never have been able to do the deed with you, and then he would have died a few years from now and left you a rich woman."

Lyn looked sidelong at her friend.

She glanced around to make sure her parents weren't near enough to hear their conversation. She was in enough trouble with them as it was, although Lady knows the man had dropped dead of his own accord. She had nothing to do with it, beyond rejoicing when it happened.

"That wouldn't have been the way of it at all," she reminded Ailys. "I would only have been left rich if I had produced an heir, and that, you know, would have depended on him being able to do the deed, as you put it," she said.

"Lyn. You are the most naïve person I know," said Ailys.

Lyn looked at her uncomprehending.

"There are ways, you know, Lyn," said Ailys.

"Ways?"

"Certainly."

"What would you have done?" said Lyn, put out by the smug look on her friend's face.

"Taken a lover. Had a child by him."

"You're forgetting, Ailys. Forgetting a couple of practical matters," said Lyn.

"What practical matters?" scoffed Ailys.

"For one thing, suppose this babe were a girl?"

"Keep trying until you get a boy."

"And if the poor earl died before I could do that?"

Ailys nodded thoughtfully. "Yes. You're right. That would have confounded the plan."

"Besides. Say I had a baby boy and the earl died. Do you think I could have kept his grown son from disinheriting my babe or somehow baffling the entire thing?"

"Huh," said Ailys. "Have you seen how the man looks at you? He'd have just waited until something unpleasant happened to his wife, and then he would have wed you himself."

"You mean he would have done away with her?" L:yn looked over at Ailys, incredulous. "You have quite a lurid imagination, Ailys."

Then her lips began to twitch into a grin. "Besides, I just heard his wife tell him he was naught but a mannikin, and she'd cut it shorter if he looked at me again."

Ailys stood astounded.

Suddenly the two of them were laughing so hard Ailys had to hustle Lyn away so nobody heard them.

"Lyn, just when I think you're a complete simpleton, you prove me wrong," she said when she could catch her breath.

"Hush up," said Lyn.

The two stood back in the shadow of a building as noisy conversation told them others were coming.

Around the corner came four young men, talking and laughing. Then they turned down another lane.

"It's those lads," Ailys breathed. "The prince and his friends."

One of them is John, thought Lyn, her heart beginning to pound.

The real John, not the fantasy one.

She stood on tiptoe to look after him, but the four lads disappeared at the bottom of the lane where it curved toward the forest, and were gone.

JOHN

CHAPTER THIRTY-FOUR

An Audience

They'd all gotten the word. *Make ready!* As soon as the spring storms were past, Ranulf would assemble his campaign for the conquest of the Western Isle. He had subdued a tiny part of the southeastern coast and had taken a port city. Now it was time to use that coastal strip as a base to mount a full-scale invasion into the interior.

Avery had gone through his vigil and had pledged his fealty to his father and brothers. Avery and Dru had long since been knighted, and Conal had pronounced John and Rafe efficient soldiers. They were ready. They'd all go over together, Conal included, under the leadership of one of the most battle-hardened of Ranulf's captains.

"Why not Conal?" muttered Avery to the others. "He's the best leader. Can't my father see that?"

Conal heard. He turned to them all with a smile. "I'm young yet. I'm the king's arms master, because I'm good at all the forms of fighting. Good in all the practice bouts and all the displays of arms." It wasn't boasting. It was just true. "And good at putting up with you lot." Conal grinned at them. "But I've only gone on one of His Majesty's campaigns," he continued. "Let the more experienced men lead us. I'll be proud to fight shoulder-to-shoulder with you lads."

When he said that, John looked over at him in wonder, and something he'd thought before came to him. *He's not much older than we are.*

They no longer all gathered in the practice courtyard for formal training, but Conal still worked with them there individually. A veteran who walked with a limp from an old battle wound would remain behind to train the young boys until Conal could come back and resume his regular duties. This man had already begun his work with the boys.

And still Wat is excluded, thought John, and his anger rose. But he stuffed these feelings down. There wasn't much he could do about Wat's situation, not officially. Unofficially, he trained Wat himself every afternoon, worrying it would not be enough. Sometimes Dru and Avery joined him.

Often Rafe did. Wat was a lot younger than Rafe, but Rafe was closer in age than the rest of them were to Wat. John could see the two of them were becoming close. He loved Rafe for it.

Rafe had his own problems. He didn't have to take on John's and Wat's.

"You don't understand," murmured Rafe. "I've always wanted brothers. Now I have them."

The comment baffled John. John knew, from some things Rafe had said, that Rafe did have brothers, over in the Baronies. Three of them. But he also knew that at a young age Rafe had been sent away from his family to be fostered in Gilles's household. Gilles de Rais, the most powerful noble in the Baronies.

Still, wasn't Caedon supposed to be a brother to Rafe, more or less? The thought gave John the shivers. What kind of brother would that be. He already knew that Caedon beat Rafe. They all knew it. One time Rafe disappeared for a fortnight, and when he returned, although he wouldn't talk about it, they found he'd been in the hands of a healer, repairing whatever it was Caedon had done to him.

Or maybe. John had heard hints of it. Maybe Rafe had been sent discreetly across the Narrows. Maybe Gilles had done it to him, whatever had caused him to need a healer. He remembered what Rafe had said once. *I answer to Gilles.* And the shiver that had taken John, when he heard Rafe say it.

John feared for Rafe. That was one fear he had, as they prepared to leave. He thought it was a good thing the war would get Rafe away from Caedon.

And John worried about Wat.

What will Wat do when we're all gone off to war? John thought. He made Wat promise to keep practicing.

Wat has friends, but his friends are those two girls, thought John. Eris, their bastard half-sister, born of a bondswoman his father had brought back with him from some exotic place, and Keelie, the daughter or maybe it was granddaughter of one of the servants who lived nearby. Those were Wat's closest friends. *He needs boys to tussle with, the way the three of us had each other*, John thought.

Wat laughed when John talked of these misgivings.

"Keelie, yes, she likes to hunt and fish with us, but she likes girl things too. Eris, though. She's as fierce as any boy. You should see her, Johnny. She and I will practice together."

John had nodded skeptically but he didn't voice his skepticism. No point in discouraging his brother.

Meanwhile, he and his friends were all practicing their skills, practicing them furiously. It was about to get real.

Yet today when John went to the practice courtyard, the others weren't there. Only Conal.

Conal took John aside. "John, the king has commanded we come to him for an audience. Dru and Avery have already gone. I stayed behind to wait for you. Come with me."

In the excitement and anxious flurry of emotions John felt at being summoned to his father, a man he rarely spoke to, he didn't realize something important until he and Conal were halfway to the main hall of the fort.

"Where's Rafe?" he said.

Conal shook his head. Now John realized Conal had been looking unusually subdued.

"Master Conal—" John began.

"Johnny. The king isn't allowing Rafe to come with us on campaign."

"What?" John stopped in the middle of the path to the fort's inner bailey. "What do you mean? Why?"

"It's Audemar. He asked the king not to send Rafe. Said he needed him."

"Need him?" John was dumbfounded. "Audie doesn't need Rafe. He never has before. Why now?" Over the past year and more, John had noticed Caedon paid little attention to Rafe. Caedon and Audemar used to set Rafe to constant small tasks. Hardly ever, now. It was as if Caedon, or maybe Gilles, had decided that Rafe should train with Conal and take lessons with the other lads, and had forgotten about him.

"Just between us, I don't think Audemar gives a rat's sard whether Rafe goes to war with us or not," said Conal.

"So why."

"I think it's Caedon. Master Caedon." Conal's voice dripped sarcasm. "Flexing his puny muscles. He doesn't like it that you and the lads are friends with Rafe. He handed Rafe over to us, and now he wants him back. That's my guess, anyway."

John stood considering. Rafe not to go. It was unthinkable. "But Rafe is good. He has gotten better than I am," he said. "He's a really good fighter."

"Yes," said Conal, kicking the ground morosely with his toe.

"Conal," said John suddenly, forgetting to call him Master Conal. A strange thought had occurred to him. "Avery is going. Why isn't Audemar?"

He didn't bother to ask about Artur, the crown prince. The king had his obscure reasons, but Artur had not trained as a warrior. He had trained as a scholar.

"Audemar would get his sorry ass killed, maybe?" said Conal. "However he begged off, I'm glad of it. I've seen him fight. It's a pathetic sight. I was even asked to work with him once, but he always seemed to find some excuse not to attend our sessions together. If Audemar showed up on a battlefield, he would just get the man on the right of him killed, and the man on the left of him killed. Probably himself. I'm glad no one will be put in that position." Conal heaved a sigh. "Although if he did get himself killed, the world would be a better place, and you didn't hear me say that."

John looked over at Conal. Ever since the night Avery was attacked, Conal had made no secret of his contempt for Audemar, even to the point of speaking treason. *And Conal is a prudent man*, thought John. He must, John realized, feel really strongly about it. But John's mind shied away when he thought what might have happened to Avery, that night, to make Conal feel so.

"Well, lad. We best hurry. You don't want to keep your father waiting."

Conal presented them both to the guards at the corridor leading to the king's private audience chamber, and the guards took the two of them in.

Conal and John stepped through the big doors together. Conal bowed deeply. John looked over at him and saw with a jolt that he should do likewise. He tried to mimic Conal.

Avery and Dru were already there.

The king sat in his ornate carved chair, raised on a dais at one end of the room.

"Approach," said Ranulf softly.

The four of them moved closer.

"We're about to head to war, my boys," he said to them. He looked from one to the other. "Avery, my son." He paused and regarded his youngest son somberly. "And Drustan. You are like a son to me. Your father, my friend, has entrusted you to my care. He'd be proud of you this day."

Then, remembering, he turned to John. "And you, John," he said.

He looked past John to Conal, who had fallen discreetly behind the other three. "I've asked you here as well, Master Conal," said the king, "because I want to thank you personally for helping my son and young Sir Drustan become the strong warriors I see they are."

When has he seen that, wondered John. And then, *Why am I even here?*

Ranulf motioned to a man standing in the shadows, who now stepped up to the king with several bundles, and handed them to him.

"Avery. Drustan," said Ranulf. He held out one of the long silk-wrapped bundles to each of them. They came forward and took them with thanks, at Ranulf's nod unfolding the cloth to reveal richly chased baldricks. "For your swords of knighthood," he said to them, smiling.

"And Master Conal," he said. The servingman handed another, smaller object to the king, and the king handed it to

Conal. It appeared to be a plump leather bag that John was sure must be filled with coin. Gold, probably.

"Thank you, Your Majesty," said Conal.

"And for you, John," said the king. The servant stepped up to him again with a bulky object. "The royal falconer has told me of your love for this creature," he said, pulling aside the covering.

It was a cage. With a leap of his heart, John saw it contained Striker.

"Thank you, Your Majesty," said John.

Striker! John exclaimed.

About time, Striker said grumpily. *That awful man complained about you to the king. The king thwarted him. But when will we be able to hunt? You must go to war, boy.*

I know, said John. *But I'm still happy that you are mine.*

I belong to no one, hissed Striker.

Of course not, my lady, said John with great deference.

As they left the king's audience chamber together, John caught Avery and Dru staring at him. He could tell they thought the king's gift to him a shabby one.

"You don't understand," he told them. "I love this little hawk."

Avery and Dru looked at each other angrily. But John saw Conal understood. Conal knew.

"It's fine," John told them.

"John, how you keep your temper—" began Avery, but Dru poked him in the ribs, and he stopped.

"I'll have to take her back to the mews, though," said John, realizing. "That's the only way she'll be taken care of, when I'm off at war."

Don't be downhearted, said Striker. *The falconer will have to take good care of me now he knows I've received special treatment from the king.*

He'd better, said John.

And there's a go-between who will get word from me to you, and you to me, when it's needful, said Striker.

John remembered the blackbird who had warned him Avery was in trouble. *Little Bird told me to tell you*, this blackbird had said.

Yes, said Striker. *Little Bird. I'll send her, when you need it.*

I've heard of her, said John carefully, *but I've never seen her. How will I recognize her?*

She takes many forms, said Striker. *When she comes to you, you'll know.*

So John was relieved about one thing. About the other, though. His good mood disappeared. "So tell me, brothers," he said to Avery and Dru. "What do you make of it, that Rafe won't be allowed to go with us?"

Then they all turned gloomy. As they walked through the big hall of the fort, there was Audemar at one end, and there was Master Caedon beside him, as always. But Rafe wasn't with them.

"Where is he?" muttered John.

"Probably off doing some silly errand a servant could have done just as easily," said Avery. "It's pure spite, that he's not being allowed to come with us."

"I heard Master Caedon let it be known their guardian the Baron Gilles didn't approve of his wards being sent off to fight in another monarch's war," said Dru.

"That's just an excuse," scoffed Avery. The four of them gazed down the hall at Audemar and Caedon. John carefully schooled his expression, but he saw Avery's stare was overtly hostile. Those two stared back, Audemar sneering, leaning over to murmur something in Caedon's ear.

"Let's get out of here before I do something I'll regret," Avery muttered. "I could beat Audemar bloody, if I'd a mind to."

Conal gave him a warning look, and Avery went on across the great hall. John and Dru and Conal followed.

They went their separate ways then. They all had many preparations to make, and only a few days now to get them done.

CHAPTER THIRTY-FIVE

A Song

The air turned mild; the skies turned blue. The word went out: *our ships sail on the evening tide tomorrow.* John had said goodbye to everyone he knew. He had gotten his gear together. His mother had cried. Now he had almost two days to get through. A whole day to himself, and then another until early evening, when he was due at the port. He wandered the lanes at loose ends.

There was one person he wanted to see. Rafe. Somehow Rafe had been hidden away. He hadn't seen Rafe, and none of the other three had, either.

Nothing to be done about it. John imagined waylaying Caedon and throttling him until he revealed Rafe's whereabouts. That was not going to work. He talked to the other friends; they'd all had the same impractical wish. Maybe, if they had more time, they could think of something. Time had run out.

The whole matter haunted John. He worried ferociously about Rafe.

But in circumstances like these, John had a way to calm himself. His rebec.

On such a fine day, he decided to walk out to the little meadow on the other side of the fort to play and sing to himself.

When he got there, he saw he was not alone. Just beyond the stone wall, a group of mostly grown girls sat in the grass, having a picnic. Their cloaks and clothing almost shimmered in the sunlight. Blues, reds, yellows, greens.

How fresh and bright they all look, thought John, admiring the picture they made. And there, on the far side of the field, stood a few grooms holding the girls' horses. He peered across the field at the little group. He recognized a few, girls who had crossed the boundary to womanhood and would soon be presented at court.

He smiled to himself, remembering the snowy day they'd spent huddled around the hearth in the fort. Some of these same girls had been there that day, too. Flirting with Rafe.

When he thought of Rafe, though, his mood turned somber again.

But then he sat against the stone wall of the field, tuning his rebec. He climbed up on the wall, so he could bow his instrument freely, and began to sing. He didn't even bother to sing softly. The girls were pretty far across the field. If his voice carried to them, he doubted they'd care or be very curious. They looked like they were all having a fine time together.

She stepped away from me as she moved through the fair, sang John.

> *And fondly I watched her*
> *move here and move there*
> *and she went her way homeward*
> *with one star awake*
> *as the swans in the evening*
> *move over the lake.*
>
> *The people were saying*
> *no two e'er were wed*
> *but one has a sorrow*
> *that never was said,*
> *and she smiled as she passed me*
> *with her goods and her gear*
> *and that was the last*
> *that I saw of her here.*
>
> *I dreamed it last night*
> *that my true love came in.*
> *So softly she entered*
> *her feet made no din.*
> *She came close beside me*
> *and this she did say,*
> *It's a cold grave we'll have, love,*
> *on our wedding day.*

He was caught up in the song now, no longer noticing his surroundings.

A voice at his elbow startled him so badly he nearly fell off his perch on the wall.

"That's a pretty tune."

He looked over to the person standing beside him. His eyes met the eyes of a girl, a tall girl with a tumble of red-gold hair, and at the moment when their eyes met, a shiver ran down his body from the top of his head to his toe tips.

Some of John's songs were of love, and they were always about things like that.

A glance between strangers, leading to the immediate and overpowering thrill of desire.

But who took these songs seriously?

Poets made these things up. Nothing like that happened in real life, to real people.

Yes.

It only took John an instant to find this out. *Yes, it did*.

He couldn't say a word.

The moment stretched out before him, an expanse of time he thought might go on forever. He swallowed hard.

She spoke again, finally. "Hello, I'm Odelyn," she said.

From drowning in her eyes, he moved with no pause to drowning in the honey of her voice.

"I'm John," he made himself say.

"I know." She smiled at him, a mysterious smile, as if somehow she already knew him.

How that could be, he had no idea.

He recognized her as one of the girls he had seen at the great hall that snowy day. It dawned on him then. *The only one whose eyes hadn't followed Rafe. The one whose eyes had stayed fixed on me.*

He found himself desperately wanting to lean over to her and kiss the tiny dimple that appeared then at the left corner of her mouth.

"You can call me Lyn," she said. "Everyone does."

"Lyn," he repeated. His voice felt rusty, as if he didn't know how to use it. He looked around, desperate to say something. Anything. "You're having a picnic with your friends."

"Yes," she said. "The weather is so pleasant."

"We're all of us off to war tomorrow," he said.

"That's unfortunate." Her voice dropped low.

He appalled himself by leaning over and kissing her. He didn't think about it. He just did it.

She laughed incredulously.

Oh, no, thought John. *What have I done.*

But then. Then she was kissing him back.

They sat in the meadow grass side-by-side underneath the stone wall and kissed again.

"Play me a song, John," she said.

And he did.

He wasn't sure how much time went by. A few moments. A candle measure. A year. Regular time had stopped.

But the girls across the field were staring and peering in their direction, and waving their arms at her. This girl named Lyn.

"I must go," she said with a deep sigh.

"And I must go to war," he murmured.

"Tomorrow?"

"Our cog sails on the evening tide."

"Suppose—" she hesitated. "Suppose you come to my house tomorrow early," she said, and hurriedly sketched him a little map in the dirt patch beside them.

"There's a garden," she said, "and a gate. I'll be there mid-morning."

The others were calling to her now. She leapt to her feet, brushed her clothes off, and rushed over to them without a backward glance, leaving John sitting stunned against the stones of the meadow wall.

He walked home in a daze. In a daze, he stuffed gear into a pack, and sat in a daze at his mother's hearth while she prepared something for him to eat.

Then he went to bed early, in the loft he shared with his brother.

He and Wat lay side by side, talking softly of John's hopes for Wat, that Wat would have time to practice his combat skills while John was gone.

"Rafe is to stay behind, Wat," said John. "Find Rafe. Ask him to teach you. I know he has already worked with you on many skills."

"I will, Johnny, but that's unfair. Why can't he go with the rest of you?"

"I'm not sure," said John carefully. "Something about his obligations to that baron across the Narrows."

Gradually his brother's breathing slowed. John marveled as always at this talent Wat had for dropping off to sleep whenever he felt like it. John couldn't do that. He'd lie awake candle measure after candle measure, thinking some problem over or worrying. That was happening to him now. He lay on his pallet with his arms crossed underneath his head, staring up into the thatch and saying, over and over again, in his mind, *Lyn. Lyn. Lyn.*

Before it was even dawn, he was out of bed. He was sure he hadn't slept at all, except that he remembered some confused fragments of dream, so he must have slept at least a little.

He swung down from the loft, careful not to wake Wat or his mother, and eased out the door into an unexpectedly frosty morning.

Midmorning, Lyn had said.

He had memorized her little map, and he thought of it now. The lanes he'd walk to get to her. That's when he'd realized, with a chill, that Lyn must be the daughter of the frightening Lord Piers, one of the king's most important and most quarrelsome and truculent vassals.

What would happen if he and Lyn were caught together, he wondered. For someone like him, even talking to a girl like that, in some private place, was enough to get them both into terrible trouble. He began thinking uneasily of their meeting in the meadow, and of how many eyes had seen them together there.

But that didn't stop him from drifting down the lane in her father's manor's direction, his rebec slung over his shoulder. *After all*, he told himself. *I'll be gone soon. Any talk will soon die down. Lyn and I will both be safe.*

He spent an uncomfortable several candle measures tramping the roads and fields around the manor, waiting until the day was conceivably advanced enough to be called midmorning.

At least he had his rebec. When he thought he was far enough away from Lord Piers's manor so that he wouldn't be heard, he blew on his fingers to warm them and played every song he could think of.

The skies were gray and louring, nothing like the way the sun had smiled on the world underneath the Spheres only the day before.

By the time he found himself hovering at the manor's back gate, a stinging rain was drenching him, plastering his hair to his head. Luckily, his oiled bag would keep his rebec dry. But as for the rest of him, he was soaked and shivering. He leaned against the stone wall of the manor's back garden, telling himself what an addlepate he was.

Suddenly the wooden door set into the wall yanked open from the inside, and he nearly fell into the garden. She was there in a cloak and hood.

"Holy Lady," she breathed. "You are wet."

He smiled at her ruefully. Not exactly how lovers' trysts in song and story usually went, he thought.

"Follow me," she whispered.

They both edged along the inside of the garden wall, making for a building close to the house.

What if we're seen. What will they do to me? What will they do to her? John's heart began pounding.

"Stay here," she said. She disappeared around the corner of the building, then quickly reappeared, seizing him by the arm and pulling him after her.

She pulled him into a dim barn, a stable for horses, John realized.

She motioned to him. Outside, he heard voices, the tramping of feet. She motioned again, frantically, and then he was getting up a ladder as fast as ever he could, and tumbling into a loft with her in his arms, and they were lying still and terrified as people, men, came into the stable and rustled around beneath them, only one thin platform of boards away.

The men left.

She collapsed against him, and he was holding her tightly to him.

"You'll get soaking wet," he started to say, just as she said, "You're soaking wet!"

She eased out of her cloak and handed it to him, shivering in her kirtle. "Here," she said. "Get out of those wet things."

Under cover of the cloak, John stripped off his clothes. He wrapped himself in the cloak.

"You're freezing," he said to her, realizing. He tried freeing a fold of the cloak to wrap around her, but somehow they were both in the cloak together, and John was all too aware of his nakedness against her.

They'll kill us both for sure, he thought desperately.

But then he stopped thinking about it, because they were in each other's arms, stroking each other, and kissing, and tasting.

"My lady, I—" he began, and stopped.

"Lyn," she whispered.

"Lyn," he said. "I know little of women, and I fear—"

"I've never done it either," she said.

They stared into each other's eyes.

"We'll teach each other," she whispered. "We'll learn together."

"How is it you're so brave?" he whispered back.

"I'm not very brave. But then, there in the meadow, when you played that song—" All the while she was talking, she was wriggling out of her own wet things.

Then they were both naked in the cloak.

And then they had made their first experiment in the matters of love and the body.

If only I had asked Dru about this, or Rafe, he thought miserably. Both of them knew about such matters. Avery, not at all. But Dru and Rafe might have laughed at him, if he had asked. *Wonder if Conal knows about these things,* he thought. Conal might be someone he wouldn't be too bashful to ask. Conal would tell him anything he asked him to explain.

Oh, well, he thought. *It's too late to ask for advice now.*

"I'm not sure that's how it's supposed to go," he whispered to Lyn.

"How would I know," she whispered back. "Except my friends say it's supposed to hurt a little, and it did. And I'm supposed to bleed a little, and I am."

"But you're supposed to really like it," he said, feeling desperate and stupid.

"We'll try it again, in a while," she said. "I like lying here with you. Did you like it?"

"Yes," he said. So much better than the furtive activities he'd practiced on himself.

"I thought so," she said, and her voice was full of triumph.

He looked at her, and they smiled at each other. He buried his face in her hair and discovered, to his astonishment, that he was ready to give it another try.

By the end of the afternoon, they agreed they thought they were getting the hang of it.

"But we need more practice," she decided.

"Oh, holy Lady," he moaned, as reality and the lateness of the day came crashing down on him. "I need to be aboard ship." He started rapidly pulling on his sodden clothes.

She acted lookout for him as he headed through the garden for the road.

Thank the Children the rain had stopped, but the wind was brisk, chilling him to the bone. He didn't like it, that the warmth of her was being torn out of him so quickly and brutally.

At the garden gate, he turned to her, horrified to be leaving her, and like this.

"When shall we—" she began.

"I don't know," he said. He held her in his arms and they kissed again. Then he was out the gate and running down the road, his heart beating in a panic. Part of him was still back there with her, in the loft, the softness of her, the scent of her. The rest of him was terror-stricken. He'd miss the ship, he'd be disgraced.

By the time he dashed into his own dooryard and to the house to grab his pack, the wind was approaching a gale, and his mother was waiting for him.

"Where have you been?" she said.

"There was something unfinished I had to—" he gulped. "—finish," he said.

"Master Conal was just here," said his mother. "He says you're to await further orders. The sailing has had to be postponed. The weather is too bad."

"Thank the Child," said John so fervently that his mother stared at him.

"John, you're soaked. Give me those wet things and put on dry clothes before you make yourself sick," she said.

The terrible weather lasted a sen'night. Then, as soon as it cleared and the sailing was scheduled again, another spate of bad weather kept them in port a sen'night longer.

By the time John really did see that the ships would likely sail the next day, he and Lyn had had a lot of satisfying practice and had learned quite a few satisfying new skills.

He got one or two useful pointers from Dru, too, but only by cautious roundabout inquiries.

Something frightened him deeply, though. One night, as he sat at the hearth fire with his mother and brother, his mother turned to both of them with a smile. She put a hand on her belly.

"My sons, I will be giving the two of you a brother or sister in about six turnings of the moon," she said.

Suppose that happens to Lyn, he thought. *And then suppose they see. Of course they'll see. Eventually she won't be able to keep such a thing hidden. Suppose I'm not there to protect her, if someone tries to punish her.* That scary father of hers, perhaps.

Child help us both, he thought. *I'll be so far away, I won't even know she's in trouble.*

When he told this to Lyn, she scoffed. "It won't happen," she told him.

"Why do you think it won't."

"It just won't. The fates can't be that cruel. We've only had each other for a fortnight. I know women who say they and their husbands try for many turnings of the moon to get a babe, and finally it happens. But this fast? I don't think so. I don't think it works that way."

For an instant, she looked doubtful.

Then her expression had cleared, and she had pulled him back down in the loft with her, and he'd pushed the thought away from him as they tasted and felt and stroked their way to the pinnacle of their delight.

But she was melancholy, after. "We've only had each other for a fortnight," she repeated. "When will we be with each other again?"

"Lyn—" he hesitated. "War is chancy. I may not come back at all."

She threw herself weeping into his arms. "Come back to me, Johnny. Promise me you will. I won't be able to bear it, if you don't."

"I'll be careful," he promised her.

Then, the next day, they sailed.

John looked glumly across the water as the land receded.

"Missing her already, huh?" said Dru.

John looked at him, startled. He looked to the other side, where Avery was regarding him with the same sympathetic look.

He blushed scarlet. "But we were quiet. We told no one."

His two friends began to laugh.

"How long have you known?"

"How long?" said Dru. "Hmm. A fortnight?"

"But—"

"You think no one saw the two of you kissing by the meadow wall?" said Avery, poking him in the ribs. "You think they just went on with their picnic?"

"But that doesn't mean we—" John stopped. "Who knows?" he demanded.

"Just about everybody, I'd say," said Dru. "Especially after the stable boy at Lyn's family's manor babbled everything he was overhearing to the entire fort."

"Let's hope Lord Piers doesn't know," said Avery.

Moaning, John buried his face in his hands.

"Nine Spheres, Johnny. It's not that bad," said Dru.

"No, you don't understand," John choked out. He suddenly sprinted to larboard to throw up his breakfast.

Dru and Avery laughed.

A few moments later, Avery wasn't laughing. He had joined John to larboard, retching his own guts out.

Dru shook his head at them both and rolled his eyes. He, like the two of them, was a child of the Child of Earth.

But Dru had grown up by the sea cliffs, his mother had been a child of the Child of Sea, and the sea and the heaving of its briny depths held no terrors for him.

CHAPTER THIRTY-SIX

All In This Together

The next day, John's and Avery's stomachs had settled. The three friends sought out Conal and sat tucked into a niche by the cog's mast, talking quietly. They were almost to their destination.

"I need to tell all of you something," said Avery. "Something important."

John leaned forward, listening. The other two of them did, too.

"I found Rafe before we left," said Avery.

"Thank the Lady," said John.

"Is he well? I worried about that lad. It was so strange, him disappearing like that," said Dru.

"Did you know Caedon has a little house tucked away in the woods? He was making Rafe stay there until we were gone."

"That's troubling," John said. "At first, I told myself I understood his reasoning, sort of, in forbidding Rafe to go to war with us. Rafe had been brought over to help him with Audemar, and instead, he became our friend. And then, or so Caedon claimed, their guardian didn't want Rafe fighting in our father's war. But to keep him hidden away. That frightens me. I don't understand it." He thought of the time Rafe had spent away from them, with a healer, and thought of what Caedon might have done to him to put him there. What he might be doing to Rafe now. John shuddered.

"Rafe knows things. He saw some things, important things. Caedon didn't want him telling us about them." Avery looked around at them all.

"What things?" said Conal. He had gone quiet. Now he was very obviously very angry.

"Rafe thinks—" Avery paused and took a breath. "Rafe thinks Audemar may be plotting something."

"I'll just bet he is," said Conal.

"You think so too?" said Avery.

"I've been suspicious of your brother for some time," said Conal.

Avery looked away. They all shifted uncomfortably.

Since that night, John thought.

Conal broke the silence. "Pardon me for saying so, my prince. I know what I just said is treason." He held himself stiffly away from Avery.

Avery put out a hand to him. "Conal," he said. "Don't do that."

Conal looked to John to be a man just barely containing himself. "I can't help thinking it," he said, low. "And I know I shouldn't be saying it in front of all of you."

"When you say that, Conal, I feel you've separated from us. That feels wrong," said John.

Dru nodded. Avery looked away.

John couldn't make Avery out. Surely he didn't think of Conal as someone separate from them. Surely he realized Conal was one of them now. Part of the *us*. He realized none of them addressed Conal as Master any longer. When had that changed?

Avery went on telling them what he'd observed, and including Conal in it. *So*, John thought, *Avery does see it. He does see Conal is part of us.*

"What Rafe tells me—well, that makes me think you're right, Conal," said Avery. He and Conal locked eyes.

No, John thought. *I'm wrong about what I thought I was seeing. Avery is even closer to Conal than Dru and I are. But something about that is making him uneasy. Whatever it is,* he thought, *it must have something to do with that night at the bridge. It has to.* But John didn't know what.

"Rafe overheard some things at Caedon's little hideaway in the woods," Avery went on. He was sounding almost ordinary, almost like the Avery of old, confident and in control of himself. "Rafe says he heard men exchanging information about where we will be, over here. Rafe thinks Audemar is trying to undermine Father's efforts on the Western Isle."

"Now that," said Dru. "That's treason for sure. Not just indiscreet talk. Real treason."

"Rafe and I have agreed on some tactics," said Avery. "He'll play the loyal servant to Caedon and my pig of a brother. Meanwhile he'll keep his eyes and ears open. For our part, over here, we four will keep our eyes and ears open too."

"Should we tell someone?" said Dru.

"Who would we tell? What proof do we have? No, we'll have to watch and wait. Agreed?"

They all nodded yes.

"We four," said John. "And Rafe. He may be separated from us by water and distance, but he's part of it too. We five. All in this together. You too, Conal."

Conal looked over at John and the haunted expression in his eyes softened.

"Yes," he whispered. "Yes," he said louder. "I stand with the three of you. And Rafe. Rafe, too. And you know something? I always have."

Avery was staring hard at the deck. "I don't like what I saw, in Rafe."

"What do you mean?" John said, alarmed.

"Caedon is doing something to him. I'm not sure what. Something bad." Avery and Conal exchanged a look that John couldn't decipher.

"I think so too," said John in a panic. "I've been thinking so for a while. What can we do about it?"

"There's nothing we can do about it. Not from here," said Dru.

The four of them moved to the top strake of the cog and looked out, where the Western Isle was a smudge on the horizon growing larger and more distinct by the moment.

That's where they would be tested, John realized. And their loyalty to each other was the weapon that would help them fight through it.

He looked at the three beside him. *My brothers*, he said to himself. Avery, his actual brother. But the others, too. Rafe too.

He thought of Rafe with a sick worry. Somehow they must help Rafe.

Then he thought of Lyn. *That*, he thought. *That's a different loyalty, but it's no less strong.*

He remembered telling her that, the last time they met. "My feelings for you, they're my rock," he told her.

"I feel the same," she had replied.

"How can this be? We haven't known each other long."

"It just is," said Lyn.

"But how did you know? I never would have been brave enough to walk up to you and introduce myself, let alone kiss you. Or this." They were on their backs together in the loft, looking up into the shafts of sunlight as they poured through the crannies in the roof's thatch. She was lying against his chest, toying with the lock of hair that always fell down in his face.

"You are brave," she insisted. "You did kiss me. We had just met, and you kissed me."

"I must have been crazy," said John.

"I knew, though."

"How?" he remembered demanding.

"I don't know. I just did," she had said, and a secret smile played over her lips. "That winter day, in the fort. That's when I knew."

As for John, he felt trapped betwixt and between. No longer a boy. Not quite a man. He wondered if these bonds he had forged—to his brothers, to Lyn—were the way forward to manhood. He wondered how strong they were, and whether they'd sustain him in the crucible of battle and blood they were all soon to face.

Foaming breakers were beating against the ship now, and he didn't feel very brave. Suppose he let his brothers down. He stepped away and crouched miserably by the mast in the center of the ship, praying to his Child the voyage would be over soon.

Very soon the four of them stepped out onto the shore of a green land not their own, and John felt better with land underneath his feet. If Ranulf had his way, they'd make this land their own. Right now, it was slipping from the grasp of what some might call its rightful owners, but it had not yet come into the grasp of Ranulf.

"Power belongs to those who can take it and keep it," the king told them all. Ranulf himself, stepping out of his tent to rally his men. John, along with Avery, Dru, and Conal stood listening with the others. "We'll take this land and keep it. Then it will belong by right to us."

And is that true? thought John. *And if it isn't, what then?* He looked over the heads of the others to the place where his remote father stood, outside his tent with the flying pennants and the honor guard of his nobles.

He thought about what the five friends had unearthed, a threat to this power the king his father was confidently proclaiming. He thought about how they had sworn to uphold the king in his power, not just as soldiers but privately, when they had uncovered Audemar's plot.

He glanced around at Avery and Dru and Conal. They looked as confident as the king. John wished he felt the same. Instead, somehow he felt separate from the three of them, and that discomfited him. "All in this together," he whispered to himself.

Several days in, and they'd yet to be tested. They had plenty to keep their minds off what they'd soon be facing. Tents to erect, trenches to dig around the tents to handle rain runoff, wood to collect for fires. Many small tasks.

The day before the battle, John was on firewood detail, away from the camp and his friends. The search for firewood was taking all of the men assigned this task further and further afield, and now John found himself wandering through a little meadow and into a wood. The air was mild; the birds sang.

The idea that the landscape would soon be littered with corpses seemed distant and improbable. John padded further into the forest, hitching his rebec more comfortably against his shoulder. If he had time, he hoped to find a downed log and sit there and play it a bit. That would settle him. It always did.

He'd had a strange dream maybe a sen'night earlier. A dream where he found himself in a forest clearing, a strange man beside him. He'd waked in his own tent, his heart pounding. Then he'd forgotten it. In the way of dreams, it fragmented and scattered.

Now, in the forest, the dream and its frightening feelings came rushing at him. It almost seemed an event he was just now remembering. Not a dream. Something real.

John shrugged the bad feeling away from him. He was just feeling spooky. All of the friends had confessed disturbing dreams and feelings and itches.

"The eve of battle," Conal said. "That's all it is."

John blundered through the forest into a little clearing, the dream or whatever it was forgotten again. The clearing was almost a magical place, he thought. A shaft of light slanted down through the trees, illuminating a downed log. The perfect place to sit and play his rebec.

He had just found a comfortable seat on it, was just reaching over his shoulder for the embroidered bag that held his instrument, when he became aware he wasn't alone.

A man stood under the trees, watching him.

His heart pounding, John hove to his feet. The enemy, come to take him captive or kill him? There was something too familiar about the man.

"Do not worry yourself, young master," said the man, tall and thin, hooded, a long saturnine face. "I mean you no harm."

John briefly wondered whether the man might be a kind of priest, dressed as he was in a robe of dun material. John knew little of the beliefs of the people they were to fight here in the Western Isle. Perhaps this was one of their holy men. That was frightening in itself. There were tales about what enchantments the shaman and priests of the enemy called up to entice men of Ranulf's army into some remote and isolated spot, and once they had captured such men, what they did to them.

He opened his mouth to say something, he hardly knew what, but then he stopped.

The man's voice. His accent was much like Rafe's and Caedon's. It had that distinctive Baronies lilt to it.

"Come closer," said the man, beckoning. "I'm a friend. You're John, are you not? I've met you before, you know."

John stood up, hesitating. When had he met this man before? Something inside him told him he had. He couldn't recall when. He reached down for his rebec.

"No," said the man. "Leave that."

The hair on the back of John's neck prickled. But he found himself obeying. He put his rebec down.

"John." The man's voice was low, insistent. "Come to me, John. Now."

The man made a strange motion with his hand, sketching some shape in the air. His eyes were eyes intent, his lips parted to show the tip of a tongue unnaturally red.

As if in a dream, John found himself moving forward. *That dream*, he thought in a panic. That's when he had met the man, in dreamtime, a dream landscape. He thought he might have moved into such a landscape now. He couldn't feel his feet, his legs. They moved of their own volition.

John opened his mouth to speak. To say something. What? To say yes? A strange buzzing blanketed him, cutting him off from the world he thought he knew.

Before John could say a word or reach the place where the man stood waiting for him, his hand outstretched, a frenzied screeching erupted around them. It seemed all the birds of the forest were roused by something, some enemy, and they were screaming out their warning cries.

"Sir," said John urgently, coming to himself. "We must get away from this place. Someone must be coming. Maybe the enemy." He grabbed up his rebec and began to run.

Out of breath, he crashed through the underbrush of the woods into the meadow and bent gasping against a tree, trying to catch his breath. When he looked over his shoulder, he saw the stranger was gone.

John hesitated at the verge of the forest. Should he go back in? he wondered. Might the stranger be in danger?

The forest had quieted now.

But something inside him kept insisting. *You know that man. He was in your dream. And here he has come to you again.*

Before he could make up his mind what to do, a patrol from his unit came marching through the meadow. John ran to the men and worked his way through the column to the side of the grizzled old pikeman who led them.

"Sergeant! Sergeant!" he cried, tugging on the man's sleeve.

"John, is it?" said the man. "Keep in line, lads. I want to see some discipline," he yelled past John to the rest of them. "Yes?" he said as John loped alongside him, trying to keep up.

"There was a man in the woods," said John, gesturing.

The sergeant-major wasn't listening. "What did I tell you about that pike, Peada Smalls? You're not on your farm, lad. Don't hold that pike like some hay rake."

John fell back toward the end of the column and took up the cadence. He didn't know what to do. He couldn't even explain what he had seen and heard, not in any way that made any sense. He glanced over his shoulder, hoping to see the man in the woods come bursting from the tree cover, hoping at least to know what the man was or intended, but by then their leader had marched the whole patrol out of the meadow. Caught up in the anxious thoughts and frenetic preparations that assailed them all, John tried mostly successfully to shove the whole incident to the back of his mind.

It stuck there, gnawing at him with sharp little teeth. John had no idea who the strange man was, but in some place deep inside, he knew the man meant danger. And the birds had recognized it, too.

No time for thoughts like that, thought John with an impatient wave of his hand. No time for strange thoughts arising from strange dreams. He had a war to fight.

"What are you doing, John?" said Drue. He had come into their tent.

"Chasing away a bad thought," said John.

"And aren't we all having them," said Drue, picking up his pike and taking it outside.

Not like this one, John said to himself. But he forced the thought away.

The next day dawned misty. The mist soon burned off. Today would be the day they'd meet their test. The four friends were gathered at the foot of a secluded valley with the rest of their cohort, their captain standing before them. He was scarred from many battles in Ranulf's wars. Conal trusted him, so then John trusted him, too.

"Men," their captain called out. They all stepped a little closer and crouched down to listen, leaning against their spears. "Today we face the enemy, the first time this campaign. Many of you have faced these savages before, and know who they are and how they fight. Many others will be facing them for the first time. For the rest of you, this will the first time you've fought, against anyone."

"That's us," said Avery, nudging the others. Conal smiled at him. Conal was the only one of them who had fought, the only one of them in the captain's first category.

"I have a case of the jitters," John confided in Conal. Would this be his last day on this earth, he wondered. Would he be with his friends and brothers again, once the sun had set on this day? Would he ever hold Lyn again in his arms? And then there had been the strange man in the woods. He didn't want to explain the man to Conal. He didn't try. How could he make Conal understand when he didn't understand it himself? Battle jitters were bad enough.

"Oh, the jitters, Johnny. Get used to it," said Conal, lightly. Then he stopped. His expression turned somber. "No. Forget what I said, about getting used to it. I'm not used to it. Look around you at these men who've fought in many battles. They all feel the same. I'm thinking the day you do get used to it may be the day you let down your guard. And that's dangerous."

"If we think this waiting around is bad, what will battle be like?" said Dru.

"You'll find out soon enough," said Conal, with a grim smile. He put out a hand and laid it against Avery's knee. Avery covered it with his own hand. A strong white hand gripping a calloused brown hand. Their eyes met.

Oh, thought John, looking on. *Nine Spheres*, he thought.

"But I'll be there with you, every step of the way," Conal said. "All three of you," he added after a pause so slight John wondered if he had imagined it.

Conal will be there to help us. He'll be there beside Avery, always, John realized. But then he thought, *Not just Avery. All of us, the other two of us just in a different way.*

"Here's what is going to happen," said the captain, so then they stopped talking among themselves to listen, and John set his realization about Avery and Conal aside, no time to think it through. So many things to set aside. Lyn. Rafe. The man in the wood. This new understanding. He tried hard to listen to his captain.

"We're going up this valley, men. At the head of it is a fortified place. We'll overwhelm it and take it."

John drank in the greenness of the place, its peace. But then he stared at the narrow defile, big boulders and escarpments of rock rimming it. This was the place they'd meet their test. The place they'd maybe die.

"Now listen to me, and listen carefully," said the captain. He eyed each one. "You may hear talk. This valley is a bottleneck. Look around you. Brush. Hiding places. You may hear murmurs. How easy it will be for us to be ambushed here. If you're thinking that, you're right. But here's what I know, and here's what you're to trust. Our king has other ideas."

"I was wondering about that," Conal whispered to them.

"Down that end of the valley, that other king, I hear him now," said their captain, stepping forward to address the whole troop. He put a hand to his ear, as if he really could hear what the enemy's leader was saying. The eyes of all the soldiers were riveted on him.

"That savage king, he says to his men, says he, *Men, fear ye not. We're impregnable here.* And his counselors say to that savage king, say they, *We can ambush Ranulf's men in the valley.* The king, that savage king, he says, *But wait. That's just what they think we'll do. We'll not.*" Their captain looked around at the soldiers in his charge, and the four of them, Avery, Conal, Dru, and John, looked aside at each other.

"Now, this end of the valley, our own king's counselors gather around," their captain went on. He put his hand to his other ear, as if he could hear Ranulf and his counselors. "And these counselors say to our king, say they, *O Good King Ranulf, keep ye our men, sire, out of the valley lest those savage warriors set upon us there. How is it we should go upon this road, the way being so narrow? Will not horse come behind horse, man behind man? There are other roads we can take.* But the king, the good king Ranulf, says to his counselors, says he, *Those savage enemies, they know we know that.*"

All around him, John saw heads nodding.

Their captain smiled. "So now these savage men are thinking, *We'll out-fox that good king Ranulf,* all think they, the savage enemies of our king. Those savages take their men from out the middle. They set their men on the left flank. They set their men on the right. *See how we'll out-fox this king, this old King Ranulf,* say our savage enemies."

The captain was speaking faster and louder, pounding his fist for emphasis. Beginning, rhythmically, to pound his spear against his shield. "*Men, my brave ones,* says the king, the good King Ranulf. *We'll do what they don't expect,* he says, says he. *Who'd think us so stupid as to sweep in our numbers up the perilous path? As my Child loves me,* says the king, *as the Child of Earth favors me,* says he, *as my nostrils breathe life in the faith of my Child, I choose the dangerous way. If you're afraid, go around. If you're valiant, follow me!*" The captain paused. He fixed them with his eye. His voice rose to a bellow. "Men, are ye valiant? Brave men of Ranulf, what say ye?"

Everyone was standing now. They cried out, cried til their voices grew hoarse. "Ranulf! Ranulf! Ranulf!"

"Your father knows what he's about," John heard Conal murmur aside to Avery.

"My brave ones, my brave lads, follow me!" the captain screamed out. John grabbed up his spear. His friends grabbed up theirs. They all did. They began jogging up the valley, and as they went, they met with all the other cohorts of the king's army in an onrushing stream made up of screaming men. At every step, John wondered if, in spite of their captain's words, the enemy would come swarming out of ambush. They did not.

The day had grown warm. John wiped the sweat from his eyes. His heart was pounding. Ahead of them loomed the fortification wall of the enemy, a warren of ditches and palisades. The king's men began to yell even louder, and John was yelling with them.

"To me!" screamed their captain. "On!"

From over the tops of their fortifications, the enemy came boiling out like hornets from their nest. The men of Ranulf thundered against the wood of the enemy fortifications with a mighty roar, and bore them down, and leaped them, slashing and jabbing with their spears as they ran. Too late, from the left and right appeared the army of the enemy, weakened and divided. Ranulf's rear guard split and took them, and then the main force of his army swiveled and turned on them too in a slashing, pounding swirl of blood and noise and nausea. It seemed to go on for a candle measure and more. For many candle measures it seemed to go on.

As if cut with a sharp knife, it stopped.

John stood leaning on his spear, breathing hard. Avery and Dru and Conal stood beside him. They looked around them, stunned. After a long shocked silence, the roar began, a ragged sound that swelled and filled and echoed against the steep sides of the valley, voices lifted in triumph. The four friends grinned at each other, thumped each other on the back, embraced. They'd come through it. The day was theirs.

Around them lay heaps of the slain, most of them the ill-armed, out-fought enemy.

As John turned with his friends to tag after their captain to their newly established camp at the head of the valley, amid the demolished broken boards and shards of the palisades of the enemy, he stepped over the contorted bodies of the dead.

He looked down at the blackened, twisted limbs and smashed-in faces. These men had owned the land they fought over. Now the king did. *This is the king's justice*, John thought.

Dru flung an arm about him and walked beside him. Just ahead walked Avery and Conal.

The day had clouded over. From the valley they'd fought all the long way up, through the incongruous beauty of its green lushness, the flattening land at the head of it seemed a grim trap now. John looked to the low gray clouds pressing down overhead. Then he narrowed his eyes against the glare.

A small shape, small as a midge, soaring from the underside of the clouds. Arrowing down to the four of them, where they trudged with the other soldiers of their cohort. Growing larger, taking shape. A swift bird of prey. A falcon or hawk of some type.

Avery stopped and pointed. "A gyrfalcon," he called out to the others.

The bird opened its beak to scream as it strafed the cohort, missing them narrowly with its talons.

The soldiers all cried out and cowered in fear, those dedicated to the Lady making Her warding sign against evil.

John's friends exclaimed. They crouched and drew their cloaks over their faces.

John did not. He stood up and laughed, raising his arms to the bird. Everything came clear to him now. The hooded stranger of his dream. The same man in the wood. And the mighty falcon, summoning all the birds of the forest to oppose him.

The bird made another pass overhead, and when it did, somehow John took wing beside it and soared up too. He became the bird. Free of all constraints, all fears, he soared, rising to the underside of the clouds, skimming along the valley, swerving up to the coast, dipping just to the tops of the breakers, gyring back again over a land as green as he'd ever seen.

It seemed to him the bird spoke in his ear. *You are part of them, but you're part of something else. Something bigger. You and I and all our kin. We're kings and queens of creation, the guardians of the Spheres. One guardian, that Little Bird, moved across the River. Now here's another. You, John. On this isle, you'll play your part, and back across the water, on your own isle, too. Don't fear. Don't fear anything, John. All of us, your true kindred, will be with you through everything. We've already driven off one of your enemies.*

The strange man in the woods. The one with the compelling eyes and voice.

That one, yes, the bird-voice assured him. *That man will be back, a mighty foe. You will help those others, your brothers, as you fight at their side against the forces ranged against them. But hear us, John! Your role is bigger than theirs. Trust that when you need it, a power will pour out of you, a true justice, and you will prevail.*

There was a tugging at his cloak.

"What is it, Johnny?" It was Dru, tugging at him. "You're lagging behind. We've got to get to our spot in the camp."

John looked around at his friends in amazement. The voice, the sensation of flying, fled from him as the fragments of a dream. "Did you see that?"

"See what?" said Dru.

"The bird. The falcon."

"I think it was a gyrfalcon," said Avery, pausing to look over his shoulder. "Yes, a beautiful bird. But really, Johnny. We can't stand around gawking. Our captain wants to give us our orders for tomorrow. Come on."

John realized he'd stopped again to gaze up into the skies.

"I will," he said, scanning the skies for the gyrfalcon, to tell it so. He looked around at his friends. "I will," he said to them.

He scrutinized each of their loved faces in wonder. Had he imagined their fear and cringing, as the bird had soared over?

Avery and Dru were laughing at him, and at each other.

Conal wasn't, though. He was staring at John in some kind of recognition.

"You brought your rebec with you, didn't you?" he murmured, dropping back beside John.

"Of course I did," said John.

"Maybe tonight, after we eat, you can play and sing for us," said Conal.

"Yes, I'd like that," said John.

"You know what they say about minstrels, John," said Conal.

"What do they say?"

"Some are just entertainers. But some—" Conal gave him a long look. "They call on powerful forces. They see things others don't see, things of the mind, and then they sing them into reality."

John looked away from him, unsettled. The gyrfalcon had mentioned some enemy, some role John would be called upon to play. Strange, unsettling words. The battle they'd just fought had been fierce. Dangerous. The king's justice had prevailed.

A hidden voice inside him kept insisting on a different vision. *You'll be required to fight a battle much fiercer, more dangerous than this. And the justice you'll be required to uphold? The true justice.*

But the memory of the gyrfalcon and the strangeness of its message was fast fading away from John into the place he kept his dreams.

He could smile now. He thought of Lyn, and how he'd see her again. He thought of how he and his friends had come through the battle together. They'd left the Sceptered Isle as almost-boys. When they came back, they'd come back men. They saw a wrong. They would come back to right it.

"All in this together, brothers," Avery said to them, his eyes shining.

"Rafe too," John whispered.

"Rafe too," the other three repeated. They flung their arms around each other. With the other soldiers, they moved to the place their captain had designated as their camp, to get themselves something to eat, and ale for their throats parched with screaming and with fear.

Before sleep, they all sat down together by their fire to listen to John as he played and sang their battle song, and their song of home, and of longing, of blood, of brotherhood, of love.

GARDE

T here," said Dee, standing up from his golden chair to move to the edge and look over, down past the nine crystalline layers of the Spheres. "There he is."

Myrddin, or Merlin, or Mervin—whatever you may call him—stood up to look too, to peer down at John, tiny beside the fire of a new land, sitting close beside his friends.

"You're right. There he is," Myrddin agreed.

"And he doesn't even know yet," Dee said. "What he is. I'm worried about him."

"He knows more than you think."

"You've helped him?"

Myrddin nodded. "A bit," he admitted. "I sent him a messenger."

Then they turned at the sound of a soft footfall.

"Hello, Gilles," said Dee, his eyes narrowing. "What are you up to?"

Gilles de Rais didn't answer. He too looked down through the Spheres. "What are you watching, down there? Who is that?"

The other two regarded him warily.

"Oh," said Gilles. "One of those." His eyes widened in mock-surprise.

Seeing it, Myrddin felt a surge of fear.

Gilles smiled, a cynical smile. "Most mages have no idea what they are, what their powers do. Many of them misuse their powers before they realize." Gilles stared at the other two. "It's dangerous for them. You know what the graybeards say about mages, tampering with forces they don't understand. They try some things, and they fail, and they die. Sometimes horribly."

"Yes," said Myrddin.

"But some of them learn," said Dee.

Gilles peered down again at John. "I know that boy," he said, nodding to Myrddin. "You think I wouldn't have seen, Myrddin? You think you could have hidden this from me? I know his origins. I know what you did, too, sending Little Bird into the forest to set her feathered minions screaming. To jostle him awake. Interfering, are we, Myrddin? Not allowed. Isn't that what you're always lecturing me about?" He smiled, a big smile showing all the gleaming sharp teeth in his mouth. He turned to Dee. "You know what else the graybeards say." He turned to Dee. "I seem to remember some graybeard saying it, at the trial of a trivial man, a king who had done wrong. The curse of the father descends to the son."

His eyes and Dee's met. Dee was the first to look away.

Gilles laughed. He gave Dee a shrewd, knowing look, wrapped his long dun-colored robe about him, and walked back into the mist.

Dee stood watching after him, a worried line between his brows.

"Dee," said Myrddin, shaking his head in warning. "I did maybe a bit too much. I sent some protectors to John. But that's it. I will not do more. And you're not to interfere. Gilles is right. These are the rules of our kind, decreed by the Three, and I must abide by them."

"You think Gilles will abide by the rules?" Dee said.

"He'd better," said Myrddin. "Balance depends on it. The very structure of the Spheres depends upon it." Then he too took his leave. Only Dee was staring over the edge now.

Would Gilles stay out of it? *He'd better*, Myrddin had said. "But what if he doesn't?" Dee whispered to himself. He stepped back and sank into his chair.

Those words Gilles had spoken. *I know that boy.* When had Gilles encountered John, and how had he known to?

The movement of the Spheres clicked from morning to afternoon to dusk to night as the Spheres chimed with the unearthly music of their crystalline movement, singing their unearthly song.

A chill ran up the back of Dee's neck. In the very midst of harmony, a discordant note struck, a tiny sound, far off. A faint cracking. Dee stepped to the edge again and shaded his eyes. Far away, almost too far for the keenest sight, one of the chains holding up a star where it was attached to its sphere had broken off. Its star dropped, fell free. The star hurtled in a crazy path from its proper place. Trailing behind it, the star's chain burst into flames, a fiery tail chasing after a fireball of a star.

It's very far away now, thought Dee. *But it's coming closer.* One of those harbingers in the heavens. He thought of the last time he had seen such a thing, when Ranulf the king had been a youth the age those lads far below were now.

These hairy stars, these comets. They were said to be portents of evil. Back when Ranulf had been a young man destined for a throne, Dee remembered thinking how unusual it was for The Three to send Their avenger to chastise Ranulf over his misdeeds. Surely many of Ranulf's kind had done the same, and worse.

Dee remembered the tribunal the mages had convened, at the direction of The Three, to judge Ranulf. Kings bore great responsibilities, true. It seemed this king's malfeasance posed some dire threat only The Three understood. Dee for sure didn't understand it, bad as Ranulf's behavior had been. Dee himself had passed along the judgment of The Three. *Let him be cursed*. And then the other part of the judgment: *The curse of the father descends to the son.*

But now that was all over, wasn't it? The king had repented his bad deeds. He had embraced his Child. Surely The Three had lifted Their curse. Surely They would not visit it upon the king's sons. Not on John. Surely not.

Dee thought of the wrath of The Three, and he squeezed his eyes tight shut. Something was going on, with this particular king of the ordinary folk, something involving Gilles de Rais, and Dee could not fathom what it was.

Below him, did he feel the first tremor of a cataclysm that might grow strong enough to shake the very Spheres? Dee prayed to the Children that was not what he felt. He prayed to the Children that he was only a foolish old mage whose fears gnawed at him and had started to turn him timorous.

He shook his head. *I should get some sleep*, he told himself.

Then he felt it again. A tremor. Stronger this time. He opened his eyes.

The malign star with the fiery tail blazed up. Blazed on.

READER, Before you go!

DON'T MISS A BOOK! SIGN UP FOR MY NEWSLETTER, shrikepublications@janemwiseman.com. Just put **sign me up** in the subject line.

The sweep of the nine novels in the **Stormclouds/Harbingers** series, and the two companion novels (**Betwixt & Between**) starts with the sighting of the comet of 976 CE, recorded in the British Isles. Except for that one reference, we know almost nothing about this hyperbolic comet, known as x976, but it did show up, and you can read about it in the historical record.

The events of the nine novels progress from the appearance of x976 to the famous sighting of Halley's Comet in 1066 CE. Halley's, one of the most-studied comets in human history, seemed to the people of the British Isles in 1066 to presage the regime change ushered in by the Norman Conquest, and it was observed in the Americas, too. These two comets frame my series of novels—with this difference, that the sightings of the two comets in my novels occur in the fantasy-verse, not in real-life history.

The nine books of the three interconnected series and the stand-alone novel are all available in print or for Kindle at www.amazon.com. For more information about the novels in the series, and for a playlist that includes many of the songs the characters play and sing, go to my author web site, https://janemwiseman.com. To see the way people, places, and things may have looked in the Stormclouds/Harbingers world, go to my ten Pinterest boards: *Medieval Life—Gyrfalcon, Medieval Life—Shrike, Medieval Life—Stormbird* (for the **Stormclouds** series); *Medieval Life—10th Century* (about *Blackbird Rising*), *Medieval Life—Halcyon, Medieval Life—Firebird, Medieval Life—Ghost Bird* (for the **Harbingers** series); *Medieval Life—Martlet* and *Medieval Life—Nightingale* (for the **Betwixt & Between** companion series), and *Medieval Life—Dark Ones* for *Dark Ones Take It*, the stand-alone novel.

The "flavor" of the three series varies a bit. The novels of the **Stormclouds** and **Betwixt & Between** series (and *Dark Ones Take It*) are a bit darker and more adult, while the novels of the **Harbingers** series are a bit more YA/NA in flavor. Even though, chronologically, the **Stormclouds** novels come first, you may begin either with the **Stormclouds** novels or the **Harbingers** novels, and may want to read the **Betwixt & Between** novels last.

And for those who want to know about the series villain, Caedon, and how he got that way, the stand-alone novel set in the same fantasy universe, *Dark Ones Take It*, will give you all the grisly details of Caedon's origin story and the story of how his brother Maeldoi became the Dark Rider of the Wild Hunt.

The Novels:

A Gyrfalcon for a King (Stormclouds, book 1): King Ranulf may be cursed, a curse of his own making, through his own misdeeds. Which of his sons will redeem him and which will be his undoing? Artur, the crown prince, scholarly and retiring? Audemar, the second son, conspiring to unseat him? Avery, the third son, alert to the dangers that surround the throne? Or John, Ranulf's bastard son—John the minstrel, John the mage.

The Call of the Shrike (Stormclouds, book 2): Ranulf's true-born son Prince Avery and his bastard son John band together with three friends in the guerilla action they name The Rising. The young warriors of The Rising set out to right a great wrong that threatens the realm. They face a mighty enemy—not the enemy they thought they were fighting, but one more dangerous than they could ever have imagined.

Stormbird (Stormclouds, book 3): The ragtag band of The Rising faces near-impossible odds in its quest for justice. How can the Six hope to prevail when they fight without resources; when they are picked off one by one? When they face an evil man backed by an unimaginably evil force? John's young brother Wat must take up his brother's fight, struggling against not only the powerful enemies of The Rising but his own self-doubts. Meanwhile, in the grasp of their enemy, the Princess Diera and the man she loves must do the same.

Blackbird Rising (Harbingers, book 1): An orphaned young girl, a band of spies and assassins, a sister lost, a queen found—in the midst of chaos and treachery, Mirin must somehow learn to trust. Only then can she fulfill the mission John the minstrel left her. Only then can she live up to the promise and the magic of her music.

Halcyon (Harbingers, book 2): On the run, Mirin and Wat try to carve out a new life together. But when everything is taken from Mirin, she must find the strength to go on alone. Her music sustains her, and so does the mysterious power of the fisher-bird, the harbinger of her god.

Firebird (Harbingers, book 3): Keera has one goal—avenging her parents—and boundless confidence. After all, she has her magic powers, and they are second to none. When she finds she must fight her battle with only her wits and her grit, how can she possibly prevail? But the girl has friends: an old mage who helps her, a young man with a twinkle in his eye who can't get her out of his mind—and a ghost.

Ghost Bird (Harbingers, book 4): Keera and Gwyl voyage in Gwyl's dragon ship to the heart of a new continent. But their enemies from the world left behind are not done with them yet. The two of them have to fight for the life they want, pursued by a powerful evil, relentless and closing in. Lucky for them Keera is an ornithomancer like her mother, Mirin, and like her uncle, John—the kind of mage who calls upon the mysterious powers of birds.

The Martlet is a Wanderer (Betwixt & Between, book 1): Who is Silence? He can't speak to tell anyone the role he played in the conspiracy called The Rising, and he can't remember it anyway. He knows only that he needs to find two people: a friend, and a woman who means more to him than life itself. How can he possibly carry out this mission? Especially since he might be dead. (The events of this novel take place in parallel with *Halcyon*.)

The Nightingale Holds Up the Sky (Betwixt & Between , book 2): Say you've been kidnapped and dragged to the underworld. Say the man who loves you wanders the realm looking for you. Say he finds a way in. But suppose you don't want to be found. As for the fate of the realm in the grip of evil, the fate of the world underneath the Spheres; as for justice—suppose you forge your own. (The events of this novel take place in parallel with *Halcyon* and *Firebird*.)

And finally: **Dark Ones Take It**, *being the origin story of Caedon and his brother Maeldoi*. Caedon and Maeldoi are gwrgi— creatures who look like the rest of us, except for their amber eyes. When they get into a rage, they transform. Like werewolves? Not exactly. To an out-of-control bestial form of themselves. As they reach manhood, the dangerous age, the brothers are separated. Caedon is adopted by Gilles de Rais, a powerful mage with powerful secrets, a sorcerer who values Caedon's rage and schemes how to use it. Maeldoi is taken off by his fellow gwrgi to be taught how to control the rage inside him. **Brother against brother**. When Caedon and Maeldoi meet again, the fate of the Spheres Themselves hangs in the balance.

A younger, more light-hearted read. Oh, no! The fantasy world of the Stormclouds/Harbingers characters intrudes into our own! Read the novella *Witchmoon* to find out more— available only in ebook format.

About the Author

I hope you have enjoyed *A Gyrfalcon for a King*, Book I of the **Stormclouds** series, the prequel series to the **Harbingers** fantasy novels and the companion **Betwixt & Between** novels. Please leave a review of my novel on amazon.com and other web sites for readers and book lovers. I care about what my readers think! Please visit my author page on amazon.com and my author web site, https://janemwiseman.com. Follow my blog about speculative fiction, https://fantastes.com

As always, I welcome reviews posted on amazon.com, goodreads.com, and other web sites for book lovers, and on my author web site.

Jane Wiseman splits her time between Minneapolis and the Sandia Mountains of New Mexico. She loves fantasy in all its forms, enjoys her family, reads all the time, and writes in many different modes. As for fantasy, she writes books that she would like to read. She also paints.

A NOTE OF ACKNOWLEDGMENT

Thanks to my wonderful daughter, Margaret Govoni, for your editing eye. You steered me away from many mishaps and missteps, Margaret, especially in the early novels. All the remaining mistakes are mine alone. And now you have revolutionized the cover!

Many, many thanks to Bob, friend and marvelous beta reader!

Thanks for all the helpful suggestions I've gathered from a number of online Litreactor workshops, www.Litreactor.com and from other writing workshops, especially the Tinker Mountain Writers workshop, www.hollins.edu/academics/workshops-online-writing-courses/tinker-mountain-writers-workshop-residential/ , and the (sadly now defunct) Taos Summer Writers' Conference. The instructors' comments and suggestions were of course incredibly helpful, but I have valued beyond measure the comments and suggestions of my fellow workshop attendees. Thanks to all of you! You may not have been able to save me from all my writing sins, but you saved me from many. Thanks also to the Anam Cara Writer's and Artist's Retreat, www.anamcararetreat.com, on the Beara Peninsula of Ireland. What a peaceful and lovely place to write! Thanks, Sue!

And finally, thanks to all you Norrathians out there. You are my true battle buddies. You know who you are. You are my fantasy friends in the purest sense of all.

Thanks to Margaret Govoni for designing the cover of this book. She created her composite illustration using royalty-free, free for commercial use art and fonts made available through Canva Pro, as well as art acquired through Pixabay.com. The cover was produced using Canva Pro and BookBrush.com.

Thanks to this talented artist for a royalty-free, free for commercial use photo made available through Pixabay:

Image by <a href="https://pixabay.com/users/slightly_different-2006397/?utm_source=link-attribution&utm_medium=referral&utm_campaign=image&utm_content=2136095">slightly_different</a> from <a href="https://pixabay.com/?utm_source=link-attribution&utm_medium=referral&utm_campaign=image&utm_content=2136095">Pixabay</a>

NOTES ON **A Gyrfalcon for a King**

from the author

This novel is a work of fantasy, not historical fiction, although it is indebted to history.

THE TIME-PERIOD of the novel is roughly early medieval. The novel begins in a geopolitical environment resembling several of the Frankish, Anglo-Saxon, and Scandinavian kingdoms vying for power in the 10th and 11th centuries.

TWELVE REALMS:

> THE SCEPTERED ISLE stands in for the united Heptarchy (seven main kingdoms) of mainland Anglo-Saxon England, but also includes the northern part of the realm (Scotland), the Western Isle (Ireland) and the northern isles (islands off the coast of Scotland— Inner and Outer Hebrides, Orkney, and Shetland Islands). It does not include the area around Lunds-fort (London), however.

> THE EASTERN BARONIES stands in for a loose confederation of powerful feudal lords spreading across medieval France and parts of Germany. In my tale, the Eastern Baronies also own territory on the mainland of the Sceptered Isle—the land around Lunds-fort (London) and along the eastern edge of the mainland—in addition to their strongholds across the Narrows (the English Channel).

> THE SOUTHERN PRIMACY stands in for medieval territories in Italy (as well as Portugal and Spain), the homeland to which the Old Ones (ancient Romans) pulled back as their empire dwindled.

> THE LYRE-LANDS stands in for the vestiges of ancient Greece and the lands rimming the Aegean in the medieval era, including that vast metropolis the Vikings knew as "the Great City," Constantinople (earlier, Byzantium; later, Istanbul).

> THE REALM OF THE ASP stands in for the ancient Near and Middle East.

> THE BURNT LANDS —a vague concept to people of the Sceptered Isle and similar northern realms. It stands in for North Africa and below, through Sub-Saharan Africa, but people in the northern realms know little of these lands.

> THE ICE-REALM stands in for medieval Norway and, in a loose sense, the other parts of Scandinavia.

> THE FIRE ISLE stands in for medieval Iceland.

> THE MOUNTAIN FASTNESSES stands in for the Alpine regions of Europe.

THE TRADE ROAD FORTIFICATIONS stands in for the old Silk Road of the late ancient world through the Renaissance, stretching along the Eurasian steppes.

THE SILK LANDS stands in for China and southeast Asia.

THE FORGOTTEN KINGDOM stands in for the Indian subcontinent. No one in the world of this novel knows much about this place.

ALSO:

UNKNOWN LANDS (the Americas) across the Great Sea stretching to the west. Travelers have come back with tales of these lands, but no one knows much about them.

THE CONCEPT OF TWO COMPETING RELIGIOUS GROUPS, worshippers of the Lady Goddess vs. worshippers of an elemental universe controlled by earth, sea, fire, and sky, is fantasy but based on some actual bits of information about belief systems in the post-Roman British Isles and medieval beliefs in general, especially medieval ideas about the body and healing. These derived from very ancient sources such as the Greek philosopher Empedocles. The head of these elemental gods is Trioditis, the Three, the goddess of the crossroads. For Empedocles, the three faces of this triple godhead are Strife, Love, and the overarching Harmony that binds them together. For others, they are the three faces of Hecate, or the Triple Goddess Selene, Artemis, and Hecate. (Present-day astrologers and neo-pagans have their own settled ideas about these matters, as do anthropologists and folklorists. I know nothing about their ideas, or nothing deep, and don't pretend to—I'm writing fantasy, not philosophy or theology or anthropology. Apologies too, Matthew Arnold!) There is a sense that older gods once ruled the lands, but no one remembers much about them.

THE OVERALL CONCEPT OF MY NOVEL'S UNIVERSE is Pythagorean: nine revolving crystalline spheres carry the heavenly bodies (sun, moon, stars, planets) around the earth at their center. This idea, originating in the ancient classical Near East, was widespread in the medieval period, obviously long before anyone knew anything about the way the physical universe really works.

THE FALCONRY LIST that begins this novel comes from *The Boke of Seynt Albans*, a 15th century manual of hawking, hunting, and heraldry, three topics necessary for a gentleman of the time to understand. You can look at a version of it at https://archive.org/details/cu31924031031184/page/n29 (see p. 28). Different versions and similar manuals of the times give variations on the list, so my list is not necessarily the only or most historically accurate. What caught my interest was the overall idea that different social ranks were due different perks in all areas of life, such as hunting. Although *The Boke of Seynt Albans* was published in the 15th century, it presents much older traditional social arrangements and rules of falconry: who got to fly gyrfalcons, who got eagles, who got the larger female peregrine falcons and who got the smaller males (tiercels), what lesser orders got lanner falcons, and which even humbler ranks were only allowed the ignoble hawks, the sparrow hawks and others. I'm applying the principle of a highly stratified society with rules like these to my fantasy 10th century. Whether these same rules literally applied to the actual 10th century or were more like tropes of hierarchy I leave to the experts.

COMET X976 is the bare-bones designation for a hyperbolic comet that was observed over the skies of the British Isles in 976 CE. There are one or two written records of it. No one knows much about it, but comets (literally, "hairy stars") were widely believed in the ancient and medieval worlds to presage world-shaking changes such as regime change and the deaths of monarchs. Comet x976 is probably a periodic comet (that is, it will return again and again in its orbit about the sun unless it breaks up), but observations of it were too vague and inaccurate in 976 to suggest when or whether it would return, and as far as anyone knows, it never has. This means it may have broken up through some internal or external force. Alternatively, its orbit may be so huge that we haven't seen it again in recorded history—yet. The fantasy comet that begins the novel is based on this real comet. That invaluable source, Wikipedia, gives a full list of hyperbolic comets, including x976:
https://en.wikipedia.org/wiki/List_of_hyperbolic_comets
Even better, sources at the end of the article direct you to primary material. (Wikipedia is unfairly maligned, in my opinion. It has its drawbacks, but so do general printed reference works—just different drawbacks. The best thing about a Wikipedia article is the list of sources that usually follows—and that's true of any general reference work worth its salt.)

GARDE is a really old, obsolete term used in chess to alert an opponent that they are in big trouble.

MINSTRELS WITH MAGICAL POWERS—There is a long history of medieval belief that minstrels could exercise magical powers through song. The Pied Piper of Hamelin story is a good example. In medieval Ireland, minstrels were often seen as "rat-rhymers" who could rhyme and sing the rats away from a town or from crops. To run down the origins of the idea, see Fred Norris Robinson's ground-breaking critical essay, "Satirists and Enchanters in Early Irish Literature," *Studies in the History of Religons Presented to Cawford Howell Toy*, ed. D. G. Lyon and G. F. Moore (New York, 1912), pp. 95-130, reprinted in *Satire: Modern Essays in Criticism*, ed. Ronald Paulson (New Jersey, 1971).

MEDIEVAL BEDDING CEREMONIES took place after actual medieval weddings, not just weddings in fantasy literature. Consummation of a marriage, especially a

royal marriage, was a matter for public concern; the bodies of kings and queens were more or less public property, and all of a realm's subjects had a vested interest in making sure the marriage was consummated. No consummation, no son. No son, no continuity of power. No continuity of power, social and political chaos. Here is a quick read:
https://www.thevintagenews.com/2018/06/30/bedding-ceremonies/

BOUNDARY POSTS AND ROAD MARKERS in the British Isles of the 10th century: there probably weren't any. Just in fantasyland.

HUGGING YOUR CHILDREN, breastfeeding them yourself when you're a member of the nobility, and other contemporary child-rearing practices: these are fantasy, not usual 10th century practices among parents and children. There were accounts of noblewomen who breastfed their own children, but these women were seen as exceptional and pretty odd (for example: the 10th century noblewoman Saint Ida of Lorraine, who turned her righteous wrath on anyone with the nerve to breastfeed her children besides herself). This essay gives a good overview, with helpful references at the end if you'd like to read more:
https://www.representingchildhood.pitt.edu/medieval_child.htm

CAUSES OF MATERNAL DEATH: Post-partum hemorrhage, the condition that kills Emilde in my novel, is real, the leading cause of maternal deaths in the world. It's a scourge of undeveloped nations now and is a big problem even in developed nations (especially in the U.S., which at the time of this writing has a soaring maternal death rate from all causes, by far the highest in the developed world and growing higher—except in California, which has enacted life-saving regulations that put its rate on a par with Sweden, half the rate of overall U.S. maternal deaths per 100,000 births). Post-partum hemorrhage would have been virtually unstoppable in the medieval world. In severe cases, a woman can die from it in 6-10 minutes. Other maternal deaths are caused by infections which go by several names now, depending on the infectious agent, but in earlier times were grouped under one term, **puerperal fever**. This condition, which kills both Aderyn and Eris's mother in my novel, still afflicts new mothers, not only in developing countries but also in developed countries. As an American I'm passionate about this situation because the high maternal death rate here represents such a blot on our national delivery of health care, health care for women in particular, and national health care policy in general. It's a complicated issue, however. Read about it here, if you're interested:
https://www.health.harvard.edu/blog/a-soaring-maternal-mortality-rate-what-does-it-mean-for-you-2018101614914

BASTARDS in the actual historical time-period of this fantasy novel would not have suffered the stigma that John and his brothers do, although some of the stigma John endures is due to the particular emotions of his father and not the general practices of the (fantasy) time. In the actual medieval era (which is huge, stretching from the fall of the Roman empire to the Renaissance in the 14th-17th centuries—a period of easily a thousand years), the stigma about bastardy came much later. Here's an article by Sara McDougall that explains the matter quickly and well: https://aeon.co/ideas/the-strange-story-of-inventing-the-bastard-in-medieval-europe

THE ROMAN WRITER HYGINUS, in his *Fabulae*, writes about how dissension fomented by the god Hermes resulted in human societies becoming fragmented by language, much in the way that the Tower of Babel story explains it in the Hebrew Bible. Hyginus is the writer Bren is trying to think of.

NORMAN INVASION OF WEXFORD: The fictionalized battle for which Ranulf praises Conal's bravery. The Normans fought the actual battle in 1169 during the reign of Henry II, besieging the Irish-Viking port of Wexford (Waesfjord). They broke through the city walls and fought hand-to-hand to subdue the city. They were then able to establish a Norman foothold in southeastern Ireland.

THE REBEC is a real medieval musical stringed instrument from around the 10th century. The rebec preceded later stringed instruments such as the lute, the gittern, and the citole. Unlike the lute, which is built of strips of wood, the rebec's bowl was carved from a single piece of wood. It may be the precursor to the violin, but musicologists have had a lively debate about this, and I'm not qualified to weigh in. This web site gives a fantastic overview: http://crab.rutgers.edu/~pbutler/rebec.html

THE BALLAD OF CHEVY CHASE, Child Ballad 161, probably composed in the 15th century about the actual Battle of Otterburn in the 14th century (much later than the fantasy era of my novel), is the Scots song John mangles and turns into a battle song for his friends. You can listen to the actual song on *A Harbingers/Stormclouds Play List*, which is posted on my web site, http://www.janemwiseman.com. You can read the whole thing (the real ballad) here: http://www.luminarium.org//medlit/medlyric/chevychase.htm

SCOT-FREE is an expression with a troubled history of misunderstandings. It has nothing to do with the Scots, with anyone named Scot, with the Dred Scott decision, or any of the other crazy references people think they are making when they use it. (I'm using the phrase anachronistically, myself.) Here is a link:

https://www.washingtonpost.com/nation/2018/12/04/who-is-scott-free-search-meaning-after-trumps-misuse-medieval-idiom/?utm_term=.844d75d6009e

THE SPORT OF FALCONRY (see the earlier note on the falconry list) is such a complex activity that I hesitate even to include it. Apologies for the many places I have probably gotten some technical detail wrong. There are a few areas where I know I have sinned: for example, *The Boke of Seynt Albans*, previously mentioned, was written later than the time period of my novel and probably wasn't to be taken literally, even then. Gyrfalcons probably weren't even introduced into the British Isles until the Norman Conquest, right at the end of the time period of my two series of books. I plead my usual excuse, that my books are not historical novels but fantasy novels tinged with history. Some of my sources: that amazing memoir by Helen Macdonald, *H is for Hawk*; Shawn E. Carroll's article "Ancient and Medieval Falconry: Origins & Functions in Medieval England," posted on http://www.r3.org/richard-iii/15th-century-life/15th-century-life-articles/ancient-medieval-falconry-origins-functions-in-medieval-england/ and especially valuable for its bibliography; and wonderful sites like these:
https://www.youtube.com/watch?v=kJIMhsoNjOE
https://www.youtube.com/watch?v=sFqf-_IS8j0

"SHE MOVED THROUGH THE FAIR," a traditional song collected in Ireland and Scotland, is listed as 861 in the Roud folk song index. Although the song is known in many variations, the Irish poet Padraic Colum is credited around the beginning of the 20th century with writing some of the lyrics usually sung in recorded versions today. John sings the song (with variations of my own) in this novel, and also in **Stormclouds** Book II, *The Call of the Shrike*. You can listen to the song on *A Harbingers/Stormclouds Play List* posted on my web site, http://www.janemwiseman.com

THE ENGLISH SWEAT, so-called, was a feared epidemic of late medieval-early Renaissance northern Europe (in the real world, as opposed to the fantasy-verse, occurring later than the time period of my novel). "Merry at breakfast, dead by supper" was the phrase describing the rapid progress of the symptoms, which contemporary researchers believe may have been caused by the hantavirus. Here are some interesting accounts—a quick read and a more extensive discussion:
http://discovermagazine.com/1997/jun/thesweatingsickn1161
https://www.ncbi.nlm.nih.gov/pmc/articles/PMC3917436/

ORNITHOMANCY is, literally, divination using birds, a practice that goes back to ancient times and exists in many cultures and religions. I have broadened these practices of sortilege (telling the future) to include all sorcery based on and using birds. The idea of ornithomancy and the magic associated with birds permeate the two fantasy series, **Stormclouds** and **Harbingers**, and in the two companion volumes called **Betwixt and Between**. Although in this novel John doesn't know it yet, he is the type of mage known as an ornithomancer.

THE BATTLE SCENE that ends this book is based on an actual battle fought over three thousand years ago, a battle during which Pharaoh Thutmose III of Egypt defeated the Canaanites at Megiddo (the basis for our word "Armageddon") in 1479 BC. British general Edmund Allenby used the same tactics during World War I, at the same place, with the same outcome. You can read about it in Eric H. Cline's *1177 B.C.: The Year Civilization Collapsed*. (Thanks for pointing me to this fascinating book, "Tacitus.") In my novel, the captain's speech paraphrases the words of Thutmose III in an inscription translated by J. H. Breasted, *Ancient Records of Egypt*, vol. II, pp. 180-81, https://archive.org/details/BreastedJ.H.AncientRecordsEgyptAll5Vols1906/page/n575
Plus ça change, plus c'est la même chose.

APOLOGIES **for my petty and not-so-petty thefts!** (As always, lawyers, I playfully use the word "theft" for the literary figure of speech known as "allusion." The technical term is the "mash-up.") In this book, I stole from the traditional folklore of the British Isles; from the 15th century *Boke of Seynt Albans*; from Milton; from Chaucer; from Shakespeare; from western Christianity's traditional marriage vows; from words attributed to Queen Victoria, who almost certainly didn't say them ("Close your eyes and think of England" as the appropriate response of virtuous, chilly young women to sex); from the poetry of W. B. Yeats; from Edmund Spenser's 16th century *Faerie Queene*; from John Donne's 17th century love poetry, especially "The Indifferent"; from J. H. Breasted's 1906 *Ancient Records of Egypt*; from 19th century poet Matthew Arnold's *Empedocles on Aetna*; from a variety of sources on Arthurian texts and lore, especially the lore surrounding Merlin the Magician (aka Myrddin Wyllt); from the life of Dr. John Dee, a real mathematician, astrologer, proto-scientist, believer in all manner of crazy mystic theories, and advisor to Queen Elizabeth I; from the life of Gilles De Rais, a real fifteenth-century French baron who supported Joan of Arc but later became fascinated with the occult, going down in history as one of the most prolific and chilling serial killers (especially of children) the world has known. Mervin/Merlin/Myrddin, John Dee, and Gilles de Rais play more important roles in several other novels in the **Stormclouds** and **Harbingers** series.

And a final thank-you to Warren Robinett, the inventor of the easter egg.

Excerpt from

The Call of the Shrike

Stormclouds Book II

prequel series to the **Harbingers** fantasy novels

W hen John woke up that first morning back, he lay sprawled across the furs, rubbing the sleep out of his eyes and trying to clear his head. The three of them had returned late, too late to do much more than rouse a few servants and strike the bung off a new barrel of ale.

The three of them.

That's the way they had thought of each other when they were lads. John smiled at himself, shaking his head. In the crucible of war, they'd gotten used to thinking differently. He corrected himself.

The four of them.

And then, if you added Rafe. . .

John began worrying, yet again, about Rafe and how he fared. The rest of them hadn't seen Rafe in two years. They'd received word from him only rarely, and they all knew he was facing a difficult situation, bound in service as he was to a very dangerous man. But John forced himself to put this worry aside. They'd all see Rafe soon, and then they'd know for a certainty how he did. Avery had made it his first task to send a summons to Rafe.

John looked across the room at Avery and Conal, where they lay entwined in the piled up furs of their low platform of bedding just as they had fallen onto it the night before. Then at Drustan. Dru was awake, too, propped on an elbow.

Absently John raked the hair out of his eyes. It always insisted on flopping down into his face. He exchanged a wry smile with Dru. Dru clambered out of his own bedding and stumbled from the room in the direction of the jakes, trying to be quiet and doing a piss-poor job of it.

John lay back, his arms crossed behind his head, and watched with amusement as Avery shot up into a half-crouch, tumbling Conal off him onto the stones of the floor.

"Morning, brother," said John.

"Nine Spheres," muttered Avery.

Conal lay on his back on the floor, blinking up at Avery. Avery reached a hand down to him and pulled him to his feet. "Sorry, Con," he said. "For a moment I thought I was back there."

"You're going to undo everything I patched up," Conal said.

Avery felt about his rib cage. "Doesn't feel too bad," he said.

"Your voice sounds as thick as my head feels, Aves," said John, trying to make himself sound light-hearted. But he glanced over at Avery and worried about him. The slash some kern's sword had made across Avery's torso actually did look pretty bad.

Conal chuckled, though. That reassured John. If Conal wasn't worried, John decided he wouldn't be, either.

Avery caught Conal around the neck and pulled him close. "Morning," Avery whispered into Conal's ear.

A blush rose into Conal's stubbled cheeks. John was guessing Conal was having a hard time getting used to it, too, this openness among them after so many secrets.

"My lord—" Conal began.

"Don't go my-lording me, Con," growled Avery, feinting a punch to his gut.

Conal looked across at John. "Tell him, John."

"He's right, Aves," said John, but he couldn't help grinning at them both. They were so happy. "The sun and moon and all the stars shine brighter through the Spheres in Conal's mere presence. We all see that it does. But brother, now that we're here at the fort, you've got to— "

"I know, I know," said Avery.

He knows, John thought. *He does. He'll be careful. But then.*

He remembered what had happened, the time King Ranulf's two favorite jousters were caught in the hayloft together. He remembered their heads, rotting and swarming with flies, on the spikes above Tam Fort gates. Would the king act any differently if the malefactor were his own son? Maybe, but Conal was for sure putting himself in terrible danger.

John tried to drive away the other disturbing thoughts that wanted to come crowding in. The strangeness of the battle. And the other thing. The dangerous thing they'd found out, over there across the water.

No, he decided, the morning was too glorious. Time to think those dark thoughts later. John shook his head hard, as if that would drive them away. As if it could. He thought instead of Lyn. He thought of seeing her again. The red-gold of her hair. The way she smelled, warm, like apples and honey and something more mysterious. The way she felt under his hands. . .

Before he could lose himself in thoughts of her and turn himself into an utter ninnyhammer and bondslave to love, Dru staggered back in. "What a night. My head."

"We're home," said Avery. "We're alive. Life is good."

The bright morning sun sent glittering shafts filled with dust motes down on them from high slits of windows. John reached for his rebec and began picking a tune out on it. A sense of well-being descended on him, riding those shafts of sunlight. The few notes on the rebec were turning themselves into a song.

"Johnny, no," said Dru. "It's too early for that." He squinted up against the light.

"Never too early for a little music, Dru," said John. He strummed a phrase, not bothering with his bow. "*When wilt thou blow, o western wind,*" he sang.

Dru groaned and dove for the furs again.

"I'm guessing it's close on noon," said Conal.

"We've missed breaking our fast," Avery said.

"Don't speak of food to me, villains." Dru's voice came to them half muffled from underneath the furs.

"*The small rain down can rain*," John sang.

"Someone shut him up." Dru.

Conal, Avery, and John smirked at each other.

"*Nine Spheres, if my love were in my arms. . .*" sang John, moving over to just above Dru. He strummed wildly on his instrument. "*And I in my bed again.*" He finished with a flourish as Dru rose from the pallet; neatly skipped aside as Dru charged him.

And ran headlong into the slender young man who had just stepped into the room.

"Rafe!" they all shouted.

The young man named Rafe made a mock-leg to them all and whipped off his cap with a twirl.

"The king your father says, says he," Rafe announced in his lilting Baronies accent, "Tell that drunken lad of mine to sober up and present himself to myself, forthwith."

"Lady take it," said Avery.

"My lord, I'll get some hot water," said Conal, with a small formal nod.

"Shut it, Conal," said Rafe, his gray Sea-Child eyes twinkling. "You think I don't know? Good sweet Lady, it's written all over the both of you."

"Nine Spheres," Conal muttered. "Does the whole fort know my private business?" He was pulling on his tunic, then his trousers.

"Nay, Conal, just us. Just us. Welcome back!" said Rafe, and caught up Conal in a bear hug, and then they were all surrounding Rafe and thumping him on the back, and they were all talking at once.

John watched Rafe narrowly. He seemed well, thank the Child. Older, more mature. He didn't seem in any way damaged. It ate at John, how he hadn't been able to get to Rafe, when he had come back across the water for that brief time.

"But really," said Rafe, stepping away. "Ranulf the Good, may the Children bless his sacred name, really did summon you," he said to Avery. "And he really is quite put out that you're lying abed so late. My lord," Rafe added with a little smile.

"Avery. I'm getting you some hot water. I need to do that. I need to be seen doing that," said Conal.

"I know," said Avery with a sigh. "I don't have to like it, do I?"

"Bring me some hot water, too, Conal. I promise to like it," said Dru. At Avery's look, he raised a placating hand. "I'm joking."

Conal had been the Royal Arms Master, when they were lads. Their teacher in the arts of war. Now he no longer held that position. While he was away at war, another man had assumed it. Some in the fort probably considered Conal a glorified servant in the retinue of Prince Avery. The five of them knew that wasn't true. But Ranulf's courtiers thought differently.

It would be prudent to let them think so, thought John. *It would be very prudent indeed.*

"Nine Spheres, it's good to see you all back," said Rafe.

Trying to stand on one leg and pull on his leggings, Avery turned to John. "John—" he hesitated. He looked back at Rafe. "Rafe," he said. "We discovered something, Rafe. Something big."

Dru moved over to Avery and steadied him. "You're going to open up that wound, you know," he said.

John wasn't listening to any of this. He was trying to get Rafe's attention on an entirely different matter.

"Rafe," said John.

"Can it wait?" said Rafe, turning from Avery.

"You know it can't."

"She's fine. Blooming," said Rafe.

Dru overheard. "Odelyn!" he moaned, mock-clutching his heart. "Odelyn, my love, where art thou?"

"Stop." Rafe bit the word off.

John gave Rafe a hard look. Rafe's expression was serious. Something was wrong. John's mouth went dry.

"Tell you later," Rafe murmured, trying and failing to smile. Then he clapped his hands, drawing the attention of the others. "Get dressed, knuckleheads. You're wanted below in the audience hall. Not just Avery. Him especially. But all of you."

Conal was back in with a basin of water and towels. "Not me, though."

"Yes, you. You too," said Rafe. "All you vermin. His Most High Majesty wants to hear all about it, and from your own lips." In an undertone, he said to Avery, "Aves. Our suspicions. Are there grounds? Audemar?"

Avery closed his lips in a grim line. He nodded. He yanked his tunic down over his head.

"Good sweet Lady's tits," said Rafe, with a low whistle. "I've been seeing the same signs over here, the ones we talked about, but—if they're acting on their plans over there, on the battlefield—" He took a deep breath. "Then it's not all boast and braggadocio, is it?"

Avery looked around at them all. Their festive mood was gone. They'd all heard. They all knew what he was about to say.

"We're going down there, to the court," he said, his eyes glinting. "I'm making my report to my father. But nothing about this. Nothing. Just the usual. Glorious battle. We win, they lose. March of empire. Hurrah, hurrah. Does everyone understand? Too many ears down there, too many tattling mouths."

They all nodded.

Avery said as if to himself. "Poor savage kerns. What were they armed with? Scythes and hoes?" He looked up at Rafe. "But then, out of nowhere—" he started to explain. He stopped. "Later we'll figure out what to do," he said. "How much we'll say we saw. What steps we can take next. Agreed?"

They all nodded again, although Conal cast a look askance at Avery's ribcage, where the blood was blooming again into the cloth of his tunic.

"Let me see to that, Avery," said Conal.

"So not a word. Especially you, John," said Avery over his shoulder as Conal led him off and sat him down on a joint-stool. "You know how he is." He meant Ranulf. Their father the king. Ranulf the Fourth. Ranulf the Good.

John grinned, but it was a mirthless grin. "I know. Divide and conquer. *What's your brother up to? Tell me everything, boy,*" he mimicked.

"He really does listen to you, Johnny," Rafe said.

"Who, me? The bastard?" But John smiled inwardly, fondly, at Rafe and his familiar ways, his Baronies accent. *Yanny.*

"He does," said Rafe.

"Now Children, stand up for bastards," said John. He knew his tone was caustic. He tried to turn the remark with a laugh. He saw Rafe was not fooled.

It had not always been so. In his boyhood, he'd been pretty much ignored by his father the king. But that had changed during the time he'd had to come back across the water to see to his mother.

Somehow, while they were over there fighting, Ranulf had conceived a distrust of his third son, the legitimate third son Avery.

Avery had always been—not his favorite, because he loved and valued all of his three legitimate sons, but the one of his sons most like himself, a strong young warrior. But during that visit of John's back home, Ranulf had pumped John for information, and John had realized the king thought Avery was opposing him or flouting him somehow. Ranulf was just as unsettled by John as he always was, but his need to find out about Avery seemed to override that.

How was it the king distrusted Avery so much, John had wondered. It wasn't fair. Of all his sons, Avery was the one who deserved his trust most.

Then, as John spent time around court, he saw the likely reason for the king's suspicions. Audemar and Caedon, the sharp-featured ferret of a man who followed Prince Audemar everywhere and did his bidding.

The two of them had been spreading rumors about Avery, John was almost sure of it. That had to be it.

Ranulf had had to come home from the Western front, leaving that war in the hands of his commanders, to deal with some civil conflict or other on his borders.

Or maybe, some said, because his healers made him come back. The king was getting old.

That's when the rumors had started, and Avery, over the water, couldn't defend himself.

Avery was rash and pleasure-seeking, the court gossipers whispered. Avery slacked his duty. Avery spoke lightly of the king. Avery was a coward.

John had also begun wondering about the civil unrest that had brought Ranulf back home. Who had provoked it? Might Audemar and Caedon be behind it?

Now a chill settled on John.

What if Caedon and Audemar learned of Avery's feelings for Conal. What they could do with that kind of ammunition made John's blood run cold. He had no illusions about Audemar's malice toward his younger brother Avery. None of them had. Not after what they'd all seen over the years of their childhood and youth.

John made himself listen as Avery talked it out now, what they'd say during their audience with the king. It was important they all act together, so he needed to pay attention to Avery's thinking before the king asked them anything before the entire court.

"It will be fine," Avery was saying, wincing as Conal poked around his wound. "The king won't even go into those other matters too deeply, all that other stuff about the situation over there and how we lost some battles we should have won. You know what he's going to ask about. He's going to ask about Johnny. We can distract him with that."

Great, thought John bleakly. The freakish thing that had happened across the water, paraded before the entire court. He imagined how his father the king would take it. Really, how close were John's actions to a species of witchcraft? As it was, even without this tale to make things worse, something about him always unsettled his father. Always had.

But it didn't matter. Not really.

Whatever his father had to say, what did it matter? His feelings about his father might be—he stopped, considering. Complicated. That was the word. But his feelings about the five of them, the friends, were as solid as anything he'd ever known in his life.

He thought about it. Feelings about his brother and friends.

And then there were the feelings he had for Odelyn. That was different but no less strong. What could Rafe's look have meant? He began to worry again.

There was no time to worry. The four friends had to put themselves to rights. They had to present themselves to the king, and the king was an impatient man.

Rafe wished them luck and waited behind, to find out, later, the worst of what the other four had discovered. When the four descended to Ranulf's great hall in the massive stone pile that was Tam Fort, they went as one.

www.ingramcontent.com/pod-product-compliance
Lightning Source LLC
Chambersburg PA
CBHW021244050726
47498CB00003BB/689